W9-DBS-859

All that you are

**Center Point
Large Print**

Also by Stef Ann Holm
and available from Center Point Large Print:

All the Right Angles
All That Matters

**This Large Print Book carries the
Seal of Approval of N.A.V.H.**

All that you are

STEF ANN HOLM

NEW HANOVER COUNTY
PUBLIC LIBRARY
201 CHESTNUT STREET
WILMINGTON, NC 28401

CENTER POINT PUBLISHING
THORNDIKE, MAINE

This Center Point Large Print edition
is published in the year 2009 by arrangement with
Harlequin Books S.A.

Copyright © 2009 by Stef Ann Holm.

All rights reserved.

This is a work of fiction. Names, characters, places
and incidents are either the product of the author's
imagination or are used fictitiously, and any resemblance
to actual persons, living or dead, business
establishments, events or locales is entirely coincidental.

The text of this Large Print edition is unabridged.
In other aspects, this book may vary
from the original edition.
Printed in the United States of America.
Set in 16-point Times New Roman type.

ISBN: 978-1-60285-620-2

Library of Congress Cataloging-in-Publication Data

Holm, Stef Ann.
 All that you are / Stef Ann Holm. -- Large print ed.
   p. cm.
 ISBN 978-1-60285-620-2 (library binding : alk. paper)
 1. Large type books. I. Title.

PS3558.O35584A797 2009
813'.54--dc22

2009027881

For my husband, Greg, who proudly tells everyone his wife is a romance writer. You're my inspiration.

PROLOGUE

THE BLUE NOTE is a step above the other bars in Ketchikan, Alaska. Its elevated status comes from the fact that it's located in the marina, and has dock frontage for its sister business, Fish Tail Air—a floatplane sightseeing service.

At one time, the building housed a cannery, until it closed when the bigger processing plants began operations on nearby Tongass Highway. The Blue Note's seagull-gray siding has remained unchanged; its metal corrugated roof springs new leaks every year without fail. But none of this matters to the many locals who come to hear the sultry jazz music and they don't seem to mind a bucket or two on the floor collecting rainwater.

The relatively bright interior is due in part to recessed lights, as well as a row of windows along one side. A narrow hallway and door lead to a deck. In the warmer summer months, small tables are arranged on the small outdoor patio and customers can drop lines over the rail to fish. They watch the floatplanes fly in and out, as well as the numerous boats that motor to and from mooring spaces.

For a small-town bar, it's clean and well staffed. The place smells like hops and salty ocean air, with no choking clouds of cigarette smoke—the customers pay attention to the signs posted that threaten offenders with expulsion.

The Blue Note retains the integrity of its original purpose: a platform for the smooth sounds of Grover Washington, Miles Davis and the master of jazz—Mr. John Coltrane. The place was born from a love for jazz. The original owner, Oscar "the Sax Man" Jackson, sought to make his mark in Alaska, having hailed from Louisiana in the early seventies.

Today the Blue Note is run by a family member. She is an unlikely woman who doesn't tolerate disorderly conduct, fights, drunken behavior, political debates—especially jabs to Sarah Palin, their state's infamous governor—or religious preferences that bash one belief over the other.

So it was no surprise to the regulars one June evening that the owner grew irate over an altercation that needed resolving.

"Who are *you*—" the woman inhaled, grabbing on to an angry breath "—to come into *my* place, break *my* glasses, knock over *my* chairs and dirty *my* floor? You're both too drunk to clean this up, but you can be damned sure you'll be paying for what you broke."

Her low and silky voice owned the barroom's heavy air, leaving no doubt she meant business. She had a determined look and her posture spoke volumes about the plate of spilled Buffalo wings and pieces of glass. She addressed her remarks to

8

the two bruised men wobbling in their boots, one nursing a growing knot on his cheekbone from a sucker punch, and the other a bloody nose he received after taking a header into the table and tipping it over like a tiddlywink.

What had instigated the fight seemed to be a distant memory. All eyes were focused in on the slight woman with the spitfire personality. A sweet trumpet melody played through the jukebox, the music a background serenade for all the coughing and breaths being caught.

With an exasperated sigh, she tossed her long hair over her shoulder, revealing the profile of her oval face.

At that moment, bystander Mark Moretti felt as if he'd taken a blow to his gut, only nobody had delivered the punch. The second he saw her clearly, his mind lost every thought but one.

Good God, she was gorgeous.

He hadn't noticed her thirty minutes ago when he and Jeff Grisham had entered the Blue Note, a watering hole with ocean-blue walls and coral-tone vinyl-covered bar stools.

Black hair fell down her back, stopping just below where the lacy band of a bra would hook. Or unhook. The forest-green knit shirt she wore clung to her breasts and upper body.

His gaze lowered slowly, drinking her in.

Dark denim jeans hugged her curved butt and a purely physical response assaulted Mark. The reaction felt as if a hand had grabbed his throat, crushing his windpipe, making swallowing difficult.

Her skin color reminded him of unstained oak. Golden-brown and warm toned. He thought her heritage might be Chinese, but he wasn't positive. Her features were more Anglo, except for the sexy slant of her eyes.

Even with a flipped-over table and some distance between them, Mark could make out those killer eyes. The irises were silver-green, rimmed with a darker color he couldn't discern. Her mouth pouted, the lips a natural pink shade. The lower lip was fuller, but the upper appeared just as sinful. That mouth made a man wonder right then and there what she'd taste like if he kissed her.

With an irritated wave of her hand, she gestured to the exit. "Go beat on each other outside, fishbrains, before I beat the crap out of you myself."

For a woman whose height probably marked at five foot three on a tape measure, give or take a half inch, she had some guts.

There were very few women in the place. The bar was mostly full of men who wore rubber boots, having clocked off at the canneries or having just come in from fishing boats. Then there were guys like Mark, visiting from the lower forty-eight to feast on Alaska's untamed beauty, and right now the scenery wasn't the only thing worth looking at.

Jeff shuffled in front of Mark, his cheek swelling. "Am I cut, bro?"

"No, but you're turning a ripe shade of purple."

"Son of a . . ." Jeff ran a hand through his rumpled hair, then shot his opponent a mighty glare.

Mark reached forward and jerked Jeff by the shirtsleeve to make him face away. "Leave it alone."

"That guy hit me for no good reason," Jeff moaned, his legs not quite stable. He'd put away an undeterminable amount of beer and was feeling no pain.

Mark's dry tone cautioned, "It might have been you saying guns should be banned and him saying people like you should be banned."

"He's just a Wild Bill who doesn't have any common sense about the dangers of guns in a big city."

"You left Seattle behind. This isn't a big city."

Disregarding that information, Jeff gathered his vest. "I'm out of here, bro. Come on." He trudged through the door onto the pier, a gull squawking overhead.

Mark held back, his gaze seeking one more glance at the dark-haired woman who obviously ran the Blue Note.

Her attention was focused on Jeff's sparring mate. Tucking her hair behind her ears, then resting her hands on her hips, she asked one of the bar's heavyweights to escort him outside. Giving a sigh, she looked at the tumbled furniture. If Mark wasn't mistaken, she seemed shaken by the spectacle of grown men pounding into one another.

She began to right the table and Mark jumped in to help. From bent knees, she looked up through her lashes as he took hold on the opposite end.

"I got it," he said, and in one motion had the table back onto its legs.

She didn't say thanks, something that struck a chord in Mark. It didn't seem rude or impolite as, instead, it made him think she rarely asked for help.

In her throaty voice—the kind that whispered into a man's ear in a way that would make him do anything—she uttered, "I could have done it myself."

They stood so close he could smell her warm skin. A light sandalwood fragrance or something earthy. Maybe it was her shampoo, its scent smelling of coconut. Whatever it was, he wanted to breathe in deeper, pull her into his arms and keep her close.

She took a step back, eyes locked on his.

In the few seconds that ticked by, he could read her as clearly as an open book. She had a stubborn pride in her, and her determined features were like an ice sculpture. But underneath the cool facade, he detected the vaguest hint of feminine frailty, as if one more scrap of trouble might just set her off into an emotional meltdown.

Arching her brow, she asked, "What are you looking at?"

"You, sweetart."

The words hovered between them; their implication meant a lot more than he'd spoken. But she wasn't stupid. He knew damn well that a hundred times a day, men must look at her. And lust.

"Quit it."

The heavyweight came to stand beside her, pointedly glaring at Mark. "Hey, he was with the guy who took the right hook."

Defiance lifted her chin a notch, as if now she had a reason to get rid of him, too. "Get out."

Sliding into body language that pretty much won over any female he set his sights on, Mark folded his strong arms over a chest that years of construction work had developed into hard slabs of muscle. He knew he was built as solid as a steel frame, stood taller than most men and had been blessed with Italian good looks.

While he hadn't shaved today, the stubble shadowing his face could be considered, by some, handsome in a movie-star way. When he smiled just right, a slight impression of dimples made brackets at the corners of his mouth.

He slipped one hand into his jeans pocket, then shrugged. "I'm just standing here."

He was surprised when she shot back, "I don't like how you're standing. So get out."

Now stuffing the second hand in his pocket, for reasons quite oblivious to her, he said, "You know, you'd look a lot prettier if you wiped that frown off your face."

An evenness marked her repeated command. "Get out."

The beefy guy's hands closed into hamlike fists. A warning that if he didn't leave, he'd be dealt with.

Mark got the message, but he didn't move real fast. Instead, he reached into his back pocket for his wallet, fingered through the bills, then dropped a hundred note on the table. "That should cover the tabs and the damage." He paused, then added in a lazy drawl, "Unless you want to make other arrangements. With me."

A fiery light burned in her beautiful eyes, and she reacted in an angry tone to his offer. "You're in Alaska, fish-brain. And you're in my bar. Inside here, it's my law. I say get out. Now go."

Mark played along and nodded. "Yeah, somebody's got to drive Jeff home—and I have the truck keys. But I'll come back another time to make you smile."

The muffled sound she made gave a crooked lift to the corner of Mark's mouth.

He always liked a challenge. Maybe it was fate after all that had him stuck in Ketchikan.

Seeing Jeff sitting on the pickup's tailgate, Mark headed for the parking lot. The soft sound of salt water lapping next to pilings and the metal clink of rigging against masts filled his ears.

It was almost eleven and a misting drizzle had taken over for the day's steady rainfall. It seemed like the sun had set only moments ago, the sky still vaguely awash in color. The days here were long, the summer solstice fast approaching.

He never would have guessed he'd be here, with a guy he'd only known for twenty-four hours, driving him home and thinking about a woman who'd caught his attention like no other ever had.

His was a long story, and he was still writing it, making up a whole lot of bull as he went.

But for the first time since his plane connection to Kenai had been canceled yesterday, the straight story looked a whole lot better than fiction.

CHAPTER ONE

SITTING AT HER SON'S BEDSIDE, Danalee Jackson tucked the Spiderman bedspread next to her sleeping five-year-old. Eyes peacefully closed, he didn't stir as she gave his forehead a loving stroke. Even as a baby, Terran had been a deep sleeper.

A soft light enveloped the bedroom, its source the night-light plugged into the wall. Two dresser drawers remained half-opened, as if Terran had been looking for socks and underwear after his bath. Toys were scattered over the floor: a vibrating and light-blinking astro-man gun, dinosaur card game and the remote-control stingray with a water puddle spread beneath it on the hardwood floor. He must have brought the toy into the tub with him. His ice skates and hockey

15

stick lay where he had dropped them Monday night after practice.

As she watched her little boy sleeping, her heart swelled with a sweet, aching love. Life before him seemed a distant memory, and Dana couldn't help reflecting back upon all the years that had brought her to this moment in time.

Everything had happened at once. One life began and another had ended. It had seemed the worst of ironies six years ago.

Dana had been earning a decent wage as a checker for the town's only Safeway grocery store, when Cooper Boyd began regularly waiting in her line. Sometimes he bought one meal's worth of food. Other times he bought paper products. Most of the time, he didn't bother with the main aisles— he became strictly a checkout-aisle shopper. He bought the stupidest things just to go through her lane so he could talk to her. Spicy corn nut packages and a sudoku puzzle book were among his purchases, and later she laughed when she discovered Cooper had zero aptitude in math.

While he did passably well in the looks department, it was Cooper's sense of humor that provided relief to her day. Working at a grocery store had been like working at a circus. Between the check staff, the managers, the various department heads and the box boys, there were a lot of issues, and many customers came with their own set of quirks.

There was the four-hundred-pound woman who clipped ankles with the wheels on her power chair. On his breaks, Scout, the morning box boy, took the electric cart out and spun doughnuts in the icy parking lot, then returned the chair to charge by the front doors. Another regular customer was the unshaven, out-of-work guy who always came in wearing his pajama bottoms and cheap rubber flip-flops.

And then there was Tori Daniel.

Without fail, whenever Tori came in wearing a thin top, black leggings and knee-high Ugg boots over her shapely calves, you could be assured every male within a ten-mile radius had her on his radar. When she turned her cart into the frozen-foods section, her headlights came on and suddenly anyone wearing boxers or briefs seemed to have business by the fish-stick case.

Grocery store work hadn't been Dana's dream job, but it had been a great employment opportunity in Ketchikan. She'd been without a college degree and had no desire to get one. If it hadn't been for . . . well, a lot of things. Who knew, maybe she would have stuck it out and applied for a managerial position.

Cooper, with a dirty-blond shock of hair over his brow, was slightly stocky but not overweight. She found out through the gossip circle at the Pioneer Café that he'd been born here, but moved to Homer in the first grade. Now that he'd returned to

Ketchikan, he planned on starting a hockey league at the local rink.

She began looking forward to seeing Cooper Boyd's smiling face in her lane.

On a rainy Saturday morning, a ginormous jar of extra-crunchy peanut butter came rolling down the conveyor belt with Cooper trailing behind it. That was the day he asked her out.

As far as first dates went, theirs had been low-key. Burgers at Burger Queen and a make-out session afterward in the front seat of his Dodge Ram at a scenic overlook. They didn't do anything other than kiss, but his technique had lit her on fire like a Fourth of July rocket.

A few days later, she brought him to meet her parents.

Dana's father hadn't thought too much of Cooper's potential, and neither had her older brother, Terrance—who'd been her idol since she'd been a toddler and able to stand and look up to him. Terrance said Cooper rubbed him the wrong way, claiming Cooper didn't readily look him in the eyes when they had a conversation. He said an honest man would have nothing to hide.

Rare were the times when Dana disregarded her brother's advice, but that had been one of them. She caught herself making excuses for Cooper, telling her brother he needed to extend himself more and get to know Cooper better.

Maybe she felt that way because it had taken

Cooper so long to ask her out. So he had a few shortcomings. Who didn't? He was easy to talk to, he always picked up the tab and the physical attraction was too hot to deny.

In the end, Terrance's final word had been she'd have to learn from her own mistakes. After all, at twenty-two, she lived on her own and took care of herself in her own apartment.

Dana's mom, Suni, had been reserved in her opinions about Cooper. A cultural thing perhaps, but since Terran's birth, her reticence had all but vanished in a vapor. Now she had plenty to say about Cooper.

Leaning forward to kiss Terran's sweet-boy cheek, Dana let memories from the past slip away. Things that had happened six years ago shouldn't be dwelt upon. She only had one sinking regret; it caused a dull heartache that sometimes consumed her. Her father and brother weren't here to watch Terran grow up.

They would have been so proud of him. Even of her, and the woman she'd turned into.

As Dana rose from the twin bed, fatigue overtook her. Even after so many years as the owner, the late hours she put in at the Blue Note still felt foreign to her. There were moments when she longed to call it quits by nine o'clock and be home to put Terran to bed herself. She savored Sunday when the bar was closed. And she looked forward to Tuesday and Thursday nights when her trusted employee, Leo Sanchez, took over her duties and she had a couple of blessed nights at home.

Tonight was not such a night.

The hour had to be somewhere around two-thirty. Walking to her bedroom, she paused, then took the stairs to the kitchen. She knew from experience it was impossible for her to come home, crawl into bed and fall instantly asleep. She had to decompress and unwind, look through the mail, make out a grocery list, mindlessly click through the television stations. After today, she might even eat a Twinkie.

Quietly heading into the kitchen, she flipped on a light, then stood bleary-eyed in front of the open cupboard. No Twinkies. No Ding Dongs. Not even a homemade cookie. Just Goldfish crackers. Not her usual choice, but she was hungry and decided to plunge into the box of processed cheese and sodium.

Today had been very, very long. Made longer by the two fish-brains belting each other this evening.

Sometimes she wanted to walk out of the Blue Note and never go back . . . but she couldn't do that to her father. Never. Ever. He counted on her, even in death. She felt it. She knew it was what he'd want. And a part of her, the part she kept hidden from everyone, even her mother, was a part of her that was afraid to let go.

"I didn't know you liked Goldfish."

Dana turned to find her mom standing in the

kitchen doorway wearing a flannel housecoat and squinting against the bright light. Her inky-black hair brushed her narrow shoulders.

"I don't," Dana replied, digging back into the bag. "We don't have anything else to munch on."

"There's fruit in the fridge. Apple slices. Terran had some with his dinner."

"I'm not in the mood for fruit."

Suni reached around her for the peanut butter jar. "You don't eat enough fruits and vegetables."

Had Dana not counted on her mother in a hundred different ways, she may have made a retort. But she kept her comments to herself. If it hadn't been for her mother helping with Terran, she'd be lost.

Her mom whipped up two peanut butter and jelly sandwiches, then poured two icy-cold glasses of milk. "Sit down, Dana. You look ready to drop."

"I'm so tired." She sank into the chair, grateful to be off her feet. "A pair of mainlanders broke two glasses and a beer pitcher and spilled hot wings all over my floor."

And a guy called me sweetart, as if I were a piece of candy.

Dana's thoughts hadn't dwelled on the man who'd said it, but now she let herself recall the sound of his voice. Deep and husky, a dose of sarcasm mixed into his words. He was good-looking and he knew it.

Quiet resistance fell over Suni's face. A long

moment passed and she said nothing, as if biting her tongue. Then, the inevitable question: "When are you going to sell the Blue Note?"

Dana didn't respond. "You don't have to get up every night to check on me when I get home, Mom. I'm okay."

"You're not okay."

Refusing to have the same discussion over and over with her mother had gotten easier. Dana had her own tactics in their verbal warfare. In a way that usually worked, she steered the conversation in a different direction.

"The bears haven't gotten into our garbage cans lately. It's a pain to keep the trash on the service porch, but at least it saves us from cleaning tipped-over cans on the front lawn."

"I'm grateful for that. Nothing worse than smelly trash in the grass." Suni put the peanut butter and bread away. "Come to bed, Dana."

"I will."

A single light on a side table remained switched on downstairs as they climbed the steps. When Terran had begun walking, Dana feared that he'd somehow get up from his bed at night and fall down the stairs. She started leaving a light on, just in case he woke and ended up on the landing. For a time she'd used a baby-gate, but he figured out how to open it, and the restraint was all but worth-less.

No longer worrying about Terran and stairs,

Dana still kept the lamp on for comfort and no other reason. The milky glow helped make the home feel guarded downstairs.

Dana had few fears, but being home alone in a dark house was one of them. There was something to be said for having a man in the house at night. Too bad she didn't know of any.

Too bad Cooper Boyd had turned out to be a bad nightmare.

Dana undressed for bed, then slid between the warmth of new flannel sheets letting go of the day. She finally relaxed.

Closing her heavy eyes, her thoughts drifted like a tide rolling back into the sea. She was too tired to keep the man who had challenged her to smile from her mind. She tried to remember his face.

He had nerve, that's for sure, and a confidence she rarely saw in men who flirted with her, and this one had done so quite blatantly. Most came on to her with a lot of pretense—cock-and-bull stories, but when it came to asking her out, many didn't follow through. Her brother had told her that since she was so beautiful, men had a difficult time with her looks. They felt threatened.

Dana rolled onto her side, hugging the pillow and settling into a drowsy warmth. She didn't think she was that pretty, but she did acknowledge she was different. Nobody else in Ketchikan was black and Chinese, with a quarter Caucasian thrown in. And that did set her apart.

"But I'll come back another time to make you smile."

Yeah, sure . . . go ahead and try.

Those were her last thoughts before falling into a deep sleep.

"I'M NOT GOING to Kenai—just thought you should know." Mark spoke into his cell phone.

From the redwood deck of Jeff's rental condominium, Mark gazed at the panoramic scenery below. Cedar and hemlock trees flanked the steep hillside, the ground alight with white and purple blooming flowers. An overcast sky hung heavily in the air, but he could make out the waterway. Earlier this morning, the harbor had been cloaked in fog. Now he could see four monstrous cruise ships, like large bleached-white whales, lining the dock space.

"Where are you?" his sister, Francesca, asked.

"Ketchikan. My connection was canceled on Monday, then I missed Tuesday afternoon's flight out. We went fishing first thing and didn't make it back on time. So I'm staying at Jeff Grisham's rental condo for the duration."

Mark fought off a yawn. He'd woken when the sun began to break just after four—six o'clock Boise time—and he could have used a couple more hours after last night's lack of sleep. Years of hitting an alarm at that hour and the habit of getting up early meant he was awake for the day.

"Duration of what?" Franci's voice reverberated through the line, concern marking her tone. "Who's Jeff Grisham?"

"A guy from Seattle I met at the Pioneer Café two days ago. I went in for lunch to wait for the next flight out and we got to talking. He's here to go fishing, so I decided to stay overnight because he hooked me up with a sweet fishing charter in town. Then I missed my re-ticketed flight because our boat was late getting back." A sparrow swooped onto the deck, pecked at something, then flew off. "Be on the lookout for a big box of frozen fish. I sent you, Robert, John and Mom some halibut and salmon."

His brother Robert owned a restaurant and would appreciate the fine catch. John was a lawyer and his kids probably wouldn't go for fresh fish, but he'd sent some anyway. His mother would cook it for sure. Francesca . . . she'd probably have her husband, Kyle, fix it for them.

"Okay, thanks." Then just like his sister, she went on with the grilling. "So why aren't you going to Kenai now?"

"What for? Fishing's great here. And that's the whole reason I came to Alaska."

The line grew quiet for a long breath. "I know why you went to Alaska, Mark. Don't try and hide the truth from me. You need time to think about Dad and what you're going to do."

"Yeah, sure. I know that." He leaned against the deck stair, his bare feet propped on the railing's lower rung.

There was a cold chill this morning, but he hadn't readily noticed when he'd stepped outside wearing jeans. His long-sleeved Moretti Construction T-shirt warded off some of the earlier morning bite, but not much. Coffee cup in hand, he'd been thinking about too many other things to bother with boots or a sweatshirt.

"So let everyone know," Mark said, watching the hundreds of tourists populate the streets like an army of ants. The hour crept toward noon now. Jeff had slept in. "You can reach me on my cell. There's no landline at this rental."

"Be careful."

Mark pushed away from the wall, a smile on his mouth. "Oh come on, Franci. I'm forty years old." He laughed. "Be careful for what? If something was going to get me, it would have smacked me on the side of the head by now."

They ended their conversation after casual exchanges about what was going on within the family, then Mark slipped his phone into a leather holder on his belt.

"We're good to go," Jeff announced, stepping onto the deck that needed a fresh coat of stain. Any hangover traces prompted by last night's beers seemed to have been curtailed by his third black coffee. But the arch of his right cheek had ripened to an eggplant color. "Bro, I got us seats on Fish Tail Air. They'll fly us to Red Creek Lodge and the charter will take us to prime fishing grounds. Depending on how we do hooking the chinook, we may want to leave the freshwater inlets and head out to the ocean." Draining the last of his coffee with a long gulp, he set his cup on the deck railing. "The rate on two rooms was cheap. Gotta love Alaska."

Mark went inside to grab his boots and wool socks, Jeff following behind.

The condo was relaxing and comfortable despite its size. It boasted a small living room with a view of the city and a gas fireplace. The tiny kitchen used up half the common space, and there was a breakfast bar rather than a table and chairs. There were two small bedrooms with a shared bath and a laundry closet.

In spite of running at the mouth in bars, Jeff wasn't a pig. He picked up after himself, kept the bathroom counter clean and didn't leave his wet towel on the floor. Actually, he'd proved to be pretty anal and meticulous about personal details.

Mark sank onto the sofa and asked, "So how often do you fish here?"

"Every year. It's a major stress reliever. I told you about my buddy who couldn't make it at the last minute. Had a tech problem to iron out in our latest beta program. He's probably popping Rolaids like Tic Tacs."

Tying on one of his boots, Mark gave an upward glance. "What do you do in Seattle again?"

"Microsoft." Jeff gave him a wide grin. "I'm a computer geek. You run Vista? That's me, bro. Had a hand in developing it."

Laughing, Mark stood. "I'm computer illiterate. I don't even have one. Couldn't tell you how anything works."

"I could get you a primo discount."

"I'm good, thanks."

"Well, if you ever change your mind," Jeff said, snagging his jacket and a ditty bag, "whatever you do, don't go to the dark side. Macs suck."

"I think that's what my sister has in her work trailer."

"Bummer, bro."

They locked the condo, stowed all their gear in the pickup, then took off for the floatplane dock.

"So you build stuff," Jeff said between bites of beef jerky—the breakfast of computer geeks. "Like furniture and those wall racks we all had to make in wood shop?"

"Buildings. High-rises."

"No kidding. Cool."

As they wound down the hillside toward town, green scenery passed in a blur. Dark rocks covered with moss created shadows on his left. A small waterfall spilled on his right, then disappeared into the trees. Gazing out the passenger window, Mark's thoughts strayed to Boise, Idaho. *Home.*

He wondered how things were going for Moretti Construction, the family construction business his Italian immigrant father, Giovanni, had built from the ground up.

They'd just completed their most ambitious project ever—the multimillion-dollar Grove Marketplace. A downtown renovation and revitalization that had been Giovanni's dream.

His father had passed away before the Grove had been completed, but he had been able to see the job get a good start. Last month, when the final building had been signed off on by the inspectors, the moment had been bittersweet.

The family had gathered that Sunday night at Mark's mom's house for dinner, giving Giovanni Moretti a toast of remembrance.

The project's formal dedication had been reserved for this September, and Mark would be there to take part in the ceremony. For now, he had the summer to think about what he wanted to do with the rest of his life.

The truth of the matter was, Giovanni's untimely death had affected Mark far more than he'd let on to his mother or brothers and sister. The father he'd been so driven to be accepted by and win approval from was no longer around to give him a pat on the back.

Mark felt as if he'd lost direction. He had to figure out a plan.

One thing for certain—he wasn't getting any

younger. Years of physical labor were taxing his body. To his annoyance, his joints had to be worked out of their stiffness in the morning, and it was harder to get going.

His brother-in-law, Kyle Jagger, and partner in Moretti, wanted to take the company in a new direction—construction management. Doing so would mean no more hands-on carpentry work for Mark. While he still found some satisfaction from strapping on a tool belt, the idea was something to consider seriously.

Mark had spent years molding himself into a man his father could be proud of. Learning the carpentry trade, he'd been taught everything his father knew about building.

Outgoing and fair, Mark recognized he was good with people, managing crews and telling the superintendents what to do. The trouble was, he hadn't managed his life well at all.

And the Grove Marketplace had literally burned him out.

Long overdue to recharge his batteries, Mark had cashed his bonus check and caught a flight to Alaska.

"Parking downtown sucks," Jeff complained, angling the rental pickup truck behind a Dumpster, slightly blocking a Buick LeSabre's rusted white fender. The marina overflow lot had signs designating slots for the Blue Note and Fish Tail Air customers.

Not realizing the businesses were so close, the idea of seeing the woman with the green eyes and sexy mouth filled his mind with suggestive thoughts. Mark fit his sunglasses on the back of his neck, glancing at the marina. "Do you know the name of that woman who threw you out of the bar last night?"

Indignance crossed Jeff's facial features. The bill of a Seattle Mariners ball cap rode low on his forehead. "I've never been thrown out of a bar. I chose to leave." Giving the dial on his complex watch a quick look, Jeff frowned. "We gotta boog. Flight leaves in half an hour."

They hopped out and grabbed the fishing gear, coolers, Orvis rods and reels, waders and tackle boxes and headed down the buckling sidewalk leading to the slips. The sidewalk also led directly toward the Blue Note.

The bar looked different in broad daylight. Definitely in poorer repair than Mark had noticed last night. Sections of corrugated roofing had loosened, slightly bent at the ends from the wind. Areas of siding had been repaired too many times and were beyond fixing. Each board needed to be axed and a whole new exterior constructed.

Gray and colorless, the place lacked life. Directly in front, at the dock, three floatplanes were in a line, propeller to tail, like yellow insects waiting to take flight.

"Dana." Jeff spoke without a reference point,

then added as a clarification as Mark cocked his head, "Her name's Dana Jackson. And don't even bother to go there. She's not interested. We've all tried. You'll have better fishing for chicks at the Arctic Bar."

The entry door to the Blue Note had been propped open, soft music spilling outside. Mark made a guess that midday didn't draw a lot of customers.

If their pilot hadn't been on the dock waiting for them, Mark would have gone inside the bar to shout out a little howdy to Dana.

Jeff conversed with the pilot, giving their confirmation info as well as heights and weights. Other sports fisherman congregated at the planes with their gear.

The pilot gathered everyone around to discuss instructions. Maybe in his early thirties, he was moderately tall, had an average build and came across as friendly. His chestnut hair had been cut short; his alert eyes were a glacier-blue. "My name's Sam Hyatt. I'll be flying you in a de Havilland Beaver—the best bush plane in the world. I'll go over seating assignments in a minute, but first we'll stow all your gear and then . . ."

Mark all but tuned out the rest of what Sam was saying. Right about midsentence, Dana Jackson appeared in the doorway looking more beautiful than any woman had the right to look.

Something about her long black hair and warm, caramel skin knocked Mark sideways. He'd always been attracted to tall blondes. If Dana were standing in a pair of killer heels, he doubted the top of her head would come to the bottom of his chin.

Looking at her mouth, those pouting lips, just about did Mark in. But she was preoccupied with watching Sam, and she didn't even notice him. Those eyes of hers were even more stunning in the daytime. A man could drown in them. She had a sense of purpose about her, a woman who wanted something. He could tell by her body language. The way she tapped her fingers on the door frame, impatient for Sam to be finished.

Then it hit Mark like a one-ton concrete slab—maybe she was hot for the pilot.

Suddenly the dock became very busy as their things were handed into the floatplane, then Sam began calling in passengers and telling them where to sit based on their weight.

Sam pointed to Mark, who was the last man to be seated. "Hop in—you'll be my copilot who does nothing. Just be careful not to touch any of the controls."

Mark listened to Sam, but his focus remained on Dana.

Just then, she looked at him and recognition flooded her features. She scowled. Her raven-black brows, with their high arch and tapered ends, made her green eyes look all the more exotic.

Mark lifted his chin and gave her a grin. "Mornin', sunshine."

"It's not morning, cowboy," she responded tartly. Then unlike any woman had ever done to him— she blew him off. "Hey, Sam. I need you to do a huge favor for me."

"Anything you want."

Their easy dialogue brought an unwelcome response to Mark.

Dana didn't elaborate. Rather, her gaze leveled on Mark as if to say, *Don't you need to get into that plane so I can have a private word?*

Sam took her silent direction and called to Mark in a brisk tone, "Climb in, Mr. Moretti. I'm on a schedule."

Stepping onto the pontoon and bracing his hand on the wing strut, Mark looked over his shoulder. "I do favors, too, Dana."

If she wondered how he'd known her name, she didn't show it. Maybe because she was too intent on harpooning him with a barbed glare. She made no response. Simply stood there, tight-lipped, very annoyed by him.

Merely chuckling beneath his breath, Mark lifted himself into the floatplane and took his seat. What looked like a flywheel and a bungee cord was at his left foot, while two yokes protruded from the dash.

On closer inspection, the plane looked like it had seen better days and had many worn stickers stuck to the metal. Years of scuff marks were on the floor, and who knew how many dirty fishermen had climbed in and out of the seat he sat in. A shorter person would have struggled to see over the tall instrument panel.

The passenger door pocket couldn't get another map stuffed into it, and the window glass had been lowered just enough so he could hear Dana and Sam on the dock.

"Can you bring me back some shaker halibut? Nothing bigger than fifteen pounds. Presley's going to make her famous crispy fish tacos tonight." A long, vulnerable sigh caught in Dana's voice. "The new state fire marshal's coming in, and damn if I don't need to soften his heart through his stomach."

"Sure thing. I know a guy who can fill a cooler for me. I'll be back in about four. Will that work?"

"That'd be great, Sam. I'll owe you one."

When Sam replied, his words were punctuated with an emotional depth Mark didn't understand. "No, Dana. I'll always owe you."

The airplane dipped on its pontoons as Sam pulled himself in. A dockhand secured the door and prepared for departure as ropes were removed from the dock cleats.

Slipping into the pilot's seat after grabbing the headset, Sam didn't immediately fit it over his ears. Staring at Mark, he addressed him with all frankness. "She's not as tough as she seems. She doesn't need a guy trying to take her for a ride." He slipped aviator sunglasses over the bridge of his nose. "Your headset is on the yoke. When you wear it, it'll cancel out most of the engine noise. If you need to say something, talk into the mouthpiece and I'll hear you."

Sam Hyatt may not have been the biggest guy with the biggest threat, but there was an underlying warning in his advice that gave Mark pause. And something did become clear to him.

While it seemed Sam would do anything for Dana Jackson, he wasn't interested in her in a romantic way. Rather, he carried a deep-seated compassion for her. Like a big brother watching out so she wouldn't get hurt. As if she'd had more than her fair share of it already.

When they returned, Mark would find out more, but for now, he settled in for the ride. He looked forward to fishing and getting out on the water, thinking, forgetting about responsibilities.

He felt good. Optimistic. His mood light.

But three days later, when Jeff led the way from the dock to the pickup, all that changed.

The truck was no longer in the parking space.

CHAPTER TWO

"A'IGHT—LISTEN UP, everyone." In his naturally grizzled tone, Bear "Roadkill" Barker called the patrons at the Blue Note bar to attention. "I got a new class startin' next Wednesday night. Pass the word around to them who ain't here and need to know how to butcher roadkill. Anyone's interested, y'all got to preregister and bring a sharp knife, saw, meat hook and a box of freezer Ziplocs to the first class. We be meetin' in the Church of Divinity's basement. Oh—and it be free to senior citizens." Bear hunkered back onto his bar stool and gave a satisfied nod. "Thanks and God bless America. Now go back to drinkin'."

Dana had been standing at the back bar, getting two beers on tap for the pair seated at the bar's end, when Bear made his colorful announcement. Every month, he offered his field expertise to those who needed free game to feed their families. The state had enacted a roadkill plan that, when a state trooper found a fresh carcass at the railroad tracks or highway, he called a person on his waiting list to haul it away. That person had to know how to butcher a fourteen-hundred-pound moose and pack it from the accident scene.

The occupation Bear had had before showing up in Ketchikan was left to speculation. Dana thought she'd heard he was a university professor from Oregon. Others claimed to have seen him getting off the "Blue Canoe"—the ferry from Bellingham that delivered cuckoos and convicts from Washington State with a one-way ticket to Alaska. If you asked Bear, he never gave you a straight answer.

In any case, he was a regular at the Blue Note, and the bar was all the livelier for his presence.

Leo Sanchez, her trusted manager, busied himself with mixed drinks for the table by the door. Without Leo, Dana would be sunk. In the kitchen, Presley Reid, her childhood girlfriend, manned the oven and stove, creating cocktail fare for a packed house.

Saturday nights slammed the Blue Note. A live band played in the corner, the honey-sweet sound of modern jazz rising to the rafters. Dana loved to feel the fluid notes through her body as she wiped off the glossy counter with a damp rag.

If it weren't for the fire marshal's visit the other day, she would have been in a great mood since she was closed tomorrow and could spend the day with Terran.

But the fire-breathing dragon had descended on her and not even Presley's to-die-for fish tacos could take a bite out of his flame.

Nobody except her close staff—Leo and Presley—knew she'd been written up, and the infractions weren't minor.

The Blue Note had once been an active cannery and, as such, the roof and walls had been constructed pretty basically. Dana's father had done some remodeling back in the early eighties when he'd opened the place, but nothing major had been done since.

Nearly thirty years later, and the Blue Note was in trouble.

Big trouble.

The fire marshal had found several violations. Most of them had been overlooked by the previous inspector. She'd been operating a legal nonconforming use of property, and had been allowed, to a degree, to run with the "illegal use."

State licensing had never encountered a problem with her stove hood, or typical operating errors with food prep and/or serving minors—a *major* no-no. Dana and her staff carded big-time, and to their credit had busted fake IDs from a few jokers trying to drink underage. The city's building department had an insurance company who frequently came on checks. Everything had always been fine.

But the new guy, Bill T. Kirk—or as Dana nicknamed him, Fire Marshal Bill, reminiscent of the Jim Carrey character in an *In Living Color* sketch—said with the number of people crowding the bar on Friday and Saturday nights, she'd have to add a new sprinkler system. Not to mention, another exit door would be mandatory regardless of her crowd control.

At present, there was only one way in and one way out of the Note—the wharf. Not good enough. She had to be prepared in case of a fire so people could get out via two exits. His bloodhound hunt had also found that her bathrooms weren't handicap accessible like they should be. And she'd have to replace the old electrical panel and bring it up to code.

Fire Marshal Bill gave her six months to do it all—or he'd close her down.

Dana felt like taking his report and tossing the papers onto her desk without a thought. But she couldn't afford to be so cavalier. Without passing a fire inspection, she'd lose her business insurance. Without business insurance, her liquor license would be taken away. And without liquor, she'd be closed.

In short—she was screwed.

Screwed by the blatant truth that she didn't have the collateral to pay for the improvements and repairs. The bar was tapped out and her floatplane service had declined in a bad economy. Fewer people were traveling, and those who'd booked a ticket last year had gotten a great price.

Dana never knew what the cost on a gallon of fuel would be until the barge arrived. Last fall, she'd booked seats estimating the price at four dollars a gallon, but it had come in at five seventy-five. Gas had gone through the roof, taking a big bite out of her profits.

Yet Fish Tail Air stayed afloat, and for reasons that were too personal to dwell on, she'd never let Sam Hyatt go. . . . It would kill the man if he had to walk away.

"Did you put Sambuca on the order list?" Leo asked, drawing Dana from her thoughts.

"Yes. And I took off the banana brandy. I found a bottle in the stockroom."

"Good deal." Leo moved efficiently, his long hair in tight curls that rested on his shoulders. She'd never known a Mexican to have a natural perm like that, but he swore it was real. She believed him.

Her curly hair had been chemically relaxed, and each time she shampooed, she had to touch it up with a flatiron. The process grew out, and she was due to have it done again if she wanted to keep her hair straight. There were days when she hated fighting it, and drew the length into a hair claw and said oh well.

Refilling the snack bowls with wasabi-coated peas, then snack-size pretzels and salted cashews for those who didn't like to set their mouths on . . . *fire* . . . Dana frowned at the reminder that she'd been smacked with violations.

She'd been trying to figure out what she could do on her own to save labor costs. It took an experienced carpenter to do sprinklers and cut in another door. But who did she know who could build an extension ramp out of steel? A trip to the library, and they'd been very helpful finding some home repair books for her on bathroom remodeling. Leo offered to help her out with that project.

Maybe she could get a bank loan, but doubtful. She already paid each month on the loan for Fish Tail, an added business her father had taken on about ten years ago. Buying the airplanes had started because they had the dockage for fueling stations just outside the bar. Oscar had always been fascinated by airplanes, and so had Terrance. But neither had learned how to fly. That's why they'd hired Sam Hyatt and his brother. . . .

But that was the past. She had the present to concern herself with.

Dana released a troubled breath. She had one hundred and eighty days to bring things up to speed. Or else.

Cardelle Kanhai plopped a giant green insect repellent can on the bar, then took a seat. "Blue Hawaiian, heavy on de rum, mon. I sold a boatload of tanzanite rings today and I'm throwing myself a bashment."

A "bashment" was Cardelle's word for "party." He used the expression often enough that Dana knew just what he meant.

"Cardelle," Leo immediately said, "I told you I don't want any of that DEET crap sprayed in the Note. We don't have mosquitoes in here."

A Jamaican national, Cardelle worked as a counter clerk in the cruise-ship-owned jewelry store—Jewels of the Nile. He only lived in Ketchikan during the peak months from mid-June to the last day of September. He never went anywhere without an Off! insect repellent can.

"You don't know dat for sure. We got Wes' Nile, malaria and dengue in my country—and Alaska has many maskittas. I seen dem swarming with mine owned eyes. I don't need no sickness, mon."

He went to pick up the aerosol can to douse his bare arms, when Leo put a hand over his.

"I'm telling you, Cardelle, that shit stinks and I don't want to be breathing it in. I'll risk the West Nile."

Deterred, he left the can alone. For now. Dana knew from experience, he'd go outside a few times a night and shoot himself with another coating of the stuff.

Looking left, Cardelle said to Bear, "Pass de buns."

"Card, them is hot nuts, not buns." Bear's broad shoulders took up the same width as his behind.

"Pass dem, mon."

Bear obliged, then inquired, "You ever figure out whose truck you had towed?"

"No. But I bet you, it was probably some chi-chi mon blocking my Buick."

Bear's thick brows knit together. "What's that?"

"What you call a girly mon without de balls to park in a straight line."

Dana left the bar gossip to say hi to familiar guests at a table. As she approached, the door opened and two men came inside. She recognized them immediately.

Fish-brain and Moretti.

Sam had called him Mr. Moretti, and the name had stuck in her head. Why—she didn't care to examine. But in the days that had passed since he'd been a passenger on Fish Tail Air, Dana's thoughts, unfortunately, had strayed to Moretti.

More than once.

Against her better judgment, she'd taken a slow inventory of his features. Black hair, but showing a faint trace of silver at his temples. Olive-toned skin. There could be no more denying, his smile kicked her heart into overdrive. His handsome face exaggerated every masculine feature a guy could have. A square jaw, a day's beard growth, strong nose, straight forehead.

He'd gotten under her skin with those looks, and the smack he talked, it had just . . . well—just everything about him had set her a degree off-course. The rest of that Saturday, when she walked, she felt unsteady. When she breathed, she was short of breath. When she tried to think, she struggled.

And here he came striding into her place as if he'd been given a formal invitation. She'd thought, after tossing him out, he'd never have the nerve to return.

Her mistake.

While the fish-brain kept a cell phone to his ear and stepped back outside, Moretti approached her, a heavy ice chest in his arms. He carried the white-and-blue Igloo with ease, walking directly past her and having the gall to head right into her kitchen.

Dana followed behind him, determination marking her steps.

Once in the kitchen, he set the cooler on the

stainless surface and Presley turned with wide eyes. "Mother of pearl! You look just like that actor—what's his name? Only better. Younger. More big. Holy cow, is the room shrinking or are you really this tall?"

"Presley, I'll handle this." Dana went around the other side of the counter.

Intimidating Moretti posed a problem. He had to be a foot and a half taller than her, so she lifted her chin to give him a hard stare. Brown and rich like a candy bar, his eyes melted her.

She blinked to clear the liquid heat in her head. "What are you doing in my kitchen?"

His response was uttered in a slow and deep voice. She could swear Presley squeaked or fainted behind her. "Why, bringing you something, swee-tart."

That ridiculously stupid name he used on her grabbed hold of her nerves, fueling her backbone. "Moretti, I didn't ask you to bring me anything."

"You know my name." His smile brightened. "You care."

"Get over yourself. I heard Sam talking to you."

"Did you hear me tell him that you take my breath away?"

She faltered a second, then snorted. "You're full of it."

Breaking into a chuckle, he lifted the lid on the cooler. Inside, dry ice blocks and cleaned fish in plastic bags. Halibut. And shaker size, too.

"Heard you had a need for these, so I brought home as many as I could catch. Funny how fishermen think the big ones are the best to keep."

Not saying thanks, she commented, "I needed them three days ago and Sam brought me a half dozen when he flew back."

"Well, I've got eight in here."

"Well, I've got spicy meatballs on the menu tonight, and hot wings on tomorrow's." Her brow arched. "And you know all about spilling them on my floor."

He leaned closer. His eyes bored into hers, his firm mouth in a set line. Hair fell over his forehead in a thick shock and she fought the urge to smooth it back. She could smell the ocean air on his skin, feel the heat coming from his gaze. If she took one single step backward, he'd know he got to her, so she remained where she was and didn't flinch.

His next comment rose the gooseflesh on her arms. "I sure don't know what to make of you, yet. But I will."

Straightening to his full and intimidating height, he rubbed his fingers on the underside of his chin as if feeling the stubble while in thought. Then in a voice exaggerated in parody, he said, "Hey, Mark, thanks for the fish. No problem, sweetart."

Before she could reply, he turned and left the room.

Presley came up beside her, leaning onto her

shoulder. "Who was that guy? Honey-honey, he's so sinfully good-looking he should be illegal."

Dana quietly drew shallow breaths into her lungs, forcing a calmness to take over the disarray to her wits. "Mark Moretti."

"WAITING FOR DE TOW TRUCK, it vex me, 'cause I'm missing my fav'rite show—*America's Idol.* I say to myself, if I ketch 'im who parked here, I whoop his bum."

The man sitting next to Mark at the bar could have fit sideways in a gym locker. He had some muscle on him, but he was as lean as a gazelle. His head was shaved to a shiny brown glean, his smile white like a piece of chalk. A short-sleeved shirt and tie hung loosely against his chest.

Mark overheard the man talking while he waited to be served. It had taken a heap of sweet talk to convince Dana to let them stay and have a drink while they were waiting to hear from the impound guy.

Jeff had called and, in fact, had made an about-face outside, diligently trying to get the man on the phone. It seemed the city of Ketchikan used more than one impounding service, and the guy who'd towed the pickup wasn't around.

Earl Spivey's recording claimed he'd be back Monday, but Jeff wasn't to be deterred and had already left six messages. He wanted that truck now because he hadn't been able to find his wallet. When they arrived at Red Creek Lodge and Jeff went to get his credit card, his wallet hadn't been in his back pocket. A call to Sam Hyatt and it hadn't been left in the airplane, so Jeff was convinced it must have fallen from his pocket on the truck's front seat.

"Card, I can't see you whoppin' anyone's butt," responded a guy with thick hands. His beefy size had Mark thinking he could have worked in a meatpacking plant, hefting carcasses.

"You've never seen me vexed, Bear," the Jamaican replied. "I could show you crazy."

Mark's gaze traveled to Dana's movements behind the bar. He liked how she moved. Never wasted a step. Efficient. Fast. It was a shame she didn't slow down. A person could miss a lot when they never stopped to enjoy what was right around them.

With that, Mark grinned. And just then she turned. Seeing him smiling at her made her frown. "So why is it we have this opposite thing going on here, Dana? I smile, you frown. I want to stay, you tell me to go. I say yes, you say no. Seems to me you make things too difficult. Might want to change your answer next time from what you're really thinking, and then we'll be on the same side of the bed."

She drew up to him, the bar separating them, and set down two cold brews. "I'm thinking that you better drink fast and go to bed with someone else tonight, cowboy."

Chuckling, Mark folded his arms over his chest. "She does have a sense of humor."

Apparently only hearing that last part of their exchange, the Jamaican added a comment. "Dis gal, she is de best."

"Thanks, Cardelle," she replied in a flattered voice.

Thanks. And spoken just as easy as that. But not one *gracias* for him. And he'd brought her a cooler of halibut—*and* chucked all the salmon into Jeff's so he could fill the stupid ice chest to the top.

Cardelle recognized Mark with a polite nod. "Jewels of de Nile offers discounts to Carnival cruisers."

"Jews of Denial—that some kind of Holocaust museum?"

"*Jew*-ry," he enunciated. "For de Carnival cruisers."

Dawning hit Mark. "I'm not on any fiesta ship." He took a cold drink of beer. "I'm here for the fishing."

As he spoke, Mark heard a sound that he hadn't anticipated.

Dana softly laughed.

An instinctive response gripped Mark—he wanted to fit his mouth over hers and kiss her quiet. Since that wasn't an option, his gaze slowly fell to the expanse of her neck, then lower to her breasts. "Are you laughing because I'm here fishing or because I fished for you?"

"Neither." She'd sobered the moment his eyes landed on her in a suggestive way. A pullover sweater with a high scoop neck and jeans might have been plain enough for the average woman, but she wasn't average. Anything she wore would attract a man. "I thought it was funny Cardelle assumed you were a tourist on a cruise. Then again, I guess you cruise for women so there's some truth to it."

"I don't need to cruise for women, sweetart. They drive right into my lane." He popped a few cashews into his mouth, chewing a moment. "And that's not my cooler, by the way. When you unload it, let me know and I'll come back and get it."

She sobered, her gorgeous face taking on a stubborn strength. "I can unload it in a sec. You won't have to come back."

"I'm in town for the summer, sunshine," he informed with a satisfied grin. "I'll be back."

Jeff nudged his way toward the bar and dropped onto the seat next to Mark's. His face red, he reported, "Still no answer. What kind of city is this that you get your truck towed and nobody's on a switchboard to answer your call? I'd even take a routing to India if that meant I could talk to a live person to get some answers."

Cardelle tilted his head, staring at Jeff. Creases at the corners of his dark-as-coal eyes, he gave a questioning stare. "What dat that you say?"

Taking a miscue, Jeff blurted, "You know

someone at Spivey's impound? I need to get my pickup truck back. Some bozo had it towed from the lot right outside."

Puffing his narrow chest, Cardelle's eyes closed halfway. His stubby lashes framed an irate gaze. "I be dat bozo."

"What the—?" Jeff jumped off his bar stool. "Why in the hell did you do that? You've caused me a lot of grief, bro."

With an intense glare, he replied, "I'm not your brother, mon." Sliding off his chair, the Jamaican stood poised like a praying mantis ready to fight. "Your stupid parking blocked my Buick and I missed my fav'rite TV show."

"I didn't park stupid. That piece of crap you call a car was over the line."

"Dat is was not, mon!"

A fist was raised for a swing, but the guy behind the bar came around to stand between the two men. Mark had heard Dana call him Leo.

"Walt!" Leo called, and the bruiser appeared out of nowhere, bearing down on the scene like a raging bull barreling into a mob.

"Break it up, girls!" Walt's wall of muscle was no match for Jeff, and he just about hefted him over his shoulder to knock him back on his feet about a yard away from Cardelle.

Dana appeared, her long hair falling over her shoulders as she squared them, looking first at Jeff, then at Mark. She hadn't been at the bar when the truck bozo discussion had occurred, but he could bet she'd make a snap judgment.

Not disappointing him, she gave Jeff a stern glare. "Get out."

"Hey, lady—I'm not even drunk. I didn't do anything! This joker—" he motioned to Cardelle with his head since his arms were pinned by Walt "—had my pickup towed, and for no good reason."

Cardelle, who'd been refraining from a bodily attack, dove onto the bar and snatched a tall green aerosol can. With the agility of a featherweight, he began spraying the stuff at Jeff.

The meatpacker intervened by saying, "Card, settle down and fork over the dang Off!."

Within a matter of seconds, the whole thing was over, both of the men grumbling their grievances to anyone who'd listen.

Mark's gaze met Dana's, and he could tell she was amping up to throw them both out. Again.

With his best you-gotta-love-me smile, he gave a humorous shrug. "Nobody spilled anything this time. Let's call it good and forget the whole thing."

With a velvety-smooth tone that sounded like the finest musical note, sweet and low, she uttered, "Let's not."

And then all it took was a glance to Walt and Leo, and Jeff and Mark found themselves standing on the dock, looking at the closed door to the Blue Note bar.

The night's ocean dampness fell over them like a

wet blanket. Their gear had been stowed at Fish Tail Air when they'd come back to the dock to figure out what had happened to the pickup. Now dark and motionless inside, the floatplane building had been locked up. They would have to retrieve their stuff tomorrow.

"This sucks." Jeff hunkered down near a faucet and turned on a stream of water. The hose that the water came from lay in a green coil. He washed off his face, blinking back the droplets that collected on his lashes. "That guy just about made me blind with that mace he sprayed on me."

"It was mosquito repellent." Mark leaned against the building and retrieved his cell phone from his belt clip.

"Who are you calling?" Twisting the faucet off, Jeff flicked water from his hands and rose to his feet. "The cops? Good idea. I'm going to press charges."

"A cab." Punching 411, Mark held the phone to his ear. As the phone rang on the other end, he asked, "What did you do before you were a computer geek?"

"I worked at Best Buy in the electronics department. Why?"

"Just wondering how you developed such a way with people."

With a deadpan expression, Jeff supplied, "Extensive training."

CHAPTER THREE

A MAGPIE FLEW overhead, its repetitive screech distracting Suni. Tilting her head, she searched for the black-and-white bird to see where it landed. She'd never been fond of magpies.

It perched in the majestic hemlock, crying and carrying on as if she would listen. She preferred songbirds, their notes soothing.

As Suni continued to tend her hillside garden, reflections of her past came to her. Most times when she tilled the soil, pulled weeds and dead-headed her flowers, she let her mind wander to beautiful things.

And her mother embodied one of those beautiful things.

As a young lady living in Chinatown, Suni's mother had been blessed with a gift for painting delicate watercolors; she also served on several committees in the community. She met and fell deeply in love with a diplomatic social worker, a man whose heritage was half Caucasian and half Chinese. Her parents, immigrants from Mainland China, hadn't approved of his mixed race.

But her mom married him anyway.

From that union, a daughter had been born. Jane Sun Li. In the Chinese culture, her name would have been written Li Jane, but her parents took pride in the fact their daughter was American—

like them. They'd taken their oath of citizenship, and proudly honored the United States flag.

When Jane had been a little girl, she loved her glorious name, grateful her parents had given her a popular choice. Ridiculous as it seemed, she'd fantasized she'd marry someone named Dick.

As she matured into her teens, she began to feel more of a pull toward her Chinese heritage. While her dad had been half white, Jane hadn't thought of herself as anything but Chinese. A desire to be less like everyone else came about the same time she entered her senior year of high school. Janes and Barbaras were a dime a dozen. Nobody was Sun.

So she began to ask everyone to call her Suni. Suni sounded cool—like the girl Windy in the hit song by The Association. She'd seen the group perform on the *Smothers Brothers Comedy Hour.*

Suni had grown up in San Francisco during a time of free love, peace demonstrations and pot smoking. Speaking out and testing the establishment went against her family's cultural beliefs. The only way she displayed her ideas was through her typewriter. She loved to write and had worked on the fourth-period newspaper staff as an op/ed advisor. Within the pages of the newspaper, she found a limitless way to express herself.

She'd also loved wearing her white vinyl go-go boots, corduroy maxiskirts, and had permed her hair to emulate Janis Joplin's look.

As years passed, she forgot about the perm, and

let her hair go to its natural straightness. She gave up the blue eye shadow, frosted Lip Smackers, and ended up being rather subdued in comparison.

But she continued with her writing. She enjoyed that aspect of her life, and felt she had a real talent for it. She tried writing plays and dramas, but nothing ever jibed. Until she wrote a piece about taking an extended camping trip to Half Moon Bay in a 1969 Volkswagen van with three friends. The words fell into perfect poetry and she'd sold it to a travel magazine.

She'd found her niche.

Suni packed a suitcase, and dropped out of college to start on a road adventure that ultimately led her to the true love of her life. She wrote travel articles, filled with slices of American pop culture, and sold them to syndicated presses, making a living for herself—much to her parents' disappointment. They'd wanted their only child to remain with them, and model herself into their expectations.

Having written about the quirky denizens of the West Coast and Pacific Northwest, Suni opted to venture farther north. She arrived in Alaska in 1973, taking her time soaking in the beauty. Articles seemed to flow from her fingertips, personal and thoughtful like life's scrapbook.

The people she wrote about were real, they had drive and determination. There was a scrubbiness, a pistol-charged energy about their communities.

Hearing about one such man who knew everyone and who had the uncanny ability to make anyone smile, Suni stepped into the Blue Note bar to talk to Oscar Jackson, formerly of Louisiana. And from that day forward, she knew she'd found her man.

Her wedding license hadn't been scripted to Dick and Jane, but rather Oscar and Suni. Two people who loved, who laughed, who were best friends and soul mates.

The magpie's caw intruded once more, disturbing the atmosphere. She looked around at the trees, the moss, the rocks. Her free spirit dominated the space. In her garden she had no cares, she embraced the earthy breeze on her face, and she was able to go forward without her beloved Oscar.

And her baby boy . . . Terrance.

She had Danalee. And her grandson, Terran. A grandmother's love and joy, that little boy Terran! Suni couldn't imagine life without him and recalled the tiny bundle she'd held in her arms when he'd been born.

Dana and Terran were all the family Suni had left. Her parents had been gone for years, and her darling husband and son had been gone for going on six years now.

Suni used a hand claw to fluff the earth around the sprouts of ferns that she hadn't planted by seed, but had grown by the hand of tranquillity. The garden comprised most of the hillside. She'd been working it for years, adding more to it all the time.

Each year, the expanse came alive with vibrancy during the short summer months. Suni loved it out here. She had a bench Oscar had built for her and paths in flat stone that led in all directions. The house sat on five acres of unfenced forest. Her garden took up the south side of the property, the whispers from the pines calling to her as she worked.

Over the years, her collection of Chinese statuary had increased. Pavers led to secret nooks where waist-high pagodas, fu dogs, temple lions, arching dragons and many Buddha were sentinels over the vast landscape.

The wind chimes hanging from the pagoda arch stirred to life. Metal tubes created beautiful notes, but the melody belonged to an old spoon, coins, tie clip—which had only been worn a handful of times—a car key and a man's plain wedding ring.

Suni paused, shaded her gaze and watched the pieces sparkle in the sun. They moved on the breeze's whisper.

"Thank you for coming to me, love. My mind is serene," she said to his spirit.

She smiled, a calming peace soothing her broken heart. The chimes had hung for many years before Oscar's passing. He'd given them to her as a special birthday gift. But she had created the other chime: the spoon—his favorite to eat ice cream. Dangling coins with tiny holes to string them—the money he'd had in his pocket the day he'd died.

The dreaded tie clip—something he only wore when pressed. An extra car key—to his '84 Mercedes-Benz which she had sold long ago. And the ring he wore on his finger for every day of their married life. These things were the heart of the wind chime.

They were Oscar.

True tranquillity was found in activity, in the midst of sense objects.

Gardening was her tranquillity. The chimes were her sense objects. And when Oscar walked in his return to earth, the things that were his moved with his presence.

She felt him come home on the wind. Happiness filled her being and she knew that he was waiting for her to join him.

Sometimes she wished she could leave right now. But that wasn't what Oscar wanted. He needed her to be here for Dana. And for Terran.

But the times when the chimes danced, and captured Suni's soul, it was like dancing with Oscar. A slow dance that she loved.

"Mom," Dana called from the side porch of the house. "We're going to town for dinner. Wash your hands and come with us."

Suni got to her feet, her knee joints slightly aching from time spent on bent legs. She used a foam pad to kneel on, but she wasn't getting any younger. Sixty next year.

Calling out, Suni asked, "Where are you going?"

Dana's hands rested on the railing, her body standing in a rare slice of Ketchikan sunshine. The smile she offered warmed Suni to the very core. "Where do you think?"

Her stomach growling over the answer, Suni replied, "I'll get ready."

Thirty minutes later, on a late Sunday afternoon, Suni, Dana and Terran sat together in a black booth at Chop Suey. The cushion needed new springs, or something to give it some lift, but none of them cared. A Chinese-American restaurant located on the far end of Front Street, the place filled a culinary gap in Ketchikan.

"Mommy, can I get fried rice and those chicken nuggets with the red sauce?" Terran asked. He'd recently had a haircut, the sides short, but the top a little longer. Cooper had taken him to a barber.

"It's called sweet-and-sour chicken, Terran," Suni clarified.

Dana nodded, her menu unopened before her. She knew the choices by heart. Their usual waitress came, visited with them and took their orders.

They'd been coming here for three years, ever since Dana and Cooper had ironed out a visitation agreement in court. Sunday was their trade-off day for Terran, and usually just after dinner. Being at Chop Suey gave Dana the chance to wind down without mundane distractions at home—bill paying, bar supply lists—stuff she felt she never caught up with. She liked having an enjoyable meal and time off to visit and talk to Terran about the week ahead at his dad's.

In the beginning, when Terran first had to go to Cooper's for a week at a time, he'd start to ask her when his dad was coming hours beforehand. Terran's disposition changed; his face expressed worry. And as the hour approached, he'd get clingy, then start to cry.

No doubt. Terran had only known her arms when he'd cried in the middle of the night, her soothing voice to calm his fears. During the first two years of their son's life, Cooper bailed. He saw him, but he hadn't taken an active role in his caregiving. Infancy to the toddler years had fallen to her. But when Terran started forming words and turning into a little man, Cooper took notice. He'd wanted to make up for the years he'd missed.

Better late than never, Dana supposed.

Thankfully Cooper had turned out to be a pretty decent dad, and now Dana didn't have any trouble on Sunday. Once in a while, there were some whimpers, but overall, the routine had turned as normal as the situation could.

Dana felt for her son. The back-and-forth from house to house was a horrible thing for a five-year-old, but it was the best solution. Even though she and Cooper differed in many ways, she couldn't be too critical of him at this point.

He had stepped up to the plate, something she

61

never thought he would do. In his own way, Cooper managed.

Cooper had Terran in preschool—aka day care— during the day, an arrangement Dana wasn't fond of, but the time was Cooper's and he could legally do what he wanted so long as it wasn't detrimental to Terran's well-being.

"Momma, how come there's no soy sauce on the table?" Terran asked, his dark eyes inquisitive.

And so it began.

"Because they bring it with our dinner."

"How come?"

"Because that's how they do it."

"But doncha think it would be smarter to leave it on the table? Because everybody loves soy sauce."

"That would be a better idea, baby, but that's not how they do it."

"Why not?"

"Because."

Suni enveloped the blissful four seconds of silence. And then the inevitable happened.

"Mommy?" Terran's dark brown hair spiked a little at the back where he had a cowlick. "*Because* isn't an answer."

Suni, an observer during the exchange, broke in with her stock response. "Terran, if your mom says 'because' is an answer, it's an answer."

"Yeah, but—"

"So," Dana began, flattening the long paper wrapper that she'd discarded after putting the straw in her cola glass, "Daddy said you're going fishing on Wednesday. He's got the day off."

Terran's warm-colored skin glowed with charged excitement. His ethnic features were subtle. The most prominent were his very brown eyes that he'd inherited from Oscar. He actually looked more like Cooper than her. Same nose, a marginally unsymmetrical lower lip and beautiful eyebrows.

"Yep. We're taking Riley, too."

Riley was Cooper's two-year-old chocolate lab. Since the day Cooper had gotten the puppy, Terran had been after her to get a dog at their house, too. But that was not happening. She wasn't around enough to take care of it, and just because Cooper did something, didn't mean she would.

Their meal arrived, and as they ate, they talked about Terran's kindergarten registration. They'd visited the school in May to fill out the paperwork, and he couldn't wait to start Fawn Mountain Elementary.

"Momma," Terran said between chews, displaying the gap in the top of his teeth. His left front tooth had fallen out and he'd been awarded a dollar bill from the Tooth Fairy. "How come the school won't let me go if I don't have that shot?"

"Because you need the booster, baby."

"What's a booster?"

He must have asked her this a dozen times. "It's a little extra medicine in the shot that makes you not get sick."

"If I had the med'cine the first time, how come I need some more?"

"You just do."

"But why?"

"Because."

Then in his sweet-boy voice, he said, "Mommy?"

Dana looked up from her plate and waited for the question. "Yes, Terran?"

He grinned, that toothless smile of his that made her want to squeeze him. "I love you, Momma."

Dana melted into a puddle, her heart warmed to her deepest center of being. She fought hot tears, resolving not to let them fall. Tears of unconditional love, tears of having to miss him being with her this week. "Love you, too, baby boy."

THE BLUE NOTE REMAINED closed on Sundays, giving Dana the much-needed opportunity to play catch-up. Normally, she filed her mountain of paperwork, did the payroll, organized ledger sheets that controlled the expenses and operating costs. She had gained a lot of knowledge since taking over the Blue Note, and the mistakes she'd made early on had merely been learning curves.

On this clear Sunday night, she had an eight-o'clock meeting with a general contractor. She almost canceled so she could enjoy sitting outside. The day had reached nearly sixty degrees, and had been sunny. Days like this were to be savored down to the last second of a late-evening sunset.

But Bruce was going to meet her at the Blue Note and give her a bid on adding an exit door.

She'd gone to high school with Bruce and had known him and his wife, Sandy, for years. When she called, he'd said no problem to coming out at this hour on the weekend.

Dana unlocked the bar, stepped inside and switched the lights on. When nobody was around, the place looked entirely different. A vast empty space of tables with chairs turned upside down on their tops, a vacant bar and the musician's floor where the jazz notes of the Sax Man's woodwind still filled Dana's memory.

Sadness assailed her, and she wished her dad would come out from the back room and give her a bear hug.

The heavy silence in the cavernous space hurt Dana's ears. She turned on the jukebox and selected a CD recording of her dad playing. Listening to the notes, she lost herself in the song. Then the nostalgic sound of Glenn Miller and his orchestra overtook the ghostly shadows. "Moonlight Serenade" breathed life into the room.

Pouring herself a sparking water with a twist of lime, Dana barely had a moment to think about the fire marshal's demands when Bruce showed up.

He was once the captain of the football team with a promising pro career, but an injury had wiped out that dream and Bruce had stayed behind in Alaska. He'd married Sandy, the head cheer-leader, and opened a contracting business. They had four kids ranging in age from fourteen months to eight and a half.

Time hadn't been kind to Bruce. He'd grown a soft belly and his dark hair had thinned. The bridge of his nose had been broken during the game against Juneau, and what had been considered so cool in high school, looked misaligned in later years.

Striding forward, the first thing she noticed was the saying on Bruce's navy T-shirt, and she stifled a laugh. In big block lettering over his chest: *It Takes A Stud To Build A House.*

"Hey, Dana. You're looking great, as always." He'd brought a metal clipboard, the kind that opened and folded back to expose the notepad inside. A yellow tape measure hooked onto his belt, and he wore a Denver Broncos ball cap.

Never comfortable acknowledging her appearance, she let the comment go. "So, like I told you on the phone, Fire Marshal Bill hit me with some stuff I need to do."

His gaze lingered on her face then, for a few seconds, lowered before moving back to direct eye contact. She'd worn a short-sleeved Ed Hardy T-shirt, loving the colors and the lively skull with hearts. A pair of blue jean capris encased her lean legs, and she'd kept her wedged leather flip-flops on from earlier in the day.

She noticed a slight chill in the bar, or maybe it was the feeling she got when Bruce gave her a closer look. But she disregarded the tinge of vague discomfort. She was being stupid. She'd known the guy practically her entire life.

"So here's his report." She led Bruce to the table where she'd laid out the papers.

Bruce studied it, shifted through notations, then said, "You've got some pricey problems to tackle."

Dread sank her emotions and she felt as if she were drowning. How could she make this work and not go broke? "Even more than what's there?"

"Yeah. I add an exit door and you're going to have to widen the hallway."

"He didn't say I had to."

"It's code. You make a door, you better have the room to get out of it. After I do that, you'll need to slap up some fireproof rock down the corridor." He gave her a placating smile, something that she would have warmed to, but she sensed it had nothing to do with what they were discussing.

He wanted to nail more than drywall.

With a brawny exhalation, he said, "It'll be a fairly straightforward job, but I'll have to put in some hours. And I'm thinking it'll disrupt your business operation, so mornings work well. What time do you get here?"

"I'd really like an estimate, Bruce." She didn't add that she was tight on funds and needed to make every penny count.

"Not to worry about that." His gaze fell on her breasts once more. "I'd give you a discount." He took a step closer to her; she didn't flinch.

"Don't do me any favors," she said flatly.

"We all need favors, Danalee." With that comment, Bruce took down a chair and made himself comfortable. "Damn, it feels good to get off my feet. Sandy's had me doing junk for her all day. You'd think the woman had two broken legs. It'll be good to work for a woman who appreciates me."

The idea of Bruce being here every day left her cold.

"It's nice to get out and be understood. Sandy doesn't give a rip about me, what I want. You were lucky you never married. You can do whatever you feel like."

"Not true, Bruce. I have a son."

"Yeah, that's right. Cooper Boyd's kid. He was some lucky son of a gun to have hooked up with you." Leaning back in the chair, he slowly spread his legs, as if for her to get a view of the bulge in his jeans. "In high school, you would have killed to go out with me, only I never had the brains to see just how damned gorgeous you are. I'd like to treat you right, Dana. I know you'd like it."

Her heart beat in her ears, a thunderous pounding. The very air in her lungs seemed to be growing thinner. She knew she came across as don't-mess-with-me during business hours but, in truth, it took a lot of craft and acting to appear unfazed. Deep down, she had a tender heart, and she hated this kind of manhandling, even if it was only vocal.

For a scant second, she feared he might try something and she'd never be able to get him off her. *Don't panic.* She struggled to not bolt for the pepper spray she kept hidden behind the bar.

His hands cupped either side of his inner thighs and he gave her a smile that—yes—she would have loved to have received in high school, but that was then and this was now.

Now, he made her feel sick. She'd trusted him to come over here, had never even given him the slightest encouragement or led him on.

Damn him.

"Bruce, I think—"

"I'd like to propose something." His eyes shone with a glassy purpose and hunger.

"So would I, slick."

Mark Moretti's muscled body fleshed out the doorway opening, his voice like a drop of honey. All the tension within her seemed to let go at the same time, and she almost gave a short laugh.

Trusting on blind faith was a stretch for her, but that's what she had to do right now. Deep down, she sensed Moretti wasn't a threat. There was an honest quality to him, and because of that, his unexpected presence brought her relief.

She kept her emotions in check, and then quite

matter-of-factly said, "Moretti—good, you're right on time to talk about the construction job."

An unspoken question flickered in Mark's gaze, but he didn't counter her comment.

She acted as cool as a spring tide, not making eye contact with Bruce as she dismissed him. "Work up an estimate and mail it to me. Thanks for coming out, Bruce. Tell Sandy I said hi."

With a jerking motion, Bruce grabbed his clipboard, then shot Mark a long stare. The lettering on his T-shirt seemed to scream off his chest.

"That shirt sums you up, doesn't it, stud?" Mark strolled into the bar as if he'd had an appointment to be here. "And I bet you're into performance evaluations."

Dana gritted her teeth. Mark should have let it go. Now he'd pissed Bruce off.

"You know what, pal," Bruce said through thick lips, "I wasn't finished here."

"Sure you were." Mark halted dead in front of him. The men were matched in height, but Bruce had Mark in bulk twofold. "You want to know why?" Moretti's voice sluiced through the bar, assured and easygoing.

"Why?" Bruce grunted.

"'Cause I've got a hunch that the shiny four-wheel drive out in the parking lot with the bumper sticker that says *Building America, One Erection at a Time* is yours."

"What of it?"

"Some kids were taking a piss on your tires and writing 'ride me' on your tailgate with the cans of fluorescent paint you had in the truck bed."

Bruce bolted for the door, bearing down on it as if he was running for the end zone. As soon as he was out, Mark hitched the lock in place and folded his arms over his chest.

Dana's mouth opened. "Is that true?"

"He'll find out when he gets there."

"You were lying?"

"Dana, I don't lie very often. Only to men who have heads like buffalos and who think with what's below their belt."

Unbidden, Dana laughed to the point where she couldn't stop. And it felt so good, she didn't want to.

CHAPTER FOUR

WHEN MARK HAD SEEN the fearful wariness on Dana's face as Bruce propositioned her, a foreign rage had hit him. If he hadn't controlled himself, he could have done something he would have regretted.

Mark remained stationed at the door in case Bruce decided to come back and use his fist to give it a pound. "How'd you find that dum-dum? The yellow pages?"

Dana sobered, her easy laughter fading. Instantly, he missed the lighthearted sound. "I went to high school with him. He was the captain of the football team."

"He's the captain of dirtbags now."

"I never thought I'd say this to you—but I agree. I didn't realize he'd changed so much when I called him. But I needed a contractor."

That information gave him pause again. He only had one explanation for how she knew what he did for a living.

"The Internet makes it easy to find out about a person," he said with a half ounce of sarcasm. "Nobody's got any anonymity anymore. Not that I care you looked."

"I don't know what you're talking about."

"Type in a name, click on the search. For a few bucks on your Visa, you can find out all sorts of stuff." He went toward her, a grin on his mouth and a slight dimple on his cheek. "All you had to do was ask, and I'd have told you anything you wanted to know about me."

Her eyes narrowed, and she lifted the chair back onto the tabletop, as if she needed something to do. Then she accused, "How do I know you're not here for the same thing Bruce was?"

He felt a shadow of annoyance touch his face. "Do I look like I smash beer cans on my forehead?"

"I'm not sure."

"Is that your final answer?"

"Maybe."

"Then you aren't as smart as I thought you were, Dana. You don't advance to the next round."

"I'm not playing games with you."

"Too bad. Sometimes it can be fun if you pick the right game." Mark's gaze traveled across the ceiling and over the walls. "So what do you want done? I noticed the roof's shot in a few places."

Her standoffish demeanor was evidence she didn't want to talk to him about her remodel—or whatever it was she needed.

Mark's guess, having overheard her talking to Sam about the fire marshal coming in for an inspection, was she'd been written up. Having taken just a cursory look at the Blue Note, Mark thought she was fortunate the guy hadn't closed her down.

"You must have gotten written up longer than a wish list for Santie Claus," he said, glancing at the papers on the table. "Show me what you have."

She made no move for the folder or its paperwork. Doubt set lines in her forehead. "What are you doing here? We're closed."

"Lights on, music playing. Looked open to me."

"Well, we're not."

In an easy voice, he said, "I went to the aviation office to grab our stuff. Nobody there. Saw lights on in the bar and hoped someone inside would have a key. My lucky day—" he gave her a compelling smile "—I found you."

For a long moment, she said nothing, as if she

were mulling over his intervention and whether or not to comment on it. She gave him a slow and hard study. Her almond-shaped eyes grazed over his body, heating his blood to the marrow of his bones.

Mark would have given anything to be able to read her mind. He watched her face, the different expressions that played into her eyes and caught on her mouth.

At length, she said tartly, "I could have handled Bruce."

"I'm sure of it," he scoffed, her words not the ones he would have liked to hear. "He's got to be pushing two-sixty, wears a triple XL and you're what—ninety pounds soaking wet, and five feet on tiptoes?"

The comment had her bristling, something he'd probably set out to do only he didn't want to admit it. But her lack of falling all over him in gratitude for saving her from a construction moron who had ground beef for a brain put a dent in Mark's male pride. Women had always gone out of their way to appreciate him.

"Five foot three, and a hundred and eight." A blush crept over her cheeks as if she'd said too much. Apparently sensitive about her petite stature, a mixture of distress and irritation crossed her face.

Disarming her with a smile, he simply stared. He fought the urge to compare her to the women he'd dated in the past. But there was no help for it. She was a tiny package with a quick wit and a hot temper that could ignite him. She was nothing like the women he usually felt himself drawn to; he couldn't be more attracted to Dana if she walked naked in front of him.

And that was a thought worth thinking about.

He liked the print shirt she wore. The colors and artwork had attitude. Just like her. White knit fabric caressed her waist and emphasized her slender shape.

Taking in a sharp breath, she folded her arms over small but attractive breasts.

The defensiveness had to have been perfected over the years. While all people had a history, hers had to have been tough. He wondered what she'd be like without hidden scars. She must have been hurt pretty bad to be so protective of her emotions.

Moving past him, she said, "I've got a key to Fish Tail."

She went to unlock the door, and he laid his hand over hers on the knob.

This close, he absorbed her body heat, and her fragrance filled his senses. His shoulder width and height devoured her, but she didn't move. Her lips, delicately made, looked soft and full. He fought the urge to pull her into his arms and kiss her, stroke her glossy hair and keep her close.

"I'll go first." Gravelly and thick, his voice didn't sound like his own in his ears. When she narrowed her eyes, he clarified, "In case Paul Bunyan's still around."

Outside, the evening had turned damp and cold. The harbor lights were like fuzzy yellow orbs bathing the Blue Note's entry in a pale glow. Shadows cast murky shapes on the walkway. You'd have to be a cat to see clearly and know if anyone was moving in on you.

In earnest concern, he took her fingers, knitting them within his own. Surprise widened her eyes, but a swift jerk couldn't get rid of his protective gesture. He held fast. "You walk to your car alone after you close?"

She no longer flinched, but turned loosely toward the aviation office and continued to head that direction. Her stiff posture begged him to release her. "Usually."

A buffered anger welled inside him. "You shouldn't do that. Anything could happen to you."

"I'm still standing. So far, so good." And then she slid out of his grasp to open the floatplane building.

She switched the light on, and the booking desk came into view, strewn with brochures and paper-work piles. It was the airplane model that caught his attention.

"Your pilot make that?" he asked, wondering about the connection between the two of them.

Casually responding, she spoke while heading for the back. "Yes, it's Sam's."

"Cozy that he gave you a key to his office," Mark said, unable to contain an unwanted jealous note.

"It's not his office. It's mine." Then she smiled, as if gloating that she'd gotten the better of him. Surprise must have marked his eyes, giving him away. "I own Fish Tail Air. The three airplanes and this building. Sam and two other pilots fly for me."

Mark digested her news. She spoke with an emotional pride; he felt a tenderness in her words, as if there were more meaning to the place than what she let on.

Contrary to her tough talk, she had a softness inside that came to light. He'd only seen traces of this emotion in her before. The layer added yet another complexity about her he found interesting.

"Well, aren't you the complex woman," he remarked after a long moment.

While Dana shifted things in the back room, Mark gazed at the surroundings. Framed photos on the wall drew his eyes. Celebrities standing next to a floatplane. He recognized some of the actors from a hit television show. With strings of salmon and halibut raised behind them on scales, they mugged for the camera with a pilot—not Sam. Someone else. Looked like Sam though. Had the same eyes.

One photo demanded his attention and he zeroed in on it. An African-American man stood with his arm around another guy. The younger of the two men resembled Dana in many ways. Lifting the frame off the wall, he angled it toward the light to study the images closer.

"Put it back." Dana's voice held a strong note of reproach.

He held on to the picture, neither looking further nor replacing it on the wall.

The next thing he knew, Dana was lunging toward him, trying to swipe it out of his hand. He drew back, the photo high in the air with his arm extended.

Tackling his chest with a body thrust, she knocked him into the door's edge, her breath heated against his neck. Hands grappled to take the picture from him, but her sloppy effort was only a minor nuisance. He could take her down over his knee before she had the chance to suck in another breath.

Mildly confused by her outburst, with one hand he angled her in a different position away from his shirtfront. With her energetic charge, the hard point of her elbow had been dangerously close to a certain area.

With a husky whisper, he informed, "Simmer down, Dana. I'll put it back."

He slowly released her and she didn't fight him anymore.

The photograph resumed its spot on the cluttered wall. Using his knuckle, he corrected the tilt.

Getting the top level, he skimmed the photo for clues. He couldn't figure out why she'd gotten so bent out of shape.

Turning to Dana, he asked, "If you don't want anyone looking at it, why do you have it hanging on the wall?"

The steady rise and fall of her breasts, the soft sucking of her wet lips trying to catch her breath, almost made him forget what he questioned her about. Black hair fell around her face, a tangle of sexy wisps. Raking it back, she took in a gulp of air.

"There's all your stuff." She pointed to gear piled on the floor. "And your ice chest."

"I take it you're not going to answer." It was a curiosity to find a woman so damned standoffish, yet fascinating.

Going around her, he hoisted two ditty bags on his shoulder, then grabbed the tackle boxes and rods. He couldn't manage the Igloo at the same time. "I'll have to make another trip."

Silently, she gathered the ice chest and followed behind him to Jeff's rental truck. They'd gotten it back late that afternoon and Jeff's wallet had been on the truck floor. A credit to Spivey's integrity, no money had been taken—until Earl asked for the impound fee, and handed over the ticket from the police department.

Jeff had been so irritated by the amount it cost him to park in a public lot he went back to the condo to have a beer and mess with the software on his laptop. At that point, Mark volunteered to get their fishing equipment.

The parking lot's asphalt glittered with busted glass pieces by the Dumpster.

"Watch where you're walking," he cautioned over his shoulder. "You're going to step on glass and cut your foot."

"Not hardly."

Settling the tackle into the truck's bed, he snorted. "So we're doing that dance again—the 'I say one thing and you say another'?"

"I walk in this parking lot with my flip-flops on all the time and I've never had a problem."

"You should have a problem with it." He frowned, glancing at the black-cloaked veil of the parking lot. Set off from Dock Street, a person would have to scream at the top of their lungs to be heard. "It's dark out here. Any degenerate might be sitting around waiting to jump you. That potbellied quarterback could be hunkered down behind the wheel of his four-by-four, pumped up to rush you."

She gave the area a furtive glance, biting her lip as if he'd made an impression on her to be—at the very least—momentarily concerned.

As if to validate her lack of concern, she declared, "There's nobody here."

Lowering his mouth intimately close to her ear, he whispered, "I am."

• • •

NOT SINCE COOPER TOOK HER to court over his visitation rights had Dana felt such frustration, compounded by the feeling of total lack of control.

A glance out the window, and she saw Mark's truck was still there.

For the past thirty minutes, she'd holed herself up inside the Blue Note, hoping he'd drive away and leave her alone. Trapped with only her thoughts to pass the time, she was going stir-crazy. The harder she tried to ignore the truth, the more it persisted.

Tonight had been a turning point.

Mark had touched her, held her hand within his own. She'd fought to disguise the internal tremble she'd felt over the smooth warmth of his flesh. No man who came to the bar was allowed to get physically close. While it wasn't something she'd made an announcement about, everyone knew Danalee Jackson was off-limits.

She'd never gotten involved with a customer. Nor would she. As the owner, she set herself apart from the crowd. She didn't mind if Presley or Leo and Walt made connections. She just felt that as the proprietor, people ought to have propriety around her. It was all about respect.

But there were times when a good-looking man came in, and she wanted to amend her personal rule. Many had tried to get her to change her mind. She had never yielded.

She'd dated plenty before Terran, and while not so much after his birth, she wasn't seriously looking. If the right guy happened to come along, it happened. She wouldn't shut the door. There had been a few guys who'd been nice enough, but the spark just hadn't been there. Not even in their good-night kisses . . . Kisses she'd hungered for, had put her best effort into, but she'd felt nothing more than a crackle—not a snap and pop.

There was something to be said about a hot kiss that could curl her toes, make her want to fuse herself into the man delivering it. Too bad she hadn't felt that since . . .

Damn.

Stupid Cooper Boyd.

Dana checked the time, then glanced out the window. The watchdog was still out there. Didn't he have anyplace to go? The loser.

With that, she laughed at her false misnomer.

Mark Moretti was anything but a loser.

The contact of his hand, the strong feel of his fingers wrapped around hers, had done strange things to her insides. She'd felt as if her blood sped in different directions. The second he touched her, a cocktail of emotions invaded her body.

That he could evoke such a strong awareness in her, and by only taking her hand—God help her if he ever tried to do anything else physical. If a simple touch could affect her, how would she react to his kiss?

Dana groaned.

Her wildly beating heart was the only sound in the bar. She'd shut off the jukebox long ago. All the lights were off except the one at the back bar. Everything was good to go. Just like she was.

Another glance out the window. Still there.

Leave, Moretti! she screamed inside her head.

His talk about the parking lot being a danger zone had given her a mild case of paranoia. She had never had a moment's trouble leaving the bar at night. Usually Leo or Walt was walking out with her, and on those nights they weren't, she hadn't felt afraid to head for her car.

Ketchikan had its fair share of transient drunks who tried to stay dry in various buildings. For the most part, they were harmless. And the crimes were more often to property and not people. Although assaults occurred. She wasn't stupid. She'd got into the habit of carrying a can of mace in her purse, as well as a whistle on her key chain.

Tired and stressed, she wanted to go home. But she had the sinking feeling that Mark would wait her out. And win.

There was no point in stalling any longer.

So, on a resigned sigh, Dana locked the bar, then headed for her 1989 blue S-10 Chevy pickup.

Ignoring Mark, she walked past him with her gaze straight ahead. But she could make him out in her peripheral vision. Muscular and on the alert, he stood with big arms folded over his chest and leaned into the tailgate of his truck.

She didn't want to talk to him anymore.

Trying to fit her key into the lock, she didn't like that her aim was unsteady. What was it about this man that could unhinge her so badly? Her response toward him encompassed more than chaos in her heart. His presence rattled her thoughts, her actions. She couldn't prevent her pulse from triggering swiftly and misfiring.

Glancing at Mark, she tossed her purse onto the bench seat then turned over the engine, anxious to be out of here.

Only the engine didn't start.

She tried once more. Nothing.

And again. Nothing, not even a click.

Dead, dead, dead.

Of all the unbelievable luck. Her battery was dead.

Her hands on the steering wheel, she saw Mark push away from the full-size truck, his tall figure heading toward her. Under the low lights, his hair seemed blacker. A recollection of the faint strands of silver caught in her mind.

He had on a lightweight black jacket that remained unzipped, displaying his broad chest and the crew-neck T-shirt underneath. Boot-cut jeans fit him nicely in the legs and hips. And everywhere else.

She was digging inside her purse for her cell to

call Leo when a soft rap on her window made her stop. Mark stood directly outside and motioned with his hand to lower the glass.

Dread over the inevitable filled her as she cranked the window down a few inches.

"Pop the hood," he commanded, and she was all but ready to tell him no. But the heavy-lidded look in his eyes was serious—he meant business.

She felt for the release and pulled it.

Mark leaned over the engine, fiddling with wires.

She gave him a few seconds to feel macho about trying, then she slipped out of the S-10 to stand beside him.

"It's dead," she announced with a sinking feeling in the pit of her stomach. "It's been touchy lately."

Turning toward her, he cocked his head. "And you're driving it knowing it's not reliable?"

Indignance furrowed her brows. "Hey—it starts most of the time and when it doesn't, a jump will get it going."

Raking his hair back from his forehead, he smirked. "Now if that isn't just like a woman."

Rather than say another word, she released a slow and deep breath. Closing her eyes, she began to count to ten, something she did when she got angry with Terran when he did something wrong. Usually, that ten-count gave her enough of a lapse that she calmed down to talk reasonably with him.

Three . . . four . . .

Thinking about anything else but her truck, she let her mind drift. *Seven.* The aviation office. The photograph. Yes, anyone could see it. She loved that picture.

But she didn't want Mark asking questions about her dad and her brother, Terrance. She hadn't been up for the inquiry . . . and the inevitable "I'm sorry." Nobody was more sorry than her, but it had happened long enough ago that she'd moved on the best she'd been able to. She wasn't healed. She didn't think she'd ever be.

Eight . . . nine . . .

Ten.

She opened her eyes, watching Mark's wrist-watch glint under the parking-lot light as he moved something over the battery. Her concentration to keep herself in check shattered as she caught a hint of his insufferable grin.

"What are you doing?" Against her will, she peeked over his shoulder to see what he was up to.

Facing her, he stated his observation. "You've got yourself a problem."

"You?"

The response was uttered before she could take it back, and she had to admit, watching his smile disappear did add a slight satisfaction.

"No, smarty. Your battery cable's corroded. You got any tools in that box behind your cab?"

The diamond-plated toolbox had seen better days. It was the catchall for stuff she didn't want getting wet from the rain. To her credit, she did keep a small tool kit in there, but nothing fancy.

Without answering, she pushed the button latch and one of the sides popped up. Rummaging around in the dim light, she felt for the tool chest and handed it to Mark.

He lifted the lid and examined the contents, then gazed at her. "This all you have?"

She didn't care for the way he made her feel inept. She didn't have an inadequate bone in her body. She was an unfailing survivor and always managed to figure out a plan. "A hotshot like you should be able to make something in there work."

He stood to his full height, dominating the space around them. She no longer felt the night's chill. To the contrary, warmth seeped through the barriers of her clothing, touching her skin and making her feel hot. Not only towering in size, his shoulders were wide and powerful. Just looking at him caused her throat to go dry.

His height dwarfing her, he said, "I can use the pliers, but you don't have a wire brush in here. How about in the truck?"

All rational thought escaped her and she couldn't seem to work out a response. "What about the truck? It won't start."

Placing hands on either side of her arms, he turned her to face him. With his knuckle, he notched her chin upward to make her look him directly in the eyes. Her entire being shivered. Mortified, she willed herself to be still.

His intent eyes watched her, studying every facet of her fragile features. Brown and fathomless, his pupils were large as he drank in the entire fullness of her mouth. Ever so slightly, his thumbs ran across her skin. She could feel the calluses on his fingertips, the rough-warm sensation of the raw strength he possessed.

Dismayed, she realized she wanted him to touch her like this. She couldn't remember the last time a man had held her face. Her lips fell apart, and she fought for breath. He stood close and his touch felt so . . .

Tension wound through her muscles. She couldn't imagine what he was thinking, didn't want to know.

"What about the truck?" she babbled, repeating her earlier question.

Momentarily tangling his fingers in her hair, he smoothed the pieces behind her ear. "A wire brush. Would you have one in the truck?" His enunciation came across slow and clear, as if she were some kind of half-wit not understanding a basic question.

A dip of her shoulder and she broke free of him, and of the insane feelings bordering on lust that fell over her. "I have a hairbrush."

"What kind?"

Thoroughly out of sorts, she muttered, "What difference does it make?"

"Let me see it."

Dana sat on the truck's narrow seat, rifled through her purse and brought out her hairbrush.

Mark only made a cursory look toward her offering, then shook his head. "It won't work."

Not seeing his reasoning, she put the plastic-bristle brush back in her purse. Then a white lunch bag she'd forgotten about on the front seat caught her attention. Terran's dentist bag.

He'd gotten a good-boy checkup earlier this week and they'd given him a goody bag with stickers, a small bouncy rubber ball that he'd taken into the house to drive her batty as he bounced it off the hardwood floor, dental floss, mini tooth-paste and of course a—

"I have a toothbrush," she offered, extending the unopened package.

Nodding, Mark said with approval, "That'll work."

He peeled the plastic wrap away, took the tooth-brush out, then gave a low laugh from the back of his throat.

Clenching her jaw, she found herself instantly annoyed. This wasn't the first time he had made light of something she'd done or said, using a sense of humor she didn't find entertaining.

Dana snapped, "What's so funny?"

"They were all out of Barbie?" He held the toothbrush for her to view.

Terran had picked the Captain Jack Sparrow

toothbrush as his choice. A plastic replica of Johnny Depp formed the handle.

She wouldn't get into any discussions about her son, so she simply replied, "I like Captain Jack Sparrow—savvy?"

"I like Cameron Diaz but I wouldn't brush my teeth with her."

Dana's hands covered her face for short seconds, then as she lowered them, her posture slumped . . . defeated.

There was no winning with Mark tonight. He always seemed to have a better comeback line than she did. She silenced the few retorts that came to mind, knowing it was futile.

Through the gap where the hood met the dash, Dana could view Mark working on the truck. With the pliers, he removed the terminals from the battery, then cleaned them with the toothbrush. When he was finished, he put the cables back on.

After he checked all the fittings, he said, "Give it a try."

She turned the key over. It started on the first attempt.

Never had the tired engine of her old S-10 sounded so good.

After a final once-over of the engine, Mark lowered the hood. He fit his arm above the cab and leaned in to speak with her.

"Cap'n Jack's got a nasty problem." He handed her the dirt-blackened toothbrush.

She pitched the toothbrush on the seat. "I'll get another one."

Mark didn't readily step aside so she could close the door. She knew she should thank him, but the words didn't form. Instead she asked, "How'd you know how to fix it?"

He scratched his forehead with the back of his thumb and she noticed he'd gotten greasy. "My dad had a lot of old construction equipment and something was always breaking."

A half-used paper towel roll lay on her truck floor—among other things. A crumpled dinner bag from Burger Queen, a set of plans for the Blue Note that she'd had copied and countless items belonging to Terran that he hadn't taken in with him at home. She didn't keep the interior very neat.

"Construction . . . Really?" she asked, tearing off a paper towel and handing it to Mark.

"I thought you figured that out already." He wiped his hands clean, a motion that fascinated her for reasons she couldn't fathom. Maybe because his hands were very masculine. Or the way he went between his fingers, slow and drawn out . . . that she imagined those hands working over her . . . slow and drawn out.

Dana blinked, trying to capture her composure. "I didn't look you up on the computer."

"Well, if you had, you would have found out that your white lie to your high school buddy wasn't a lie at all. I'm your all-American construction worker."

"You could have fooled me."

"Why do you say that?"

"It's your attitude. I would have bet you did something inside. Desk. Chair. Office with a view."

He laughed. "I've got a chair and a desk. It's a beat-up piece of metal crap that my sister tries to keep clean, but that only makes me wonder where everything is. And the chair, the wheels fall off and it gets old putting them back on. The only view I have is through the dusty miniblinds covering the trailer windows on the construction office."

Dana didn't quite know what to say.

Turns out, she didn't have to say anything. He shut the door to her truck, reaching inside to push down the old-style lock on the frame. Peering through the barely open window, he commanded, "Do me a favor, drive straight home. It's too late for you to be out, Cinderella."

The uneven purr of the Chevy's motor idled in the night, the exhaust misting from the tailpipe. In spite of everything, she had a difficult time drafting the words she knew she must say. But to be indebted to him, of all men. The one who could turn her stomach inside out, make her light-headed, cause her the most grief—it was nothing short of warped irony.

"So . . . uh, thanks, Moretti."

She was rewarded with an intimate smile as he backed away from the truck. "Anytime."

CHAPTER FIVE

MARK MORETTI WAS A natural-born charmer.

In elementary school, he had worn his hair too long, like a surfer's, dressed in board shorts year-round, and never cared that girls were always trailing him. At ten, he had better things than chicks on his mind.

Skateboarding rocked his world.

The quarter-pipe plywood ramp his father had built him occupied half their double garage—something his mother disapproved of. But she didn't have to park her car in the driveway—Giovanni's truck had that spot.

His father's goodwill gesture hadn't been forgotten by Mark. In later years when their relationship changed, he reminded himself that his father had built something for him. The boss ramp became a sanctuary, and Mark's posse of friends were always over perfecting tricks on their banana boards.

Teachers liked Mark, but rarely took him too seriously. He got moderate grades—ask him if he cared. Life revolved around various sports—mostly football, but he'd liked baseball season, too. But in the sixth grade, he decided not to re-sign for Optimist football. That summer, he'd settled in on skateboarding, and a dream he had to become the next Ty Page.

Too bad that year he took a face-plant that resulted in a closed fracture of his radius. His arm had hurt so bad when the bone was set that, in spite of telling himself not to, he'd cried. His mother lost it during the procedure, vowing she'd insist his father disassemble that death ramp.

But over dinner, when Mark's two brothers and sister wrote "get well" and "you stink like bugger" on his cast, Giovanni had told his wife to forget it. A boy needed some form of athletics in his life. It could have been worse—he could have landed on his head.

His bone healed, and life went back to normal. Except he no longer had the determination to be a freestyle skater. In junior high, he considered himself fairly uncomplicated and pretty simple. He gave a modest attempt at garnering straight C's—something he felt was a reasonable goal. He attained a little more on his final report card and was rewarded with a ten-dollar bill. He'd blown it on candy and a *Playboy* he'd paid a kid at school to give to him. Known as the family clown, he always joked or played pranks and teased his peers.

Wanting to be taken more seriously, he entered high school and strove to mirror his father's ethics: disciplined in what he did, and doing it the best he could.

Throughout his twenties and thirties, he'd dated a parade of model-type women. Unable to stick around for long in a relationship, he attributed it to the fact that the ladies he involved himself with rarely challenged his intellect. Probably because he never felt as if he had much of his own.

He knew he needed help in the communication department. Practically every girlfriend he'd ever had told him he just didn't understand what they were feeling, and when they asked him how he felt, he said he was fine with how things were. After that, things went south and the relationships ended.

To Mark, it seemed as if he'd set himself up to be treated as nothing beyond the funny guy, and the squirt of the Moretti boys. There was no turning back the clock, but even when he grew more serious about life, nothing felt as if it had changed.

When he'd taken over Giovanni's respected role at Moretti Construction, Mark hoped it would give him satisfaction and the sense of accomplishment he sought.

It hadn't.

The time had come for him to accept responsibility for himself rather than try so hard to fill the big-man shadow his father had vacated.

Sitting on the rain-soaked deck of Bud's Bait and Beer, Mark lit a cigar and let his memories fade. He waved the match to snuff it, thinking the last time he'd enjoyed a cigar had been at his sister's wedding a couple of years ago. He'd never been a cigarette smoker, but sometimes the taste of tobacco appealed to him.

Rain ran down the gutters, into the mud, creating mini-ravines along the tackle shop's decking. Monday had been marginally sunny, but in the three days since then, it'd been raining almost non-stop.

Most people didn't realize Ketchikan was part of a rain forest. The town's lush beauty and that of its surrounding area came from the density of moisture in the air nearly every day.

Rain fell in a nail-pounding sound, the tackle shop's roof awning being buffeted in the late afternoon. Mark sat alone, Jeff having gone inside the shop to buy some beers. They'd driven fifteen miles north of Ketchikan this week to Elk Cove, and had been staying in a rustic cabin here. Yesterday, nearly two inches of rain had fallen, but they'd still headed out in charter boats and hauled in plenty of cohos and kings.

The day before, Mark had thrown on a slicker and hiked in the nearby woods. He'd walked along the river, spotted roaring waterfalls and smelled the pungent mossy banks and regional wildflowers. Not necessarily a great photographer, he'd taken quite a few pictures.

Today, he and Jeff agreed to sit and do not much of anything. Two old men played cards at the far table. Even though it was a hell of a day, sitting outside was a lot better than staying cooped up inside.

Taking a few puffs on the cigar, Mark let his reflections drift once more to Boise.

Kyle's suggestion that the company take a new direction had merit, but Mark questioned if he wanted to go into management. It would be entirely different from what he'd been doing—foreign to what he knew.

After the magnitude of the Grove Marketplace, paring down and taking on smaller projects seemed more attractive to him than throwing himself into something big again.

"Two cold ones, bro," Jeff said, setting beers onto the wooden table situated between their chairs. "Beer nuts, king-size Snickers and two copies of the *Ketchikan Daily News*."

"Thanks," Mark replied, Jeff's gesture considerate.

Jeff Grisham had moments when he could be affable, and it was nice to be in a town with someone to chill with and who wanted to do the same things. Jeff proved to be a veteran fisherman, and he'd taught Mark a thing or two.

They would return to Ketchikan tomorrow, then Jeff planned on flying back to Seattle on Saturday. Mark thought he'd have to find another place to stay, but Jeff called the leasing agent and had been given the okay to transfer the rental into Mark's name through August.

At this point, Mark had no immediate plans. He didn't have to be back in Boise until September.

He'd already told his family he'd be gone for a large chunk of the summer. His sister was taking care of his house and handling his mail. About all he got was utility bills. He had zero debt. With commonsense investing, he'd managed his money well. And after his father's passing, the family had equally divided Giovanni's stock options in the company.

Leaning into his Adirondack chair, Jeff twisted the cap off his beer and immersed himself in the newspaper. Their chairs backed onto the tackle shop's rough-hewn wall, and Mark stared at the deep blue water.

Mark enjoyed his beer, not necessarily thinking about anything as Jeff thumbed through the newspaper and talked under his breath, a comment here and there about something he'd read.

A full-size SUV pulled onto the gravel lot, its tires crunching as the driver manipulated it close to the building. Behind the SUV was a long-bed trailer covered with black visqueen, anchored down with rachet straps. The uneven lump underneath was large and curious.

Getting out of the rig, a big guy made his way over to the deck in a half run, half walk to beat the pelting rain. He wore an oilskin hat that had water dripping off the brim. A charcoal raincoat constructed from heavy fabric parted open in the middle to show his stomach paunch and silver belt buckle the size of an oyster shell.

"Whoo-wee! It's raining buckets at the falls." Under the awning, he removed his hat and slapped it against his thigh to get the water off. His canvas trousers were a beige color that was stained pink lower on the legs. Work boots, worn leather and scuffed, carried the same crimson markings. "I almost couldn't see where I was goin'. S'pose neither could that spankin' new Ford Expee-dition. Didn't even have the plates on her yet. Dang shame."

The geezers looked up from their card game. "Howdy, Bear. You got a fresh one called in?"

"Was home and heard it on the scanner. Miz Rathbone was next on the list, and that seventy-two-year-old broad couldn't never quarter up a moose, much less load it out. Bony as she is, she don't have the strength. I called her and said, 'Ma'am, I'll go get that roadkill for you.'"

"Right neighborly of you, Bear."

Bear nodded. "That ain't the half of it. Then that old gal told me sumpthin' that I'm passin' along to y'all in case one of you lugheads takes the notion to pay her a call. She told me she just redone her will and left instructions for no male pallbearers. Ever since Wilber went to his reward, no men have come to ask her out when she was alive, so she swears no men will take her out when she's dead."

"I don't get it," one of the men mumbled.

"Take her out—carry the casket," Bear clarified. "Dang sorry shame, that widow woman is a lonely old bird. One of these days, I'm buildin' a retiree home for geezers to live in so's they never have to be worryin' about who's heftin' the load on their departed bones. I be thinkin' it be a fishin' hut, too." Working his jaw, Bear added, "Anyway, I saw your Chev-ro-lay in the lot and reckoned I'd swing in for a quick hand of rummy."

The two elderly men welcomed him as Bear pulled out a chair as if it were homecoming week.

Almost immediately, Mark recognized the grizzled man in the long coat. He'd been at the Blue Note. Meatpacker physique.

Roaming his gaze over Bear, Mark internally congratulated himself on his initial summary. He'd thought this guy could heft carcasses for a living. Looks like he'd been dead-on.

"Bear, you ever fix to butcher one of them dead animals and have it come back alive on you?" A man wearing a Skoal brand ball cap and sporting a stubby white beard questioned Bear. "You know, like in that movie *Tommy Boy*. That deer was only stunned when they put it inside their car."

"No, Merrit." Bear settled a thin toothpick in between his lips. "That's only sumpthin' made up in them Hollyweird movies. It ain't never happened to me. I know when sumpthin's dead."

Tilting on his chair legs, Bear glanced over his shoulder at Mark. His craggy eyes focused in, recognition dawning. "I believe we've sat along the same bar." Then he stretched his gaze to Jeff, his mouth souring. "And your partner was with you."

"We're not gay," Jeff shot over the newpaper's edge.

Bear grunted. "I didn't mean it like that." Taking his cards in hand, he fanned them out, then added, "Cardelle was dang fired up that night. You ought be glad you didn't get a full dose of his Off!."

Rolling his eyes, Jeff gathered his newspaper and snacks, then snagged his beer. "Later, bro. I'm heading back to the room."

"Okay." Mark remained, deciding it would benefit him to visit more with Bear. "You guys mind an extra player?"

Only after giving Bear questioning glances did Merrit address him. "It's okay with Bear, so it's okay with us."

Since there was no ashtray available, Mark knocked the ash off his cigar, snuffing it and setting it by his Snickers.

Sliding out a seat at the weather-faded table, Mark positioned himself next to Bear. The solid man was built like an elevator shaft. Something about sitting beside a guy with animal blood on his pant legs disturbed Mark. But this was Alaska. New rules up here made for an interesting perspective.

"So you help people get meat." Mark made a statement rather than ask a question.

"I do."

"You butcher it?"

"Not usually." Bear needed a shave and a bath, but overall, the guy didn't seem overly barbaric.

"I'm Harvey," said one of the geezers. He wore his hair in a comb-over and sported a gray Clark Gable–style mustache.

The Skoal cap responded, "And I'm Merrit— like the cigarettes but with two *R*s."

Mark acknowledged them with a nod. "Mark Moretti."

"Where you be from, Moretti?" Bear asked.

"Boise."

"That north or south from Des Moines?" With a studious eye, Bear arranged his cards, shifting them from spot to spot. "Got me a great-aunt who lives there."

"You're thinking Iowa. I live in Idaho."

Confirming the location, Bear enunciated it in his own way. "Aye-Deh-Hoe. They got a lot of taters."

"We grow them, but the best ones are exported for the fine folks such as yourself in Alaska."

Bear chuckled. "You be jerkin' our chains."

Actually, Mark wasn't. But he didn't counter the point.

"What ship are you from?" Harvey asked, but Bear answered for him.

"He ain't from a cruise ship. He flew in like a bird. Deal them cards, Harvey, or do you aim to jaw all afternoon?"

The last time Mark had played cards, it had been

strip poker with a past girlfriend. He couldn't recollect when he'd last held a hand of gin rummy. The game's rules came back to him, and he sorted his cards. Getting them where he wanted, he took a drink of beer.

Then the game got under way.

Rain pattered over the rooftop, unrelenting in its deluge. The four of them played a hand, table talk covering a range of subjects. Bear bemoaned the fact he'd been babysitting his daughter's dog, a mutt, while she and her husband had gone on an anniversary trip to the San Juans. He called himself its grand-"paw," until the *dang fleabag dawg* began dragging its hind end across his Anso-4 nylon carpet. Since then, Bear had nicknamed the dog Scooter.

Moving around the table, Harvey raved that his dividend check had been higher than he'd anticipated and he'd been able to fill his tank with premium instead of that low-octane sludge. Then Merrit praised his new teeth as being better than his old ones.

"Moretti, you doing a middlin' amount of fishin' while you be here?" Bear had laid down his pairings and won the game.

"I've been out several times."

"You ought try open waters." Then Bear snickered. His laugh brought a frown to Merrit's mouth. "Nuttin' better than bein' out in a boat on rollin' seas."

"Bear, isn't it just like you. I said my new teeth was better, so's you don't have to bring that up. I already done it for you."

Harvey's grin rounded out the dialogue as he said, "Moretti, ask Merrit why he's got new teeth."

Subtly interested, Mark took the challenge. "Merrit, you want to tell me why you have new teeth?"

Merrit grinned, clearly not all that offended. His teeth were so white, they could have lit a room. "These chumps took me out to do some deep-sea fishing and I upchucked over the boat's side. Not only m'lunch, but m'teeth. My denture cement didn't hold the way it should have."

The three of them had a good laugh in remembrance. Mark didn't run with their sense of humor, but he let them laugh it up.

Another ten-card hand was dealt, and now Mark turned their generalized conversation in the direction he wanted.

"Have you known Dana Jackson a long time?" he asked Bear.

Thoughtfully talking around his toothpick, Bear replied, "It's been 'bout ten years since I be first introduced to her by her papa. She must've been what, Merrit—nineteen or twenty? Out of high school, for sure."

"Dana's got to be hitting thirty," Harvey supplied, taking a four of hearts.

Mark didn't want to come across as overzealous,

but curiosity tugged. "Running a bar's got to be hard on a woman."

"She doesn't take no nonsense," Merrit said, discarding a queen of clubs. "I don't often get in to the Note, but when I do, she's always got a smile for me. If I were ten years younger—"

"Ten years?" Bear interrupted, his belly jiggling from humor. "You'd have to be at least thirty years younger, you old coot!"

Mark picked a card, but he didn't calculate how he could use it in his hand. He wasn't focused on the game. All he could see in his mind's eye was Dana's stunningly beautiful face, and figured there must be an endless lineup of men coming into the Blue Note just to look at her. "What does her father think about her running the Blue Note?"

The atmosphere grew quiet, the patter of rain a loud cadence on the rooftop. Then Bear spoke. "Her father died some five years ago in an airplane accident. Took her brother's life, too. God bless America, them was rough weeks to follow with the funerals and all."

"Tragedy," Harvey supplied softly.

Merrit released a sigh. "Don't know of a soul who didn't call Oscar Jackson their friend. Folks crowded the bar to hear him play jazz. He was the master of it, and God bless Dana for keeping the place going after his death."

The framed photograph of two men in the aviation office came back to Mark in a crystal-clear image. He'd thought they resembled Dana. They had to have been her father and brother.

"What happened?" Mark asked, disinterested in finishing the card game.

"As far as the investigators could tell—the weather caused the crash. Fog crept in and they had dang near zero visibility." Sucking on his toothpick, Bear shook his large head regretfully. "The plane was under full power on impact. Hyatt couldn'ta seen the hillside that hit him in the nose."

Confusion held Mark. "Sam Hyatt?"

Harvey clarified, "Jake. Sam's brother. He went down with the plane, too. All three died."

The mood at the table turned as gloomy as the gray sky. In the silent moments that followed, Mark observed three grown men fighting their emotions, fidgeting and shifting in their chairs.

No wonder Dana had come after him when he tried to take a closer look at that photo. Pain must still rip through her heart. She hadn't wanted to answer the inevitable questions or hear the usual condolences. While his dad hadn't died in an accident, Mark knew too well the gut-wrenching loss felt over the death of a parent. But he couldn't imagine losing one of his brothers.

Yanking a white handkerchief from his back pocket, Bear blew his nose into it. "Dang allergies," he mumbled, by way of an excuse for the misty eyes.

Merrit adjusted his hat bill. "She's a survivor."

"Couldn't agree more." Harvey put in his two cents.

"If it weren't for her son," Bear thoughtfully concluded, "I don't think she'd've made it this far."

Harvey nodded, continuing the game by discarding. "Terran gives her a reason to get up in the morning."

"How old is her boy?" Mark asked, lowering his cards.

"I reckon close to five or thereabouts." Bear drummed his fingers on the table, then selected a card. Looking at its face, he grimaced. "Son of a— Why couldn't I have got this card the last hand?"

Harvey took his turn, shifted cards, then grinned, laying them all down and shouting, "Gin!"

Merrit cursed beneath his breath and folded. "I was one run shy of going out."

"Me, too," Bear put in.

The trio, bent on playing another hand, turned the topic to the irritating rash on Harvey's right ankle as he shuffled the cards. Bear suggested he put some grease on it. Merrit begged to differ and told him to soak his feet in epsom salts.

As they heatedly debated the benefits of both remedies, Mark broke into their dialogue and excused himself.

Sprinting toward the rows of cabins, folded newspaper tucked underneath his arm and the cigar clamped in his mouth, he blinked against the rain pellets smacking him in the face. With every step he took, he digested the information he'd learned.

By the time he crossed the parking lot, he was soaked through.

"SEAGULLS ON THE ROOF AGAIN." Leo's blunt commentary made reference to the incessant tapping on the Blue Note's metal roof.

Dana exhaled heavily, thinking this was the last thing she needed today. Saturdays were her busiest days at the bar and it took some prep work to get ready for the crowd. Extra food had to be fixed, plenty of liquor stocked, and she arranged the stage area to accommodate live music. Most, but not all, Friday and Saturday nights, she brought in bands to play jazz.

Rain had fallen in a steady sheet all day, and she had several buckets strategically placed on the floor. The forecast called for at least two inches, possibly three. She'd have to keep her bussers on top of dumping the buckets.

Tap, tap, tap, tap!

"Doesn't sound like seagulls," Dana commented, across the bar. They weren't open yet, and she'd just set up the mike system. "But they were up there pecking a couple of days ago."

Wiping his hands, Leo asked, "Want me to check it out?"

"No, keep stocking the bar." Dana plugged in an amp cord, then checked the sound by tapping on the mike. "I'll figure it out. Where's that box of rotten limes?"

"Gave it to Presley to dump."

Dana headed into the kitchen and found Presley slaving over mini-pizzas with cocktail sauce and crab topping. Burners going full flame on the big commercial stove threw off enough heat to melt an igloo. Presley made multitasking seem effortless as she pivoted on her heels from one spot to the other. She whisked the contents in bubbling pans, then opened the large refrigerator to bring out the cellophane-wrapped dough balls. She had a helper, a young girl, who did almost nothing but slice and chop.

"Presley, where's that box of bad limes Leo gave you?" Dana went to the long countertop and glanced around.

"In the service room with the trash." She gave a puff of air to blow her fringed bangs off her forehead. "There was only about six bad ones. Leo salvaged most of them. We should ask for a refund for the limes we can't use."

"I'm going to use them—just not in drinks."

Dana left the kitchen. In the small room behind a duo of built-in dishwashers, the bar kept the evening's worth of trash that needed to be carried to the Dumpster. Since there was no back door to the Blue Note, the trash was only taken out once at night—and after closing—by a designated employee who used the front door.

Nosing around in the boxes and crates and the large trash bags, Dana finally found the discarded limes. She grabbed the small box and went through the kitchen, but not without grabbing a hat from her private office.

Once outside, the rain came at her with the light steadiness of a fine showerhead. She made a sprint to the Blue Note's front, her fedora keeping the rain off her face and hair.

Tap! Tap! Tap! Tap!

"Damn birds," she muttered.

Winding her arm back for a throw, she tossed a rotten lime at the corrugated roof. The fruit sailed over to the other side, disappearing from her view.

The roof's shallow pitch ran from front to back, creating a middle point that prevented her from seeing how many seagulls flocked to roost. She couldn't determine where the lime made impact, if it even did. But the noise seemed to be interrupted.

Tap tttt—

The seagulls didn't take flight, at least not where she could see them.

Rain doused her sweater, wet her jeans, fell in a puddle at her shoes. But she made another effort, this time, the lime pounding in the roof's middle, before bouncing over the top.

Then an unexpected thing happened.

A man's head, topped with a Carhartt ball cap,

appeared over the peak, and he called out in a growl, "What the—?"

Tilting her chin upward, the rain fell across her chin and she squinted. "Moretti?"

He rose slightly taller, and that's when she noticed the tool belt around his hips.

Disbelief held her still. "What are *you* doing on *my* roof?"

"Fixing all the holes, Indiana."

Trying to ward off the relentless rain by cupping her hand, she hollered, "Stop calling me nick-names—you're really pissing me off. And I didn't ask you to fix my roof."

"No, but your cook said she's sick and tired of you scrounging for pots and pans to use as buckets. She doesn't have anything left to cook with."

"Presley? You talked to Presley?"

"Ran into her at True Value Hardware when I bought this tool belt, among other things. I didn't need a ladder since you've got one built into the wall."

The mossy rung ladder had been permanently attached to the side of the building by her father. Years and years of repairs had made keeping a ladder in place almost a necessity.

"Presley didn't tell me she saw you."

With that lopsided grin of his that just about unraveled every stitch of common sense she tried to keep knit together, he said in a drawl, "Did you ask her?"

"Why would I ask anyone about you?"

"I thought maybe you'd be curious."

"I'm not. Now get down from there, dammit. You're going to fall then sue me for damages and I'm not paying you a cent."

"I've never fallen off a roof in my life, and I'm not billing you for a thing, Dana. You won't have to worry about the roof leaking anymore." He sank his hand inside one of the pouches on his hip, then showed something between his fingers. "I'm using galvanized roofing nails with rubber washers, and waterproof Malarkey roofing tar. It works when it's wet." He grinned. "Just like me."

"Get off the roof, Moretti."

Ignoring her request, he replied, "I've got about another half hour's worth of work left. Go inside and dry off." Then, lifting his chin a notch, he added, "I like the hat, Indiana. Now take a hike like a good girl."

Beside herself over him giving her orders, she stood for many long seconds, staring at him. His gall dug under her skin, but also she felt the shame of relief seep into every pore.

She should have called Leo to climb up and yank Mark down, but it would be so nice not to have the roof leak.

"Why?" she called to him, not understanding the motivation for such generosity.

Hammer in hand, he paused, rain running off his

slicker and the bill of his cap. His eyes were dark, unfathomable. "Why didn't you tell me that was your son's toothbrush?"

Caught off guard, she said nothing. She didn't owe him any explanations about her life, now or ever. How he'd found out was not her concern. Easy information. But the notion that he'd been asking, or making inquiries, did somewhat affect her balance.

"Go inside, Dana. Grab a cup of coffee and warm up. I'll be done here soon enough."

CHAPTER SIX

COOPER BOYD'S BLACK Jeep Wrangler parked next to the curb, and Dana stepped away from her lookout spot at her home's picture window. Her ex-boyfriend being fifteen minutes late didn't ruin her elation. Filled with smiles, she looked forward to Sunday evenings when she got her son back for her week.

Opening the front door, she breathed in the air's clean scent, thankful no rain had fallen today. She'd been able to wash off the layers of grime from her Chevy S-10—which had been running great ever since Mark fixed the battery terminals.

She wouldn't spare a moment now to think about him. She'd done enough of that last night after he'd been on her bar's roof and taken care of that for her, as well. While her many questions about his motives had been parked, she did plan on revisiting them later.

Walking down the steep front steps toward the street, she went to the picket fence to wait for Terran.

"Hey, Terran!" she greeted, happiness in her heart.

"Hi, Momma." His voice was slightly sullen, as if he were in a pout over something.

Cooper opened the Jeep door, and a big brown Lab stuck his face out from the backseat. The dog gave a reverberating *woof,* its body shaking from an enthusiastic tail wag.

"Riley. Quit," Cooper said, ruffling the dog's head. "You gotta stay here."

Terran sniffed, the kind of nose-wrinkling sniff belonging to a crabby little boy. Through rubber lips, he murmured, "How come I can't borrow him, Daddy?"

"Because Riley lives at my house, buddy."

"How come I can't live at your house?"

That innocent-enough question caused Cooper's hazel eyes to lift and lock onto Dana's.

Gone were any emotions that she'd felt for this man, but she could still catch herself falling victim to anxiety when around him. She'd reconciled to sharing her son, but aside from that, she'd never—*ever*—relinquish her parental joy at having him with her half of the time.

Terran's question threw Dana off-kilter, and she wondered if Cooper had been putting the thought in her son's head.

Giving Cooper a warning glare, she had to restrain herself from asking him about what Terran meant. The court-appointed parenting class cautioned both sides to never interrogate the other in the child's presence.

But still . . . why had Terran asked such a thing?

Keeping her wits about her, Dana remarked in an upbeat tone, "Terran, Grandma cut you some celery sticks with peanut butter."

"How come?"

"Because you love them."

"I love dogs better, Mommy." His frowning eyes pleaded with her. "Can't we *please* get one? *Please?*"

So that's what this was about. Terran wanted to live with Riley the dog.

They'd been down this road before in the past. Terran would get his mind wrapped around something he had to have, and he'd be relentless in asking for it, hoping she'd cave. Depending on what it was, sometimes he could wear her down. Other times she kept her heels dug in. Just like she'd do on this issue.

Not only was she not home enough to take care of a pet, she couldn't handle getting attached to one. A dog could develop a fatal tumor or get run over. She couldn't lose another thing she loved. It was far better to keep her life as uncomplicated as possible.

At least Cooper didn't tell Dana to get a dog, too. Instead, he lifted the window hatch on the Jeep's rear door, gathering Terran's belongings into a pile.

Dana left the picket gate to help him with her son's stuff.

It always felt awkward to stand near Cooper and remember the past, and the role he'd played in her life. His presence now was nothing more than a court-ordered arrangement each Sunday. There were the generic hellos on the phone before Cooper handed the receiver to Terran so she could check on him during the week and ask him how his day had gone.

Cooper smelled like nice aftershave, but she hardly took note. Too much had changed. When she'd dated Cooper, his physique had leaned toward the stocky side. But years of regularly playing on ice hockey teams had firmed his body into a more muscular build.

He kept his sandy-blond hair short and trimmed at the ears, but with longer-than-average sideburns. She didn't think she'd ever seen him with stubble. He shaved twice a day, morning and night. He had a more refined appearance to him now, dressing clean-cut and neat—probably due to his day job at GCI Cellular as their store manager.

Many women would think Cooper was quite good-looking.

Standing beside her ex-boyfriend brought no more memories of what had been, only what was. Things had changed between them. It had taken a long time, but she could honestly say a neutral feeling was the best way to describe her reaction toward the man who'd fathered her son.

"What's all this?" Dana queried, taking out a small box with two jars, and three plastic bags that hid mysterious contents.

"He collected a couple of things, and I bought him treats he wanted to take to your house."

Treats aka candy to make him hyper and not want to go to bed at a reasonable time. Cooper knew she didn't let Terran eat a ton of sugar, yet he always did this to her: overrode her authority at her house, on her time.

She'd have to handle it the way she always did— get rid of the offending things little by little and Terran would eventually forget he had the junk.

Dana strapped Terran's hockey bag over her shoulder and held on to his stick while managing the small box.

"That's all." Cooper shut the Jeep's rear door to come around and say goodbye to Terran.

Terran hooked his backpack through his arms and stood with his chin tucked to his chest, staring at his white-and-black-striped tennis shoes.

Laying a hand on Terran's shoulder, Cooper said in an upbeat tone, "Hey, buddy, see you at hockey practice this week."

Terran didn't reply.

Cooper gazed at Dana and shrugged, almost like giving her the same pouting look as Terran.

No, Dana mouthed firmly. Then once more when Cooper kept on with the shrug: *No!* She would not be coerced into getting a dog.

"Sorry, bud, that's a negative from the mommy."

Dana's blood boiled. She hated when Cooper called her "the mommy" as if she were the Wicked Witch of the West.

"Let's go, Terran," she said, giving Cooper the evil eye. "Say goodbye to your dad."

Only marginally lifting his chin to address his father, Terran's parting words bore the world's heaviness on his tiny shoulders. "Bye, Daddy."

A person would think the sun would set today without another tomorrow from the sigh in her son's voice.

Damn Cooper for even remotely getting their son hopeful about a pet.

She ushered Terran up the steps and into the house, relieved to get him to herself. Once in the cozy living room, she set his goody box on the coffee table and deposited his hockey gear on the floor.

Terran stood in the middle of the room, the backpack sliding off his shoulders with a light thump onto the hardwood. He made no effort to pick it up.

Suni came cheerfully into the room. "There's grandma's little boy." She gave him a big squeeze. "How are you—"

Dana mimed her finger slicing her neck, the gesture speaking volumes. *Cut the dialogue.* Her mother took the hint and quit her question.

"So what do you have in here?" Dana asked with enthusiasm, digging into the box. She needed to take Terran's mind off the dog, and if that meant letting him have a piece of his candy, she'd do it.

She opened one of the GCI bags and rooted around inside, but as she touched something suspicious, she smothered a scream. The squishy object flew from her hand and hit the television screen.

Terran's soft boy chortle filled the room. "Momma, what are you doing?"

Hand over her heart, she swallowed. "What was that?"

Running to the offending thing, Terran grabbed it. The icky object was roundish and totally gross-looking. Her son wadded it in his hand, then doubled over and made a vile regurgitating sound. He plopped the blob on the area rug.

"Doncha know what fake barf is?" Terran asked. "There's chunks of corn and ham'bugger in it. Dad got it for me."

"Gosh, Terran. That's sick."

Terran merely smiled, the gap where his missing tooth was an endearing hole in his mouth.

Dana shook her head, smiling back at him. "You're a funny guy, you know that?"

"No—*you're* a funny guy!" he said back at her, giggling.

For now, the battle of wills about getting a dog seemed to have run its course. Thank goodness.

Rummaging through the rest of the things, Dana examined the jars and discovered three flies bonking around the glass in one, and a hairy spider in the other. "You can't keep these in your room."

"Are you going to keep them in yours?"

"No, Grandma is."

Suni stuck her nose up. "I am not."

"Hey, Mommy, you ever see a wallop sock?" Terran reached into the last bag and came out with his father's crew sock stuffed with something. Fine white particles rained onto the coffee table.

"What's in there?"

"Dad and me made it," Terran proudly proclaimed, waving the ribbed white sock and depositing a talclike dust cloud in the air. "We smashed a whole bunch of chalks and now I can give people wallops. You want to see?"

"Uh, no—not in the house."

"What you do is swing it round and round and you *wallop!*" He swung at the air, pretending he was hitting something.

Dana jolted backward as Suni reached in for the sock. "You let Grandma hold on to this for you, baby. We'll wallop the weeds in the garden."

"Okay." He stuffed his hand into his small jeans pocket, came out with an unwrapped Tootsie Roll and was about to pop it into his mouth.

Suni came to the rescue, removing it from his

hand. "Terran, come with Grandma and let's have some peanut butter and celery."

"Then can I have my candy?" he asked. "Daddy said I could have it for later."

"We'll see."

Dana gathered Terran's belongings as her mother took her son into the kitchen for snacks. She'd let him keep the rubber barf and wallop sock, but the flies and the spider would have to go.

As she climbed the stairs with boy things in her arms, she had a vague wondering about what it would have been like to have had a little girl . . . and would she ever have the opportunity.

At twenty-nine, the chances were slim. While many women were having babies in their thirties and forties, she didn't have the husband needed to make this happen.

It would take a miracle to meet the right man, someone who would accept her for who she was, and that she came as a package deal with her son. She had no delusions about finding a wonderful guy who could work around her routines and be there for her in every way.

Besides, beyond Terran and her mother, her heart had no more room for love. Those empty spaces within her kept the spirit of her brother close, and her father's dreams alive. She was too busy, too focused, to put her life out of order.

With a resigned sigh, she continued to her son's room. No pink blankets, baby dollies and little girl's dresses. This was it for her. The last stop on the motherhood train.

She'd remain single all the rest of her days.

"DE VILLAGE PEOPLE BROKE UP, mon. Disco is dead."

"Is that right?" Mark replied, the handle of his clawhammer hitting his thigh as he walked toward the bar. He wore his new tool belt, a T-shirt and stone-washed jeans—not a shirt with the sleeves torn out, ropes of gold chains and a prop hard hat. "Here's another news flash, Marley. The Jamaicans have never medaled in Olympic bob-sledding."

Cardelle laughed, a Jamaican melody. "All right, mon. You got me. And de name is Cardelle, not Marley. Dat be de guy who sang with de Wailers."

"I knew your name."

"I'm t'inking you did, mon." Cardelle extended his chocolate-brown hand from his bar-stool perch. "Even d'ough you not be on de cruise ship—I give you twenty percent discount on all bling."

Grasping the man's pale palm, Mark gave his arm a friendly pump. "I'll take that into considera-tion."

"If not for you, mon. For de gal of your heart."

Mark didn't have a girl of his heart, but he did have a woman who got to another part of his anatomy.

"Weh is dat chi-chi mon friend of yours?"

Cardelle asked, eyes narrowing warily as he sipped on a drink garnished with a pineapple wedge.

"Gone home to Seattle."

"Good. I did not like 'im."

The song on the jukebox changed to something up-tempo, the brassy sound of horns carrying the mellow jazz notes through the Blue Note.

Cardelle drummed his slender fingers on the edge of the glossy bar, keeping time. "Don' you jus' love de magic from Oscar?"

Mark listened closer, thinking the artist had an excellent style. The music had to be from an Oscar Jackson recording. Hearing the song must have been surreal for Dana, but kudos that she kept her father alive in the bar.

Bear's wide girth occupied the stool next to Cardelle's. Mark nodded a silent hello to the mammoth guy, momentarily thinking back to their card game at Elk Cove.

"Has anyone ever really looked at a fly?" Bear asked, staring into a mason jar real close. "They's awfully hairy little bits with bug eyes. None too smart, neither."

Not necessarily wanting to know why Bear had brought in a jar filled with flies, Mark replied, "No, Bear, I haven't. The only time I've paid much attention to a fly is when I whacked it with a fly-swatter."

"Dem is filthy t'ings. De be right up deh with maskittas." With that, Cardelle snagged his bug repellent can and glanced toward Leo, who was giving a few shakes to a mixed drink in the shaker. Seeing that he wasn't being watched, Cardelle shot a few chemical *psphts* on the back of his neck.

"Card," Bear cautioned, shaking the jar with his eyes glued to the bouncing insects responding inside as he emulated the cocktail shaker in Leo's hand. "Leo catch you doin' that and you're goin' to be sittin' over at the Arctic from now on."

"I risk it."

Bear grunted. "Your call, Card." Then, "Hey, Moretti. How come you're packing a hammer?"

"I'm going to be doing some renovation work around here."

"Is that so?" Leo came down the bar and poured a beer from the tap. "Men's room john's been dicey lately. The second urinal has a problem with the flush valve."

"I'll make a note of it," Mark responded tightly. Plumbing was Mark's least favorite thing, and starting a job in the men's restroom was low on his priority list. "Is Dana around?"

"In her office," Leo replied, heading down the bar to serve the beer.

Mark quit his exchange with the men and headed for the rear of the building on a hunt for Dana.

Monday night didn't pack the bar like a sardine tin, but plenty of people occupied tables enjoying an evening snack and alcohol to wash it down. Mark had come by earlier in the day, but the place had been locked tight until opening a short time ago.

He found Dana sitting behind her desk, an all but worthless swing-arm lamp illuminating her scattered paperwork. Sensing someone standing in the doorway, she looked his way.

Rather than the grateful smile, and arms thrown around his neck in the hug he'd dreamed about getting from her, he was met with a frown and not a single move to jump on him.

"Now is that any way to say howdy to the guy who patched your holes?"

Sitting straight, she licked her lips, grazing the lower with her teeth. The innocent-enough gesture heated everything inside him. "I said thanks last night when you left."

And so she had.

He'd finished the repairs about an hour after she'd discovered him on her roof, and he'd only come into the bar for a quick few to report he was done. She'd been suspicious of his motives, her body language guarded. Accepting his generosity had been hard to do. In the end, she'd given him a relieved thank-you, but a slight hitch in her voice held on to her words as if unsure what to make of him—but she remained more than grateful.

He'd gone home for the night, taken a hot shower and slid into bed, sleeping the best he had since arriving in Ketchikan.

"What are you doing here?" Her black hair had

been drawn into a clip, messy pieces falling next to her face. She'd put on very little makeup, yet her complexion was flawless. He loved her skin's toasted-sugar color. Desire flooded him as he thought she'd taste just as good as she looked.

"I came to get a copy of your fire marshal's report. I'm going to start working on the violations and bringing them up to code for you."

A long moment passed where her gaze remained locked on his. Then finally, without fanfare, she questioned flatly, "Why?"

"Because I want to."

"I think you want more than my violations."

Irritation colored his reply. "Has it ever occurred to you that I might just want to help you out—no strings attached?"

"Not really." She spread her fingers over an adding machine's keys, punching in a few numbers and talking while she got her total. "I liked you better when you were gone fishing."

He couldn't help laughing to himself. "I didn't know you liked me at all."

Dana's chin lifted, her brows darting into a frown. "Dammit, Moretti. You twist everything I say into a tangled ball of BS." She tore the receipt from the calculator, stapling it to a bill. "For the record, I don't like—*like*—you. I've tolerated you. I'm not hiring you. And I know what you're up to so you might as well quit the handyman act."

Relaxing into the door frame, Mark folded his

arms over his chest, not going anywhere. "Have you ever trusted anyone?"

"Plenty."

"Then trust me."

"Not a chance."

"Why not? Be honest."

She propped her booted feet on the desk's corner. With her almond-shaped eyes angled directly on him, she owned the word *exotic*. Her Asian facial features were stunning, her mouth a beautiful rose that should be kissed. The shape of her nose, carved very delicately, flared slightly at the nostrils.

"I've met you before," she stated, her voice silky and low. "Not personally, but I know your kind. You come to Alaska, you recreate all day, then want to flirt all night. You want to take me out and get into my panties. I've never agreed to that. Although I've been tempted—just for the pleasure of sex, that is." She lowered her legs, her feet once more planted onto the floor. "Is that honest enough for you?"

"Any more honest, and we'd be bolting this door and you'd be showing me your undies."

"Get over yourself, Moretti."

Mark took a step toward the desk, standing over her with his hair falling at his brow. "Sweetart, you've been around the wrong kind of men. If I want lingerie, it's easy to find it. In fact, it finds me. I've never had to work at getting a woman. They seem to like me just fine." He reached into his back pocket for his wallet, pulled out his business card from the fold and held it out for her.

It would have been easier to drop the card onto her desk, but he wanted her to take it, to accept him. "I'm bonded and insured."

Her hands remained crossed on her lap. Confusion seemed to weld together in her as she mulled over his offer.

When she spoke, her voice had faded to a hushed stillness. "Why help me?"

"I have the money to spend. It's time I did something in my life that I want to do, not because I'm obligated or asked."

She bit her lower lip again, that catch of her white teeth, the thoughts in her head apparently swirling in varying directions. The extended card in his hand remained. Then she slowly raised her arm to take it. Afterward, she shifted through the papers, found a folder and handed it to him.

With a nod, he accepted the folder, relief flooding him like a river. Up to this point, he hadn't realized how much he wanted this. "I just fixed that ladder on the building front and replaced the mossy rungs. A guy could've really hurt himself slipping off it."

"Nobody ever has."

"And now nobody ever will." Optimism and promise fueled his purpose, and he was anxious to get started fixing up the bar. "Let's go to lunch tomorrow and talk about what needs to be done."

"Sorry—I have to take my son to get a booster shot."

Exhaling, Mark asked, "Can you get away for dinner?"

"No—I spend Tuesday nights with my family."

"The next day? Dana, I will need your input on this. How about breakfast?"

She looked away, her gaze distant. There was no question she struggled with this, with him. But in the end, she uttered the reply he wanted to hear. "Okay."

CHAPTER SEVEN

"DANA, DO YOU EVER THINK it's weird you wiped my butt and now I'm serving you breakfast?" Tiffany asked, setting down a menu.

When Dana was in the sixth grade, she'd babysat Tiffany, who'd been in diapers.

At nineteen, Tiffany had turned into a very pretty girl. Tall and lanky, but precious in demeanor. Three years in braces had paid off in spades. She had a winning smile and rosy-apple cheeks.

"No, Tiffany. I don't think about your butt when I'm ordering. And I don't want to." Vaguely looking at the menu, she added, "I'll need another menu. Someone's meeting me."

"I'll bring one right back. Two coffees?"

Dana didn't know if Mark drank coffee or not. "Uh, sure."

"Regular or decaf?"

"Well, damn . . . I don't know. I'll take regular and . . . make his a regular, too."

"His?" Tiffany scrunched her face, her nose wrinkling with a grin. "Do you have a breakfast date?"

"Not even close."

Tiffany left and Dana stared out the windows, waiting for Mark to appear.

Pedestrian traffic was quite heavy for this hour. The *Royal Caribbean, Regent Seven Seas Mariner* and *Pacific Princess* all had docked before eight o'clock this morning. Different languages could be heard through the cafe's open door as people peeked inside the small restaurant to see what it was—as if it were some interesting must-visit place like the fudge shop. Some of the old people looked absolutely dense, eyes squinting and trying to figure out if the menu was worth their time away from the Tanzanite R Us jewelry stores.

Dana could only wonder what the town looked liked through the eyes of those who didn't love it the way she did.

Ketchikan resembled an old shoe, its leather worn and in need of polish. The buildings could use a fresh coat of paint, the rooftops new shingles, and some asphalt poured into the downtown potholes. But its sole still had a lot of tread left, and these minor imperfections gave the port a soul to be proud of.

Those who called the city home embraced it for all that it was. A community for the arts, showcase for talented musicians, bagpipers, a symphony, great performances in plays and a chorus where anyone could apply. Locals endeared themselves to the ocean and its gentle swells. Most everyone had a sailboat to race in competitions.

While some traveled to warmer places during the winter, those who stayed enjoyed the town's quiet beauty with the tourists gone. Dana loved the new vibrancy that filled the quaint restaurants, the handful of year-round shops and the empty harbor berths. People used the time to catch up with dear friends, and do normal daily routines they hadn't been able to keep up with while taking ship passengers on paid trolley tours or working in kettle-corn booths.

Dana vaguely wondered what Mark Moretti had thought of her town when he'd arrived.

Coming in from the airport ferry, there was a lot of industry along the highway to the town's center—rock quarries, canneries and a sawmill. The site where the old pulp mill stood now put on lumberjack shows. But when the season ended, no longer did the chainsaws buzz and crowds cheer at the Great Alaskan Lumberjack Show—its owners had returned to Wisconsin until next year.

The former salmon capital of the world, Ketchikan's natural beauty was postcard perfect. A mountainous place with panoramic lush greenery.

And love it or hate it—it was a cruise-ship port for thousands of tourists who put revenue into their economy.

On Front Street, also known as Jewelry Row, the Pioneer Café had evolved into something of a landmark where Dana had many memories to recall. For over thirty years, the Pioneer had withstood restaurant closures in a town where an eatery was lucky to be around after six months.

Its decor was pretty standard. Some basic tables and booths, a long counter where singles were encouraged to occupy a spot rather than take up an entire booth. Lighting the wall, a neon sign blinked *Route 66—America's Main Street.* A person could get a decent meal for a decent price, and that included reindeer hot dogs, reindeer sausages and reindeer steaks.

Tiffany returned with two coffees and two waters, another menu and a happy smile. "I hardly see you anymore, Dana. What've you been up to?"

"Nothing much. Just working. How about you?"

"I have a boyfriend now. We should double-date."

Softly smiling, Dana shook her head. "I don't have anyone I'm interested in, Tiffany."

"I could see if Ray knows of anyone your age."

"I'm good." Dana had to inwardly laugh over Tiffany's effort. Nothing like nineteen and thinking the world was awesome with a boyfriend and a Saturday-night date at the Coliseum Twin Theatre.

When Tiffany went to retrieve an order, Dana resumed her view of the street outside, noting the people who passed by.

Within a few minutes, Mark appeared outside the door, a cell phone next to his ear. He seemed to be deep into a conversation, a very intent expression covering his face. Not yet noticing she sat in the restaurant, he carried on with his call.

She used the time to study him.

Against her better judgment, she admitted he was beyond the best-looking man she'd ever seen. It was just her luck to think this way about a lower-forty-eight man.

Here today, gone tomorrow.

She'd seen it a million times. Guys came to Alaska, fell in love with it, fell in love with her, stuck around a handful of weeks and moved on. To her credit, she'd never fallen for any of them. It had been difficult at times to completely ignore a nice-looking guy bent on getting her attention. She'd received lavish flowers, dinner invites, fudge—ugh. Mostly they flirted; many came to the bar every night they were in town. It got to be almost embarrassing when Leo or Walt would take bets on who'd come back the following night to try and wear her resistance down.

Sometimes it was mortifying to be a woman.

And to be different in a town where Caucasian women were the predominant ethnicity. The majority of Filipinos worked mostly at Wal-Mart,

133

and of course clerks like Cardelle came to stay, but just for the summer.

There was only one of her. Maybe that's why men found her so intriguing. God knew she didn't lead any of them on by flirting back.

But as her gaze pored over Mark, she amended that thought. She could squeeze in time for lust. Just looking at the guy made her think of a dozen ways to kiss his mouth, to lean over him, push him back on a bed while she straddled his hips.

The most bone-shivering seductions began with clothing on, at least in her mind. Denim could hug a man's butt and legs in a sexy way, and a T-shirt's soft cotton knit stretching over his chest was wildly attractive.

Lowering her eyes, she noted that Mark favored a boot-cut jean that offered a tempting view. His lightweight black jacket had been left unzipped. The shirt underneath was knit, but not a T-shirt. The fabric looked softly worn, a charcoal color that didn't stretch taut on his chest, but rather, loosely gloved his skin.

He'd shaved today; a smooth jaw and lower half of his face caught her attention. The hair at his neck brushed his jacket collar. Smoky-lensed sunglasses rode at the top of his head.

The easy smile that curved his lips captured her undivided attention. His mouth was sinful. She hated him for it. With a slight tilt of his head, a resonant laugh carried from his throat.

Who was he talking to? Why did he look like he was enjoying them so much?

Unexpected jealousy pricked and she didn't like it one bit.

With a slight nod, Mark then disconnected the call, slipped the phone into his jacket pocket and entered the café.

Seeing her, he headed for the table.

"Have you been waiting long?" he asked, sliding into the chair opposite hers.

"Long enough to watch you talking to someone on the phone. Was it your girlfriend?" The words were out before she could take them back, and she chastised herself for the slip.

One arm halfway out of his jacket, Mark paused then laughed so loudly the couple at the next table looked in their direction. "If I'd've known you cared, I would have brought you a Hallmark."

Dana closed her eyes a moment, her displeasure solely caused by her juvenile question. As she refocused on Mark, she called upon every ounce of effort she had to maintain her composure.

He measured her with his gaze, a mixture of humor and intent in his rich brown eyes. "I was talking to my sister."

He'd mentioned having a sister before.

Spying his coffee cup, he reached for the cream and added a splash. "She's going to ship me my tools that I'll need to do the job for you."

Dana stared into the depths of her murky

135

coffee, a myriad of thoughts in her head, with one prevailing.

Addressing Mark, she put care and effort into her words lest he think her ungrateful. "You don't have to do this. Lots of guys I meet in the bar seem to think that they have to impress me to get me to notice them." With a hard swallow, she admitted, "I noticed you, okay? It's kind of hard not to."

The warmth in his smile melted her very center. "Dana, I'm doing it for me as much as I'm doing it for you." He drank a little coffee, then said, "Back in Boise, I inherited the job of running our family's construction company. I've worked for my dad my entire life, and probably would still be there if he hadn't died a few years ago. He had a heart attack that threw us all off center. We counted on my father to be at Moretti Construction's helm."

She made no comment, but she wanted to confide in him that she, too, knew what it was like to lose a father unexpectedly.

"My sister and I partnered to get a big project completed, and we did. It just about burned me out to the point where I thought I might quit. But then my brother-in-law offered me a deal that would get me away from the trailer and into that cushy office you assumed I had." Mark's expression grew reflective. "I'm here to figure out if I could be that guy. It's been so long since I built something because of a desire to do it rather than from a sense of obligation. I don't know if that makes any sense to you." He let out a long breath. "Hell, I'm not even sure I understand it myself."

This time, she spoke from her heart. "I understand more than you could imagine."

Tiffany arrived at the table, bubbly and cheerful. "Hi, have you had a chance to look at the menu?" While she talked, she gave the eye to Dana, as if to say—*Wow, he's cute.*

Dana ignored the wink. "I'm not sure. Do you know what you want?" she asked Mark.

The question carried far too much weight, and she regretted her word choices as soon as they spilled from her mouth.

Mark's gaze consumed her, a hidden meaning in the stillness of his eyes. "Four eggs—over medium, ham, white toast with grape jelly and extra butter."

"Sure thing," Tiffany said, snapping to attention. She clearly liked a customer who knew what they wanted and how.

"I'll have the pancakes," Dana replied, sliding her closed menu to Tiffany. "And some orange juice."

Pocketing her order pad and taking the menus, Tiffany left them to their interrupted discussion. Dana was glad it had been interrupted; she had felt herself getting too personal.

"You must order the same breakfast a lot," Dana commented.

"I know what I like."

The implication of his reply spoke volumes above what he'd actually said. There was no denying he could affect her with innuendo, and it galled her to distraction.

From the stereo on a shelf near the register, Brian Hyland sang "Itsy Bitsy Teenie Weenie Yellow Polka Dot Bikini."

"So," she said after several long seconds, "what do you have for me?"

He quirked his mouth into a sassy smile. "I've got plenty for you. What do you want to have first?"

On an annoyed gasp, she replied, "Why is it you turn around what I say to you and make it seem base?"

"Not my intention, sunshine. Must be you thinking naughty thoughts in your head."

Keeping herself in check, she forced an evenness to her tone. "Right now I'm thinking meeting you for breakfast was a mistake. At this point, I would have accepted a brick of fudge."

"You like fudge?"

He had no clue as to why she'd even suggested the candy, but in true Mark form, he ran with it anyway. The guy could rally even the worst come-back and leave her sputtering.

"No, but I like it better than you."

"Well, you can't kiss a Milky Way and tell it to quit hogging the covers."

Her blood heated to a frustrating degree. Dana

would have stood and gotten out of the café had Tiffany not poured warm-ups for their coffees— and with goofy eyes for Mark and that sly wink again for Dana.

Mark reached over the table, laid a calming hand over hers, and she felt as if her skin burned with the contact. Not because she didn't like the masculine touch of his fingers, but because she did. Too much for her own good.

"I'll stop messing with you," he said, his deep voice sincere. "It's just that your eyes shine real pretty when you get aggravated."

"No, they don't."

"Yeah, they do."

To her immediate relief, he moved his hand and leaned back. For a brief moment, she acknowledged that it had been pleasant having him touch her. If his hand felt this nice, what would his mouth do to her?

She staved off a shiver.

Thankfully Mark produced a small spiral notebook from his jacket, and he opened it to discuss the notations he'd made from the violation reports she'd given him. He'd written pages and pages of ideas, suggestions and ways to go about bringing things to code.

"So if you add a door here, you're going to have to widen that hallway." He pointed to a rough sketch he'd made. "But it's better to do it before your reinspection. Those guys tell you to do one thing, and they don't mention that when you do, you create a new situation."

All she could manage was a nod, feeling completely at a loss over the extent of things.

"As for your second exit, I put in a call to a structural engineer I know to draw up a quick set of plans for the fire exit. I told him to make it good-looking, not just utility."

"I don't understand."

Mark scribbled a rendition of her current patio. "We'll have to build the exit here—see?"

She leaned forward and he turned the drawing so that it would face her as he continued to add to it.

"You're going to need to come off this point, add steel girding, then bring it to the wharf. Thankfully you have that patio. Without it, you would have had to start from scratch."

Everything seemed overwhelming to her. The changes would be drastic . . . and cost a lot.

Before they went any further, she had to confess, "I've got five thousand dollars that I can put toward the expenses. Beyond that, I'm tapped out right now." Admitting her funds came up short gave her a humiliating, deflated feeling, but she had no choice other than to be up-front with him. "Can you bring the project in for less?"

"Honey, five grand won't touch it."

Her heart sank.

Mark laid his palms on the table in front of him. He eased his fingertips toward her, so close they lightly touched her knuckles where she'd knit her hands together. His contact sent an electrical jolt through her. "Don't worry about the cost. I already told you I'd take care of it."

Inching away from him, she replied, "I don't want to owe you anything."

"You won't."

"Yes, I will. More than five thousand." Bruised pride left a bitter taste in her mouth, the despair hard to swallow. "How much, Mark?"

He studied her at length, as if contemplating whether or not to be truthful about it. "Forty— probably closer to fifty."

"Thousand?" She gulped.

"It's not nickels, sunshine."

Smothering a groan, she almost wished he'd answered with a lie to placate her. She tried to regain her composure as the weight of his words settled in.

She hadn't seen this moment coming. Certainly not from the first she'd laid eyes on Mark Moretti two weeks ago.

That night when he'd come into the bar, she'd noticed him long before his friend had gotten into a stupid fight. She'd been at the bar for some reason, unimportant now, and he'd entered the Blue Note with a tall presence that she hadn't been able to ignore.

Right from the start, she'd been attracted to him, but denial had been easy to manipulate. She had grown to be an expert at it. She'd watched him for a long while, noticing the ease with which he moved, the way a smile fell naturally on his mouth. There'd been an envious pang that had filled her, something she'd long since tried to forget.

So what had led to this moment now, them together and sitting across a table . . . and what had he proposed? She trusted few. Herself least of all. She'd made too many mistakes in the past. Would this be one of them?

If she didn't let Mark make the repairs, she would lose the bar.

She had no other option.

Reaching into her jeans pocket, she produced a key. Setting it on the table, she slowly slid it toward Mark. His brow quirked with a curiosity she thought unfounded given what they'd been discussing. "You'll need to have access to the bar," she informed him.

With a lopsided smile, he said, "Shoot—I thought you were giving me a key to your place."

She felt a frown work over her mouth, almost glad he'd been crass. Far easier to be annoyed by him than humbling herself.

"You wish," she retorted, pinching the bridge of her nose to rid herself of the headache that seemed to slap her all at once. The dull throb made her lose what little appetite she'd had.

Of all the guys she didn't want to be indebted to, Mark was on her short list. Applying pressure to her forehead, she gave him a heavy gaze. "If this is some elaborate plan to get me to—" She didn't know how to finish the thought without visually spelling it out. Regrouping, she continued, "Look, if all you're trying to do is hook up with me, then you're going to a lot of trouble and expense—"

"Dana, for fifty grand, I could buy a whole lotta love." For the first time since she'd given him crap about his motives, he got angry with her. Clearly insulted. "Trust me. I have no ulterior motives. I want to do this for me as much as you need it for you." He raked his hair from his forehead. "And if I wanted to get you into bed, I could have talked you into it a long time ago."

Conviction laced his voice, and the air between them snapped with tension. She wasn't altogether sure he was wrong.

CHAPTER EIGHT

OSCAR'S DEATH had changed Suni. She saw beauty in things she'd taken for granted. She became more forgiving, more patient. Past scars were healed, hard feelings forgotten. She recognized that life could be taken, breaths ceased. Live for today.

And she had much to be alive for.

A daughter. A grandson.

Her health. Happiness. Moderate prosperity.

In death, Oscar had made sure she'd be taken

care of with the modest life insurance policy he'd secured. Most of the money stayed in a savings account for Terran's college education.

She'd paid off the loan on the house, gotten rid of Oscar's old Mercedes and bought herself a reliable Toyota. She didn't let Dana pay for utilities or things pertaining to the home. But as prideful as she was, Dana wouldn't let Suni buy her a new car. That junker S-10 was held together by rust and hope. How it even still ran was anyone's guess.

Suni enjoyed providing a place for Dana and Terran that they could feel special in. Build memories. She loved having them with her. Without them, her life would be very empty.

She remembered the evening that Dana had sat her down and told her she was pregnant. There had been no guessing who'd fathered the child. Dana had been seeing Cooper for less than a year, and she'd been infatuated with him from the start. Suni had never cared for him, and he did not have a lot of good qualities.

He procrastinated.

He was lazy when not prodded.

He needed some strong energy.

Dislike for him tainted the fabric of her path. Because of him, each fold of her life now unraveled. She would have loved to have seen him sail away on a paper airplane, but the moron had fathered her grandchild. From that day forward, she'd have to concern herself over what Cooper did. Now his thoughts, speech and actions would affect their lives forever.

Over the past five years, the first two being most difficult, Suni had learned to accept the new path. And much to her desire for it not to be so, Cooper had turned out to be rather "okay."

He'd finally taken responsibility, entered Terran's life, and did indeed make a difference. And for the better.

So Suni did have many things to celebrate. She kept Oscar's memory alive, telling Terran stories about his grandfather. And about his uncle Terrance, whom he'd been named after.

"Grandma!" Terran called, racing ahead. "Why are you walking like a turtle?"

"Terran, you slow down, baby. It's slippery."

Rain had been falling off and on that morning, but the annual July Fourth festivities never faltered. For Ketchikanites, it was a huge holiday featuring a big parade.

Terran paused on the sidewalk, bouncing in tennis shoes with impatience, waiting for her to catch him. He wore his hockey uniform, a black-and-gold jersey with the number 4 on the chest and sleeves. Gripping his hockey stick, he swished it over the sidewalk, chasing an imaginary puck.

As Suni set her pace faster, he hollered, "Grandma, how come you aren't running? Doncha want me to get you some candy at the parade?"

Suni didn't need any candy, but Terran seemed to

think he could hoard more if he prefixed it with the intention of collecting handfuls for his grandma. Besides, the candy toss wasn't until the big parade, not the kiddy one. "I'm not worried about candy."

"How come you don't worry?"

"Because worry isn't wise."

Terran made a slap shot toward the curb, banging into a streetlamp base. "What's wise mean?"

"Smart."

"How come you didn't say that in the first place?"

Striding next to him, she frowned. His endless questions did tax a person's patience quota. "Come on, we're almost there."

The Federal Building loomed on Mission Street, a massive tarp-covered monster at the moment. At a public meeting this past April, the few people in attendance had voted to repaint the building in its current pink shade rather than a proposed cream. The National Register of Historic Places gave the city some leeway in arguing for the pink—since cream would have matched the sky's dreary color most of the time.

Suni thought the building looked like an L-shaped block of Pepto-Bismol.

Children, accompanied by adults, crowded near the entrance, organizing who would ride on deco-rated wagons pulled by parents, and who would race along on scooters or zip past on bikes. Everything had been decorated with red, white and blue crepe paper, and there were all sorts of waving flags, stars and whatever patriotic symbols the kids could find.

Terran's group had a banner to carry. His ice hockey team, the Chinooks, would be led by their coach—Cooper. Whenever Terran saw his father, his eyes lit brightly and he dashed ahead to give his daddy a leg hug.

"Hey, buddy!" Cooper said, lifting his son into his arms for a brief moment before righting him on his feet.

"Daddy!"

Suni held back, having done her part by bringing Terran to the parade start by ten-thirty. Dana had secured a spot complete with camp chairs and umbrellas for them near the tunnel on Tongass Highway where she waited, camcorder in hand, to video him as he marched along.

Glancing Suni's way, Cooper waved, then busied himself in the task of wrangling a dozen hyper five-year-olds into a rough formation.

MARK LEISURELY CHECKED OUT the booths on Tongass Dock, a mix of carnival games and food stalls. He learned what *lumpia* was—a Filipino egg roll. The roasting smells of reindeer sausage came from portable grills. The Indian taco stalls serving fried bread and fixings had quite the lineups. Other stalls offered seasoned turkey legs that had just finished cooking, gathering a crowd ready for their lunch. Mouthwatering aromas filled the damp air, and rain threatened in the clouds that hung low in the sky.

People lined the street running along the dock. Most sat in folding chairs; some had bedding on the curbs and rain tarps pitched just in case. Some kind of parade made its way through town to the cheers of those watching.

Moving toward the street, Mark was tall enough to have a decent view from the dock. Children let off steam, waving at proud parents and darting like spring-loaded pinballs within the confines of the street.

Mark smiled as one little dude pumped his legs faster on his scooter to keep up with the rest of his pals. He looked wobbly and ready to take a header, but the grin on his face split it in two. He was clearly loving the parade.

His own childhood memories settled over Mark.

Every once in a while, Mark thought about what it would be like to have kids. It wasn't an idea he'd dismissed as a possibility, but at the same time, he didn't dwell on it.

For the most part, he was okay with never being a dad. He'd learned a lot from his own dad, and sometimes he thought about passing down his knowledge to a son of his own.

He was glad he'd had the opportunity to work for his father all those years, but sometimes wished they had bonded in other ways, as well. It wasn't as if he faulted Giovanni, but as the last boy in the family, Mark kind of felt left by the wayside at times.

Mark left the booths and walked toward the tunnel. He passed cruise-ship berths, their gang-planks and banners attached to the docks. It felt good to walk, so he continued through the tunnel, bypassing the crowd that had gathered at the end.

Exploring Water Street, he found the Arctic Bar. Rock-and-roll music spilled onto the street from its open door. The bar was a vastly different place from Dana's. It seemed more modern with a grid ceiling, neon lights, pool table and lively patrons.

In his younger days, Mark would have gone in and made some new friends. This had been his kind of place. Beer, shots. Women with some nice hardware. But he didn't feel like going back to old habits. So he turned around and went back through the tunnel.

He really shouldn't be wandering around, anyway.

He needed to take measurements at the Blue Note so he could order the Sheetrock. He'd already placed an order for an electrical panel and circuit breakers with the town's union electrician. For the larger projects—the updated sprinkler system, steel deck and exit door extension, he'd have to hire help.

The crowd thickened around him. A woman caught his attention, and he should have known by the way his body reacted, it was Dana. She was such a petite thing, it was a surprise he could even find her in the press of adults.

Her hair was different today. She'd let ringlets frame her face and cascade down her back. They were ethnic curls, appearing soft and tempting for a man's fingers to wrap around. She had on a thick moss-green sweater, no jacket. Dark denim jeans, with back pockets that hugged her butt in a way that left little to his imagination. Black boot tips peeked out from the jeans. To his recollection, it was the first time he'd noticed her in heels. She wore casual shoes to the bar, but now she had on a pair of come-to-papa boots.

She turned to a woman with Asian features who had to be related, maybe her mother. Then Dana smiled, laughed as a little boy ran to her and she scooped him into her arms, pressing a soft kiss on his temple.

Dana's green sweater contrasted with the boy's jersey. No doubt the boy was her son.

The feminine features on her face took on an entirely different appearance. A total softening from pure love. What would it be like if she ever loved a man and looked into his eyes like that?

She smoothed the boy's hair from his brow, and he rambled on about something in an animated way. He had the pleading expression that little boys get when they have to have the newest toy out of the catalog—ASAP. Mark knew he'd been just like that kid many times. Whatever her son asked for, Dana must have said all right, because he began to jump in place as if he were on a trampoline.

Lively little guy.

Dana turned to retrieve something from her chair, and it was then that she noticed him. Their eyes met and he didn't falter. He knew she'd know he'd been watching her. And he was glad.

He liked looking at her. Liked watching how she moved, how her face lit, the way she smiled. Those occasions were few and far between, and when she showed happiness, he drank it in like a man parched for water.

Mark went toward her and said his howdy, waiting for her to say something.

"Hey," she finally offered.

"Hey, yourself."

Then awkwardly, her gaze skirted to the woman beside her. It didn't seem she had a choice, so she said, "Mark, this is my mom."

"Hello, Mom."

The woman wasn't sure about his response, but Dana had left out her mother's name.

Quickly rectifying that, Dana added, "My mom—Suni."

"Nice to meet you, Suni," Mark said cordially. Then, brows raised, he waited for Dana to introduce him. When she didn't, he filled in the blank. "Mark Moretti. I'll be doing some construction work at the Blue Note for your daughter."

"She didn't mention you," Suni replied bluntly, giving Dana a questioning stare.

"I've been busy, Mom." Dana's hair fell about her shoulders. Her eye makeup shimmered in golden-green, a color that brought out her eye color intensity. He could lose his entire focus staring into her eyes.

The boy's chin lifted and his mouth—purple from some food—hung open while he studied Mark with a pucker to his brows. "How come you're so tall? Was your dad a giant?"

"My dad was an Italian."

"Did he have green slime for snot and six eyes?"

The comment threw Mark for a curve.

Dana clarified with a shrug, "He thought you meant alien. Sounds like Italian. He doesn't know what that is."

Nodding, Mark said, "My dad was a pretty tall guy, but I'm a lot taller than him."

"How come?"

"Uh, because I just turned out this way. So what's your name, dude?"

"Terran. Are you going to be in the parade?"

"No."

"How come?" But he moved on in rapid-fire, not giving Mark the opportunity to reply. "The grown-up parade people throw candy to the kids. I already got a grape lollipop from my dad."

That news about a dad halted his thoughts briefly. So Terran's father was in the picture, living in Ketchikan and obviously here. Mark hadn't connected that dot this far.

He hadn't spent any time considering how Dana's ex fit into her life—if he was around or what happened to their relationship. In a way, the news was satisfying. A boy needed his father. But Mark did feel a sharp pang wondering how much Dana relied on the guy.

Suni eyed him from top to bottom, taking in every noteworthy piece of him. Hair, eyes, mouth, shirt, pants and shoes. He felt as if he was under a microscope. He couldn't imagine why she wanted to dissect him like a bug. Unsettled, Mark got the distinct impression she didn't approve of men talking to her daughter.

"You think it'll rain, Suni?" he asked, trying to draw her into a polite conversation.

"Yes." Her obsidian eyes settled in on his, searching, then she asked, "When did you move to Ketchikan?"

"Just here for the summer. I'm from Boise, Idaho."

With those words, she seemed to view him differently. "Boise's inland from Seattle and Portland. Drier climate."

Not since high school had Mark felt like this under a watchful parental scrutiny. No wonder Dana was a pistol—she got it from her mother.

"High desert."

"Ketchikan's a rain forest," Suni said in the tone

of a dour weathercaster. "It rains—a lot. Not many can handle it."

"Probably not."

The ping-pong conversation might have kept on bouncing back and forth if Sam Hyatt hadn't arrived toting a deck chair and backpack. He hadn't seen Hyatt in a week. The man flew back and forth like a bird, landing and taking off for Fish Tail Air. While Mark had listened to Sam's advice regarding keeping a safe distance from Dana, he still thought the guy felt more about her than he let on.

Seeing Mark, Sam paused. "You're still around."

"Looks that way," Mark replied caustically.

"Hi, Sam!" Terran exclaimed. "Are you going to get some of the candy, too? If you find Smarties, can I have them?"

"Sure, Terran."

Dana seemed at a loss over what to do about his being there. He'd invaded her little world of family and friends, and he knew a need for an exit when he felt one.

"Have a good Fourth." He nodded to Suni, then gave Dana a smile. "I was heading over to the Blue Note to start work."

But before he could take a step, she called out to him.

"Don't. It's a holiday. Watch the parade."

"Hey, uh, alien guy? If you watch the parade, can you get me some Smarties or bubba'gum?" Terran asked, a gleam in his eyes. The gap in his mouth made the boy's smile seem lopsided. "But only the wrapped ones. My mommy won't let me eat the dirty ones."

Mark curved his mouth into a half grin. "Maybe I could." To Dana, he gave a questioning look. He wouldn't invite himself.

"We have an extra chair you can use." Dana's shoulder held a proud line. She evidently wasn't used to inviting men onto her turf. "Terran never sits in his—he's too busy grabbing free candy. I don't even know why I bring him a chair."

Mark glanced at Suni, then Sam. Neither would have made it on the welcoming committee, but they didn't tell him to take a hike.

"Appreciate it," Mark said, then went to arrange his seat. But not before Sam angled his chair between Dana and him.

So that's how it was going to be.

Mark kept his thoughts to himself as a new parade began its procession.

Suni, of all people, gave him the lowdown on the floats. The Misty Thistle Pipes and Drums— bagpipes and drummers wearing kilts. A group of Muskeg Marchers, forest service employees with band instruments that added some local color.

Some guy holding a live bald eagle on his hand, standing in a utility truck bed, waved to everyone. Even the cruise ships had built floats. Local politi-

155

cians rode in vintage cars that crawled along. There were the customary fire trucks, complete with sirens and flashing lights, along with Harley riders with badass tailpipes ripping it up.

Everyone threw candy into the crowd, and each time, Dana or Suni or Sam would say to Terran, "Watch for the cars!" or "Get out of the street, baby!" as another float crawled on past.

From his chair, Mark extended his arms and fisted flying candy being thrown at him—mostly from the women riding in the parade. He scored some candy necklaces, snack-size M&M's and assorted other kinds that Terran eagerly took from him.

It had been a long time since Mark had sat back and relaxed long enough to watch something like this. Boise had a Fourth of July parade, but he hadn't gone in over thirty years.

Finally, a cop car inched its way along, signaling the parade's close.

When it was over, Terran came screaming toward the chairs to check on his loot. He'd double-fisted a good bucketful of sugar—all dumped into a Lightning McQueen backpack.

"Hey, giant guy—you know what?" Terran said with gusto.

It took Mark a sec to realize the little boy was talking to him. "What?"

"You rock, dude!" The statement set Mark back a bit. It was funny when he thought about it.

Something as simple as the act of getting candy made this kid think of him as a hero.

"Mommy! I got so much candy!" Terran declared. "You want to see it? Want to?"

Dana peeked into the stuffed backpack. "Wow, that's enough to last until Halloween."

"How come I can't eat it all today and tomorrow?"

"Because you'd get sick."

"If I promise not to get sick, can I eat it all?"

"No, baby. You'd get sick, trust me."

"Can I eat four . . . no, five—" he held up his fingers "—pieces today?"

"One now, the rest after lunch."

Mark observed the easy way she spoke to her son, the evident love in her voice toward him. He felt a stab of . . . he wasn't quite sure. Maybe envy. As stupid as that sounded. Envy that she had a kid to call her own, a kid to love her. A kid to be there with her.

Back home, his house was pretty basic. Nobody lived there but him. No mess to clean since he was hardly ever around. He ate out a lot, visited his mom. Went to lunch with his sister. Hung out with a couple of guys from the job, but he didn't really have a close bud. He worked too much, took on too many things for Moretti Construction.

Dana did a lot, too. And yet she had a little boy who counted on her to be his mom. And from what Mark had seen, she seemed able to handle it.

157

"So we're going to St. John's Church for pie and coffee," Dana said, entering his thoughts. "You can come, if you want."

Dana—so gorgeous and confident. He loved the curly hair.

He loved looking at her. But these were her people, her parade. Her town. Not his.

"No, that's cool. You go ahead." Rising from his chair, it felt good to stretch his muscles.

If she was disappointed he'd passed, she didn't show it. But Sam seemed happy about Mark's departure, collecting his things to make ready to leave.

"Mark," Dana said, and to his recollection, it was the first time she'd called him by his name. "The Blue Note's operating hours are from two to two." Her teeth snagged her lower lip, a gesture that he read as her uncertainty about discussing business within the earshot of others. "Can you renovate outside those times?"

"Yeah—maybe," he replied. "The outside stuff's going to have to continue after two in the afternoon. The inside shouldn't be that big of a deal. I'll arrive early to get a jump on it. Probably six in the morning."

"That would work." She allowed Sam to gather her things, as well as Terran's. "How long do you think it'll take to complete?"

"It has to be done by the first of September."

"Why's that?"

Puzzlement creased her smooth forehead, an inky black curl teasing her brow. Heat flashed through him, fierce and strong. The set of her mouth, the flesh-pink color, tempted beyond reason. If he hadn't been on a public street with people milling around, he would have taken her into his arms and kissed her.

He damned the direction of his thoughts.

Dana could make him forget obligations to his family, and the life he had back in Boise.

" 'Cause that's when I'm out of here, sunshine," he said, then left her to enjoy the rest of her afternoon.

CHAPTER NINE

"HOT TAMALE, BABY. Somebody should take that man's picture and put it on a calendar." Presley's animated *caliente* reference to Mark brought out a frown in Dana.

"Who'd buy it?" Dana stood in the Blue Note's kitchen, her friend and cook assembling an order of seviche.

"You know you would."

"Not even."

"Uh-huh."

Dana was annoyed by Presley's throaty response that meant something like *yeah, right.*

Knowing herself the way she did, Dana was sure of her reply. She wouldn't buy a hunk calendar.

Never had. But she did have to admit one thing—if only to herself. Tracking Mark with her gaze as he worked around the bar was a nice diversion.

She'd hired help in the past to repair something here and there. Those guys had had beer bellies, or had been scrawny with a visible butt crack. Mark was neither of those.

Tall and muscular, he moved with a commanding presence that said he knew exactly what he was doing. His shoulders were wide, his muscles evident in the long-sleeved T-shirts he wore.

He'd been deep into the demo for two weeks, having knocked out the one wall and tarped the bare studs and conduit with plastic sheets as he installed a doorway and widened the area. Dust floated throughout the bar, a pain to stay on top of. Mark managed to keep the renovation as functional as possible, so as not to interrupt her normal business operations.

"I told him not to get here so early," Dana remarked, the warm scent of toasting bread filling the space. Which was very true. Mark's strong work ethic, while admirable, was going to run him into the ground with exhaustion. "He said he'd start work at six o'clock. But when I'm locking the door just after two and leaving to go home—he's coming in. The guy doesn't sleep normal hours."

"He doesn't strike me as the type to listen to anyone's advice," Presley said, squeezing lime juice over her creation just as a waitstaff worker whisked the tall glass away for serving. Glancing at her next order, Presley added in a yummy voice, "Have I mentioned, that man is smokin' hot?"

"That would be a yes," Dana said shortly, leaning into the stainless counter. "And remind yourself you aren't shopping."

Presley Reid had had the same on-again, off-again boyfriend since their senior year. Ten years of yo-yo dating had left Presley strung along, waiting for more. Dana wouldn't have tolerated it.

A gleam lit the cook's bright eyes. "No, but I can look at the beefcake." Then in a rush, she added, "Which reminds me—I saw Tori Daniel at the Chevron station this morning. Her skirt was so short you could see her goodies when she leaned over to pump her gas."

"Seriously?"

"Well, she had tights on. You know how she is."

Dana had seen Tori around town since her Safeway days, but the woman was a nonentity in her life. She had a glossy starlet look but a brain the size of a whiskey shot.

Sometimes Dana wished she was tall and blond, but she had no imagination when it came to that sort of thing. She'd lived with what she'd been born with, and she'd gotten used to it.

There were always high heels to add inches to a woman's confidence.

She didn't often wear them to work, but on her

off days she loved heeled boots or pumps with jeans. Practicality won most of the time when it was pouring rain. Nothing beat Gore-Tex on a slippery sidewalk. Dana feared she'd kill herself in some designer heels if she dared wear them during a typical Ketchikan deluge.

Another round of orders arrived at the counter, and Dana left Presley and her assistants to fill them. Out in the barroom, she scanned the crowd and found Mark.

He'd quit working early today after his materials hadn't been delivered when they'd been promised. He must have gone home, napped, showered, and now he'd returned to the bar as a customer.

Mark sat at the end of the bar, talking to Bear and Cardelle as if they were old buddies. He'd integrated himself nicely into their small town, making friends.

Friendships weren't easy for her. She had too much to do, so little time to do it. Each day was filled before she could take a deep breath. The weeks she had her son, she spent every minute with him that she could. When he was with his dad, she tried to catch up on all the mundane things. And every hour in between—she was here at the Blue Note.

Aside from her mom, Presley, Walt and Leo were the closest things to confidants Dana had and, even then, there was only so much she'd discuss with each of them. Her true best friend had been her brother. They'd shared a closeness growing up that would never be duplicated by anyone else.

Sometimes she missed Terrance more than she could bear; her dad, too. Oscar had been the bar's soul, and his presence was missed to this day by the patrons. It seemed like holidays were the worst because they had special meaning. But a day like July Fourth had created new memories because of Terran, and that helped heal a place in her heart.

Dave Brubeck's quintuple-time rendition of "Take Five" played through the expensive speakers, and customers' voices carried across the room. All was well. Everyone appeared happy.

The need to visit with Mark tugged strongly. She could ask him how things were falling into place. A legitimate question.

Although she'd never admit this to anyone, like Presley, Dana thought Mark was "hot" as well when it came to his looks.

But that day at the parade, she'd seen a different side to him. The easygoing interaction between Mark and Terran hadn't gone without her notice. They had somehow formulated a joint effort to collect candy, although it had been unplanned. Terran had caught on quickly, dodging left and right, and staying out of the line of fire for Mark to snag flying candy.

Smiling in remembrance, Dana gave Mark another glance, and this time she found he was looking directly at her. His eyes caught hers, and he gave her a look that said more than she cared to know. Too intimate for words. He did that to her, all too often. She didn't like it. Or maybe she liked it more than she dared admit. The way he made her feel without even being close by or talking to her.

Dana changed directions, and went into her office to work on her six-month expense forecast. With the economic downturn, every dollar had to be accounted for the best way she could. She had made a detailed cash flow list with food receipts, beverage sales and sales receivables. She'd tallied her cash disbursements and the controllable expenses such as operating—including utilities and the music entertainment she hired, and miscellaneous expenses, payroll and . . . contract labor.

Settling back in her chair, she stared at the spreadsheet on the computer screen. Mark was saving her a fortune. She could never have afforded a loan to get everything completed.

His generosity still perplexed her.

What was he all about? Too many whys kept circling through her thoughts. There were times when she wanted to get to know him better, to find out what was behind his offer to help. Not just any guy would do this for her. Motives were a strange thing. She knew too well how a false motive could manipulate a situation.

A person had to want to do something for themselves. When they did it for someone else the result could get emotionally messy.

Mark drew her attention like nobody else had in the past. He was an enigma of sorts. Maybe she could invite him out for dinner or coffee . . . talk to him about himself.

Dana rolled her eyes. *Stupid idea.*

Still reclined in her chair, she rolled the computer's mouse to minimize her document. In its place, she visited an Internet site with pages of shoes she'd been looking at earlier. She loved the ubber expensive cranberry-red, peep-toe pumps with the stiletto heels.

The spreadsheet forgotten for the moment, she clicked on the shoes to enlarge the photo. The heels were four-inchers. That was about her limit. Any taller, she'd risk falling while walking in them.

"Those are some sexy pimp kicks, boss." Mark's voice drawled through her office with a honey smoothness. As he leaned next to the door frame, his black hair fell over his brow. "You'd look good in them. Little black skirt—"

"Why are you like this?" she snapped, sitting upright with a jolt of her body.

"Practice, I guess."

With a fast click, Dana minimized the shoe images. Her cute desktop background photo of Terran came into view.

Heart beating, and not just from being startled while salivating over a pair of Christian Louboutin shoes—which she could never afford anyway—

she glowered at Mark. Just his appearance in this small nook of her life, her tiny office, affected her sensibilities. She felt as if he took over the entire space with his presence.

"What do you want?" she asked bluntly, not meaning to sound so cold, but he'd snuck up on her. She hated being surprised.

He wore a button-down shirt, a soft grayish color that brought out the few silver strands at his temples. "How's life treating you, sis?"

"I'm not your sister."

"And then they all said—Amen." He gave her the rakish grin that went straight to her . . .

"So what is it you really want, Mark? I'm busy."

"I can see that. A little shoe shopping on company time. But you're the boss so you shop all you want."

Flustered, she replied, "I wasn't interested in any of them. I was just—"

"Looking." He pushed away from the door. "Nothing wrong with that. Giving something a look over before you buy it is actually damn smart."

"Are you talking about shoes?"

"Are you?"

Closing her eyes, she held her breath for a ten count. Then when she was ready to face him, she blinked. "Is everything okay with the remodel? Leo said you cut out early."

"Lumber delivery didn't make it like they promised. Happens all the time."

"I'm sorry."

"What for? You didn't do it."

Mark examined the office walls, taking in the numerous framed pictures of Terran.

"He's a good-looking boy." Mark studied the Halloween photo featuring lit pumpkins on the porch steps and her son outfitted in his Batman costume with the muscled chest in gray flame-retardant fabric. "But so is his mom."

She accepted the flattery without comment.

Mark's gaze drifted from the photo. "Bear had told me you had a son. And about what happened to your dad and brother."

That news caused her to impose an iron will not to show any reaction. While it was common knowledge about her brother and father's deaths, she didn't care to discuss it with Mark.

Mark went on, "That's why you were bent out of shape in the aviation office that night. My dad passed away, too. I understand."

"You don't understand anything about me."

"If that's what you want to think."

He gave a cursory examination of her desk and the contents strewn on top. The items on the floor. A briefcase. Black patent leather heels she'd kicked off one afternoon when she needed to help haul in beer kegs. In the corner, a musician's case leaned against the wall.

"Satisfied?" she questioned. "I'm not the best housekeeper, but I know where things are."

"I suppose you do."

He managed to make himself at home without being invited or even sitting in the other chair in the room. The confines were tight and she wished he'd say his piece, then go.

"So what's up?" she inquired pleasantly, hoping that kindness would disarm whatever intent he'd had when he'd entered.

His day's stubble had been shaved, his jaw's razor smoothness beckoning. She ignored the lure.

Mark leaned next to the doorway once more. "I want to buy you a drink and get to know you better."

"I don't drink when I'm working." On a pretext of being overly involved in paperwork, she shuffled paper around to look busy. "And that reminds me, I hope Leo's not charging you at the bar. I told him you could have anything you wanted. Just don't abuse it."

"I haven't gotten stupid drunk since I was twenty-three." His dark brown eyes lowered, traveling across her narrow shoulders to the dusky-rose sweater that fit over her small breasts. "And never tell a man he can have anything he wants, unless you mean it."

Fire sparked through her every nerve ending and she shot to her feet. Needing to stand up to him, or rather trying to, she only came to his chest. "I was talking about liquor, and you know it."

This close to him, she could smell his aftershave

or body soap. It didn't matter which. He smelled too good and she didn't like that she thought so.

She tipped her chin upward, holding her ground. "You bring out the worst in me when I'm trying to like you for all your help."

He got that cocky grin on his face that infuriated her. "If you get this excited about my worst, I could really make you happy with my best."

While childish, she shoved him just to get her frustration out. His hands clamped over her arms, holding her still. Pumping fast, her heartbeat betrayed the calm she presented. She could feel her pulse at her neck, the obvious sign she was affected by him.

Trying to slow her breathing, she remained motionless while his face loomed over hers and his breath caught on her cheek.

For the longest time, he drank in her features, looking at her face as if he wanted to memorize it. She grew nervous, unsure how to respond. Her mind said one thing, her body said another.

She wasn't immune to his startling good looks, the feel of him this close. His warmth, his scent, the dark glint in his eyes. But she wasn't going to jump him, not for anything.

Dana had a lot of reserve in her. She could wait this out for as long as he wanted. She wouldn't flinch or bolt. She could stand still and simply breathe.

In the end, Mark's hands slid over her arms and

toward her chin. He caught the point in his strong fingers, then lightly brushed his thumb over her mouth. She couldn't suppress the shiver that came with a thousand hot pricks of assaulting pleasure. Angry with her lack of resolve, she finally jerked back, needing to be free of him.

"Get out—go have a drink," she ordered.

Then in a tone that both exasperated and caressed her like a light kiss, he replied in a rich timbre, "I'm not the one who needs it, Princess Bubble Gum."

"What did you call me?"

"Pretty sweater. You look amazingly good in that color."

Then he turned and left as quietly as he'd appeared. Dana let herself watch him retreat, standing still. Her chin lowered and she gave her pink sweater a glance. Its cable knit was delicate and woven with ruby-pink metallic yarn to create a startling pink illusion of rich color. It was probably the most expensive sweater in her closet; her mother had bought it for her.

For long seconds after Mark left, Dana stood wondering what all this had really been about.

But she didn't have time to overly ponder it because the hour had grown late—it was nearly eleven o'clock. Opening the hard-shell black case, she took out her father's saxophone. She had her own, back at the house. He'd bought it for her and taught her to play. But she kept Oscar's sax at the bar. This was his place, his music, and when the notes on his saxophone filled the Blue Note, it was as if he was here again rather than on the recordings.

Finding Leo, she told him to cut the music when he saw she was ready. This was their standard operating procedure when she opted to play. Normally she did so a couple times a week, but it had been nearly a month since she'd played.

Standing on the short riser where other performers played live jazz, Dana held her shiny saxophone, and Leo was right on cue to cease the jukebox tune.

Posture straight, head erect, she fought to stave off the flush that had crept over her face. Mark sat at the bar once more, and she could feel his eyes following her every move.

When she'd prepared, taking her place, she had it in her mind to play "Somewhere Over the Rainbow," but as the room stilled to a hush, she heard rain pounding on the rooftop. Fat drops fell on her corrugated roof, sounding like a brass-tack staccato over metal. A thought hit her—they didn't need the buckets anymore.

Mark had fixed the leaks.

Now everyone in the Blue Note could enjoy the sounds of the rain as it fell overhead.

Taking a few silent beats, she collected herself, then began to play. "Here's That Rainy Day" came alive as the crowd gave her an encouraging round of applause.

Breathing from her core's center, she played with a loose embouchure and a strong airstream. Fingers close to the wind holes, she went after tone and purity.

Air and fingers met. She had a perfect understanding of open and closed so the melody was in constant motion. Her father had taught her that the notes she did not play were as important as those that she did. Sometimes, technique only served to stifle. Use your sense of rhythm to make the song come alive.

As the song wrapped around her she forgot about everyone in the room. Her father's voice came to her ears, blending with the sweet notes of his instrument.

"Put your heart and soul into it, Danalee-honey. Otherwise it's just noise."

She liked to imagine she could play as well as Oscar Jackson, Louisiana musician extraordinaire, but she would never emulate the sound he had perfected as his own.

As the last note rose from her chest, traveled through the reed and created a soothing sound, Dana held still.

The crowd gave her rousing applause, and the noise broke her dream world. When she played, she grew lost in the music. It became a part of her she grabbed hold of, bringing her closer to her father.

Tonight had been especially hard, and for reasons she didn't understand at the moment. Stinging tears flooded her eyes, and as she lowered the sax onto its stand, she blinked to keep them at bay. She knew she had to get out of here. Fast.

Head down, chin low, she wove her way out the front door and gulped in the clean, wet air. Rain fell in a veil that clung to her skin, her face, her sweater.

She sprinted to the aviation office and stood under the awning that offered little shelter. She didn't realize she was crying until she tasted the salt on her lips.

Losing her father had been more than difficult. Keeping the bar going in his memory was even harder. There were times when she didn't want any part of it.

She wasn't smart enough to figure out a business budget.

She wasn't talented enough to play the saxophone her father had lovingly taught her.

She didn't have it in her to meet people and think of them as old friends when they sidled up to the bar—not like Oscar had.

Oscar Jackson was the one and only Sax Man. He had lived and breathed jazz. The Blue Note was his dream, his vision.

Dana kept it going—for him. And for Ketchikan. They loved this place. She couldn't close it. Why she even let herself think of that right now . . .

A weak moment. One that allowed her to release her true inner feelings rather than hold back.

She understood Mark when he'd said he did things out of an obligation. If he only knew how alike they were . . . if he only—

"Dana," came Mark's voice through the rain.

He approached, the rain spotting his shirt as he met her under the awning.

"Go away," she said in a biting tone.

Mark pulled her to him, his fingers digging into her shoulders, the contact a searing heat through her wet sweater. His mouth was inches from hers, his breath caressing her trembling lips.

"You're crying." He took her face in his hands and held her, easing his callused fingers over her temples. She closed her eyes and allowed him to stroke her. Standing still, she could barely take in a breath. He moved his hands lower, tracing the shape of her eyebrows, eyelids and long lashes, cheekbones, nose and, finally, her mouth. She parted her lips as he continued to trace her jaw and slim neck.

His touch returned to her lips again and she involuntarily pressed a featherlight kiss on his thumb, tasting his skin.

"I want something that's mine and only for me." The words seemed to be spoken by someone other than her, but Dana had felt them well inside her. Then she whispered, "Kiss me."

She melted into him and he pressed his fingers

into her hair that now curled down her back. Pulling her face closer, he brought his wide mouth down on hers.

He kissed her slowly and skillfully, sapping any common sense she might have had. Everything inside her skittered in a warm fusion of senses. She breathed deeper, the night smelling of minerals and earth as she dragged in a half breath.

There was a strong hardness to Mark's lips as he blended his warm moisture with hers. The pit of her stomach tightened as she let herself enjoy without thought, without guilt. It had been so long since she'd kissed a man . . . yet badly wanted to.

From the beginning, she'd been attracted to Mark, but she'd held that reaction in check. Now, she let go of reason.

Shocked by her own eager response, Dana kissed Mark back, shadowing his movements. She grew only slightly startled when he forced her teeth to part, his tongue invading her mouth's velvet recesses. The contact made her dizzy, and she tightened her grip on his muscled back. She wanted him close, so close. She worked her hands over his spine and across his heavy shoulders, feeling the thick cords of his neck.

It was as if her blood had turned to fire, fueling some hidden desire she never knew she possessed.

This was insanity . . . the emotions of the moment had caught her unawares. She'd been too vulnerable, discouraged that she hadn't played as well as Oscar. All she wanted was something for her, to be a woman who needed and wanted.

And she'd wanted this.

But it would be a bad choice to give in to.

Cold rain pelted them, giving her the chill she needed to allow the reality of the situation to set in.

Breathless, Dana broke free. It took her several long seconds to compose herself, unable to disguise her body's reaction to him in the way her cheeks had heated. Without looking away from Mark's face, she staggered to break free from his grasp.

Gasping, she said, "I didn't mean it. I didn't want you to kiss me."

Eyes dark, like stones on the beach, he swallowed thickly. She could see from the way he slowly worked his jaw, he was trying to figure out what happened. "I could take it back."

"No," she rallied, not wanting him to kiss her again. Then in a defensive cry, she urged, "Leave me alone."

"Whatever you say, Princess Bubble Gum."

"Stop calling me these ridiculous nicknames."

"You want to know why I do?" He leaned in closer, his voice like a flat chord, but strong with sharp meaning. "Because it makes your eyes shine and you react . . . and you look like you've been—" He slowly shook his head, as if in disbelief over his blunt honesty. "God help me, I love that look on your face."

"Well un-love it."

"Not so easy, sweetart. Once I get something set in my mind, it stays there. For a long time."

Rain fell over his face as he stepped back, then left her to her own ruminations over what had just happened.

CHAPTER TEN

THE BLACK RUBBER WHEEL didn't pivot on its axis like it should, causing Mark to grip the cart's handle tighter. The blue Wal-Mart cart didn't want to steer in a straight line down the jeans aisle. He came to a Levi's table and fingered through them, finding his size and length. Chucking two pairs of 501s in the cart, he moved on to socks and T-shirts.

Doing laundry a couple times a week had gotten old.

When he'd arrived in Alaska, he hadn't given himself a specific timetable to be here, but he'd figured he would've been back in Boise by now.

Several weeks should have been ample time to figure out what he wanted to do about his role in the family business. The trouble was, in the month and handful of days that he'd been in Ketchikan, he'd barely given his situation back home his attention.

His mind had been wrapped around Dana and her current set of problems, not his own. Ever since last night, entirely different thoughts had clouded his head. And they had nothing to do with her renovations.

This morning lying in bed, in a state of half asleep and half awake, he could almost feel her pliant sweater beneath his hands. The strands of her wet hair curled around his fingers. The warm feel of her mouth over his. Visions of their heated kiss, of her sweet body pressed against his, had invaded his dreams.

He'd woken strongly aroused and staring at the ceiling. The dreamlike images became crystal clear in his thoughts. He was a fairly tall man, and with Dana in his arms, he felt too big and too tall. As if he'd crush her. She was so short and slight. It had been with effort he'd bent his knees to accommodate her in his arms while pressing his lips to hers.

Not since he'd been in junior high or high school had he spent time reliving a kiss. Back then, he'd thought with what was behind the fly in his jeans. Zeroing in on sex had been the focus of puberty. He thought about sex as an adult. But a guy wasn't programmed to repeat a romantic scene in his head over and over. What happened, happened. Then the moment was over. Sometimes a kiss was okay. Sometimes it was mind-blowing. But it wasn't worth dwelling on after the fact. This morning's dream went beyond the normal for Mark. Dana's effect on him was like nothing he'd experienced in the past.

There was nothing about her that he couldn't find interest in. He was attracted to the way she walked, with sure, easy steps. The way she managed the Blue Note with a firm yet friendly approach. Her voice, sometimes rough and scratchy, other times a soft purr. The delicate features on her face, her long hair with its changing texture, her love-me sweet body. And when she'd played that saxophone . . . holy hell.

Sweat beads popped out on Mark's brows.

Maybe it was because he knew things would never work out for them that he was drawn to her all the more. Dana had a life here in this town. His was back home. The explanation for all his thoughts was easy. It was that wanting something not attainable that made it all the more appealing.

Feeling relatively assured he wasn't going over the deep end, Mark shoved thoughts of Dana from his mind.

Moving the cart around the corner, he narrowed in on the sundry aisles. He needed deodorant, razor blades and shampoo. Like most guys, he was pretty basic.

He would have thrown in some food items, but unlike the Wal-Mart back home, this store just had one cooler case with limited items and, for dry goods, only basic stuff like crackers, nuts and teas and coffee. Guess he'd have to hit the grocery store.

Winding his way down an aisle, he mindlessly

glanced at the products, and as he did so, he recognized a voice at the other end of the aisle before he saw who was talking.

"Momma, how come we have to buy namp-kins and not snotty tissues?" a little boy asked.

"Because our last name starts with a *J*."

Mark held back, inching his way forward, watching Dana and her son wheel a slow path ahead of him.

Dana wore jeans that fit her in a way that defined her hips and thighs, offering a suggestion of curves beneath. They rode moderately low on her, a chocolate-brown belt woven through the loops.

Swallowing the tightness in his throat, Mark noted she had the kind of shapely booty that a man could take hold of in both hands as he held her close.

She wore a brown cable-knit sweater and a cream-colored vest, also boots; and she'd twisted her hair into a messy ponytail. Just the sight of her caused him to react in a physical way. And she was oblivious to the effect she had on the man behind her.

Her son sat in the large basket, items surrounding him as he stacked and restacked them into a makeshift fort. Sitting cross-legged, his jeans rode high on his ankles, cowboy boots on his feet. He wore a Teenage Mutant Ninja Turtles sweatshirt and Dana's battered fedora hat, which swam on his head.

Terran asked, "How come Dad's last name starts with a *B* and I'm not a *B?*"

"Because that's how you were born."

"How come I was born a Jackson and not a Boyd?"

"That's just how it was, baby."

"But why?"

"Because you know why. Mommy and Daddy aren't married."

"Why not? Everybody else is married."

"Grandma's not married." Dana selected plain white napkins in an economy package and tossed them into her cart.

"But she was married to Grandpa, wasn't she?"

"Yes."

"Then how come you aren't married to my daddy?"

The cart stilled, Dana's back straight and proud. She drew in a breath, taking in a few beats before replying. "Sometimes I wish I had been, Terran. But things just didn't work out that way."

Mark's thoughts worked over that piece of news, but he didn't hold on to them.

"How come?"

"Let Momma see the list, baby." Dana took a wrinkled sheet of paper from her son. "So we got the hand sanitizer. Next we need to find six glue sticks and one bottle of Elmer's white glue."

"Who's Elmer?"

"Oh, I don't know, Terran," she said with an exasperated sigh. "Some guy who invented the glue."

"How come he 'vented it?" Terran peeked his head around his mother's side, saw Mark and said, "Hi."

Turning with a jerk, Dana caught sight of Mark as he rolled his cart behind her. "Hey," he greeted.

"Hello." Her response was uttered almost shyly, softly. Her eyes lowered, as if she didn't want to meet him directly in his gaze.

Mark addressed Terran, allowing Dana to focus on something other than him. "Whatcha doing, dude?"

Lifting his chin, he knocked the hat brim back with his hand so he could have a better view. "I'm buying my kinny-garden supplies. I don't bring any snot tissues, I have to bring namp-kins because I'm a *J*. What are you?"

"I'm an *M*."

"Is your dad an *M*?" Terran asked, his face masked with a veil of seriousness.

"Yes, he was."

"See, Mommy. Everybody's the same as their dad's letter but me."

Smiling uneasily, rolling her eyes briefly, Dana struggled with an evidently deflated feeling.

Mark directed the conversation elsewhere so Dana didn't have to keep addressing the subject. "So, Terran, you're starting school?"

"Yep. I'm five." He displayed five dirty fingers with orange sticky stuff on them. "How old are you?"

"Forty."

"How many fingers is that?"

"That'd be forty." Mark flashed ten splayed fingers four times.

"You're old." He grinned broadly, the gap in his mouth pink and empty.

A frown caught on Dana's mouth. "Terran, what did I tell you about being polite to people?"

"He's not people—we know him." Terran stuffed his hand in his jeans pocket and revealed an unwrapped sugar candy. "Want a jellybean?"

"No thanks. I'm trying to cut back."

"Huh?" he replied, his orangish lips pursed. Then he asked in a loud whisper, "Mommy, did he just cut one? You told me never to talk about when I'm tooting in the store."

"Gosh, Terran, he's not doing *that*." Dana's eyes widened, embarrassment spreading across her face. Adjusting her leather purse in the cart's seat, she apparently needed a distraction to get her out of the awkward situation. She tucked a stray piece of hair behind her ear, a silver hoop clipped into the lobe.

Addressing Mark, she said, "Have a good rest of your day."

"You do the same." Mark looked into her eyes, ever unique, a soft and glittery appeal in them. Whenever he let himself get caught in those eyes, he could forget where he was, do things he shouldn't.

183

He had feelings for her. Feelings he hadn't expected or sought. They would be his worst enemy if he didn't keep them in check. Yet this close to her, he wanted to feel her arms around his neck once again, have her flush against his—

"Hey, Mark? Mark?" Terran called again when Mark didn't readily acknowledge him. When Mark transferred his glassy gaze, the boy asked, "Do you like the toy aisle?"

"Uh, sure." Mark let the intricacies of his thoughts slip away.

"Can you play hockey?" Terran scooted forward on his knees and batted down the wall of assorted products he'd erected around himself.

"No."

"I can. Is that your cell phone?" He pointed to the black case on Mark's belt.

"Yeah."

"Did you know that GCI Cellular has the best plan for you?"

"Uh, no."

"Terran, stop," Dana broke in. To Mark, she shrugged. "He likes to ask a lot of questions."

"Ya think?" Mark smiled, not particularly bothered by the little boy's inquisition.

"Hey, Mark? Do you like cheesebuggers?"

"Sure, I like cheeseburgers."

"Can you get a cheesebugger with us today?"

"No," Dana clipped, interrupting Mark's "Sure."
Snapping her head in Mark's direction, Dana

glowered at him. "I don't think it's a good idea."

"Why not?" He gave her a half grin. "I'm hungry. My treat."

"But you can't have your treat until after you eat your bugger," Terran added soberly. "Mommy says—no sweets before eats."

Tipping his head in Dana's direction, Mark replied in an easy tone, "Your mom's right. Sweets are a nice treat. Especially when they're from her."

If looks could kill, Dana's would have shot Mark down right in the middle of Wal-Mart.

BURGER QUEEN WAS a Ketchikan institution. Located outside the tunnel and across from the cruise-ship berths, the place drew both tourists and locals. The building didn't look like much to an outsider. Its exterior was pale in color, like vanilla ice cream, and with blue trim that reminded Dana of her mother's hydrangeas.

Parking there was a nightmare. The restaurant was built in a shallow cutout of the shale that rose tall behind it. The dark gray rocks were covered with wild greenery and flowers at this time of year. Three picnic benches with red umbrellas were available for the customers who dined outside. Inside the small restaurant, there were four booths with seats as hard as the shale itself.

Since there was a break in the rain and the temperature was moderately pleasant, Dana, Mark and Terran sat outside. The side door to the restaurant

185

was open, and Dana had placed their order at the counter. Now they waited for their meal ticket to be called.

One thing could be said about Burger Queen—the food was the best, and if you wanted to eat here, patience was a virtue. Nothing on the menu was cooked fast.

Terran and Dana occupied one side of the table, while Mark sat on the other. Dana had bought Terran a coloring book to go along with an extra box of twenty-four crayons. He'd had a mini-fit over not being able to use the new crayons and having to save them for the first day of school. Gone were the tears that had swum in his eyes. Now his demeanor was as happy as a clam as he colored a picture of a dump truck.

Dana easily knit her fingers together, still not quite sure what had prompted her to have lunch with Mark Moretti. She was a big girl and could have said no, but she hadn't. She'd agreed, and for whatever the reason, here she was.

Vehicles and tourist buses zoomed over Tongass Highway, the traffic pretty steady for a Saturday afternoon. Located the way it was, the restaurant was less than ten feet from the road.

"Do you eat here often?" Stylish sunglasses covered Mark's eyes, making them unreadable.

"A couple times a week. Mostly I have dinner at the bar. Or my mom saves me something for when I get home."

"You live with your mom?"

Almost apologetically, she explained, "It worked out better that way because of Terran."

Terran kept his head down, intent on his coloring and tuning out the grown-up talk.

"How about you?" she asked. "Where do you live?"

"I've got a house in Boise. My sister's keeping an eye on things for me. It's nothing fancy, but it's paid for."

Dana had often dreamed of having her own place again. The days when she'd been single, she'd had an apartment, but then she got pregnant and all that changed. One day, she'd like to buy a house. But for now, such a situation was unfeasible.

"Does all your family live in Boise?" In the weeks she'd known Mark, she hadn't wanted to touch deeper on this subject. He'd told her he worked for his family's construction business, but beyond that the details hadn't been something she'd pressed him about.

"Two older brothers. Sister and brother-in-law. My mom. I told you about my dad." She could see her reflection in the lenses of his smoky glasses. "It was a tough one. We've all had to adjust. Just like you had to."

She didn't want to talk about herself. She'd always found that difficult, even as a child. Her mixed heritage had been a source of embarrassment when she was a young girl in grade school. Now she embraced it, proud of who she was. But she still didn't like to dwell on facets of her personal life with people she didn't know well.

And while she'd invested a lot of faith in Mark to renovate her bar, confiding in him about personal matters was awkward.

Actually, her reasons were more than that: she didn't trust herself with him. Better to remain as neutral as possible.

"Momma, is it almost done yet?" Terran expelled a troubled sigh, as if he were starving to death.

"Pretty soon, baby."

Mark studied the drawing. "Nice truck. I have a real one just like it."

Terran's nose crinkled. "You drive it?"

"Yes. And I have backhoes, SkyTracks, forklifts—any kind of heavy equipment you can think of. I know how to use all of it on a job site."

"Hey, Mark? That's cool."

Mark smiled. "Not as cool as how you color, dude."

"I stay in the lines," he replied somberly.

Dana gave the colored page a mother's kind glance. Her son hadn't stayed in the lines very well, but his effort was a sincere one.

"Good job, Terran," she offered with enthusiasm.

She fervently hoped he'd thrive in kindergarten. She couldn't believe that the day was fast approaching when she'd drop him off in front of the school. They lived close enough that he wouldn't have to take a bus.

"My dad colors good," Terran said, chin down and scratching a streak of red over the truck's tailgate.

At moments like this, when Terran made an offhand remark about Cooper's abilities, Dana winced. She couldn't pinpoint why, exactly. Maybe because of the reminder that she and Cooper co-parented from a distance and Terran had to jump from house to house, doing individual things with each of them rather than together as a family. Loyalties had to be a struggle for her son at times.

"That's nice that you and Daddy color together," Dana said, unable to look at Mark when she spoke. Discomfort filled her.

"Yep—we do lots of things together."

Mark's gaze followed her every move and it unsettled her. She didn't like attention focused on her—definitely not on her single parenting. She loved her son dearly, but not being part of a loving and traditional family for her baby did serve as a source for regret more often than not.

She didn't want Mark prying, asking questions about things. Her life was what it was. Making the best of it was all she could do and things worked out.

As these thoughts swirled in her mind, Mark didn't release her from his observation. Self-conscious, she felt like a tiny bug under a microscope. All she could do was sit there, not react, and hope he'd move on and find something better to focus on.

She wished their food would come so she could eat and get out of there. Especially when Mark steered their filler conversation in a direction she didn't want to go. She could do without reminders of last night.

"I never knew I liked saxophone music," Mark commented with a half grin, bringing to life an evening she'd wanted to forget. "I equated a saxophone with that perm-haired pans—" He sliced the word off.

Pansy. Nice, Moretti. She glared at him, grateful he didn't spell it out in front of her son.

"—uh, that guy, Kenny G."

Informing him tartly, she said, "Kenny G's a pop artist, not a jazz musician."

"Okay, good. I feel better. If he was into jazz, then I'd have to like him because I loved the jazz you played. Unbelievable. You're great."

"I'm passable."

"No—you're great."

She wasn't sure if he was talking about her music abilities or her. Thankfully a server brought their order and she didn't have to give it any more thought.

Dana had ordered the halibut with chips. It was the best, even compared to anything on the menu at the Cape Fox Lodge or from Annabelle's Restaurant. Both Terran and Mark had picked the shakes and cheeseburgers.

Burger Queen had the largest variety of milk shakes in the state, maybe the country, including flavors like passion fruit, toasted marshmallow, root beer, Kahlúa, macadamia nut. If she liked ice cream, which she didn't really, she would have gotten one. Instead, she'd ordered a diet cola.

Mark tried his peach shake. Beneath his breath, he said, "Mmm. Tastes sweet. Just like you."

Dana refused to show any reaction and, instead, helped her son cut his burger in two. He'd ordered his fairly plain. Just meat, cheese and ketchup.

Fitting the straw into the gap of his mouth, Terran sucked his chocolate shake. "How do they get the choc'late in here, Mommy?"

"It's a syrup."

"Mine, too, Mom?" Mark teased, licking the shake off his top lip with a slow grab of his tongue. She aimed the point of her boot at him and kicked his shin. Trouble was, he was faster, and before she knew it, his knees pressed her calf between his strong legs and held her tightly. Without causing attention, she tried to break free. No luck. His hold on her was like a vise.

"That'll teach you." He laughed, enjoying the moment.

Ketchup bracketing his mouth and an arch to his brows, Terran asked, "Teach what?"

"Never mind," Dana quickly responded.

She had to eat her lunch with Mark keeping her leg captive. Every so often, he slowly rubbed his knees together, evoking shivers across her skin and scalp. He knew exactly what he was doing, this toying with her, and she hated it. Perhaps hate wasn't exactly it . . . she hated that she responded to him. Everything inside her warmed to mush. She felt hot and annoyed, wanting him to let her go so she could cool off and enjoy her lunch.

The instant she felt Mark slightly relax his grip during a long-running exchange of questions with Terran, she yanked her captive leg free and gave Mark a smug smile.

"I can ride things out—I have patience," she said in a low tone, gloating.

"Good for you, but I have more, sunshine."

She almost snorted. Why did he always have to one-up her? It drove her crazy.

Terran was finished eating before them, and he asked if he could check out the rocks. He enjoyed hunting for treasures when they ate outside. He'd poke loose shale pieces with a stick. She'd cautioned him on touching broken glass—that was a big no-no. But he did seek things that shone and caught his attention. If he wanted to pick up something, it could only be the rocks.

"Baby, you stay where I can see you." Her caution was stern and brooked no argument. "Like only as far as the top of the stairs and your bedroom door. You understand that distance? No farther than that, okay?"

"Okay." He went off to scavenger hunt.

Mark popped a long French fry into his mouth, eating with an indolent relaxation she wanted to cuff him for. She'd watched every bite and chew, making sure she didn't have food where it shouldn't be or spill on herself. "So I've been wondering something. What'd you do before you ran the bar?"

Taking a drink to quench her parched throat, she set her cup down. "I was a checker at the Safeway."

"No kidding."

Somewhat perturbed, she questioned, "Why would I make that up?"

"Don't know. I was thinking of you as a hostess in some fine restaurant. You'd look killer in a black cocktail dress."

"Well, since Ketchikan doesn't have any fine restaurants with a call for hostesses, I chose to go into another line of work. And I'd have to check in my closet, but last time I looked, I didn't own a black cocktail dress."

"Why's that?"

"No reason to wear one."

"I could think of a few."

The suggestive comment warmed her to the tips of her toes. It was just like him to hint at something that heated her skin. Like the strike of a match head, she felt herself burning with visions of their mouths fused together in the rain. That kiss had rattled her, shaken her to the core. She didn't want to remember it. She refused to let it happen again.

She couldn't put more into this relationship than there was. Not technically his boss, he did work for her in a roundabout way. He'd proved himself skillful in many things relating to carpentry. Already he'd added the door, widened the hallway and fixed her leaking roof. If their arrangement hadn't been founded on conditional terms, she might have invested something emotionally. Then again not. Boise was too far for a long-distance thing. And she had no intentions of a one-night stand. That wasn't her.

So there was no purpose in romanticizing their relationship. It wasn't realistic.

"You get along all right with Terran's dad?" The unprompted question infiltrated her thoughts and brought her back with a zap.

"Well enough."

"That could mean anything." Mark leaned forward. "How do you feel about the guy? You still love him?"

Mark's words smacked her emotions and she quickly hid her true feelings. She had once loved Cooper Boyd with all her heart and mind. But that was no more. Now she tolerated him for their son's sake. *Love?* She didn't think she knew the meaning of the word—if she ever had.

"You're overstepping," she replied. "I wouldn't ask you if you ever loved anyone."

Not breaking a beat in the friction surrounding them, he threw out, "Why not?"

For long seconds, neither of them spoke, then she broke the silence. "Okay, hot stuff—have you?"

"Many times. I've loved long hair, short hair. Any length of hair in between. I've loved curvy women, thin women. Blondes or brunettes. Some with smoky-black hair." The latter was spoken in a honey-sweet tone that sluiced over her like warm water. "Women with some spice, women who were nice. I guess you could say I've loved all over the menu."

Eyes narrowed, Dana contemplated whether or not he was just jerking with her or being honest. She could see him dating a lot but never settling down. He didn't come across to her as the home-body type. Another strike against him. If she ever fell in love again, he'd have to want to deal with chicken nuggets for dinner once in a while and Spiderman blankets.

Caustic in her reply, she summarized, "So you just love to love women."

"In a manner of speaking." The straw on his shake was taken out and he licked the bottom so it wouldn't drip. She couldn't help being fixated by the swirl of his tongue. Finding her eyes on him, he gave her a smile. "But I can be taught new tricks."

Dana didn't want to teach him anything. She'd much rather he find his own—

A woman's voice called, breaking the mood between them.

"Oh, hey! I thought that was you. Hi."

No mistaking the purr belonging to Tori Daniel.

Dana turned on the bench to watch the woman come toward their table wearing a short-sleeved knit dress and sparkle flip-flops. Her bare legs were coppery as if she'd been soaking in some UVs in a tanning bed. Today, not even the leggings would hide her goodies. One sneeze and she'd be showing the world all she had.

While the dress wasn't exactly short-short, it was short enough to make Dana wish she had the long legs that could wear a dress like that. Not that she would in public, but just for her man's eyes only. If she had a man to rev an engine for.

"Hi," Mark replied, giving Tori a light smile.

To Dana, Tori said, "Hi, Dana. What've you been up to?"

"Same old, Tori," she replied blandly. "You?"

"I'm working at a day care. I love kids." She glanced over her shoulder, her fine blond hair falling midway down her back. Dana knew Tori could do a shampoo and air-dry and her hair would retain that stick-straight look, whereas it took her forever with her iron to achieve the same result. "Where's Terran?"

"Collecting rocks."

"Terran!" she called.

Squatting over a rock pile, Terran gave her an enthusiastic wave. "Hi."

"Aw, he's so adorable." Then she addressed Mark. "Did you find the detergent?"

"I did."

"You were going the wrong way, silly." The flirtatious note to Tori's voice bristled Dana's composure. "You were heading toward the produce when you needed to go the opposite direction."

"I would have figured it out," Mark said.

"I'm sure. You're a smart man." Tori flicked her hair over her perfect, narrow shoulder. "Well, I'll see ya."

Tori went inside the Burger Queen and Dana slid the rest of her uneaten lunch aside. She'd lost her appetite.

You're a smart man. Dana might just puke.

Giving Mark a hard stare, she'd assumed he was better than one of the panting idiots following Tori in the grocery store. "You needed laundry soap by the fish-stick aisle?" Dana snapped.

"I hate fish sticks," he grunted.

"Doesn't stop a man from heading that way, now does it?"

Puzzlement lit in Mark's rich brown eyes. "I don't know what you're talking about."

Grabbing the food wrappers and balling them into her fist, she stuffed the garbage in the sacks. She abruptly rose to her feet, then dumped the bags into the trash can. Fitting her elbow through her purse strap, she called too loudly, "Terran, we're leaving now."

Terran came scampering over with a big smile, his shoelace untied, fisting rocks and indiscernible junk.

Mark stood and gave Dana a strong stare. "I don't know what you think happened, but nothing happened." With an exaggerated motion, he raked his fingers through his hair. "Not that I even have to tell you anything."

Dana fumbled for her car keys. "Thanks for the lunch. That was nice of you."

"I wasn't doing it to be nice," he said, following her to her car. Terran skipped ahead, unaware of the discord behind him.

"Of course not." She unlocked her truck and situated Terran in his booster seat so fast he hollered *ouch!* as she snapped the buckle closed. She gave quick kisses to his fingers and told him she loved him, then closed the door and walked to the truck's other side.

Mark gently caught her arm and made her stop. Though the cars zoomed past loudly, her erratic pulse beat in her head even louder, a rhythmic cadence that was near-deafening. She sighed to slow it down, and looked Mark directly in the eyes.

He'd removed his sunglasses and the depth of his brown eyes was placating, soft. "I don't know why you're thinking I'm into that chick, but I'm not."

"You'd have to know how Tori operates."

"I already know how she operates. I used to date anything in a short skirt."

"Yes, that's right. Well—you have a good rest of your day. I believe I said that earlier. I should have stuck with it."

"Dana, you're wrong about me."

"I don't think so."

The words were barbed, and she grew guilty when she saw a streak of hurt flicker in his expression. He quickly wiped it away, and his handsome features sharpened. Remorse settled into her chest along with anger over her lack of tact. She was at fault for reacting in such a way, but she didn't have the grace to admit it to him.

"You're running scared, Dana." With an ease of motion, Mark fit his sunglasses over the bridge of his nose.

He was so good-looking with the way his black hair brushed his ears and shirt collar. His mouth's firm set said more than words.

Finally he spoke in a low tone. "I get it. You've been hurt." In a soft and low voice, his words carried in a strong whisper. "But you want to know something—a person never knows the meaning of love unless someone's broken their heart."

CHAPTER ELEVEN

SWEATY AND TIRED, Mark sat backward on a chair at the Blue Note, drinking a bottled water. He and a three-man crew were taking a lunch break from installing the sprinkler system. They'd added smoke detectors, as well.

"You've got at least ten psi flowing through this, right?" Mark questioned while studying the open wood beam rafters above. The outdated network of sprinkler pipes and heads had been removed and the new equipment was being installed after lunch.

Anything less than ten pounds per square inch would render a system inadequate because of deterioration in the water supply. Installation standards only contained minimums and Mark wanted to overkill on this job. Property insurance carriers often had more conservative standards than typical codes and local jurisdictions, so Mark wanted to make sure that after he was gone and Dana got her inspection, she wouldn't be written up for any non-compliance issues again.

"Absolutely can handle that," one of the workers pronounced.

Mark nodded, eating a grilled halibut sandwich on a French roll that Presley had fixed for the four of them. She'd come in early today to get things started in the kitchen. As always, she'd had a friendly smile for him and came across as genuine.

Glancing at his watch, Mark noted it was just after eleven o'clock. He hoped to get the new pipes in before two when the bar opened for business. Since the brackets were already in place, the possibility was good they'd get it handled.

Overall, he was happy with how things were progressing. The exit door had been cut out and installed, but was unusable until the exterior steel sections arrived by barge and the decking could be expanded. A skim coat was needed on the hallway to finish the drywall. Then it'd have to be painted. Mark hadn't seen the requirement for widening the exit door hallway in Dana's report and it chapped his hide. How would Dana have known that a twenty-four-inch opening needed to be three feet wide on an exit?

Inspectors weren't Mark's favorite people. He knew they had a job to do, but he'd been red-tagged too many times in situations that needed attention yesterday. Some inspectors tagged for minutiae, and their fixation on a detail that was really nothing was annoying.

One of the last things Mark hoped to repair before he left town was the building's siding. Although not noted as a violation, the gray boards needed to be replaced or covered.

Time was short. Both in Alaska and toward making a decision to stay with Moretti or not. Kyle had called yesterday and wanted to go over some ideas on restructuring. Mark didn't mind the consult, and it had actually felt good to discuss something familiar. He knew the family business inside and out, and Kyle's projections on future projects and the way he saw Moretti Construction going weren't far off the mark. It made sense to get into management. But Mark still had no idea if he wanted to follow his family down that road.

Working on the Blue Note had reminded him why he'd stuck with carpentry all these years. He enjoyed working with his hands, he enjoyed building things. The end result was satisfying and he could look at all he'd done and know it would be around for a while.

He'd never minded shooting the bull with guys who strapped on tools all day and did the grunt work. He'd always liked sitting on a drywall stack, eating out of a lunch pail and talking about what needed to be done.

Maybe somewhere down the road he'd lost his focus about this. He'd tried too hard to pull up in the ranks and be a Giovanni figure to the crew. In hindsight, Mark never would be his dad, nor should he have tried. He was his own man, with his own honed skills and weaknesses. Valuing his own abilities and talents should have been his priority. But he hadn't. He'd doubted. He'd wanted more. And, in the end, he'd cheated his family by not showing gratitude for what he'd been given: the opportunity to master a family trade.

Mark drank a soda pop.

"How dis afternoon be for you, Boise carpenter?" Cardelle's voice sliced through the room. "I'm stopping by to give you a holler, mon. See weh you are in dis place of changes."

Cardelle Kanhai strolled toward them, long-sleeved dress shirt and tie outfitting his thin-as-a-feather frame. His bald head gleamed as if it had been oiled after being freshly shaven. The color of his skin was like dark-roasted coffee beans, his teeth white and bright.

Mark had grown fond of the guy. They'd spent time together at the bar over drinks and had discussed a variety of topics. Neither of them lived in Ketchikan permanently and that kind of set things up between them.

Standing, Mark shook Cardelle's hand when he reached them. "Making some headway."

With a wide arc of his berry-black gaze, Cardelle nodded. "You be jammin' in no time, mon."

"Not so sure about how fast I'll get her done, but we're trying." Mark acknowledged the three-man crew with him and gave each a quick introduction to Cardelle.

Cardelle adjusted his salmon-print tie, his expression solemn. "My fadda, he be a great wall painter in Jamaica. I don' know how you say it right. But maybe—wall pik'tures."

"Pictures? You mean murals?"

"Yah, mon. Dat is it. He show me how to do it, too. I paint on walls, as well."

Up to this point, Mark hadn't thought about painting anything except the hallway expansion after it had been taped and textured. Dana had paint cans in the workroom to match the bar's current color. The rest of the walls were in good shape.

"You a pretty good artist, Card?" Mark asked, folding his arms over his chest.

"I be fairly good. In fact, I'm one of de best."

"Then no offense—how come you're selling bling? Why not paint murals for a living?"

"How do you not know I do dis in my home country?"

"I guess I don't."

Cardelle flashed him a smile. "I jus' be funning wid you, mon. Deh is not so much use for murals in my town, but more use here for de jew'ry to sell. America's people—dey buy anything if you tell dem it is de best."

Smiling, Mark asked, "What's your top seller?"

"No doubt, de tanzanite. All ladies want it. And at my store I work at, we don' samfy you, mon."

"Samfy?"

"Dat is de word for 'con.' You can't trust all de jew'ry stores in dis town, but you can trust Cardelle." His full lips split into a broad grin. "I still give a discount for you."

Smiling back, Mark relented. "Maybe I'll get something for my mom."

"Ah, for de madda, you buy pearls." Card

scratched the back of his smooth neck, taking one more look around. "Well, I best be going to work."

"See you, Card."

"Yah, mon. See you."

Mark finished his lunch, returned the plate to Presley and thanked her again for making him a sandwich. She gave him a happy face and claimed if she didn't have a boyfriend, he'd have to look out.

Back in the bar, Mark was buckling his tool belt on when Leo came toward him. "Hey, Moretti, I wasn't kidding about the men's john. That urinal sucks. The women's latrine could use some help, too. Sink is plugged."

"It's not a priority for me right now. But it's on my list. They need to be handicap accessible and I'll take a look at it when I can."

"You going to have all these pipes off the floor when we open?" Leo questioned, markedly glancing at the mess.

"That's the plan." Mark began to move materials into place as one of the workers climbed a ladder.

Leo turned, paused, then faced him once more. His dark hair, tightly curled, rested on his shoulders. The bridge of his brown nose was flat, his mouth wide. "Thanks for doing this for Dana. She does appreciate it."

"No problem." Mark then immersed himself in getting those sprinklers in.

Some time later, Dana came to the bar but

headed straight for her office. Within a few minutes after her arrival, her mom arrived.

Suni Jackson wasn't a woman to screw around with. Mark got the feeling she was direct, had an opinion that she wouldn't hesitate to share, but she was fair, and if she held you in her regard, it would be high. She had a spiritual nature about her, as if her beliefs were celestial and she burned incense or something.

She was short in stature, but tall from the way her gaze could measure a person. That look she gave a guy could freeze steel if he didn't live up to the standards she'd sought for her daughter. Mark was cool with that. Moms liked to give their opinions, but being the one Suni put under a magnifier didn't sit well with Mark. He'd done all he could to be cordial at the parade, and he'd figured she'd think what she wanted to about him no matter what he did.

So when he found her standing there staring at him, he gave her a friendly hello but didn't initiate a conversation. He kept working from the ladder. Eventually, she moved forward and disappeared into Dana's office.

With ten minutes to spare before the Blue Note's opening, the sprinklers had been put in, as well as the smoke detectors. Packing away his tools, Mark had been bent on one knee depositing things into a toolbox when Suni appeared.

"Since Oscar died, I haven't been in the bar very

much," she said wistfully as she gazed down at him. "There's a continuous pulse of movement in here. Life has gone on without my husband. He lives within these walls, but I can't see him."

Mark rose to his feet. "Have you heard your daughter play the sax?"

"Many times." Suni held her purse as if she needed to use it as a shield against the memories that must haunt her in the Blue Note. "She sounds like Oscar, though she doesn't think she does."

"I'd agree with you." Mark studied Suni's face, searching for emotions he could read. She hid them well. "After my father died, it was hard for me to go in his work trailer, especially when I sat at his desk. But he'd want me to move forward, so I did."

"How long ago did he pass?"

"Going on three years."

"Oscar's been gone for nearly six."

"I hope it gets easier for you." Then playing on something that Mark knew would bring a light into her face, he added, "You've got a grandson that's a kick."

"Terran is my blessing."

"I could see that at the parade."

Suni cast her eyes down. She was obviously pondering the moment, then looked at him once more. "Why are you helping my daughter?"

Giving her an easy smile, he said, "I'd've figured by now that you'd be onto me. I'm doing it so she'll go out on a date. I've asked before and she turned me down flat. Kept asking her—still no dice. So I thought to myself, I'll spend some time fixing up her place and then she'll give me her undying love."

Without cracking the expression on her face, Suni said to him, "Give me a break. I know crap when I smell it."

Mark burst into a laugh. "Is that right?"

"You're doing this for her because you have to. Because it's in you to do it."

"I guess you could say it's something like that."

Coiling a power cord, Mark moved around Suni to gather the rest of his tools. He didn't know how Suni had pegged him. Those eyes of hers drank in a lot more than Mark had guessed and she wasn't as quiet as he'd initially thought. She had depth to her, and an understanding that he'd probably never figure out. His mom was a lot like that. Kind of stood back and observed, watched things unfold, then tallied it all inside her head and sorted things out.

"Just don't do anything to hurt her," Suni cautioned, bringing Mark back to the present. "She's been through too much. Stay on the path."

He wasn't sure what she meant, but he knew he'd never mess with Dana's head in a malicious manner. Tease and flirt with her, yes. But hurt, no.

With his things put away, Mark was ready to go home—but before he left, he addressed Suni once more as he grabbed a cocktail napkin off the end of the bar. Using a pen from his jeans pocket, he said, "Here's my mom's phone number in Boise. Her name's Mariangela. Call her. Ask her about me. Trust me, she'll give you a straight answer."

Suni stared blankly at him. "What would I ask?"

"Whatever's on your mind." Mark stalled before handing Suni the phone number. "Better yet, do you have a computer?"

"Yes."

Mark scribbled another line on the napkin. "She just got an e-mail address and she doesn't have a lot of people to write to. Go ahead and send her your best shot. I honestly don't mind."

Taking the napkin, Suni stood there and didn't reply. For the first time since meeting her, she seemed at a loss.

"Don't worry about it. She's a nice lady. She'll be thrilled to have someone to talk to. You have things in common with her."

Without another word, Mark gathered his tools and headed for his rental truck. After stowing his gear, he sat behind the wheel and didn't immediately turn the key. He gazed at the marina, watching the boats and seagulls.

Taking a few minutes, he replayed the conversation with Suni in his head. Before he could counter his decision, he climbed out of the truck and made his way to Jewels of the Nile.

Laid out in a tight rectangular shape, the store

was small and cramped with lit cases of sparkling jewelry. Five clerks manned the counter, three of which were busy with customers from the cruise ships. A fourth rang an order at the register. The fifth was the man Mark wanted to see.

Cardelle lit up like one of the cases, bright faced and with eyes that were glittering black jewels. "So, hey, mon. You come for de pearls."

"No, Card, not today."

"De tanzanite?"

"Nope."

Cardelle's dark face waited expectantly. "Okay den, we have de jade earrings, gold necklaces, ruby rings and de sterling silver to not make your skin turn tarnish."

"Sorry—none of that." Mark moved in toward the semiprecious stones display where the Jamaican stood reed thin and proud of the goods within.

"What den?"

"I've got a proposition for you."

THERE WAS NO DOUBT about it—Dana had been avoiding Mark. She came to this conclusion by Thursday after not talking with him for the past five days. At first, she reconciled that she'd been busy in her office and she hadn't run into him. Then she recognized that she had made sure she wasn't around when he came in at night for conversation at the bar. She had places to be, things to do.

But the truth came to her this afternoon as she'd watched him work in the bar. He hadn't been able to see her as her gaze followed his every move. She'd held back in the hallway leading to her office. In that moment of hiding, she knew she'd done whatever she could to avoid a confrontation with him.

More important—she knew why.

He'd been right on target about her. She'd been hurt in love, and she ran from feelings about anyone else. Since Cooper broke her heart, she hadn't gotten close to another man. Saturday at Burger Queen when Mark accused her of not wanting to deal with things, she'd been in denial and thought for sure he was wrong.

But he'd been right.

Dread filled her soul. She couldn't let one man alter her life or its direction. Especially not Mark Moretti. She knew better than to get involved with a lower-forty-eighter on vacation. Even though Mark was charming and different, the end result would be the same. Here today, gone tomorrow.

The fact that she'd felt herself growing emotionally entangled had been a wake-up call and she'd probably used Tori as the excuse to get out of that situation quickly.

So what to do about it now?

Mark came to the bar every day for hours and worked so hard. She had begun to feel guilty, as if she were not only taking advantage of his money but his physical time and energy. The least she could do was be cordial, grateful. Express her thanks and gratitude.

Instead, she'd holed herself off in various corners of the Blue Note, avoiding him at all costs. This wasn't her method of dealing with men. She'd never run before. Most definitely never hid.

So today she decided to confront the situation head-on and she searched for Mark midday to ask him a question. However, it was difficult for her to form a plan of action, or just how she'd ask him. After running several scenarios in her head, she opted to wing it.

She found Mark outside with steel pieces that had been on a delivery truck that morning to the Blue Note. She had no idea what they were for, but assumed Mark knew.

The day was gray and overcast; a light drizzle had been in the air since sunrise. Without bothering with her coat or hat, she went through the front door and headed directly toward him.

"Mark, I need to talk to you," she said, almost too loudly.

He raised his chin, his eyes friendly and warm as soon as he saw her approaching. She never tired of the way his whole facial expression could smile without his mouth even moving.

"Look who decided to pay a call," he drawled, rising from the stacks of steel.

His denim jeans fit him in an indecently sexy

way in the butt, and a long-sleeved T-shirt draped his chest in white with a logo for some electrical company. A short tear at the elbow revealed his skin and a barely discernible cut where he must have bumped into something sharp. Even in work clothes, she found him more than appealing.

"I've been busy this week."

"Busy lurking," he replied, infuriating her that he could be so intuitive.

"I don't lurk."

"What do you call peeking at me from the edge of your office door? Hiding behind the bar when I'm at the front of the building? Or conveniently heading for the kitchen when I'm coming down the hallway?"

She had no response that would satisfy him because the truth was the truth and she had done all of those things. Frustration gave her pause, and she wondered if it had been a bad idea to make an attempt to communicate with Mark.

Rather than try to substantiate any of her actions, she simply plunged in with the question she'd silently dared herself to ask. It would prove once and for all that she was afraid of no one, that she ran from nothing. "Terran has hockey practice tonight—would you like to come and watch him?"

Mark cocked his head, rain dampening his hair and causing it to curl slightly at his collar. "What was that?"

She could tell he'd heard her the first time, but he was making her repeat it. Making her be uncomfortable all over again inviting him to do something with her. And that the event involved her son. An aspect of her life she kept mostly private.

Private. It didn't really mean much around here. Ketchikan was a small town. She ran into people she knew all the time. She really had no secrets, no privacy to speak of. Everyone knew most everyone's business. Daily tidbits were a given fact to be traded at the various local hangouts.

So why not just put Mark in the loop, right out in the open in her everyday events? He was working around the bar for her. The natural course was that he had become her friend.

"Tonight my son has hockey practice and I wondered if you'd like to come."

Without hesitation, Mark easily replied, "Sure, what time?"

Dana's heart sank, a mixture of dismay and confusion. In the early hours of morning when she'd lain in bed trying to fall asleep, the scene she'd repeatedly played out in her head had Mark declining her invite. She hadn't really thought Mark would want to watch a bunch of five-year-olds scramble and splatter on the ice.

The whole point had been to prove to him she wasn't afraid of anything between them. Or of being seen in public with Mark as if she were romantically interested in him.

Damn, she should have known he'd respond with the opposite of what she'd anticipated.

In a tone that held no preamble, she replied, "Practice starts at seven."

"Sounds good. I'll pick you up and drive you over to the rink."

"I can drive myself," she sputtered. She'd wanted to be in control and she found herself being led by Mark, not guiding him.

"I know where you live, so I'll be by at six-thirty."

Curiosity melted her resolve to stay unaffected by him. "How do you know where I live?"

"I'm resourceful." He gave her a charming half grin, raking damp hair from his brows. "Hell, sweetart, don't look so shook-up about it. A while back, I asked the right people—just in case."

Mouth half-open, she blurted, "Just in case, what?"

"Just in case I had a reason to come pick you up."

RINK TIME HAD BEEN FORMED on a giant level sand bed, then a massive layer of concrete had been poured on top. Mark had never built an ice rink, but he knew enough about them to know that pipes underneath carried an antifreeze to keep the surface chilled.

The indoor rink seemed fairly new. The entry had a pro shop for equipment, and there'd been a rental desk, as well as a snack bar and arcade. Mark couldn't remember the last time he'd been at an ice-skating rink. Boise had only gotten its rink some ten or so years ago, long after he'd been young enough to want to hang out there.

Sitting on a bleacher, Mark stuffed his hands into his coat pockets. Dana sat a body-width distance between them, having barely said a few sentences on the way over. She wore a pale cream down vest, black turtleneck sweater, a pink scarf and mittens.

"What number am I looking for again?" Mark questioned while staring at a sea of black-and-gold uniforms and helmets. It was hard to discern which boy was hers among those on the ice.

"Four."

"How long's Terran been playing?" Mark asked, making small talk.

"Since he was three."

"They start that young?"

"His dad's into it and got him on the ice at a young age."

Mark chewed on that information, realizing that co-parenting a child with a former partner must be challenging. He knew these situations were pretty commonplace, but he didn't have firsthand experience himself, nor did he know of anyone going through the same thing.

The thought had crossed Mark's mind to check out the GCI Cellular store in town just to see who worked there. He didn't have the guy's name, other than knowing his last name started with a *B*. But he'd opted out of going. It didn't matter to him who Dana's ex-love was. She'd moved on, or so she led him to believe. And he did believe her.

You didn't kiss a man the way she'd kissed him if your heart was elsewhere. Mark had known many women in his past and he knew which ones were jerking him, and which ones had another guy on their mind. Then there were the ones who just wanted to feel good in bed.

There'd been plenty who'd simply wanted him. And he'd hung around for a while enjoying that.

"Hi, Dana," said a woman on the bleacher bench in front of them.

"Hey, Laura," Dana replied in a friendly tone. But then said nothing further, and made no introductions.

Apparently the woman was another enthusiastic hockey mom. Mark noticed he'd become surrounded by parents encouraging their kids, who skated and took headers chasing pucks sliding over the ice.

Mark felt somewhat out of place within the group.

Times like these, he wondered what it would have been like to have a kid. He could go either way about it—there had been no bio-clock-burning desire to father a child before he'd reached a certain age. He'd always figured if it happened, it happened.

As a Catholic—even though it had been a long time since he'd attended a Mass, he believed in the sanctity of marriage, and would never have let the woman who bore his child go it alone. No matter what, he'd promise to make their relationship work. In a perfect world, he'd find the right woman to love, marry, then have a family if that's what they both desired.

He didn't judge Dana. Everyone was different. God knew he was no saint.

Leaning back on her elbows on the bench behind her, Laura addressed Dana. "Coach is having them practice their cut-across drill. They need work on it, but Terran's already got it down."

"Thanks. He's pretty good."

"Must be in the genes." Laura's smile was complimentary, but her curious gaze fell on Mark when she spoke. He semi-smiled at her, then his attention returned to the ice.

Terran's ability was better than pretty good. For a little dude, he skated seamlessly, fighting the pack with an easy command of his angled hockey stick. His short legs worked hard, so when he took a tumble, he didn't have far to fall to the ice. He clambered right to his feet and off he went again.

The coach stood on the sidelines instructing the kids to get moving, and telling them where to push the puck over the blue line and who should pass a drop shot. He seemed pretty competent. Not too bad-looking, either. Dirty-blond hair, built fairly well. Tall, but not stocky. He skated without effort, going forward and backward.

Mark wondered how many of the women here had a thing for the guy—if they ever wanted some private coach time.

"You like the coach?" Mark asked, making sideways talk.

Dana's brows furrowed slightly, then she shrugged. He loved the play of her hair around her face, the long length that had been flattened into a silky curtain. "He's okay."

"Seems like he knows what he's doing."

"He does."

When the practice was finished, Dana wanted to go down to the locker room and say hi to her son. Mark learned it wasn't her week to have him.

Once in the small room where boys sat on benches and stuffed skates and socks in practice duffels, Dana found Terran.

"Hey, baby!" she called, then scooped him into a hug as she bent over him.

"Hi, Momma." He squeezed her back, then almost sheepishly slipped away from her as if, even at a young age, being hugged by your mom with your buddies around was embarrassing.

"You did really good today. I saw you doing your weave drill. You were so much better."

"Dad showed me how."

"That's awesome."

Her mood was upbeat, and she showed enthusiasm for her son's aptitude for hockey. When the coach came into the room, her bright expression somewhat darkened. And when the guy came toward them, Dana became visibly self-conscious with Mark at her side.

"Hi, Dana," he said, his hazel eyes pinned directly on Mark.

Mark got the sense that the coach felt some kind of personal attachment to Dana, as if he wanted to hit on her or something.

That didn't sit well with Mark, although he had no claims to her. He knew Dana was striking— knew men would seek her attention. Even so, Mark didn't want to be around when they did. He didn't like the jealousy he felt.

He stood close to Dana, maybe too close, as if to fend the guy off and make him take a step back.

Rather than say nothing, Mark addressed the coach head-on. "I'm Mark." He extended his hand. "I'm Dana's friend."

The suddenly smug coach gripped his fingers, squeezing tight. "And I'm Cooper—Terran's dad."

CHAPTER TWELVE

DANA PROBABLY OWED Mark an explanation even though he hadn't asked the question.

Looking at the city lights below, she stood on his condo deck, embracing the temperate evening. The daytime temperature had reached sixty-four degrees and after sunset the air had settled into the low fifties—warm by July's standards. No rain had fallen today with little in the weekend forecast.

But weather wasn't really on Dana's mind as she listened to Mark move around in the kitchen behind her. The tall panoramic windows in the condo's living room weren't covered by blinds and the light from the kitchen poured onto the deck. At the railing, she watched the cars in the distance drive along the streets bathed in the fuzzy glow of double-headed streetlights.

She could actually see the Blue Note bar from here, a vague outline shadowed in the marina.

Slipping hands into her vest pockets, she thought back to the hockey practice tonight.

While Mark probably hadn't noticed, Seth and Jacob's parents had studied them with curiosity. From the interested look Laura gave Mark, she definitely wanted to know all about who he was. Dana had never brought anyone to Terran's practices except her mother. Suni came on the weeks they had Terran, and on others, she chose not to. But she never missed one of his games.

Tonight Dana had invited Mark—not to meet Cooper or to even remotely have Cooper see her with someone else. She'd done it to move forward in her life, to mix things up and just do the normal things a single woman did—like socialize with men as friends.

The look on Mark's face when Cooper introduced himself had spoken volumes. Mark hadn't been happy about it, clearly feeling as if she'd duped him into an awkward meeting with her ex-boyfriend. This simply wasn't the case and she was obligated to set that part of the night straight.

When Mark had invited her over for a drink, she would have easily declined if there hadn't been static between them. After leaving the rink, Mark hadn't said but two words in the car. So here she was. Perhaps because she wanted to clarify things—or maybe just to have some quiet time with a man she liked looking at.

Mark joined her on the deck, handing her a glass of red wine. It wasn't often she drank. Because of serving alcoholic beverages at the bar, she shied away from drinking any night she was working. And when she wasn't, one glass could relax her to the point of falling asleep on the sofa.

She took a sip, enjoying the fruity flavor swirling around in her mouth. She knew wines, and this vintage tasted excellent. It had a currant flavor with full body. Definitely a Cabernet.

"You warm enough?" Mark asked, standing close.

"Actually, yes. It's nice outside."

Arching a brow, he suggested, "I've got a cozy fireplace I can flip the switch on."

Dubious, she slanted her gaze over him and didn't address the intended message. "I'm good."

There were two deck chairs and he offered her one. She sat, a small round table between them.

For a long while, as the air lightly whispered in the boughs, they sipped wine and kept their thoughts to themselves. In the distance, a float-plane headed for the channel, its white strobe lights blinking in an indigo sky. The berths were void of cruise ships and the shops had long since closed for the day.

While Dana struggled to find the words to explain herself without coming across as vulnerable, Mark took the effort away from her as he spoke first.

"So what did you want me to be tonight? Your boy toy to show off to the ex-old man?" His hooded eyes glittered in the dim light, a dark brown that didn't carry the usual mischief and twinkle. Clearly he was perturbed.

"I don't need a boy toy," she countered. "It wasn't like that. It didn't matter that Cooper was there—I wanted to go with you and be . . . normal."

He nailed her with a hard stare. "What's normal?"

Choosing her answer carefully, she said, "Going out and doing the things women do. They hang out with guys, as friends. They—"

"Are we friends?" he cut in.

"Well . . . I suppose."

"After I had my tongue down your throat—you suppose." His statement was about as blunt as a dull knife blade.

In a smooth motion of his legs, he propped his heavy feet on the deck railing and slid lower in his chair, his muscles taut, while he chewed over what she'd said.

"Why do you have to be so crass?" she queried, then drank a long sip of wine. The alcohol warmed her to the core and instantly took the edge off her scattered nerves.

"So why'd you call me?" Mark's voice sliced through the night in a whiskey-smooth tone. "I'm sure there's a lineup of guys in town who would have gone with you."

This was the truth, but Dana hadn't wanted to be with anyone else tonight. She wouldn't readily admit it, but she enjoyed being in Mark's company. Talking to him about a variety of things came easy. On the other hand, when he was in a teasing mood, he sent her blood to boiling.

"I wanted to go with you," she responded quietly. "It's been a long time since I went out with anyone. Not since Terran was born. You do the math. Being a single mom plus working a lot means I don't have time to date. And I just didn't want to involve my son with anyone." She swallowed, staring ahead and not making eye contact with him. "What you said at Burger Queen bothered me. I had to prove to you that I wasn't afraid of getting involved."

"I understand—but why not give me the heads-up on Coach Hockey Puck?"

"I don't think much about Cooper. I have to deal with him but beyond that, he's nothing to me. I didn't parade you in front of him for any ulterior motive. He just happens to be my son's coach."

Mark grew quiet, then finally replied, "Next time you want to try some kind of experiment, Freud, let me in on it first so I can be prepared. I would have put on my best shirt to look good."

He spoke the latter in the same monotone as his cautionary words and she wondered if he was serious—until she glanced his way and saw a grin splitting his face.

Rolling her eyes, she couldn't help but smile. "You sure find humor in things I don't."

"Baby, life's too short not to be in it for the chuckles."

"Life's filled with things I can't chuckle about."

That sobered their humorous atmosphere, and she instantly regretted her remark.

"So, tell me about Cooper. How'd you meet him?" Mark had settled in comfortably in his chair. He clearly had no timetable and wanted to hear her life story.

Dana wasn't sure she wanted to tell her history, but she made a snap decision to trust Mark with details she rarely shared.

"I met Cooper in the grocery store. He always came into my lane and I thought he was funny the way he said things to me."

"You don't think I'm funny."

"I do, too," she countered. "I've laughed plenty at what you've said before."

"Sweetheart, you don't laugh much."

Dana didn't know whether to focus on the fact he'd actually spoken the endearment right for a change, or on his observation that she didn't laugh very often.

That simply wasn't true. She laughed a lot with Terran. He was a funny little boy.

"I do laugh."

"Not much," he reiterated. "I know you think things are bad, but they could be worse."

"I don't think that." Growing uncomfortable, she took another drink. Inadequacy swept her briefly. It felt as if she'd had the chair pulled out from under her and her butt had smacked on the decking.

The past had been challenging and difficult, but she didn't dwell on it. She didn't sit around at the bar drinking her sorrows away like her customers sometimes did. She'd never wallow in pity, never ask anyone to feel sorry for her.

Bristling at Mark's gall, she finished her wine and asked him to pour her another.

He went into the kitchen and snagged the bottle, topping off his wine after filling hers.

"So you thought Cooper was funny. Then what?" Mark's feet resumed their perch on the railing and he eased into his chair once more.

"We dated," she went on. "And I liked him."

"Did you love him?"

"Of course."

"Just wondering. Sometimes love and lust are confusing."

"I know the difference." She tamped the surge in her pulse, her heartbeat accelerating. Mark had a way of confusing her and heating her emotions to a point where she couldn't make heads or tails out of what she was trying to say. "I loved him and we made a baby together," she said in a rush, "but he didn't want to marry me. I told my brother, Terrance, what happened, and he wanted to beat the crap out of Cooper."

"Your brother said the right thing. I'd've killed any guy who got my sister pregnant and didn't do right by her."

"My brother didn't get the chance because of the accident. So I had Terran, and my mom's helped me ever since. I honestly don't know what I'd do without her. Then when Terran was two, Cooper had a change of heart and wanted to be an active dad. And that's where we are today. Split custody."

Mark nodded. "Terran seems okay with everything."

"He has his days where he's not. I can't imagine what goes on in his head sometimes." She drank more wine, then dared speak the ultimate truth. "I live with guilt."

After a span of breaths, Mark replied, "Don't we all for some reason or another."

Dana looked at him, drinking in his chiseled features in the marked light and thinking this was different. Being here with someone who didn't hold back his thoughts, who was brutally honest yet also tender.

Time stretched between them, both immersed in their own thoughts once more. Dana didn't talk about her intimate feelings with anyone. Rarely even with her own mother. It felt strange yet oddly comfortable sitting here with Mark.

Mark broke the silence. "So how'd you end up with Fish Tail Air? Was your dad a pilot?"

"No. He stumbled onto it. We're one of the few places in the marina with prime water dockage. My dad started with a couple of gasoline pumps to supplement his income from the Note. Later, he added the floatplanes. He took out a loan—I'm still paying it."

"Sell one of the planes."

"Not so easy—buyers have to have a lot of money to afford one. Each is worth a half million. I have two that seat seven, one that seats five."

"Someone could get a loan."

"Not in this economy. Business is way down. It's cheaper for me to just make the payments rather than give the planes away at a deflated price. Sam knows what he's doing. I pretty much leave it up to him."

Mark didn't carry that subject any further, but she could tell his mind was still wrapped around it.

Probably wondering just how Sam Hyatt fit into her life. He was a dear friend and they'd shared the same sorrow, but beyond that, nothing remotely romantic.

"You want to go inside now?" Mark asked, lowering his legs then standing and not really giving her the option to decline.

"Uh, sure." Dana stood, as well, her legs feeling mellow under the wine's effect. She hadn't drunk more than a glass in who knows how long.

Mark slid the sliding glass door open for her and she stepped into the living room. The modest room was sparse—just the basics for a rental property. Sofa, chairs, cabinet and television. Mark's things were scattered throughout the area. His work boots by the front door, a coat thrown over a chair back, brown leather wallet on the breakfast bar with car keys and paperwork—no doubt for the bar's remodel.

"You hungry?" he asked, standing in the kitchen, ready to get her something to eat.

Elbow deep in washing and folding laundry, she'd only had time for a bowl of cereal for dinner.

"Are you?" she replied.

He grinned, a white flash that gave her cause to look at his full lips rather than into his eyes. "Don't I hate that when a woman can't just say she's starving."

"I wouldn't say I'm starving. . . . What do you have?"

The refrigerator was opened and he stood in its low light, hand on the top and body posture bent to peer inside. "Beer, eggs, bacon, smoked salmon, cheese, chocolate milk, butter and apples."

"Cheese and apples. Do you have any crackers?"

"It's your lucky day." He moved to the cupboard and came out with a box. "Pizza flavored."

The hunger in her stomach soured as she wondered why boys liked artificially flavored food. Terran would have been all over those crackers. "Just cheese and apples."

"Coming right up. Take a load off, sis. Toss the shoes and try out that sofa. Slip into your comfortable."

Only Mark would make a comment about a couch and have it be an innuendo. She had no intention of lying down on the thing. She did remove her vest and boots, but kept on her socks. Wiggling her toes, she relaxed, feeling the wine overtake the day.

This was actually nice—to have someone fix her something. She was always doing things for Terran, getting up constantly from the table to get him something: ketchup, juice or milk. It was a rare treat when someone served her. When she and her mom cooked, they dished their plates from the stove and not at the table.

Shortly, Mark brought her a plate of thinly sliced red apple and cheddar cheese wedges—with some crackers on the side. He joined her, his masculine weight depressing the cushion with little room to spare as his thigh touched hers.

"In case you changed your mind about the mini-pizza bites in a box," he said, gesturing toward the crackers. Setting the plate on the coffee table, he went to pour more wine into her glass but she put her hand in his way.

"No more. I can feel it."

His brow rose and he gave her that slightly dimpled grin that could infuriate her. "Really? Can you show me?"

Exasperated, Dana stared at him. "Dammit, Mark. Why?"

Through a smile, he countered, "What?"

"You know what. Cut it out. You're acting like a five-year-old. I can hang out with my son if I want to be around someone who's a goof."

He took a piece of cheese. "My brothers have always said I had people laughing wherever I went. I was the kid who made farm animal noises during American Lit."

"Why?"

"Because it got me attention."

"Why? I don't like attention."

"I can tell."

"So why do you?"

"I don't anymore." The cheese disappeared, then he ate an apple slice. "It was a way to get my dad to notice me."

"He didn't?"

"Not in the same way he noticed my brothers."

This was very telling news about Mark. Clearly a larger family had more kids vying for parents' time. Terrance had never been that way. She and her brother had received equal time from their mom and dad. Probably more from Dad because he'd been eager to show them how to play the saxophone and learn jazz. Terrance had played ten times better than her.

Sampling an apple slice, Dana thoughtfully chewed the crisp, sweet fruit. "Do you have any regrets?"

"Sunshine, *that* is a loaded question." He finished his wine and poured another, adding Cabernet to her glass before she could stop him. She'd finished almost all of her second glass, just because it was there. "Sure I have regrets."

"Name one."

"You," he responded easily. Too easily for her comfort.

She drank more wine, its fiery heat sliding into her belly, then she turned to meet his eyes. "Why pick me?"

Intense brown eyes held her captive. "I wish you lived in Boise so I could get to know you better."

"You'd lose interest in me after a week."

"Not hardly."

"Sure you would. I'm just a challenge—something you can't have, so I'm appealing." She drank another sip, the wine drugging her senses.

"I don't think you're appealing. I think you're sexy as all hell. And I want to kiss you again."

Dana swallowed, the apple in her hand pausing midway to her mouth. "I don't think that's a good idea."

"That's just your opinion." Mark's body leaned into hers and he took her wineglass from her, setting it down next to his.

Her heartbeat slammed in her chest and she fought to calm herself. She didn't want to fall for him. Didn't want to think about how attracted she was to him. And she refused to acknowledge he was easy to talk to.

In a desperate attempt to stave off the inevitable— her melting into him—she said flippantly, "Maybe I didn't like the way you kissed me."

"You're a liar and you know it."

He had her and he did know it. She couldn't figure out how to stop him, stop this . . . Probably because she didn't want to. "I don't lie," she replied, her voice mottled with emotions.

"Yeah, you do." His intense face hovered over hers while his heavy arm draped over her shoulder.

Whether it was the wine relaxing her resolve or the need to be blatantly honest, she admitted, "I have found myself thinking about that kiss . . . wanting to touch you." Heat burned her cheeks. "But I'll get over it."

"You don't have to get over it. You can have some more."

She cast her eyes down, unable to meet his stare. He cupped her chin in his callused hand and gently tilted it up.

"Touch me," he commanded softly.

For the briefest of moments, refusal coursed through her, but it was gone as quickly as it had come. Just this one time she would succumb to the feelings for him that had been haunting her.

Tentatively, her hands rose to his shirt collar. He wore a T-shirt beneath a button-down. She caught the superfine material in her fingers and felt the weave. It had been a long time since she had touched a man like this. Her movements were slow and fragile, unintentionally bringing a grimace of arousal across his face as if she were deliberately trying to seduce him.

The feeling of the round shirt buttons was cool beneath her skin, and she rolled one between her fingertips. A low guttural noise rose from Mark's throat.

She gingerly slid her hands over his torso, feeling his warmth seeping through the fabric. He ignited under her slow exploration, burning her palms with his body heat even through the cloth.

Slowly she moved to his flat abdomen, fingering the trail of buttons and wondering . . . what if . . . she undid them. She marked each rib with her fingers, moving to the slight rise of his solid chest, tracing the dark hair at his throat. He was all man.

Strong and virile, without an ounce of unwanted flesh.

She heard Mark's ragged breath catch in his chest. Her hands grazed him with a blend of innocent sensuality, but she knew damn well what she was doing.

It had been so long since she'd been with a man.

"Dana." Mark's rough voice fell on her ears. "You're taking me to heaven and hell at the same time. You better stop."

"Shh." She put her fingertip to his mouth, surprised by her own daring. It must be the wine, or the aching loneliness, or just because it felt so good to touch him—she didn't want to stop.

In a testament to Mark's willpower, he continued to let her roam his body freely, discovering what he was made of.

Dana moved up to the tendons of his neck and buried her hands in his thick hair. Coarse and silky at the same time, it smelled like a hint of outdoors and shampoo.

He didn't move as she felt his face the same way he had felt hers that night they had kissed in the rain. His forehead was smooth and bronze from the sun. She ran her thumbs over his eyebrows from where they were fully arched to the outer part where they tapered, making him look like he was scowling. He had closed his eyes, his lashes surprisingly soft and full as her own. She felt the strong, straight bone of his nose.

As she tenderly caressed his face, she ran her fingertips over his full mouth and finally over the stubbled beard that—

Abruptly, his eyes shot open and the vise grip of his fingers circled both her wrists. "Dammit," he moaned deeply. "Do you know what you're doing to me?"

He gently but firmly pushed her back into the sofa, lying on top of her with a pleasant weight, one she welcomed. This time it was she who briefly closed her eyes.

She felt the hard length of him behind the fly of his jeans. He rested on his elbows and caught her face, then took her mouth.

There was an urgency to the kiss this time, not like the softness of before. She welcomed him, her coaxing lips eager to pleasure him, as well.

He tasted of cheese and red apples and the hard sweetness of wine. She moved her hands down the broad expanse of his shoulders and back, clutching his waist and finally feeling the tight muscles of his backside. She shivered in his arms, passion radiating in every nerve ending of her body.

Mark's hands burrowed into her hair, the straightened black length that she'd softened with products. He cupped her head in his wide, rough hands, kissing her and tracing the soft fullness of her lips, then changing the slant of his kiss. His tongue invaded her mouth and she was lost. She met him, sparring with him, drawing him deeper into her mouth.

It was all she could do not to wiggle out of her clothes to feel the velvet warmth of his bare skin next to hers. He slid his hand down her neck and shoulder, kneading her with his fingers, savoring and exploring. When he came to her breast, he moved slowly and artfully over its fullness.

Dana's cry was lost on his lips as Mark gently stroked her breast. Her nipple sprang into a hard, tight peak against the thin layer of her bra. For a long moment, he caressed her over her sweater, kissing her with deep, drowning kisses. Only after she thought she would die if he didn't touch her bare skin, did he slide his hand under her top. He managed to move her bra aside and covered her breast with his hand. She burned from the contact, arching her back to him.

The motion brought a groan from Mark, who pulled the knit aside to reveal her breast. Her skin seared under his gaze. She'd always been a little self-conscious about the size of her breasts and the dark nipples.

She moved to cover herself, but Mark shook his head, tracing her with his fingertip and vaguely smiling with pleasure.

Dana felt herself falling into a sexual pool she had never known existed. Kissing and touching had never felt this recklessly sexy with Cooper. Never this bone-marrow melting. Her body was damp from sweat, the core between her legs aching with need and wanting.

But as delicious as the sensations Mark evoked in her were, they were taken away. He righted her bra, smoothed her sweater back into place and lowered a leisurely kiss on her parted lips.

The cloud of desire waned and her thoughts scattered. She would have gone to bed with him. No doubt about it. And that sobered her—angered her—that she could just throw caution to the wind. She wasn't on any kind of birth control—until now there had never been a need.

Mark moved off her, a fine sheen of perspiration covering his brow. His heart hammered in his chest, she could see it in the pulse at his neck.

"It's time I take you home," he said in a raspy tone.

Dana gazed at him, her face flushed. Suddenly she became self-conscious of her actions. How could she have let herself be so transparent? She'd let her guard down. In fact, she might as well have used dynamite on it. It was gone, obliterated. All that she had left was a painful vulnerability and the sweet ache inside her that still wanted to be satisfied by his body on hers.

Mark combed his hair with his fingers, taking a long shot of wine to clear his head. "Let's get your coat."

"I need to get my shoes on first," she replied, slightly abruptly. The guy was pushing her out the door and she grew perturbed.

Standing and moving into the kitchen for his keys and wallet, Mark threw on his coat then came to wait for her by the sofa. She slipped her vest on and grabbed her purse.

Before she could take a step to the door, he put his hands on her shoulders and kissed her sweetly on the mouth. With a tilt of his chin, he rested his forehead on the top of her head.

"Go out with me next week," he said, his words surprising her.

She didn't think she could be around him anymore, not alone. She couldn't trust herself. Thankfully, she had an out. "I can't. I have my son."

"Bring him, too. We'll go to dinner. And whatever else there is to do in this town that Terran likes to do."

"Why?"

"Because I'm asking." He lifted his face and stared into hers. "Because it will give us something to look forward to."

CHAPTER THIRTEEN

"KAH-POW! MOMMA, I just tasered you!" Terran aimed a dead cell phone at her hip and made a garbled detonating noise from his mouth, blasting her again.

A large shocking orange vest swam on his little boy frame with *SECURITY* spelled out in big letters on the back. Cooper had given him a defective phone that had been returned to GCI and Terran had created a pretend gun with it.

Five minutes late, Cooper had pulled to the curb to drop their son off, and Dana had come down to greet them. Terran had spilled from the Jeep in an animated fashion, eager to show her what he'd been up to.

"Hey, Mommy—watch this!" He spread his legs apart at the curb and aimed at Cooper's stomach. "Hannah Montana is a stupid butt."

"Terran," Dana cautioned, collecting his belongings. "Don't say 'butt' and don't say 'stupid.' "

Cooper added his opinion. "But Hannah Montana is stupid." He didn't back her in the discipline department—no big surprise. Hair touched his brow as he bent down to tie his shoe. "That Miley chick makes bank—and for what? Looking like a dweeb on the Disney Channel."

"Mommy—I'm security for Miley Cyrus's concert and I use a Taser on anyone who tries to kill her on the stage."

"Honestly, Cooper," Dana hissed beneath her breath. "Do you really think that's a positive role-play game for our son?"

Rising to his feet, Cooper shrugged. "He found the security vest at Ben's and he wanted to wear it home. Ben said he could. That night Terran was flipping from Nickelodeon to the Disney Channel, he wanted to know who Miley Cyrus was. I swear to you, he got it into his head to be security for her. Not my fault."

Ben was Cooper's friend and the goalie on their adult league team. Not the brightest crayon in the box, Ben worked for Tongass Sanitation. Cooper had been buddies with him for years, and while Dana didn't necessarily think Ben made the greatest impression on her son, there were worse friends Cooper could hang out with.

"Well, I don't want him going around saying he's going to kill people." Dana grabbed the backpack from Cooper's hand. "That's not normal for a five-year-old."

"Hell, yeah it is. When I was Terran's age, I set ants on fire with matches," Cooper said in a low tone. "And I laughed when I watched them sizzle and fry."

"Terran's not allowed to play with matches."

"Neither was I."

With a slightly disgruntled tug, Dana took the lumpy plastic grocery bag from Cooper's grasp. "What's in here?"

"I had to buy him some new tennis shoes. His old ones are shot. They're in the bag."

"Thanks."

She and Cooper didn't have a limited amount they spent on Terran each week. No game playing with checkbooks and crying broke. Both of them were pretty good about buying him what he needed if he needed it, and the expenses seemed to balance out.

Neither of them paid the other financial support for their son, but Cooper was responsible enough to carry medical insurance that covered Terran's doctor and dental visits. They'd had to use the E.R. once when Terran, wet and horsing around, slipped in the bathtub. His top teeth had cut into his lower lip, requiring stitches inside his mouth. Dana didn't know how much that bill had totaled, but she assumed it would have been significant even after the deductible. Cooper had never asked her to pay half the cost.

Terran climbed the cement steps by the gate and pointed the Taser at the newel posts, with gusto-filled sound effects. His red Kung Fu Panda T-shirt had a dark stain down the front—possibly grape jelly or cola and whipping cream. Beneath the hems of faded-in-the-knees blue jeans, he displayed black-and-lime sneakers with spanking new rubber soles.

"So who was that guy?" Cooper asked with a snort, closing the Jeep's tailgate after shoving Riley's face back in. The dog gave a short and deep-chested bark.

Thankfully Terran's preoccupation with the security vest and gun had kept him from mentioning his desire for a dog of his own.

"What guy?" Dana replied, having a good hunch she knew just what Cooper was talking about.

"That guy you brought to Terran's hockey practice."

"Oh, him." Dana feigned a casualness in her tone she didn't necessarily feel. Her cheeks heated in remembrance of the other night on Mark's sofa and she did her best not to clue Cooper in on her thoughts. "He works for me."

"Bartender?"

Cooper never came into the Blue Note. He wasn't a party-boy drinker and, even if he had been, he wouldn't have set foot into her bar. He would have gone to the Arctic where he could play pool.

All Dana offered was, "He's doing some remodel work for me."

"I just wondered if you were dating him."

"Would it matter, Cooper?"

"Momma, I'm going to go get Grandma with my Taser."

"Go ahead, baby. She's in the kitchen waiting for you with milk and carrot sticks."

"Barf," Terran muttered with a gagging expression. Then he dug into his pocket for foil-wrapped candy kisses.

When he'd climbed all the steps and had gone inside, Dana confronted Cooper. "I wish you wouldn't give him candy, Cooper. I'm trying to keep him off too much sugar."

"He's a kid. He can have candy."

All but snapping, she tossed back, "But you won't have to deal with him tonight when he's hyper and can't fall asleep."

"He doesn't have any problems at my house."

Cooper slid aviator sunglasses over his eyes. "You're such a control freak. Everything has to be your way or no way at all. Jeez, Dana. Lighten up. No wonder you don't have a boyfriend."

Then he slipped into the Jeep and drove away.

Dana watched his vehicle disappear, rattling off a few choice swear words in her head. Cooper could really piss her off.

The rest of that Sunday evening, Dana dumped Terran's dirty clothes in the washer, took his belongings to his room and sorted through the variety of odd things he'd brought home. Then her mom called for dinner and they visited with him at the table.

Suni busied herself at the kitchen counter, spooning rice from the cooker into a bowl. Often, they ate Chinese food. Suni was an excellent cook and knew just how to spice things while not making the food so hot you couldn't eat it.

When they were seated at the small table, they discussed the week ahead, what they would do together, and how many more days until school started.

The scene was intimate and warm, with laughter and fun talk, something Dana relished and looked forward to. The nights she worked at the Blue Note, she missed this terribly.

After dinner cleanup, she took Terran upstairs and ran the bath for him. He sank into the water, surrounded by tub toys, making splashing sounds for battleships, then painted bath paint on the walls and on his chest. She rinsed and dried him off, cuddling him in the towel and soaking in his clean boy scent.

Pressing her face against the silky softness in the curve of his damp neck, she smiled, holding her breath and thinking she was so lucky.

"Mommy, I'm giving you a bigger hug," Terran said, then she lost her balance as he thrust his weight at her.

They fell backward on the floor, onto the wet throw rug and tiles. She held him tightly so he couldn't squiggle away. But he didn't attempt to. He wrapped his tiny arms around her neck and nestled in, staying close.

Dana lay there, arms around her son, staring at the ceiling light. Terran played with her hair, twirling it in his fingers as he had done when he was an infant as he'd nursed. With a soft caress, she ran her hand down his back, feeling his spine and listening to him breathe.

No words were spoken.

She didn't want the moment to pass because as he approached five, and kindergarten, he could very well grow up in a little boy way and mommies wouldn't be cool anymore to hug and hold on to.

She loved him beyond description, and the sweet joy he gave her was as pure as anything she could ever imagine.

Terran tired of her lock hold and wiggled away, leaving cool air to snatch away his warm body heat that had blanketed her. In his room, she helped him get into his blue jammies, then he crawled into bed. He lay there with stuffed animals surrounding him, blankets and pillows tucked in just how he liked them.

As she sat on his bed, the night-light giving off a tiny glow, she fondled his hair, smoothing it off his forehead.

"Hey, Momma?" he asked, his face serious.

"What?"

Cuddling his teddy bear, he questioned, "Can we have a sleepover at Dad's?"

Momentarily thrown off-kilter, Dana said, "No, Terran. That won't be possible."

"Why not?"

"Because Mom and Dad don't live together."

"How come?"

"Because we each have our own houses and that's just how it is."

Terran's eyes held hers, and with the somberness too mature for a boy his age, he uttered, "That's not fair."

Her heart broke and she wished that what he said wasn't true. But his situation wasn't fair, and she ached for him. Guilt was a heavy burden on her shoulders, but there was nothing she could do. This was the way things were.

"I'm sorry," was all she could offer.

Terran rubbed the underside of his nose, then mumbled in a disgruntled tone, "How come Daddy can have a sleepover? Tori spends the night."

That startling news prickled every sense within Dana and she felt her pulse pump in a rapid surge. "Tori?"

"The lady who said hi to me at Burger Queen."

"Tori sleeps over?"

"Uh-huh. So I think you should, too. With me and Dad. And then we can all have a happy sleepover." Stifling a yawn, he added in a muffled voice, "Can you make me pancakes tomorrow?"

A FINE DRIZZLE HIT the windshield like a million gnats steadily coming at Mark. The intermittent wipers barely cleaned the glass then it was sprayed once more.

His mind drew upon an absent thought: this weather could drive someone nuts living in it day in and day out.

As he headed for the building supply store, his cell rang.

"Moretti," he answered.

"Mark, it's your brother Robert."

"Robert, hey, how's it going?"

Genuinely glad to hear from his brother, the call pulled Mark back to Boise, another time and another place, where he had roots and a home. While deep into the Blue Note's renovation, he didn't think about responsibilities in Idaho.

Robert's phone call gave him a quick reality check.

"Things are great down here."

"You staying busy?" Mark responded, clicking on the truck's blinker to pull into Talbot's parking lot.

"This economy stinks, but I'm doing a pretty good business. In fact, I can't complain. I've had steady customers every night. Another restaurant closed in Boise and it's not looking good for a friend of mine."

"Yeah, you kind of forget about things like that up here. It's a lot different, like you're in a time warp or something."

"So how's the remodel coming along?"

"Great." Robert knew about his work on the Blue Note. He'd mentioned it to their sister. "While I'm waiting for my steel sections to get here, we're installing a platform tomorrow at the fire evac access. I've got some welders lined up. I may even throw a hood on myself and do some joint work."

"Just like you did on the Grove."

"I don't mind."

And that was the truth of the matter. Mark enjoyed building things, and more important, he'd realized he liked doing smaller projects like this one. The return was faster, and he could see the changes take place sooner versus later. So far, the place was really shaping up and he was happy with how things had been going. Of course once he was finished, he'd have nothing left to do but head home.

That prospect left him flat.

"How's everybody else?" Mark asked. "Franci okay? Mom?"

"They're good. Mom says you don't call enough."

"She would say that."

"Yeah, she mentioned she's e-mailing some lady you know in town. I forget her name."

Mark turned off the truck's engine and sat in the building supply's parking lot, a fine rain covering the windshield. When he'd given Suni his mom's e-mail, he hadn't been certain she'd contact Mariangela. He'd pretty much forgotten about it. "That'd be Suni Jackson, Dana's mom."

"Dana?"

"She owns the bar I'm fixing up. She lives with her mother, whose name is Suni. She's a widow, too. I figured her and Mom would have stuff in common."

Robert paused a second before replying. "So how pretty is this Dana?"

He inhaled a deep breath, then let it out. His hands rested on the steering wheel. Robert knew him well enough to wonder about his motives. In the past, Mark would have been out to win the woman and collect her luscious gratitude with open arms, but that wasn't the case this time. Dana was different. He was different around her.

"It's not like that, Robert."

"So how is it, then?"

Being with Dana pulled strongly at him. He was attached emotionally, drawn to her like no other woman in his dating history. But they weren't dating, and she had her own set of problems with a life that was complicated enough without him in it.

If he fell in love with her, he'd mess up the tight world she'd created for herself and her son. Mark wasn't even sure if he knew what real love was. He did know that he loved being with her, and these last couple of months had been more relaxing for him than any he could remember in recent years.

In the rugged Alaskan beauty, everything seemed surreal.

The air was like taking a bite out of an apple, crisp and sweet. The water was frigid and certain mountain ranges were always capped with snow. Never had he seen a richer green than that on the trees that cloistered around Ketchikan.

Being here had helped him see some things about himself, and he liked who he was. Working on the Blue Note took him out of himself. For the first time in years, *he* was the one driving to the hardware store, the building supply house. He'd bought pizzas for lunch, brought in coffee and doughnuts in the wee hours when they stayed late. He knew all the guys on a first-name basis—something that had been impossible on the Grove Marketplace.

He'd inadvertently stumbled into discovering who he wanted to be and he was grateful for the opportunity. Dana didn't understand just how much she'd helped him, how much he'd needed to do this for her.

With an evasive answer, Mark said, "I saw an opportunity to do something, and I figured out that my effort is benefiting me a hell of a lot more than it is her."

"Does she think that?"

"I don't know, Robert." And that was the truth. Trying to get a handle on what Dana's thoughts were was about as easy as shoving a refrigerator uphill.

"Just don't get too cozy," Robert suggested. "Your nieces have been asking when their uncle Mark is coming back."

"It's hard to get cozy here when it rains every day." He gave the lumberman, who hopped off the seat of a wet forklift, a wave of recognition that was returned with a smile. "So what's the weather like back in Boise?"

"Hot. Mid-eighties. Blue skies. It's perfect here."

"Cruel." Mark laughed.

He glanced through the mottled windshield. A wet fog hung low in the sky and visibility was poor, and he could just make out the gray outlines of lacy spruce trees through the mist.

"So I need a favor, favorite brother."

"That's a line of bunk," Mark said with a smile.

"John's your favorite brother." Their oldest brother was an attorney and always had a logical response when asked about his opinion.

"Well, you're my favorite right now." Robert laughed into the phone. "I was wondering if you can ship me any more of that fish? It went over so great at Pomodoro, I've had requests."

Pomodoro was Robert's restaurant in downtown Boise.

Mark absently flicked the wipers so he could see the channel and watch a gigantic cruise ship as it slowly progressed north.

"Sure, I can do that. What kind do you want?"

"Anything that you've got that's fresh caught. I'll pay you for the overnight shipping."

"No need. I got it covered."

"Thanks, Mark. We miss you, you know."

"Yeah." Mark felt the stubble on his neck, and suddenly home seemed the miles away it was. "I miss you guys, too."

CARL "BEANS" PINTO WAS A regular at the Blue Note. Regular in that he regularly got escorted off the premises after being cut off at the bar. His regular drink was a White Russian. After two drinks, his standard remark was, "Run a tab for me, Leo." Regularly, Leo closed out the check after the fourth White Russian.

Beans wasn't a big man—average size in height and stature—so how he managed to stay coherent after four strong liquor bombs was anyone's guess.

The reason Dana let him sit at the bar was because, as odd as it sounded, he drank responsibly. He never drove himself to the Blue Note. He always had a cab drop him off and pick him up.

Still, that didn't eliminate the regular disruption Beans seemed to cause after Leo cautioned him he was ordering his final drink of the evening.

"You know what, Dana?" Beans asked, his words running into one big connection of syllables.

"What's that, Beans?" she returned, filing a receipt in the cash register behind the bar.

"I drink so much, my blood type is AA."

Closing the cash register drawer, Dana faced him with a shake of her head. "Maybe you ought to try an AA meeting."

Dana rarely, if ever, gave advice like this, but Beans had been coming into the Blue Note for years, even back when her father ran the bar. It wasn't uncommon for patrons to have drinking problems, and she usually let things slide, as it wasn't her business to tell them what to do. On occasions when commotions started—which weren't often—it simply took a call to police dispatch for help. Thankfully, those evenings were few and far between.

The Blue Note had a reputation for being a class joint.

"AA is a twelve-step program for wussies."

Beans sneered with a pinched face. "I could stop drinking if I wanted to." He lifted the glass to his mouth. "But I don't want to."

Dana motioned to Leo, a silent signal and nod that Beans would now be cut off. Then it would be time to call the taxi for him.

"You know what, Miss Dana?" Beans said in a very loud voice as she began to walk away. "You're a lot prettier than Candy, Miss Racktober with the big hooters over at that other bar. Beauty is in the face, not in the chest and I think you're love-r-ly."

"Thanks, Beans." Dana gave him a bemused smile. Only he'd know how to give a thumbs-up that included hooters belonging to a different woman.

Making eye contact with Leo once more, Dana left the bar and headed for the kitchen to check on Presley.

"What's going on out there?" Presley asked, plating an order. "Is that Beans shouting?"

With a grimace, Dana replied, "You know how that fish-brain gets when he's buzzed. He thinks people can't hear him unless he yells."

"Gotcha."

As Dana helped Presley collect some plates from the stainless rack above the long counter, she mentioned, "By the way, I bought the wrong pads for the ladies' room. I meant to get the regulars, but I ended up with extra long."

"Good Lord, they'll be like wearing the *Titanic* with wings."

Biting back a smile, Dana didn't respond. She'd been distracted today. All day, her mind had been drifting to tomorrow night.

Mark was taking her and Terran out. He'd told her to pick out a fun restaurant that Terran would enjoy. That had been easy. She'd suggested pizza at Oceanview, a favorite eatery for her son. Terran had hockey practice at seven, and Mark said he'd be at her house at five.

Just the thought of him coming over and picking up her and her son to take them . . . *out* . . . Dana warded off shivers. The whole concept really rattled her. Terran had never gone out with her and a guy. *She* hadn't gone out with a guy in ages.

"I'm going to be in my office if you need me," Dana said, then left Presley to her orders.

Once in her office, Dana opened a page on her computer. She found those red Louboutin shoes she absolutely loved and drooled at the extravagance, knowing it would be ridiculous to spend the bucks on them.

Engrossed in the image, she didn't notice Mark Moretti filling her doorway, watching her unblinking face while she drooled.

"You sure are gorgeous," he said, shooting her off her cloud.

She about jolted sideways off her chair.

"Dammit, Moretti, you scared the crap out of me. What do you want?"

"Well, hello to you, too, sunshine."

He'd left the bar hours ago and she hadn't expected him back. The fact he stood less than a few feet away, spying on her, rose her hackles a bit.

"You went home," she stated.

"I came back." His sexy smile soared straight into her heart; those vague dimples of his got to her when he really put his charm into his curving mouth. She wanted to kill him . . . kiss him.

"How come you came back?" she asked, rising so he wouldn't stare down at her. She always felt short enough around him.

"I wanted to tell you something."

Cautious, yet concerned, she replied, "Is there a problem with the construction? Did you run out of something and can't get it? It happens here a lot. Everything has to be shipped in."

He came toward her. "Nothing like that at all." He stood tall, taller than she could imagine a man could be next to her. Standing over her slight frame, he looked into her face. "I was just thinking."

Her breath hitched in her throat. "Thinking what?"

She could feel the heat radiating off his body. He wore a rain-damp button-down shirt and jeans, dark lace shoes. No jacket, as if he'd run into the bar real quick. A light rain had been falling most of the day, and his hair was wet from that or the shower. "I was at the building supply today and I was thinking about you."

"What?" The word escaped her lips, confusion marking her tone.

Mark put his hands on her shoulders and brought her close. "I was just thinking that you're my sunshine on a rainy day."

Bewildered, she blurted, "Is that a song lyric?"

He laughed, shaking his head. "No. It's a compliment. When it's raining, you're my eighty degrees and I don't mind the clouds. I just wanted you to know."

Then he lowered his head and kissed her. Gently and light as a whisper. Before she could feel the heat of it and suction herself next to his broad chest, he pulled back.

With the faintest of smiles that left her puzzled, he said, "I'll see you tomorrow."

Then he was gone and she stood there alone and, strangely, wishing he was still there.

CHAPTER FOURTEEN

AFTER WORK ON THURSDAY, Dana dashed home and changed into dark denim jeans, heeled black loafers and a black turtleneck. The humidity had ruined her hair, frizzing the carefully flattened curls to an annoying degree. Giving up trying to fix the damage, she opted to pin her hair into a messy twist at the back of her head. She needed to have the chemical relaxer applied again, but doing that was such a long ordeal she hadn't made the time.

A few hours ago, Mark asked if he could come at four rather than the five o'clock he'd originally planned. He had a surprise for them. Dana wasn't one for surprises, but Mark wouldn't budge and tell her what it was, only that he'd learned about something fun that her son would like to do before dinner.

The doorbell rang and her mom rose from the chair to answer it, Terran close on her heels. He'd been very excited to go out for pizza, and moderately interested in Mark coming with them. He'd asked her questions about Mark since the only adult male he was around on a regular basis was his father.

To a little boy, a new guy was a novelty. Did he like trucks or motorcycles? Did he like Spiderman or Superman better? Did he hate broccoli and did he love pizza? Innocent inquiries that Dana had no answer for. She didn't know.

Dana rushed down the stairs wanting to get out of here quickly without allowing her mom the chance to question Mark herself—or to make something more out of this when it was nothing.

Suni had been surprised when Dana mentioned the evening, only a few hours ago even though she'd known for a week they'd be going out tonight. Dana surprised herself. She wasn't one to go on a date, especially not with Terran. This was all new territory for her.

Part of her still reeled over the information Terran had spilled about his daddy's cozy "sleep-over." The news that Cooper would have a woman spend the night with their son in the house had incensed her. Couldn't he have waited until his off week? The jerk.

She'd called him out on it that Sunday night, reading him the riot act over the telephone. Anger had simmered through her veins. He'd told her to chill, and claimed he could decide what he wanted in his own home, and she had no right to tell him what to do.

Dana hadn't mentioned the incident to her mom—Suni would have gone off the deep end. Instead, Dana had put in a call to her lawyer to see if she could get an injunction or something against Cooper. Her attorney told her that since there was nothing in the custody agreement stipulating overnight guests, Mr. Boyd was free to use his "own discretion" when the minor child was in his care. That just didn't seem right.

"Hi, Terran. How are you?" Mark said from the doorway as Terran swung the door open with his grandmother.

"Hi. What's our surprise?"

"You'll see," Mark replied, his voice easygoing.

Dana drew next to the door and addressed her mom. "Back in a little while."

"I'll see you at the ice rink," Suni responded, studiously giving Mark a long gaze. "I suppose you'll be there, too."

"That's probably likely since I'm driving them." Mark smiled a deep and warm smile, his words not in the slightest condescending, but rather strong and unyielding as if he wouldn't take an argument about his involvement with her daughter—no matter how casual.

Dana appreciated Mark's straightforwardness and very relaxed manner. In fact, she admired him for it. She wouldn't have been so matter-of-fact if she had to talk to some guy's mom. Having dealings in the past with parents who were curious about her mixed heritage, she'd had some unfortunate experiences that put her on guard in new situations.

"I'll get that," Mark said as she reached down for the booster car seat Terran had to use. "See you later," he called to her mother.

Suni stood on the stoop, watching them walk down the steps toward Mark's pickup truck. Settled in, they headed off.

Once more, Terran asked, "Hey, Mark, what's the surprise?"

Keeping his eyes on the road, Mark replied with a half smile, "I asked around and found out where the *bestest* place to go before dinner is."

"Where?"

"You'll see."

"But I want to see right now."

Mark softly laughed. "You aren't very patient. Just like your mom."

Dana fended off a frown. She sat directly next to Mark in the truck's cab, while Terran filled the window seat. He gazed through the glass, counting trees as they passed by. He'd only get as high as ten, then pause and start back on tree number one.

They weren't headed toward town. Dana knew it was too cold to hit Rotary Beach, although that was a favorite of hers on a sunny day—or even an overcast one. The rocky beach was fun to walk along and collect pretty stones, as well as sand-washed glass pieces. She was collecting the various colored-glass pieces and putting them in a jar. The playground there was really great, too.

Mark drove farther, turned and took a side road. Dana knew where they were going. Terran wouldn't have known the landmarks, but Dana smiled. "Thanks. He's going to love this."

Pulling the truck into a vacant space, Mark said, "That's what I heard."

The Ketchikan Recreational Center had quarter- and half-pipe skateboard ramps next to the building. Kids, mostly boys, skated the length doing tricks, wiping out and laughing. Inside, there were basketball courts, Ping-Pong tables and a walking track. For smaller guys like Terran, the playroom was popular with its toys, tumbling mats and Little Tikes slide and playhouse set.

Terran's face split into a grin. "Hey, Mommy. I know where we are!"

"Where's that?" She smiled back.

"The play place!" He wiggled in his car seat, anxious to be free and run wild.

Mark stepped down out of the truck and came around to help Terran, then her. Dana felt self-conscious as Mark's hands reached out to her to guide her to the ground. The contact was hot and over all too soon.

Once standing, she backed away and forced herself into a calm she didn't feel. She held on to her purse handles with one hand and Terran with the other so she wouldn't have a free hand for Mark to take.

They went into the rec center and Terran shot off like a pistol when they came to his section. Dana and Mark took seats as her son busied himself on the slide and made quick friends with those who'd arrived there before him.

"This was nice of you." Dana felt slightly unsettled by Mark's generosity and she couldn't pinpoint exactly why. She didn't know why it bothered her that he'd gone to this trouble to please her five-year-old boy. Maybe because she wasn't used to a man thinking of others before himself.

Cooper put himself number one on a list of important people. Not that she cared—that was just his way.

"No problem," Mark replied. "He's having fun."

"He loves it here." Dana settled in, her purse at her feet. She slid out of her lightweight coat and folded it on the vacant seat next to her.

With her agile movements, she could smell the perfume she'd sprayed at her neck. Very subtle, very soft in its floral composition. After coming home from the bar, she wanted to spend time freshening her makeup and adding a spritz of fragrance to her skin. She wanted to look nice and appealing.

Her thoughts hadn't wandered far from that night in Mark's condo, and they strayed there now. She was insane to revisit them. It had been lunacy that night to get that close to him and to want to be that close once more.

The way his mouth had fit over hers, his hands covering her breast and—

"Dana?" Mark's deep voice broke through her thoughts. "You okay?"

"Huh, yes. Sure. Fine."

"You looked far-off."

"Uh, no. Just thinking about the . . . remodel." She watched as Terran strung a line of toy trains together.

"Are you worried I won't have it finished in time?"

"No."

But she had thought about what it would be like when he'd left and gone back to Boise. In the early morning hours when she tried to fall asleep after a long night in the Blue Note, oftentimes her wild thoughts veered to Mark, and how much she'd come to rely on him being around.

Those were dangerous thoughts to have.

She counted on no one but herself—and her mom. God knows what she'd do without her mother's help. Beyond that, there wasn't a thing she couldn't handle.

Until the fire marshal's report.

That had been something that would have put her under. If it hadn't been for Mark . . .

"Good, because you have nothing to worry about," Mark said as he waved to Terran.

"I wasn't worried."

Mark turned to her, his eyes locking into hers as he gave her a serious examination. "Dana, I don't think there's a day that goes by that you're not worried about something."

"That's simply not true."

"Prove it. This morning you were going nuts over some order that Leo said hadn't arrived and you were wigging out on the phone to figure out what had happened to it."

In her defense, Dana said, "That was my liquor order. And without it, I'm in deep trouble. We cut the timing way too short and it was imperative that alcohol shipment arrive today. The freighter was due to be here by noon. But when I called, they assured me it would be there no later than five o'clock tonight."

Mark's brows raised. "How many times have you checked on it since you got home?"

"Only once, Mark." Dana gave him a smug smile. "And it had arrived."

"But you worried about it, sunshine."

"Oh, whatever." She dismissed him, knowing he'd pegged her right.

"Momma, look!" Terran attempted to do a somersault on a rubber mat. He went halfway over, then tilted sideways.

"That's awesome, baby!" she called out to him.

He made another attempt, and with the same results. While the other kids played in pairs, he pretty much remained a loner.

"You ever thought about having another kid?" Mark asked, his very personal question shaking through her mind.

"Not today," she replied, rather smartly. "Maybe next week if I meet the right guy."

"Funny." Mark rested his forearms on his knees, watching as Terran bounced from one activity to another. "I was just imagining what it would have been like to not have brothers or a sister to play with."

"I wouldn't know, either. I had a big brother," she remarked in a voice riddled with angst. As soon as she said it, she felt like crying. She would have done anything to have her brother back. "But that's why only children can make friends in school. So they don't have to feel like they don't have anyone else."

At least that was her fervent wish for Terran. That he make a good buddy for life. He had friends on his hockey team, but not many of the boys lived close by. Their modest house was located in a densely wooded area without benefits of a subdivision teeming with kids. Terran's biggest event in his life was a slumber party. It had happened a couple of times—with the teammates from his hockey league. She'd hosted one at her house, and about went bonkers that evening trying to settle all those boys down after pop and pizza. She'd finally lined them up in sleeping bags on the living room floor and she'd slept on the sofa, or rather, tried to sleep through the giggles, burps and farts. She was wasted the next day.

Dana had hopes that kindergarten would bring Terran a new set of friends.

"I like your shoes," Mark commented, drawing her from her thoughts. She followed his gaze to her black heeled loafers.

Thinking his remark unusual, she challenged, "Men don't usually notice women's shoes."

"You're right. But I did notice you have a fetish for them." A lift of his brows and lighthearted amusement filled his good-looking expression. "Yesterday when I stopped by to say hi, I saw what you were looking at on the computer."

She wanted to shrink into nothingness. First, he hadn't just stopped by and, second, she'd wanted to stick herself to him like chewing gum and he'd probably known it. Rather than clue him in to her true thoughts, she said vehemently, "I don't look at shoes all day. You caught me at a bad time."

With a shrug that dismissed the subject, he said, "Don't need to explain yourself to me."

Feeling helpless to rationalize her love for heeled shoes, Dana silently watched Terran happily interact with the other children, lost in a myriad of thoughts. This had never happened to her before. In her dating past, she must have hung out with men less intelligent than her, because she mostly controlled their conversations. But Mark gained the upper hand on her every time. She was always left bemused and wondering how it had happened.

Before long, it was time to leave.

Once outside, Mark paused to watch kids speeding along on the skateboard ramp. "Terran, do you know how to skateboard?"

"Nope." He shook his head, the missing tooth in his mouth emphasizing the *o* in the word to a slight lisp. "My mommy said I'll break my bones 'cause we live on a big street."

"We're on a steep hill," Dana clarified.

Mark nodded at Dana, then addressed Terran,

"Yeah, she's right. A little dude on fast wheels, you could take a nasty header and bust yourself pretty good." No facetiousness marked his tone. "That sucks though. Can you ride your bike?"

"I got one at my dad's house." Terran rubbed his nose. "Do you know how to skateboard?"

"Yes, but I bought it on the quarter-pipe my dad built for me and broke my arm."

"Bought what?" Terran's eyes squinched as he tried to figure out what Mark meant.

Mark vaguely smiled. "Fell down and had to have my arm in a cast."

"I want my arm in a cast!"

"No, you don't."

Then Mark called to one of the teen boys, drew closer to him and the next thing Dana knew, Mark was borrowing the skateboard.

"Whoa." Terran uttered the word in awe as Mark hopped onto the pipe and began to move the board along the flat edge, then bring things up to speed and curl over the top and back down. Knees bent and arms out, he mastered the ramp without effort and took another run at it.

His beaming face expressed the joy and freedom he must have felt to accomplish such a feat.

Dana had never seen a grown man do such a thing. She knew that boarding was hugely popular, but Mark's presence on the ramp took her by surprise.

After several runs, he handed the teenager his

board back, and the boy gave him a high five. Mark smiled and hopped down to join them in the paved area.

"You rock and roll!" Terran breathed with an excited grin, the expression one of his dad's.

"Wow." Mark laughed, his voice deep and happy. "I haven't done that in nearly twenty years. That was awesome."

"Hey, Mark? Mark?" Terran all but jumped like a rubber ball in the parking lot. "Can you show me how to do that?"

Walking toward the truck, Mark's smile remained planted on his face. "I don't know. You'd need a small quarter-pipe ramp in your garage and you'd have to wear a helmet, elbow and knee pads. *And* your mom would have to say okay." The latter comment was directed specifically at her.

"Mommy? Can I? Please?"

Dana drew in a breath. She'd never thought about Terran and a skateboard, but it made sense he'd be interested. He knew no fear on the ice thanks to Cooper's encouragement. "How do I get a ramp in the garage?" she asked as Mark opened the truck door.

Looking into her eyes, Mark simply replied, "I build you one."

And so the world between them became another inch smaller, as she nodded her agreement to have Mark Moretti build her son a mini-ramp in her garage and teach him how to skateboard.

• • •

MARIANGELA WROTE:

I went to Italy after my husband passed. It was good for me to see the Old Country and have memories of Giovanni and where we first met. I didn't immigrate to the States until my early twenties. When I was home, I stayed with my Aunt Romilda. She's a funny woman who wears thick support hose. I recall my mother wore the same. Panty hose, especially that control top nonsense, bother me and I'd rather go without. In the summers, I do wear the thigh-high ones to Mass. Other than that, I stick to cotton slacks. I never thought I'd wear pants. I was raised to believe you must respect your gender and wear a dress. Giovanni didn't mind the pants. In fact, he bought me my first pair.

Would you like to visit China one day?

Are your parents still living?

Do you enjoy living in Ketchikan?

Mark called this afternoon. He said your grandson plays hockey. I have four granddaughters by my son Robert and a granddaughter and grandson by my son John. My daughter, Francesca, is recently married, but has had plenty of time to get something started. If you know what I mean without my saying it. I hope she wants to have a lot of children.

It is pleasant weather today. Do you have snow?

Do you know how to e-mail a photo? I do not.

This contraption of a computer is so confusing to me. I would love to see a picture of your grandson.
  Ciao, Mariangela

Suni wrote:

The sun is shining today and the temperature reached 55°. It was beautiful to sit among the Buddha and listen for Oscar's spirit in the wind chimes. The breeze was ever so slight, but enough to call him. I suppose that would sound strange to you, but my husband is in my heart wherever I go. I will never remarry, as I could never find a more wonderful man. I spend most of the afternoon in my hillside garden. Do you have a garden? Do you plant flowers or vegetables?

No, I have never been to China. I have thought about it, but don't know when I would have the opportunity to go. Dana counts on me to help with Terran and it wouldn't be on the wind right now. We get snow, but in the winter. Our summers are cooler and rain is prevalent. I am used to it.

My parents are deceased and in the Heavens. They were good people. I wish they could have met Terran. He is such a cute little boy. I do know how to e-mail a photo and I have attached one. This is him in his hockey uniform. He's quite the player. I'm very proud of him.

Ketchikan is my home so I cannot speak unkindly of it, but I have grown to love this tiny fleck on

God's earth and am happy to call it my space. I believe in the spiritual path of righteousness and this is my right place.

You brought a smile to my soul when you mentioned panty hose. I do agree with you and I do not even own a pair. I love my gardening shoes and I wear them more than I should, even to the supermarket. Terran calls them Grandma's blue rubber shoes.

Mark came by last night to take Terran and Dana to dinner. Your son seems to be a very nice man. His help on the Blue Note is invaluable. I would like to ask you some questions about him.

Has he ever been engaged?

Does he see himself getting married?

Is he serious about his life?

What does he want to do for his future?

Please understand my concern for my daughter. While she is a mother and is a wonderful young lady, she has a vulnerable side and I would hate to see her heart broken. I am aware your son plans on leaving here at the end of this month. I just worry about how Dana will do after he's gone.

Thank you for your kind answer.

May your day be filled with light, Suni Jackson

Mariangela wrote:

I understand your concern about Mark. Let me assure you, he is an honorable man. While he's remained single late in life, I believe he intends to settle down. Sometimes it takes a man longer than others to recognize the value of a wife and a home. He took the death of my husband quite hard, as I imagine your daughter did in regards to her father.

Mark has never been engaged to be married. I wish he had been to one of his girlfriends. I rather liked her. But they parted ways. Mark has immersed himself into the family business, Moretti Construction, and my son-in-law is holding a spot for him as we transition into a new phase. I'm quite confident Mark will embrace his new position.

I miss my son and look forward to having him home. Thanks for welcoming him into your house. I appreciate your generosity. How is your daughter coping with running her father's founding business? From what you have described in your previous e-mails, she seems very strong.

Warm wishes, Mariangela

P.S. Your grandson is too darling for words! He must be your delight and joy! I'll bet you love to spoil him. I know I do my precious angels.

CHAPTER FIFTEEN

"I PISS ON MASKITTAS," Cardelle declared, relaxing at the Blue Note's bar with a rum and Coke between his thin brown fingers. An insect repellent can was positioned by his right hand, and Mark watched as Card looked out for Dana. When her back was turned, he shot himself with a light spray.

"Cardelle," Leo cautioned, approaching the spot where the Jamaican sat. "I can smell that DEET crap and you're making it stink in the bar."

"Mellow out, mon. It was just one small shot. De sky is thick with dem vermin today. Wes' Nile. Bad obeah—de witchcraft."

Mark had finished construction for the afternoon hours ago, had gone home to shower then returned to the bar for some dinner and a beer.

There was always someone at the long bar to talk to. Usually Cardelle and Bear, and tonight Sam Hyatt had joined them. He sat at the end, in a conversation with a guy Mark didn't know.

Settled in on his coral-colored vinyl bar stool, Mark enjoyed watching Dana as she moved about her domain, keeping folks happy and smiling for most everyone who glanced her way.

Even him.

His body warmed whenever she met his gaze, and he couldn't help but think how sensual she felt in his arms with her mouth over his. He'd like to have her there again, and soon. He sensed from a look she gave him earlier this evening that her mind wasn't focused on tonight, but rather private thoughts of her own.

The more time he spent with her, the more he wanted to be with her every second. It was that attraction thing, so strong he didn't readily know how to handle it. He couldn't recall ever feeling such a sexual pull, such a desire to wrap all his thoughts and energy around one woman.

He liked it, liked how she made him feel with a simple look or a soft smile. Her subtle yet interested reaction to him gave him a sense of power and command. Never one to put more into flirtation other than meaningless fun, he felt a deeper intimacy here. Something rare, if ever, for him.

"Maskittas are de plague of de earth. I piss on dem," Cardelle repeated.

Mark glanced at him over his raised beer glass, an idea in the back of his head. "Card, how's that mural coming?"

"Good, mon. It is some of de bes' work I ever do. I do it on de big canvas, like you ask. It be done soon and I can bring it to here."

Mark had commissioned Cardelle to paint the historical background of the Blue Note, leaving the details to his creativity. Mark had no idea what it looked like. He trusted Cardelle to make it come alive in whatever way he chose.

"So, have you ever painted on porcelain?" Mark asked.

"Porcelain not be my medium, but I guess it could be done wid de right paints, you know."

"Then I've got another job for you."

"Yeah, mon?"

"I want you to paint a mosquito on the bottom of the two new urinals I had installed in the men's john."

Mark had finally gotten to the bathrooms, creating a handicap access in the men's room first. The women's would take longer to get in order because he had extra work in there.

Cardelle's eyes widened, two bright white moons with dark centers. "You got be kidding me, Mahk."

"No, Card, I'm not." Mark patted Cardelle's back. "Ever seen a fly on the bottom of a urinal?"

"No."

"It gives a guy an aiming point. They usually use a decal, but I'm thinking a painted mosquito would be creative."

"And dis way dem maskittas can be pissed on for real. I can do dis." He broke into a broad grin. "I dig it, mon."

Jazz musicians took the stage and began to tune up, then Dana made an introduction for the group, Catch Step, here from Portland to perform. Tonight was a special Friday, the day before the annual Summer Beer Festival and Blueberry Arts Festival, so the Blue Note was bursting at the seams. The house was packed to the roof and Mark had a hard time tracking Dana through the crowd.

Among other notables in the community, the fish processors from Alaska General Seafoods had come in to enjoy a night of quality music. As the musicians began, Sam sidled over to Mark and took a spot on the newly vacant bar stool beside him.

"How's it going, Howard?" Mark questioned as Sam settled in.

Sam, unable to contain a mocking smile, remarked, "By now, I would have thought you knew my name."

"I do, flyboy."

"What's up with Howard?"

"Howard Hughes was a pilot like you." Leaning forward, Mark snatched the last wedge of toasted bread from his order and finished the seafood dip that he'd come to enjoy. "Figured it would make for more interesting conversation."

Tight-lipped, Sam flattened both palms on the glossy bar. "Hughes might have been a pilot, but he was a deranged millionaire. Are you fishing for some cash, Moretti? I thought you had the bar's renovation cinched with your bankroll."

Seeing as Mark needed Sam to do him a favor, he didn't take the bait. Instead, he spoke to the bartender. "Leo, set up Sam with one more of whatever he's been drinking."

Leo scooped a glass into his hand and began mixing the drink, but not without saying, "Bottle to throttle."

Mark wondered what he meant and let his curious gaze slide over to Sam.

After eating a handful of nuts Sam explained, "I can't fly if I've been drinking eight hours prior to takeoff. I give it twelve—overcautious." Then for Leo's sake, he added clearly, "I don't want to lose my pilot's license."

"Nobody said you did," Leo commented, his

facial expression stoic and focused, sweat beads settled on his brow. The constant bar orders kept him moving efficiently without an extra moment to grab a water to relieve his dry throat. "It's my job to make sure everyone behaves at the bar."

"Leo," Mark called, surmising the bruiser was stretched tighter than a drum skin, "you ever laugh so hard your sides ache?"

Cardelle laughed, overhearing the exchange. "He be laughing on de inside, mon. Leo is a'right."

Harried, Dana quickly drew up to the bar and grabbed a drink order herself to bring to a table. She barely noticed him, but in those few seconds, he curved his mouth when she gave him her fleeting attention.

She moved too fast, but not so lightning fast he couldn't appreciate her sultry eyes with their corners tilted upward and emphasized with a smoky shadow. Her lip color was a ruby-pink, sexy as all hell, and it made her mouth look too kissable for words.

She had on a fitted white blouse, its top few buttons undone to reveal a lace cami beneath. Pressed black slacks hugged her fine butt and slim thighs. Stiletto heels added several inches to her petite height. Her thick hair hung loose to the middle of her back in a flat and sleek mane that made his hands itch. She'd dressed nicely tonight, and it didn't go unnoticed by him—or anyone else.

Jealousy overtook Mark each time he watched a

guy's gaze grow hot while looking at her, trying to get her attention and coax her to stop by his table. Mark had to grit his teeth, knowing that this was something she had grown to deftly handle herself.

She expertly ducked a hamlike arm trying to fit around her shoulder. She could easily sidestep an eager guy coming full bore at her for a bear hug. When a colorful innuendo was spoken, she purred an equally suggestive response that packed a dynamite wallop with the adjective "fish-brain" attached. If the men realized they were being curbed and put in their places, they didn't show it. Because each time she made another pass through the room, she received yet another pass.

All of this dipping and dodging was done artfully—at least that's how it appeared to Mark. He still didn't like the fact she had to deal with the constant attention. He would have preferred to have her to himself at his condo.

Mark's reflections were broken by Sam telling a story to Cardelle. "So he made his choice, and he chose the first love of his life—not his wife." Sam took a quick sip of his cocktail, chestnut hair falling into his glacier-blue eyes before he shook it out. "And that's what AIDs is in my world, Cardelle."

Confusion gave Mark a frown. Sam's comments didn't make sense.

"Nuh true," Cardelle responded, speaking Mark's thoughts. "Dat is bull-sheet about de AIDs."

Sam explained, "AIDs is an Aviation Induced Divorce. My friend's too in love with his airplane and he gave up his wife for his single-engine Mooney. He lives to fly and she didn't want him flying so much. Pretty sad when a man chooses wings over a woman."

"Dat be a whole heap of ding-a-ling. I be picking de chi-chi any day."

Nodding, Sam acquiesced, "You and me both, Cardelle."

Heavyset and ambling along, Bear "Roadkill" Barker returned from a trip to the men's room, elbowing his way through the crowd. He nudged a position at the bar, angling next to Cardelle. The two friends engaged in an animated conversation with humor that Mark couldn't hear over the music.

"So how's the floatplane business going?" Mark asked, making small talk with Sam. From the onset of their first meeting, Sam had been standoffish and Mark wasn't left with much room to maneuver around him.

"We're doing pretty good. I had a tourist riding shotgun my last run and I kept hearing a popping in my headset." Sam shook his head in recollection. "I started to turn my plane back because I thought I had a problem. But the idiot was popping bubbles with his chewing gum into his mike. I about shit my pants thinking I had a major engine issue."

"I could see how that'd be a problem. Guess you gotta rethink your safety speech." Mark gave him a half grin, trying to make light of the incident, but Sam didn't crack so much as a smile.

The younger man's personality was about as icy cool as the color of his blue eyes. "Hey, Sam," Mark said above the guitar notes, "I was wondering if you could do me a favor."

"Depends." Sam's face grew curious, but cautious.

"Next time you make a run to one of the inner islands, can you buy me some halibut and salmon—and whatever fish is fresh caught that day?"

"Why not just buy it here?"

"I need quantity. Enough for a restaurant."

"You planning on opening one?"

"My brother has a restaurant in Boise and some kings and halibut I sent to him went over big on his menu. He wants some more."

Sam nodded. "I could do that."

"You ever thought about flying down to the lower forty-eight?"

"Not particularly."

"Your plane qualified to do that?"

"It can fly anywhere I tell it to." Sam's brittle smile softened a little. "But that doesn't mean I'll head down south."

"Then how do you suggest I get all that fish to Boise?"

"Commercial flight."

"Is that normally how restaurant fish is shipped out of here?"

"Depends on your definition of normal." Sam's fingertips traced the moisture trail rolling down the side of his cocktail glass. "Yeah, that's how it's usually done. Alaska Airlines will fly anything on dry ice."

Mark reached for his wallet, pulling out large bills and folding them in half before handing the cash to Sam. "This ought to cover the fish, and I'll pay you for the fuel or whatever you charge."

Sam's face grew contemplative a moment. "You don't have to pay me anything else. Just do me a favor."

Mark hadn't counted on a stipulation. "What's that?"

"When you leave Dana—leave clean."

Absorbing Sam's remark, Mark didn't respond.

"Don't leave her hanging," Sam explained. "Don't promise her anything. When you go, you're gone. You won't be back."

Irritation rose within Mark. "How do you know that?"

"Because they never come back. They're just passing through for the summer. It's always the same."

Their eyes locked, a collision of ice blue and rich brown. Each glimpsed a raw side in the other's unflinching gaze. Jaws clenched resolutely, dark brows spired over eyes and neither spoke.

Mark felt foolish being taken to task by a guy ten years younger than him who didn't know him enough to peg what he'd do and not do. He was torn between calling Sam's presumption way out of line and acknowledging the possible reality of the comment. Mark had no immediate plans to return to Ketchikan once he flew home, but in the back of his mind, he'd envisioned seeing Dana Jackson again.

After what seemed an eternity, it was Mark who shattered the tense silence. "You never know what the future holds."

At that point, Cardelle sat taller when Dana appeared at the bar once more with empty glasses on a tray for Leo to load in the dishwasher. "Miz Dah-nah," he politely addressed her. "What dat you call yourself?"

"I don't know what you mean, Card," she said, moving to the stainless mini-fridge and taking out a bottled water.

"Deh are people who t'ink I am African, but I am not. I be a Jamaican mon. You not be white, not be African, not be China, but you have de look of molasses candy dis night. Ah beauty." He sighed in compliment.

A sweet utterance passed through Dana's parted lips, as if she felt the music in Cardelle's words. "I understand now." She twisted the water bottle's top off and took a drink. "I've never thought about it, but I'd have to call myself Asian coffee with a splash of cream."

Cardelle's pearly smile was a beacon of light on his rich, dark face. "Dat be so beautiful."

Dana gave Mark a glance, and he found his focus instantly lost in her and the description she'd used to describe herself. The warm toffee color of her skin did remind him of roasted coffee with cream. He liked her gracious response to Cardelle.

She was indeed beautiful. So beautiful it brought a quiet ache in him. He battled the urge to take her into his arms, hold her close and cup her face in his hands, stroking her fine cheekbones with his thumbs. Her lips were so lush, they begged him to reach out to her and crush his mouth on hers.

His eyes never left her as she moved toward Leo, traded words with him about something, then laughed. Tonight, she shone. The music, the crowd, the feeling of success all brought a soft glow to her cheeks. He loved watching her like this—unburdened from the challenging details of her life.

Her blouse clung revealingly to her small breasts, and even in the bar's foggy light, he could see the slight pulse at her throat. He knew her skin was warm, fragrant with sandalwood and wildflowers. Her mouth tasted sweet, her tongue velvety against his. He combated his desires, keeping his hands fisted on his thighs, almost cutting the circulation from his fingers.

Mark felt every nuance of her seep into his heart, his thoughts rampantly burning as he fought to gain control over where his mind was leading him. His fantasies were cut short when she was called away by someone needing her attention.

He needed her.

In her absence, the crush of air surrounding him chilled, and he missed seeing her face, her slight body, watching a smile play on her mouth.

Sam made himself scarce and Bear plopped down on the chair beside Mark. In a low voice, as if in covert mode, he gruffly offered, "I aim to help you with that fund."

Coming back to reality, Mark finished his beer and ordered a second one. "What fund is that, Bear?"

"The fire hose fund. You know, the one where we hose down that fire marshal's flame report and revamp the Note for Dana. I seen you and Sam talkin'. I ain't heard your exact words, but I can read lips. That talent comes from fixatin' on animals in the wild. I could tell you what an elk is sayin' by the flap of his gums." He scratched the side of his ruddy neck. "I'd like to contribute some cash."

"Bear, I appreciate the offer—but Sam was just jerking me on that money thing. Besides, a few bucks won't make or break me in the long run. Just the same, it's nice of you to want to help out."

Pulling out a checkbook, Bear began to stroke his signature on the bottom line. "I'm talkin' ten thou, if that'll do you right."

"Ten thousand?" Mark couldn't hide his shock. "Where'd you get that kind of money cutting carcasses?"

Bear squeezed in tighter to the small bar space, nearly nose-to-nose with Mark. In a gravelly whisper, he confessed, "A'ight, listen up . . . Nobody in these parts knows this, and I'd appreciate it if you kept it on the QT—but I'm a well-fed man. Some four years back when I was livin' in Ar-ken-saw, I picked the winnin' lotto numbers." Lowering his voice to a decibel Mark struggled to hear clearly, he went on. "I'm worth over six million, and makin' more daily on the interest."

"What'd you just say?"

"Shush." Bear made a motion with his hand, as if to lower the level on a volume. "God bless America for my fortune, as I live and breathe, it's a gift from up above. Since winnin', I came to Alaska to live my life the way God intended me, and I ain't never saw the need to let the town folks know that Bear Barker's got dough. I moved my daughter and son-in-law here and that dang butt-draggin' dawg of hers—and thems the only ones who know I'm rich. This here check be from an out-o' state bank. Look-see, I used to be a fish and game warden back in Little Rock, and when my numbers hit, I packed my gear. It always been in my heart to be in the wilderness. And one of these days, I'm fixin' on buildin' a lodge for seniors to come and fish and do all them things that folks say they ought not be doin' at their ages. If you get my drift. I'm going to have a honeymoon suite and ev'rythin'. I'm workin' on the layout in my head, but it's goin' to be a right nice place."

Mark let out a long breath. "Bear, you surprised me. Nothing much in my life ever does."

"So I'd like to contribute." He continued to fill in the blank on the check, tore it off and tucked the paper into Mark's hand. "It be our little secret. Obliged to you for lettin' me help."

Then Bear disappeared into the crowd.

Mark stayed behind at the bar, drinking his cold beer as music played throughout the building, a mellow jazz sound that he'd come to appreciate. He mulled over Bear's generosity and Cardelle's deep appreciation of Dana's beauty. He thought about Sam protecting Dana and giving him a warning. And Leo, who'd throw himself in front of a bull for his boss. Presley, who ran the kitchen with devotion.

The Blue Note was Dana Jackson, and she'd made it hers. At that moment, Mark envied her for coming into her own and taking the risk needed to bring something forward.

What did he have to show for himself?

While he'd done the grunt work, pointed fingers and told guys what to do, the buildings he'd completed had been financed by his father's company. Nobody took a stand for him—they'd gone to his dad, Giovanni, for leadership. And when his father died, that power had sort of scattered among the ranks and there hadn't been a real definitive man on the job to own it. Mark had been a fill-in, a body count . . . .

The truth of that hit him hard, and made a decision for him. He could no longer work for Moretti Construction. It was time he carved out his own niche in life, and if he failed, he failed. He had to prove to himself, his father's memory, that he was capable of big things.

"Help," came Dana's voice next to his ear, her tone distressed. *"He's here."*

Dragged out of his thoughts, Mark blinked and dialed her into his vision. Standing close to him, her arm was pressed into his shoulder as she tried to compose herself. From the obvious upset look on her face, Mark wondered if her ex-boyfriend had come to cause trouble.

Before he went into a mental state to kick Cooper Boyd's ass, Mark needed to make sure. "He who?"

"Fire Marshal Bill."

Letting down his tense muscles, Mark paused. Bill T. Kirk. The fire marshal.

Easing back onto his bar stool, then manipulating her to stand between his open legs, he whispered, "Not to worry, sweetheart." Heat surged and pooled low in his abdomen as arousal overtook most of his coherent thoughts. "He can't give you another citation. You're already working under the other warning."

She took a step back and pushed her hands against his chest. "That's not the problem. He told me without that second exit door complete, I'm over capacity. I have to tell fifty people they've got to leave." A slender hand rose to her mouth, and she absently bit her pinky fingernail.

Feeling the loss of her body heat, he stated, "Well, hell, that's not a big deal."

"Not a big deal? I've been doing a wonderful business tonight and everyone's having a great time. How do I tell someone they've got to leave?"

Thinking a second, he suggested, "You offer them an incentive to come back another night." Unable to help himself, he traced her delicate chin. "Give them a coupon for a free drink and an appetizer."

A fiery desperation burned in her eyes as she blurted, "I don't have any coupons."

"Sunshine, that's what a computer's for. We'll print some."

Fifteen minutes later, Dana roamed through the merry crowd singling out those patrons who were regulars in the Blue Note and who would be understanding about her dilemma. She handed out the vouchers and everyone who received one was happy to comply and vacate.

Fire Marshal Kirk manned the front door and took inventory of the people leaving. Each person who left brought a deeper furrow to Kirk's brow, as if he couldn't understand how she'd managed to thin her crowd and have customers filing out with smiles.

At the end of the exodus Mark approached the marshal with a smug set to his mouth.

The man was in his late fifties, bald and skinny as a tenpenny nail. Wire-rimmed glasses sat on a beaklike nose, but his eyes were pleasant enough. Everyone had to make a living somehow and Mark had dealt with more inspectors than he could ever count. Most had a personality like an empty cardboard box.

"Got your noncompliance taken care of, buddy. We'll see you for the next inspection."

Kirk nodded. "I've got my calendar marked for the twenty-first of December."

Confident, Mark countered, "Dana will be ready for you sooner than that. Come see her at the end of October."

The marshal's gaze rose toward the efficient new sprinkler system installed in the rafters. "I noticed construction has been hopping around here. Are you a new contractor in town?"

"I'm just here for the summer."

And those words, much to Mark's regret, cemented Sam's prediction.

Marshal Kirk left the bar and Mark made his way to Dana, who waited near the band platform. Once at her side, he took her hand in his and steered her into the widened hallway that temporarily led to nowhere. The speaker system didn't impact this area as loud and they were able to talk.

"He won't give you any more trouble," Mark informed her, liking the way he stood so tall and masculine over her. She seemed slight and fragile, two things he knew she wasn't, but sometimes he liked to think of her as needing him.

Genuine gratitude filled her eyes, their soft pleading melting his heart. "Thanks so much for your help."

"Anytime." His arm rose over her head and he leaned in as far as a body length away. Tucking her hair behind her ears, he asked, "So when's a good time for me to come over?"

Her gaze darted to his, and she hesitantly asked, "For what?"

He grinned and gave a soft chuckle. "You think I want you to repay me with sex."

Drily, she remarked, "That was the first thought in my mind."

"Baby, your mind is in a romance novel. When and if we do, it won't be because you think you owe me. You'll want to for no damn good reason at all other than it'll make you feel like you—"

"Stop." She'd laid her fingertips over his lips and he couldn't help nip the flesh on them just once. "Just stop. You're making fun and I'm not in the mood for it."

"Fair enough." Mark spoke through her fingers,

and she then lowered her hand. He dragged a rascally grin back onto his mouth. "So when do you want me to come over?"

"Dammit—"

"To build Terran his skateboard ramp."

Her jaw snapped shut and she took a second to regroup. "Oh, that . . . sorry."

"I promised him. When's a good time?"

"Uh, next week." Clearly flustered, she tried to collect herself. "I'll pay you for the supplies."

"Not a chance. It'll probably cost two hundred at the most. I can afford it."

"I know you can, but I can't keep accepting your help without repaying you."

He tilted his chin in a devilish manner, locking his eyes with hers. "I've already thought of something you can do."

Suspicious, she asked, "What is it?"

"I'll let you know."

Then he released her from being pinned beneath him and left her to wonder what, exactly, he had in mind.

CHAPTER SIXTEEN

COOPER LIVED CLOSE to town on 2nd Avenue. His three-bedroom house had been built in the seventies, but was well kept for an older home. The front yard had two flowering shrubs that bloomed in the spring, and that was the extent of color—aside from the russet trim on the eaves. Cooper had painted the exterior siding a hunter-green last year and had Terran help him.

He had a screened-in patio and a moderately flat patch of grass before the downhill slope overtook the property.

A previous owner had planted a now enormous feltleaf willow next to the driveway, as if to provide shade for any cars. But that was unnecessary in Ketchikan because they had so little sun, and the tree's thick and gnarled roots had buckled the cement drive to a disastrous degree, making parking a car precarious.

Dana pulled her S-10 into the driveway behind Cooper's Jeep. The single-car garage was never used for a vehicle. Cooper kept his weight set in there, among other items.

"Mommy, could Riley ever have a sleepover at our house?" Terran questioned as he clicked his seat belt undone.

He'd mentioned the sleepover thing several times this week, and it still bothered her that Tori Daniel had precipitated this never-ending discussion. No talking to Cooper could change the situation, but she planned on making her feelings known once more when she brought Terran to the front door.

"No, baby. Riley lives here with Daddy."

"But he got to spend the night that one time. How come he can't again?"

Riley the Lab had spent the night at their house. Actually two nights, just over a year ago when Cooper had to go to a training class in Seattle for the weekend. Terran had never forgotten that big dog sleeping on his bed. Dana would have liked to. The dumb thing had chewed the leg off her sofa, eaten the garbage and scattered it all over the kitchen and peed in her mother's tranquil garden, killing a rhododendron with its strong urine stream. Naturally Cooper didn't believe in neutering a male dog.

"Because he's Daddy's dog and Riley would miss Dad too much if he came to our house."

"But how come I have to miss him when I'm not here?" Then his face brightened as if he'd come upon an utterly brilliant idea. "I know! Could Riley spend the night if Dad does, too? He could sleep in my bed with me."

"That wouldn't work out."

"Why not?"

Dana held on to a frustrated sigh. Sometimes she just didn't have an answer for her son's never-ending questions.

She gathered Terran's hockey gear and his backpack while he climbed down holding a leftover take-out box of fried rice from Chop Suey. Side by side, they walked to the front door.

The early August day had been spectacular with a temperature in the mid-sixties—and not a drop of rain. Bright sunshine swathed the sky in a clear blue palette and golden-tipped clouds floated in the distance. Everyone worked outside on their yards and homes, played outside at the parks or on the water, cooked and ate outside, and went swimming at Rotary Beach—even though the water left a line of teeth-chattering kids waiting for parents to wrap them in towels. Taking advantage of a cloudless day was a priority.

Dana didn't have to ring the bell because Cooper opened the door immediately, a cell phone next to his ear. He laughed into the receiver, waving Terran in and smiling at him, then giving another masculine laugh to the caller.

She knew the person on the other end was a woman from the fish-brain way Cooper acted. Thankfully he had the good manners to quit the call, but not before saying, "Yeah, me, too."

Dana wanted to puke.

"Hey, buddy!" Cooper said to Terran, who hugged the dog's thick neck. Riley's tail wagged forcefully, thumping into the doorway and Cooper's leg as he sniffed the take-out food box.

"Hi, Daddy," Terran replied, face pressed into Riley's ear. "Can Riley spend the night at my house?"

Dana pulled her mouth into a frown. They'd already gone over this and her son was blatantly disregarding her mommy rank, going to what he considered a higher source. Cooper could be indulgent, letting Terran get his way on most things. For

Cooper, saying no was difficult. Although he could sure use the word against her.

"No, Terran," Dana replied through Cooper's response of, "I'm cool with it, but ask your mom."

Very brown eyes pleaded from her son's pained expression. A rubber curl formed on his lower lip. "I asked her and she said no."

"Sorry, bud. Then I guess it's a no from the mommy." Cooper rested his hand on the doorjamb, his gaze holding hers. She knew that look. He had something to tell her. And she often didn't like what it was.

Cooper suggested, "Hey, Terran, why don't you throw the ball to Riley out in the backyard. We're going to barbecue steaks later."

"I had chicken and red sauce with Momma and Grandma."

"Yeah, I know. But I haven't eaten my dinner yet. You can have some steak if you want."

"Can I have a Laffy Taffy?"

"You know where it is in the cupboard, bud."

Terran turned to bolt, but Dana called after him with her heart in her throat. He'd forgotten her. "Terran, baby, give Mommy a hug goodbye."

Turning, he thrust himself into her open arms and obliged her with a tight squeeze. His smooth cheek was sticky from soy sauce, his breath smelling like sweet-and-sour chicken. But she loved him all the more as he whispered into her ear, "Love you, Momma."

She gave him a quick kiss on the lips. "Be a good boy. I'll call you tomorrow."

"Okay." He bounded after Riley and the two of them took off in a run through the house.

Cooper clicked the paneled door behind him and stepped onto the porch. Dana took a step backward. She didn't want to share the same space as Cooper. A long time ago, she would have slid her arms around him. Now that thought never entered her mind.

As he slipped his hands into his shorts pockets, a muscle ticked at Cooper's jaw. "So is that Mark guy your boyfriend?"

His offhand inquiry threw her for a few seconds before she made a counterattack. "If you're still pissed at me about the call I made to my lawyer, you can forget about it." Dana stood as tall as she could with a defiant look in her eyes. There had been a time when she wouldn't have purposely irritated him, but that had been when they'd been dating. She was older and wiser now. "I'd contact him again in a heartbeat if I thought it would get you to stop. What you're doing is wrong. And I don't appreciate it for our son's sake."

With his hair freshly cut but his jaw unshaven, Cooper folded his arms over his chest. "FYI, Dana—I can do what I want in my own house."

"Not technically," she corrected with a twisted smile. "Not when Terran is staying with you—

which I still find surprising because you didn't want him around when he was a baby."

Her anger caused her to say something she shouldn't have. He had been good to their son, and had added a dimension to his life that had been missing. She supposed a part of her would always be wounded that Cooper hadn't even come to the hospital when she'd given birth. He had been so freaked out about her pregnancy, he'd detached himself from her and their son for nearly two years.

Even so, her taunt was unfair, and she owed him an apology for it. But she didn't get the chance to say anything further.

Belligerence fell across Cooper's features as he informed her, "I'm a damn good father and you know it. That little boy loves me." He raked his fingers through his hair. "I know I started out wrong, but I've made up for it. How many times are you going to throw something in my face, Dana? Son of a bitch, get over it."

"You're right, I'm sorry. Terran loves you—" she licked her dry lips "—but that still doesn't make it right when you have Tori spend the night."

"She only did it that one time. She had too much to drink and I wouldn't let her drive home."

Dana snapped, "Did she sleep in your bed?"

"What difference does it make?"

"It makes a huge difference. Terran shouldn't be exposed to stuff like this. His mommy and daddy should live together, share a life, and a house—but he doesn't have that so we've got to give him as normal a life as possible."

"You can share my bed whenever you want." A sly smirk tugged at his full mouth.

The blood pulsing through her veins slowed and her throat thickened, making it difficult to swallow. She tried to make sense over what had just transpired.

This wasn't like Cooper. He didn't make suggestive comments to her. Not anymore. Nor did he pretend to still find her attractive or intimate a desire to rekindle their relationship. His provocative words were out of left field, and she chose to ignore them.

Cooper broke the tension. "Oh, come on, Dana, it's not like I'm seriously dating Tori. We have fun together. It's no big deal."

"It is a big deal to our son when he asks me if I can sleep over, too."

Shifting his weight on his feet, he asked in a light tone, "Can you?"

Car keys in hand, she shook her head with annoyance. "I'm leaving now."

"Dana, wait." Cooper touched her shoulder as she turned to head for her truck. "I shouldn't be messing with you."

"Cooper, you messed with me for two years when you didn't want to see Terran."

"And haven't I said I was sorry, like, a hundred

times? I was scared to be a dad." His eyes expressed a sincerity that came from the depth of his heart. Truth about his feelings didn't come easily for Cooper, but she recognized it now. He truly meant what he'd said. "I love my son more than anything. And I'd do *anything* for him."

"I know that."

"So, Dana, I want to ask you something important." His hands reached for hers and she stiffened, but allowed him the liberty. "I've been thinking for a long time about this . . . ."

Dread filled Dana like a cold claw scratching her heart.

Cooper was going to say he was petitioning the court for full custody—she felt it deep in the marrow of her bones.

She'd never allow that. Ever.

"And even Terran mentioned it the other day." Cooper's voice intruded into her private hell.

"Terran asked you . . . ?" She couldn't finish the thought.

"Did he ask you, too?"

Suddenly she wasn't sure about anything. "Ask me what?"

"If he could have my last name."

Relief rushed through every pore of her body.

Cooper went on in a monotone that she vaguely heard. "He's starting school soon and he doesn't understand why he's a *J* and not a *B*. I explained to him that we weren't married when you had him.

He knew what I meant—kind of. He said that we could fix it now if he got to be called Terran Boyd."

Her ex stood before her, his hazel eyes filled with hope. Part of her wanted to say okay, sure, because Cooper had such a vulnerable expectation swimming in his gaze.

But it wasn't simple.

And the legal description on her son's birth certificate wasn't up for negotiation.

Terran bore the family name, the last line in her family tree to carry on the Jackson name. She couldn't take that away from her mom or her dad. Or her brother, Terrance.

"Cooper, I understand this has caused Terran some confusion, but he has to deal with the reality."

"But it's your reality. I want him to be Boyd. So does he."

Quietly, Dana replied, "I don't think he really knows, Cooper. He just wants us to be a family."

And with those words, a tear slipped down her cheek. She hadn't even been aware of them filling her eyes and clouding her vision. She had to get out of here before she lost it.

Times like these, life's complexities were just too damn overwhelming.

OBSERVANT AND INTERESTED in the goings-on around her, Suni occupied a plastic lawn chair in their garage with Dana sitting beside her. They watched Mark stack plywood sheets and measure lengths of wood to cut for Terran's skateboard ramp.

A cursory glance at her daughter confirmed Suni's suspicions. Everything Suni could claim as true was written in Dana's features. Her daughter's gaze constantly tracked Mark's steady movements.

Danalee's energy was both emotionally and physically in sync with the carpenter. She'd aligned her heart with his, much as he'd lined up lumber on the garage floor. Only Dana wouldn't admit such a failing—for she'd see her attraction as that.

Growing close to a man after all the pain she'd gone through with her father and brother's deaths, then the ordeal with Cooper, wasn't something Dana actively sought.

In her wisdom, Suni had known the day would come when Dana would find someone. She hadn't wished for a stream of men in and out of her grandson's life, and thankfully Dana was not the type of mother to expose him to such things.

With running the bar and taking care of Terran, Dana hadn't allowed romantic notions into her thoughts—at least none that she'd told Suni. Dana had more common sense now than to lose herself in love without seriously thinking things through.

But the truth, such as it was, still made Dana

living the rest of her life alone quite unrealistic.

Dana was lovely and young herself, and Suni was reconciled to her wanting a family of her own, a house to call hers and a husband to share her bed and entwine her mind. While Dana wouldn't discuss such dreams, Suni knew every woman wanted to love and be loved.

"Can you hand me those sixteen-penny nails?" Mark asked as he moved to gather two-by-fours.

"I'm not sure what those are," Dana replied, rising to her feet. She nosed through the supplies in plastic bags that he'd brought over.

Leaning across a sheet of plywood with his measuring tape and a pencil in hand, he said, "The boxes are marked."

Dana found what he needed and handed him the nails.

Suni inched forward in her chair to check what Mark was doing with a keen eye. She caught her reflection in a mirror that leaned against the inside of the garage.

Once belonging to the bedroom set she and Oscar shared, the mirror had cracked when she'd moved the dresser to get a necklace of hers that had fallen behind it.

She saw herself as she was. Her blunt-cut black hair rested on her shoulders, her cheeks brushed with beige-pink—the only makeup she wore. For a woman her age, she admitted she had a timeless appeal. Both classically Anglo, yet with Chinese features chiseled in her nose and the almond shape of her eyes.

What would a man her age ever think of her . . . ?

Unlike Dana, she would never know. By choice, she had no desire to ever be one with another.

"Your mother told me you built her a birdhouse when you were sixteen and in high school wood shop." Suni's comment brought a faint smile to Mark as if he remembered that birdhouse.

"Mom," Dana said in a slow enunciation, as if to warn, *Don't let him know you and his mother talked about him.*

Dana's hidden message wasn't necessary. Too late for caution, Suni already had her pressing questions answered by Mariangela. Suni looked forward to the other woman's e-mails on a daily basis, writing her back with stories of her own life. Mark had been right. She and Mariangela indeed had commonalities.

"It's not a problem, Dana," Mark said with an easygoing tone. "I told her to ask my mom anything she wanted about me."

Dana's brows slightly arched, although why, Suni wasn't sure. She'd mentioned to Dana that she'd been corresponding with Mrs. Moretti.

Crouching, Mark wrote notations on a wood scrap, then stood. The sound of his tool belt filled the small space, the metal of a hammer and other such things that hung from the leather. "Suni, I've built a lot of things."

Suni inquired politely, "How do you know how to do it without a pattern? I've sewn clothing before and without the tissue to lay on the fabric, I wouldn't have known which way to cut."

Mark swung one of the plywood sheets onto the sawhorses he'd snagged from the Blue Note renovation. "I guess I've used wood so much in my life, I just know how it all goes together. And I watched my dad build the same ramp for me in my garage. Only this one will be smaller."

"What kind of skateboard do I get him?" Dana sat back down. "I've seen a bunch at Wal-Mart. He'd like the one with the Spiderman decals."

Suni would have had to be blind as a hundred-year-old woman not to notice the way Dana furtively moved and spoke. Deliberate actions caused reactions and Dana wanted Mark to react to her—even if she hadn't realized it.

Mark tucked the measuring tape into a pocket on his leather belt. "No superheros. You can't skimp on the board—he'll hurt himself on a cheap one. The quality sold at a toy store is garbage. The wheels are constructed from poor material. The trucks are weak and the bearings freeze or the board breaks." He took a step over to plug a saw into a power cord. "Besides, I already ordered him an Element online. It's coming by two-day air."

"That was kind of you," Suni said before Dana could protest. In her pride, she would have cut off her nose to spite herself.

Mariangela had sung praises for her son's generosity. She said his reliability toward the family couldn't be matched. They called on him to help when something needed repair. He'd drywalled his brother's basement after a plumbing flood, wired new lighting in his sister's house and built a deck for Mariangela.

"I've never heard of them," Dana replied.

And that wasn't the only thing she obviously appreciated. Suni noted Dana's eyes drinking in the curve of Mark's taut behind in his jeans. The man did have a strong physical appeal, and Dana tried to keep her interest concealed. It didn't work. Suni easily caught on to her.

Mark finished marking the two-by-fours and stood. "Element's been around for a long time. They make one of the higher-quality boards. They don't have Spiderman—" he grinned "—but their graphic style rocks with crisp imagery and colors."

"Sounds expensive," Dana interjected, taking a sip from a can of cola. "How much do I owe you?"

"Dana, you don't ask a man that." Suni turned slightly toward her daughter. "Just say thank-you."

Looking pained, Dana murmured, "Um, thanks."

Then on a whim, Suni opted to reveal something about her daughter to Mark—as repayment for the tidbits Mariangela had shared.

"I'm sure you've noticed by now that my daughter isn't one to ask for help. Because of that, she hasn't practiced her thank-yous like I taught her when she was a little girl." With a softness to her mouth, Suni added honestly, "But she's appreciated everything you've done. She told me so."

"Mom, I'll talk to you later," Dana replied, her face set with a stubborn frown.

Suni merely smiled, taking her daughter's warning in stride as she put an arm around her and gave her a side hug. "Beloved mine, do not criticize the heart of help."

"Tell you what, Dana," Mark said, looking away from his jigsaw, "you can buy him a helmet, elbow and knee pads."

"Of course."

Thick black hair fell on Mark's forehead as he reached forward to engage the saw in position. Eyes down, he added without looking up, "You know Terran's going to wipe out. Don't be chasing after him with a box of Band-Aids."

"A Band-Aid won't fix a broken arm," Dana replied. Then to Suni she added, "Mark broke his arm on his."

The dangerous angle of this ramp had crossed Suni's mind, but she'd not thought that far ahead. Too interested in watching Mark and her daughter together, she said, "And we're letting him build one for Terran?"

"Mom, half the kids on the hockey team have had a limb wrapped in plaster at one time or another. And remember when Jeremy got his front tooth knocked in and he swallowed it? If he hadn't thrown up on the ice, the Tooth Fairy wouldn't have come for a visit."

Suni gave a darting glance to Dana. "Bad karma."

Mark's laughter pulled Suni's attention. His face had a cheerful look marked with sincerity. "The two of you amuse me. You remind me of my mom and sister." Then before squeezing the jigsaw's trigger, he cautioned, "This is going to be loud."

As Mark ripped a cut through the wood, Dana's eyes never left him. Her gaze caressed the flex of his upper arm, his body, the way he crouched on the garage floor, the strong line of his legs.

Suni noticed that for the first time in forever, Dana seemed happy or at the very least, content. Mark had been good for her. Suni's admission surprised even herself. She'd never thought she would find favor in a man entering her daughter's life. If only—

Shaking her head, Suni let her thoughts dissipate in a vapor. Idealizing the facts was fruitless.

Mark Moretti would be leaving in just over two weeks.

COMPLETING AS MUCH as he could on the ramp tonight, Mark called it quits. He still had to soak the plywood pieces for about an hour in order to make them flexible enough to nail on the quarter curve framework. Dana had suggested using Terran's plastic pool for this. She retrieved it from the yard. It would work great.

"Can I get you a beer?" Dana offered, reaching for the white refrigerator in the garage.

"Sure." He sat in the chair Suni had vacated about an hour ago when she'd retired to the house.

Slapping sawdust off his jeans, Mark gazed into the near-black night through the open garage door. The evening held some warmth to it, but not much. Lights in the garage's interior beamed a pale yellow into the space. They were fluorescents, not single bulbs. The one on the end was burning out, its four-foot tube intermittently flickering.

The street in front of Dana's house was quiet—the homes across the street were invisible—tree silhouettes fringed the sky, and in the distance, winking bright stars. Mark could smell the woods and the flowers drifting on the air. Alaska nights always smelled so clean.

Dana handed him a bottle of beer and he twisted the cap. She sat next to him, crossing her legs. She had on sweats and a T-shirt, simple clothing that looked enticing on her. She was so beautiful he could hardly keep from pulling her onto his lap.

Her hair fell about her shoulders in loose curls that framed her face and cascaded to the middle of her back. When she wore it like this, he imagined her just getting out of bed with sleep-tumbled hair. She gave him a fleeting smile, then stared out the garage, too.

"No rain again," he commented. "You kind of

get used to it and then it's gone and you forget how much you like it when it's not coming down."

Dana's words filled the quiet night. "Rain is a funny thing. It breeds readers, musicians or drug addicts."

Mark held on to a laugh, but grinned. "I guess that's one way to sum things up."

"Rain's just a part of Ketchikan. Like salmon dip's a part of every party or event in town."

"Is that right, sunshine? You make it?"

She grimaced. "I hate salmon dip."

"But you like salmon."

"Go figure. Sometimes things just don't make sense but that's the way they are." As she spoke, he got the feeling she was thinking about something other than a party spread. Maybe him and her and the relationship they'd formed.

Mark had never met a woman he'd started out with as friends, then grown to admire, respect and more than likely, love. If he could be totally honest with himself, he'd admit that he was falling in love with Dana. But he saved that thought for another time. He usually went in with full-torpedo charm, setting out to win a woman over; it ended up in bed, both of them satisfied, then bored with the pursuit. Chase and capture. Conquest. No sense in continuing.

But Mark hadn't felt like that around Dana Jackson. Quite the opposite. He'd taken more time with her, done more to help her life along, and had more conversations with her, than any women in his past.

One flicker of the overhead light, the span in the middle of the long tube turned to ash-gray. The two ends glowed like the cherry of a burning cigarette.

Mark mused, "I'll change that light for you."

"I can do it. It's just a bulb."

"It's not. That ballast just died."

"What's that?"

"The metal box inside the fixture."

"How do you know all this stuff?"

"I just do." He took a sip of beer, the cold beverage quenching his thirst. "So how do you know how to run a bar?"

"I had to learn."

Gazing at Dana, he contemplated asking her a question that had been at the back of his mind for some time. The personal side of it was none of his business. But he felt compelled to ask just the same. "Dana, are you and your mom financially okay? Is that why you're keeping the Blue Note going? You need the money?"

"No—no, not at all." There was a sputter to her response, but no false answer. "My dad made sure we were taken care of, and the bar turns a decent profit to fill in the cracks. Fish Tail isn't doing so hot, but we'll be okay."

"Then mind if I ask you a question?"

She turned toward him, her eyes meeting his with their green-silver color shooting straight to his heart. Her sweet pink lips were lush, the lower full and ripe. It was all he could do to remember his train of thought.

"Why not sell the Blue Note?" Mark asked, bringing his hand over his lap to disguise his lust. "Why run the place at all? It's not a great environment for you. Granted, you're hooked up with a damn nice posse of people who'd do anything for you there. It's just that you've got your boy to look after—"

"I look after him fine," she snapped, fire lighting across her oval face. Her next comment came out clipped and tactful. "You don't know me."

"I know you pretty good."

"No, you don't. If you did, you'd know what I'm thinking, what I want, what I need."

Easing back into his chair, he gave a slight snort. "I can read you better than you read yourself sometimes."

"The hell you can."

Pulling his mouth into a smile, he remarked wryly, "That's another thing I like about you, sweetart. You never mince words. Say it like it is—unless it's something you don't want me to know. And I say there's a reason you're holding on to that bar that you're not willing to tell me."

Dana turned away, stared ahead and kept her profile somber. Her brain clicked in her head, he could tell by the arch of her brow and the set of her mouth. Blinking once, she licked her lips.

He didn't say a word. He knew better than to break the spell when she was running something through her head. He sensed if she talked, she'd dissolve. Emotions would flow. She'd have to face something she'd been ignoring. God knows everyone had a ghost they tried to outrun.

Endless minutes passed and the silence wrapped around them with the weight of a steel mesh.

Mark knew he'd taken a risk, entered dangerous territory, so he backed away a few steps. "The barge coming in with the steel should be here next week, and I've got cranes coming to unload it and put things in place, but the structure won't be done before I leave. A guy named Steve from Channel Steel is in charge and I'll be in touch with him to make sure everything gets done." He drank the last of his beer and set the bottle down. "I'm going to write down all the subs' phone numbers if you run into any kind of trouble with the second inspection. I don't anticipate problems so I rescheduled Kirk to come the second week in October. Steve said he could fill in for me, but I could fly back to be here if you want."

"N-no, not a good idea."

Not the answer he'd hoped for, but he expected it.

"All right then, once you pass inspection in October, then you'll have the winter to—"

"I can't," she blurted, tearing her gaze from the vast sky and looking directly at him. "I can't sell it." Tears welled in her eyes, then splashed down her cheeks. His heart broke. "I'm afraid if I let go of the bar, I'll lose my dad and brother forever." She took a gulp of air, shaky and trying to maintain her composure. "Dad was such a part of the Blue Note and Terrance was always there. I . . . I miss them *so* much."

Without conscious thought, he slid her onto his lap and held her tight while she cried into his chest. Her fingers bunched the knit of his shirt, her body quaking with sorrow.

He cradled her next to the comfort of his body, held her close, murmured indiscernible words. Her words were smothered by tears of anguish as she confessed, "This is the first time I've ever cried in front of someone about losing my father. I didn't cry at the funeral. I just couldn't."

Mark didn't have a lot of experience offering condolences, but he managed and his efforts were from the depth of his heart.

His big hand splayed across her back, stroking, soothing. He let her cry it out, releasing the tension that had to have been hell to live with all this time.

Warm breath caught on the side of his throat where her face lay buried against his hot skin. Her sandalwood fragrance filled his nose, the texture of her hair soft against his cheek. Her arms wound around his neck, and she kissed him without apparent thought. Then once more. Then on the lobe of his ear.

His entire body came alive, his arousal swift and hard. Mark was jolted by her lips' moist warmth and the weight of her pressing into his groin. It took him only a half second to fully kiss her back, deepening what she'd started, stoking it with the desires he'd kept banked. He tried to read the unspoken thoughts on her lips, kissing her deeply, thoroughly. His hands traveled down her back, tracing her spine and finally cupping her bottom in his large hands.

He sucked in his breath as he realized she wore a thong under the lightweight sweatpants. He could only stand so much and keep from taking her here and now.

Dana angled her head to kiss him more deeply, to make his lips mold over her own. In the back of Mark's head, he thought to himself that she knew she held a power over him. She parted his lips with her tongue, to trace over his straight teeth. His mouth opened to hers and he moved to cradle her head with his hands. He wove his fingers into the silky tangle of her hair, drawing her face closer to him, pressing his lips harder to hers, meeting her tongue with his own, teasing her, dueling with her.

He would have given anything to have her naked against him. For her to feel the hard contours of his bare chest pushing against her own. His raw strength next to her breasts. He wanted to be closer to her, to be rid of clothing between them.

She trailed her fingernails over his back,

bringing a cry from his mouth into her own. He felt a sensual smile on her mouth, as if she enjoyed holding him captive. She left his lips momentarily to move her mouth over his jaw. The rough texture of his beard made him wish he'd shaved before coming over.

Once again, she brought her mouth to the crook of his neck, kissing his earlobe and brushing her lips there. He let go of a shudder as she opened her mouth to flick her tongue over that sensitive part of his ear, lightly running the tip of it into the shelled cavern.

Mark pressed her against him so tightly, he thought he'd break her in two. She returned to his lips, and he ran his hands across her shoulders and up to the nape of her tousled hair.

Everything inside him screamed one thing—take her to bed.

But he couldn't, not in a garage. And he wouldn't, not when she was vulnerable and looking for a release.

With every ounce of willpower he could muster, he set her back at arm's length away, and held her firmly. "We gotta stop this or I'm not going to be able to."

Mutely, she nodded, her face flushed and her lips parted as she panted to catch her breath.

After long seconds, she finally was able to talk. "I'm not normally like this."

Taking slow and steady air into his lungs, Mark

tried to calm his pulse. Feeling as if he were gaining some control back, he had to make light of the situation or else he could easily forget good intentions and strip her naked.

In an indolent tone, he offered, "Maybe I just have the kind of shoulder women like to cry on."

Sniffing, she questioned almost gruffly, "You've offered your shoulder before?"

"You're not the first."

She gave him a death glare. "I hate you."

Quietly, he responded, "No, you don't."

A bony elbow jabbed his ribs as she jerked to right herself and resume her own chair. Where there was once warmth and passion, the air around him was cool.

Mark wasn't real good at giving sound advice when it came to upended emotions, but he knew something from his childhood that had helped him. Regardless of Dana kissing him, of needing to be loved and feel good, she still needed to deal with her father and brother's passing, and holding on to the Blue Note wasn't the way to get there.

"Get yourself out from behind the eight ball. You'll hold on to your sadness unless you allow yourself to let it all go." Mark didn't know how else to say it. "When I was nine, my dad took me to the upper level of the downtown Sears parking garage, and he let me go down all the ramps like a maniac on my skateboard. Anyone knows that's probably suicide, but he told me to have at it and put a little faith in myself. He trusted me to make my own way. Honey, sometimes you just have to let go and put faith in yourself you'll take the right turns and not fall on your ass."

Dana pressed her fingers to the bridge of her nose, eyes half-closed. "God, you're like a wool coat. Itchy, but you wear it anyway because you know it keeps you warm."

Laughter roared through Mark's throat. "You want to wear me? Anytime, baby."

Glaring at him, she blurted, "I meant that I like having you around for comfort, but you chafe my skin, Moretti." With a groan, she spoke into her hands. "What am I going to do with you?"

"I already have an answer for that one."

CHAPTER SEVENTEEN

"I'M ENGAGED!" Presley announced with animated excitement, flashing a princess-cut diamond engagement ring at anyone within a five-foot vicinity.

Dana moved in for a closer look, nodding her approval. "So he finally asked you."

"Can you believe it?" Presley's cheeks blushed, pink and rosy from happiness. Her light-colored hair was swept into a loose ponytail with silver hoop earrings dangling from her earlobes. "Last night he said he wanted to have a DVD night and I was like, 'There's that new Brendan Fraser mummy movie playing at the Coliseum. We never do anything anymore but stay at home,' and he just told me to quit complaining, sit on the sofa and he'd get the popcorn. So I sat there, steaming like a plate full of clams, when he pops in *Platoon*, a movie he's seen, like, a hundred times and I hate it. I was ready to just go home when he said to have some popcorn, and when I put my hand in the bowl, there was this jewelry box and I was like, what is this and then I pulled it out and when I opened it, he got down on one knee in front of the couch. He asked me and I was speechless. All I could hear through the pounding of my heart was rapid gunfire blasting from the television. He asked again and I . . . and I said yes."

Breathless from her story, Presley put a hand over her heart; of course the hand with the diamond ring.

Dana was the first to congratulate Presley with an affectionate hug. "It's about time," she said, kissing her friend's cheek.

"Don't I know it. Holy cow, I can't believe I'm engaged!" She studied the sparkling ring once more, extending her hand in front of her for a wide-angle view. In the bar's daylight, the diamond wasn't huge by any standard, but the setting was classic and simple. Much like Presley Reid.

Leo and Walt gave her clumsy hugs, as did the kitchen help staff and a few others in the Blue Note who'd heard her news.

Cardelle, who was off work today, wore an untucked printed floral shirt and jeans with leather thongs. "Let me see dat ring."

Presley flexed her wrist for Cardelle to have a look at the gem.

Rather than give the ring a nod, he pulled out his jeweler's loupe to examine it while it was still on Presley's finger. "Dis is ripe."

"Ripe?" She jerked her hand away. "Is that bad? Did he get me a CZ? Ohmygosh. I have a fake!"

"No, mon. All's good. Ripe—it mean everyt'ing well. Very nice diamond. He did not buy it from me, but dat is a'right. You come see me for his wedded ring, gal, and I give you discount."

Giddy, Presley nodded. "I will, Cardelle."

With a broad grin, Cardelle exclaimed, "You know what, mon, we should have a big bashment for dis gal before I fly back to Jamaica at de end of de next month."

"You can use the bar for an engagement party," Dana said as she watched Mark put the last of his tools away to head out for the day. She tried to stay focused on the conversation at hand, while also trying to concoct a reason to talk to Mark before he left. "I'll pick up the tab on everything."

"That would be awesome," Presley squeaked. "Well, I guess I better come back to earth and start cooking for the night." She gave a few excited hops in place. "I can't believe it! I just can't."

The small group disbanded and some resumed

seats at the bar while others paid their tabs and went on their way.

When Dana looked around, Mark had already gone. Disappointment fanned throughout her and she couldn't help feeling lonely.

The hour crept toward midafternoon. Cardelle had arrived at one o'clock to talk to Mark about something. The duo had been in a huddle by the band platform with tape measures. They'd spent a long time in discussion, then laughed and gave each other a firm pat on the back. Why she had no clue. She couldn't ask Cardelle about it now—he'd gone, too.

Cardelle Kanhai had turned out to be a joyful regular in the bar. This had been his second summer season in Ketchikan and she hoped he'd return next year. His humor and his dialogue were much appreciated around here. The white smile on his dark face could light up the Blue Note on a dreary day. Card used his wisdom in many a discussion, interjecting a conversation with a sense of humor that was different from anyone else's in town. The absurd thing he'd done in the men's room was testimony to that.

Dana had had to close the men's restroom last week for repairs. While the area was out of commission, men had to use the ladies' facilities, and then for three days this week, she'd had to divert the women to the men's room while an "under construction" sign had been posted on the ladies' restroom. Keeping tabs on what gender went where had required someone on staff to stand in front of the restrooms, much like a traffic cop.

Glad that the ladies' restroom would be finished soon, Dana was ready to get things back in order.

Propelling herself toward her office, Dana had several things on her to-do list. She had decided to have T-shirts printed with the bar's name on them. Many of the other local places had done that with great success. Tourists liked to purchase items that reminded them of where they'd been on vacation.

She was also looking into changing the Blue Note's business cards to have a free drink coupon on the reverse side. She could give these cards out to the area hotels and lodges. This was something she would consider and bring up at the next employee meeting and get other input and ideas from everyone else.

She went into her disorganized office. She had to get end-of-the-month payroll ready, and there were quarterly tax documents to look over.

Dana had barely sat down at her desk when Mark knocked on the office door frame.

"Since when do you knock?" she questioned with a smile, glad to see him appear. Over the past few days, she'd acknowledged to herself that she liked seeing him around. It felt good to be honest with herself.

He tilted his head, the black hair at his nape touching his T-shirt collar. "You got me there."

His handsome face never failed to appeal to her. His brown eyes had a powerful presence that could be serious or joking. He could use a haircut, but she enjoyed the length at his neck and the way he styled the top away from his forehead. The wristwatch at his wrist glinted as he lowered his arm from the door and came toward her.

"So, I have something for you," he said, his voice low and very seductive.

She played along, her lips forming an easy smile. "And what's that?"

Leaning over her, his callused finger traced her cheek where it curved at her ear. "The finished ladies' john, baby. Come on, let me show you."

With a good-natured frown, she rose from the chair wearing flat shoes—an everyday pair she kept beneath her desk. Standing at her full height, the top of her head didn't even meet Mark's chin.

Following him out of her office, she remarked, "I've heard a lot of come-on lines at this bar, but one about new johns has never been on the list."

"I'm an original."

"That you are," she said beneath her breath.

She followed him down the hallway and toward the restrooms, thinking this was an odd thing to be doing. A "reveal" on a new women's room? She'd already seen the men's. It had pretty much looked like it had before aside from the fresh coat of ivory paint with recently installed handicap rails. New flushing wall fixtures *and* the tiny mosquitoes painted by the drains. Cardelle had done that, the funny man. He'd taken his hate of mosquitoes to a different level.

Mark had put Cardelle up to it, and her response had been to shake her head and roll her eyes the day she'd seen what they'd done.

Now at the closed restroom door, Mark approached behind her, hands on her shoulders. She gave an involuntary shiver, his chest against her back and his groin just at the top swell of her bottom. A thought hit her hard, and she quickly stopped it as Mark slipped his hands over her eyes.

Her fingers curled around his wrists in protest. "What are you doing?"

"I'm going to surprise you."

"I don't want to be surprised in a bathroom."

"This isn't just any bathroom now, sweetheart."

He inched forward, taking her with him and entering the small restroom. She could smell paint and something else. Flowers? She wasn't sure.

Slowly, Mark lowered his hands and her eyes blinked to adjust to the light. Standing in the center of the room, she gazed at the walls and couldn't believe the beautiful transformation. There was no other word for it.

The ladies' room in the Blue Note looked sophisticated.

Aquamarine-blue, silver and gilt, with antique ivory, comprised the color palette. The countertop was a gorgeous silver-and-black granite with elegant freestanding washbasins. The faucets had large handles for hot and cold, a retro feel in their design. Large mirrors with ornate scrollwork gold frames had been mounted at the sink level. Vanity lights reminded her of glass fixtures from the twenties. Petite glassware lined a shelf along the far wall and held burning candles, their floral fragrance lending a sweet aroma to the room.

Glancing all around to take it in, she couldn't believe it.

"Mark, I don't know what to say," she finally breathed. "I had no idea this is what you were up to. I figured the plumbing was shot or something."

His head dipped toward her, his mouth close to hers. "That's the whole point. I wanted you to be surprised."

"I am." Then she slipped her arms around his muscled body and brought herself next to his chest, embracing him. "Everything is so beautiful and it feels like New Orleans. I love it. Thank you."

He felt warm and solid, and safe. Her hands rose softly to his shoulders. The stubble of his beard caught in her hair when he laid his chin on the top of her head. He smoothed her hair, keeping her close.

The moment was tender, new. She took just as much pleasure from this as she did from his kisses. She loved how he felt, smelled. She loved his breath on her neck. She loved . . . him.

Her fingers toyed with his shirt's cotton sleeve, her mind and thoughts scattered. She couldn't deal with this now. She felt a troublesome ache deep in her heart, in the very core of her body. It was something she'd never felt before. She didn't recognize it, nor did she want to.

Pulling herself together, she straightened out of Mark's hold and sucked in a breath. "So what's the plan?"

"Plan?"

"The other night you said you had something in mind when I wondered what I should do with you. So what is it, Moretti? You've done all these wonderful things for me and the Blue Note—things I couldn't possibly repay. What do you want from me?"

He rested his butt against the bathroom counter, arms folded across his broad chest. "Your time. Twenty-four hours."

For all the niceties he'd done, she wished she could just say sure, no problem, I'm yours. But the reality was, she had a business to run. She was entering the weekend, this being Friday. Tonight and tomorrow night were her busiest nights. "I'm sorry, I can't. I have to work and I get Terran Sunday night."

"Leo can keep an eye on things. I'll pick you up on Saturday and I promise that you'll be back Sunday night to get your son." He pulled her toward him, nestling her between his open thighs.

His firm mouth covered hers, kissing her gently, coaxing a response from her, softly nipping her lower lip.

Of their own accord, her arms rose to circle his neck and bring him close.

"For what?" she questioned against his lips.

"You'll see."

THE DRIVE TO EAGLE POINT would take less than an hour.

Mark came for Dana just before noon on Saturday. He set her overnight bag in the truck's bed, along with his ice chest, some things of his own and fishing gear.

They got under way, passing through town and the cruise-ship crowds that collected on street corners to cross and hit the shops. A trolley tour slowed traffic down to a crawl and impatient drivers gave a honk to get things going.

"So whose cabin is this?" Dana asked, facing his direction.

"Bear hooked me up with a guy he knew. The owner only comes into Ketchikan for the summers, but he had to bail earlier than normal this year so the place was vacant."

She teased, "Convenient."

"Honey," he said, slanting his gaze over her. "I told you this is no ploy to get you into bed. If I was angling for sex, I could have had you long ago."

She shot him a twisted smile. "So what are we going to do?"

With a low laugh, he advised, "Everything."

"That's a wide-open door."

"I'd say so."

Once they left the city streets for the two-lane Tongass Highway, they passed industrial buildings, then the airport and Wal-Mart. Beyond that, the scenery turned lush and green.

As the miles added up, they traveled through small clusters of residential areas where homes were built close to one another on addresses ending with "berry." Beyond that, a sign for Port Higgins appeared.

Mark didn't turn down that road. Rather, he continued and kept going around the point. Thickly wooded trees lined both sides of the road in places, while in other spots, the expanse of the ocean was clearly visible. They passed Salmon Falls and continued a short way beyond, then Mark turned onto the private lane that Bear had directed him to.

Once at the end of the drive, Mark turned right, then left and found the cabin nestled in a thicket of wild brush and cedar trees. A ray of sunshine cut through the clouds, shining brightly on the cabin's roof.

Mark turned off the engine, climbed out of the pickup and opened Dana's door. Tiny gravel crunched beneath her feet as she stepped down and took everything in with an expression of awe.

"This isn't a cabin," she said, her eyes drinking in the home tucked into a lush landscape of ferns and late-blooming flowers.

"I'm thinking that, too," Mark replied. When he asked Bear if he knew of any rental cabins available for a night, he assumed the grizzled guy would set him up with something rustic but cozy.

Mark took her hand and they walked toward the porch. Her fingers were slender and warm, and he absently rubbed his thumb over her knuckles. He enjoyed even the simplest of things when it came to Dana—just holding her hand made him happy.

The vacation home's beautiful wood siding had been stained a reddish-brown and it had a steep pitched roof to handle a heavy snow. A second story with south-facing dormers rose above the large main level with a multitude of uncovered windows to enjoy the views.

The tall chimney implied a fireplace in the master bedroom on the upper level. Intricately built, a deck wrapped around to the back of the house, flower baskets adding splashes of late summer. There were containers of potted ferns everywhere along the deck rail, as if someone regularly maintained the property.

"Are you sure this is the right place?" Dana asked, glancing over her shoulder at the private beach. They had an unobstructed view of a weathered dock and boathouse. In the distance, the water sparkled like silver flakes under the intermittent sun breaks. On the other side of the channel, a mountain range still dusted with snow in the higher elevations looked like a postcard scene.

"We'll know if we're at the wrong house if this key Bear gave me doesn't work."

Mark slipped it into the brass lock and the door opened. As he swung it inward, he murmured, "Damn," beneath his breath.

As far as homes went, he'd seen finer interiors and expensive luxury throughout. But considering he hadn't anticipated this, he was thrown off by a nice surprise.

Inside, the hardwood maple floors were stained in gunstock, the smooth walls a cream, and the wood trim around the windows the same medium shade as the flooring. The home opened to the great room with a vaulted ceiling and exposed beams. In the kitchen, a breakfast bar and black leather-covered chairs awaited guests. Grayish-green granite counters added richness and texture to the cooking area, along with the stainless-steel appliances.

Throughout, the owner had decorated with things that were representations of Alaska. Bear wood carvings, fish artwork on the walls along with spectacular landscapes, and a scrimshaw dolphin mounted on driftwood sat in the center of the ebony-tinted dining table.

In a quiet voice, as if she were in a library, Dana suggested, "We better not touch anything."

"Yeah, just each other," he couldn't help saying.

She shot him a frown, then smiled. "So what are we really going to do here?"

Taking her hand toward the stairs, he said, "Have fun."

MARK COOKED HER DINNER. She couldn't recall ever having such a luxury and she enjoyed every minute of it. He'd parked her on the tall leather chair at the breakfast bar, then put a wineglass in her hand. She relaxed, watching as he prepared king crab legs and a grilled halibut steak. He'd brought food in a cooler he'd stowed in the back of the pickup. He'd had the foresight to buy groceries and comfort treats such as breakfast pastries from Safeway. She knew their bakery well and must have told Mark once in passing that she liked their Danish.

The timer went off on the baked potatoes and he pulled them out of the oven.

"Where'd you learn how to cook?" she asked, after drinking more of her Merlot.

Settling the lid on a steaming pot of boiling water, he replied, "I don't know how—but who can screw up grilling meat and reheating crab legs? Throwing potatoes in an oven is a no-brainer, and the salad I'm serving comes out of a plastic bag and we've got bottled dressing."

She gave him an appreciative smile. "The gesture is very nice just the same."

"Flattery will get you whatever you want."

The response spoken in a silky tone was about as suggestive as any could get. Dana thought back to their tour of the upstairs. The master bedroom was grand yet simple. Everything had been done in ivory and beige tones. The duvet cover, the pillows, curtains and wall paint. Light wood furniture completed the room. The king-size bed's headboard rested in the dormer alcove, and with a small sitting area by a fireplace.

Mark had taken her into the room, then said it would be hers while he occupied a smaller bedroom on the lower level. Surprised by the arrangements, part of her had been disappointed. She'd never tell him that, but the moment she set eyes on the room, she imagined him lying in that beautiful bed with her, falling asleep and waking next to him.

Those thoughts were very dangerous and idealized—just romantic daydreams. But she couldn't help it. The years had crept past after Terran's birth and she'd gone without intimacy for such a long time. She missed being held by a man, his body next to hers as she fell asleep. She longed for a strong arm to drape around her middle and keep her safely tucked in.

So when Mark said she'd use the room alone, those visions all but faded. She should have been grateful for his respect. But she'd half hoped that things would have been different.

Mark finished their dinners and he took the plates to the table in the middle of the common area so they could sit and look out the windows. The views were spectacular. She hadn't been away in forever and this reminded her how much she loved Alaska and its untamed beauty.

"Mmm," she murmured after taking a bite of halibut. "It's so good."

"My brother's got the talent for cooking, not me."

"You did very well." She tried her baked potato, enjoying its texture. "How's his restaurant doing?"

"Great. I sent him a bunch of fish the other day. Sam flew it into Ketchikan for me. I shipped several insulated boxes overnight." Crab cracker in hand, he gestured toward the dinner on his plate. "You know, someone ought to look into flying fish directly from the islands and bypassing commercial flights. You could really do something with that. I know my brother would welcome a weekly shipment."

Mark cracked the crab legs for her and gave her a small dipping bowl of melted butter. The indulgence was a sweet treat. So good.

The wine Mark had brought was even better, accompanying the meal perfectly. Everything had been taken care of. All her comforts had been thought of.

Staring at her plate of yummy food, thinking

about how pretty the house was, and how peaceful the surroundings, she recognized how lucky she was to have met Mark Moretti.

"Thank you," she said, sincerely meaning the gratitude. Her eyes met his, and she grew lost in their warmth. "You have done so much for me." Emotions colored her words, and maybe it was the wine, or her feelings for Mark, but she felt an overwhelming stab of longing for the man. Longing that wasn't merely physical, but more. A tangible flutter on her beating heart.

She was in love with him.

How it had happened, she didn't know. She'd fought against it. His charming behaviors and witty comments early on had made it easy to resist him. But by degrees, he'd gotten to her. Each day, her heart wore down more and more until now he'd entered it, filling her soul and making her love him.

She wouldn't tell him. There was no point.

"I wanted to help you, Dana. You're a good woman." Mark's voice intruded on her private thoughts.

She knew her face didn't reveal any of her inner turmoil, and she continued to eat without giving away her true feelings. There was one thing that could cement her decision to remain silent, and that was to get him to talk about his life in Boise.

Far away from Ketchikan.

"So what will you do once you get home? Have

you thought about it at all?" she asked, composure in her voice.

Leaning casually into the chair back, Mark loosely held on to the stem of his wineglass. "I'm quitting. I'm going out on my own and leaving Moretti Construction."

She nodded, a flicker of unwanted hope and wonder. What did that mean in the long run? A change of location?

"I'll start up my own company in Boise— nothing that would compete on the same level as my family's business. I've got a lot of connections and it shouldn't be too hard. It's time I made my own way."

Her mute response came in the form of another nod. Stupid of her to even remotely wonder if he'd leave Idaho. Of course he would remain. It was his home.

"What will you do?" Her voice was in control and quiet, as if she were conducting a job interview with a potential employee. He'd never guess her misplaced disappointment as she internally chided herself over it.

"Small projects on the commercial end of things. Remodels. Renovations. Hell, I could even contract with Moretti on tenant improvements."

"Sounds sensible."

"Kyle's not going to like it. Neither will my sister. But this is what I want."

Unspoken words touched her tongue. They

remained there only long enough for her to taste melancholy before she swallowed them. She wanted him to say he wanted her. But she'd be fooling herself. He was like most men who came to Alaska. They loved the wild beauty of the land and the thrill of hooking a big fish. But in the long run, Ketchikan wasn't for them.

They had lives back home, jobs and families.

"Then I know you'll make a success of it." Her appetite wasn't quite as strong, but she managed to finish her dinner and truly enjoy Mark's efforts.

There was no point in growing dejected about anything. She'd known from the beginning that this is how things would end.

After dinner, they washed the dishes and Mark told her to grab a coat so they could sit outside as the sun went down.

The days were growing shorter, a sign fall and winter would be approaching in the coming months. Cruise ships would stop coming to port at the end of September. Tourists would quit flocking to town in big groups. Orca Corn—the kettle corn shop—had closed for the season, the open-air trolleys suspended business, the Lumberjack show discontinued until next season, the cruise-ship jewelry stores boarded their windows and left and the locals would settle down for the winter.

Dana always looked forward to the winter, to days sparse with sunshine and snug evenings inside. She took the time to get caught up on her life with fewer distractions and a slower pace.

Only right now, she didn't want today to end. She wanted the minutes to crawl by so she could savor every last second.

It was quiet and peaceful by the dock as the sun set that night, and Dana breathed in the tranquillity as if it were an elixir. Orange streaks shot through the clouds, a fiery show in amber and gold.

Mark had built a fire in the fire pit, and dry wood crackled with sparks flying into the ever-darkening sky. Gray smoke curled and its tangy scent seasoned the crisp air.

He'd positioned an Adirondack chair beside hers. They sipped wine together and lost themselves in distant thoughts.

Dana didn't need to talk. She felt too much churning inside to let anything come out of her mouth. She just accepted the moment for what it was. Very nice. Relaxing. Comfortable. Tranquil.

She never thought she'd admit this, but for all Mark's flippant commentaries and silly nicknames for her—he was the sweetest man she'd ever met.

When the fire began to die and an evening chill crept in, Mark doused the embers and they went inside. He flipped a switch on the gas fireplace and they cuddled next to each other on the sofa.

His large hands moved over her back and brought a light rush of warmth through her body. She felt content at the deepest part of her spirit.

She looked into Mark's face. A wayward lock of hair had made its way onto his forehead to rest above his black brow.

She ran her fingertip through it, then down over his nose and over his lips, caressing his face with her hand.

"I like to look at you," she confided in a soft murmur.

"I like you looking." His voice, a husky whisper, brought the tingle of gooseflesh across her arms.

Tracing his jaw, she said, "You smell good."

"Campfire smoke." He grinned, his white teeth giving him a disarming charm. "Manly and badass. I smell like Bear."

She playfully punched him in the shoulder. "You do *not* smell like Bear Barker."

With her face tucked into the crook of his shoulder, he stroked her hair and tucked it behind her ear. She touched his face, cupped his angular cheek.

She felt his teeth clenching down hard, as if to keep him from kissing her. In the worst way, she wished he would, but she sensed he struggled to repress an urge to do something other than keeping her folded in his arms.

He moved his hand up her back and wove his fingers into the thick depths of her hair, toying with the nape of her neck. A shiver caught her in its hold, the delicious sensation warming her. Sitting next to him, she didn't feel short. She fit easily into his arms, the side of her breast crushed into his chest. Where they touched burned her, making her want to feel his naked skin pressed next to hers.

She felt as if everything inside her turned to liquid heat and she wanted nothing more than to take his hand and bring him into that lovely bedroom upstairs. To lead him away . . . away from the responsibilities they both had . . . and to a moment where nothing else mattered but the two of them being together. Intimately fulfilled and satisfied.

She looked up and saw the intensity in Mark's eyes.

He wanted her.

Her pulse grew rapid. She glanced briefly at the stairs, then licked her dry lips with her mind racing.

"You ready for bed, princess?" he asked, his voice throaty and deep.

She couldn't speak.

He took her hand in his own. Strong and warm. Then led her to the base of the stairs. He propelled her onto the first step, turned her toward him, and she discovered her face nearly at eye level with his. He made a slight graze of the skin at her throat that sent her pulse spinning as he lowered his lips over hers.

She would have stuck herself to him like a sheet of wallpaper, but he didn't give her that kind of kiss. Instead, it was gentle and warm, light and no more than a whisper of lips on top of hers. Her knees felt as if they would buckle and she'd collapse if it weren't for gripping on to the railing with one hand.

Then he backed away from her, his brown eyes storming with emotions she recognized as her own. Desire. Lust. He wanted her so badly it consumed the features on his face to twist his mouth and draw his brows into a firm frown. Yet he didn't suggest that they . . . that he . . .

"Good night, Dana. Sleep well."

A long while later, she lay in bed alone, restless and confused. Why hadn't he come upstairs for her by now? Slipped beneath her sheets and made love to her?

As more time elapsed with her thinking about it, her ardor cooled and she felt disappointment well within the pit of her stomach. While she was burning over him, he was trying to make this easier on both of them.

No sex, no entanglements.

No foolish hearts, no heartache.

She would stay. He would go.

The setup had been defined long ago.

Why then did she want things to be so different?

Damn him . . . he has more control than I do. Even when I want to love him, I hate him for being stronger than me.

CHAPTER EIGHTEEN

MARK DIDN'T WAKE HER. Not yet. He held back, watching her sleep.

Veiled sunlight slipped through the closed wooden blinds to bathe Dana in a soft light. She slept on her side, arm around a feather pillow and one shapely leg on top of the covers. Her thighs were made for a man to run his hand down, her calves and feet so petite. She had polish on her toes, something that surprised him. She didn't seem like she'd bother with such a thing. But he liked the pink color. Very sexy.

Her black hair tangled around her neck and face, revealing a narrow face. He loved her hair. It was beautiful. Just like she was. Parted, her lips showed a small glimpse of teeth. Her eyelashes were long and dark.

It had almost killed him to walk away from her last night. He'd wanted more than anything to have gone to bed with her. Even just to hold her. But he knew better. Knew it wouldn't have only been a time for holding and snuggling. God help him, he was no saint. He would have tugged the clothes right off her sexy body and buried himself deep inside her.

Inasmuch as he wanted her, that's not how he wanted things to end for them.

In the past, sex had been uncomplicated. He'd

had no qualms about walking away from a casual relationship.

But his feelings for Dana went way beyond casual.

He'd fallen in love with her.

He couldn't remember what she'd worn, how her hair had looked, what she'd smelled like . . . it had just started to happen. He began to fall and he'd wanted to keep falling. Even knowing that it wouldn't come to anything.

Most of the night, he'd lain awake and he'd thought about what he could do, how he could change the course of his life to fit her in. The only answer he ever ended up with was moving here. She'd never move to Boise, never take Terran away from his father. He admired her for that, loved her for putting her son first.

So that left Mark having to make the choice.

If it were only that simple.

He had nearly thirty years invested with Moretti. Disengaging himself from the company wouldn't happen overnight. While the Grove Marketplace had been completed, there were never-ending side projects within the infrastructure. Improvements, repairs and management. Going forward would take time. His brother-in-law couldn't be left totally high and dry. There were complexities to a buyout that needed to be addressed.

Mark owned assets in the company, stock, and

he had a lot of joint collateral. He had potential earnings to start a decent company of his own.

Quietly approaching Dana's slumbering form, he paused. He hated to wake her up. The digital readout on the clock indicated just a little past five in the morning. In order to do everything today that he'd planned before driving back to town, they had to get started.

Mark reached for her bare shoulder, laying his hand over her bed-warmed skin. "Dana . . ."

She didn't move.

Firmer, he gripped her shoulder—fighting off the urge to crawl into the plush bed next to her . . . and damn his plans and damn the resolve he had set for the both of them. "Dana, it's time to get up."

"Whhhh," she moaned, rolling onto her back. Her arm rose and she rested a wrist over her forehead while mumbling, "What? What time is it?"

"Around five."

"Five? You've got to be kidding me. I never get up this early . . . up too late." She scrunched the covers and grabbed them with her as she changed direction and ignored him.

Slowly, he tugged the covers, pulling them down. They slipped from her fingers and revealed that she wore a flesh-colored knit tank top and pink cotton shorts.

That's all it took. He was instantly aroused and fighting a war within his conscience. Biting down, he went against every carnal instinct he had, and with a final jerk, he rid her of the covers, then turned away to flick open the blinds and let the new sunshine cast her in its yellow light.

"Dammit, fish-brain. Are you insane?"

A smile settled on his lips, and he was glad she had her spunk back. Irritation fell across her face as she sat upright in bed, a mess of black hair falling about her shoulders.

"You've got fifteen minutes to get dressed, sunshine. Coffee's on and your Danish have been calling for you."

Brushing her hair from her brow, she grumbled tartly, "Fifteen minutes? For what? I thought this was a rest and relaxation trip."

"Wrong tour company," he called over his shoulder as he left the bedroom.

HE TOOK HER BOTTOM-FISHING, something she hadn't done in too many years to remember.

Mark killed the motorboat's engine in a stream-fed bay, then dropped the anchor. Densely populated cedar trees marched down the steep shale walls, leaving little view of the land. There was very little bank, just the opening of the stream that rushed over rock in a spill of white foam.

As the boat bobbed and the wake behind them died, the quiet was beyond belief. Nothing stirred. Barely any wind on a day that promised to include an expanse of sunshine.

When they'd left the rental house and gotten into the boat, the trip across the channel had been freezing. The air slapping them in the face had a bite to it. Dana was bundled in a coat and knit hat. Thick-soled hiking boots had kept her feet warm. Mark had told her to pack a pair.

"How long's it been since you went fishing?" Mark asked, his sunglasses blocking a direct view of his eyes.

"Terran and I fish off the Blue Note's patio."

"That doesn't count."

"Then it's got to be at least six or seven years."

"You remember how?"

"Of course."

Mark moved in the boat, arranging gear and tackle. "You know how to use one of these?" he asked, showing her a pole and reel.

"Yes."

"I figured you would."

Then Mark spent the next few minutes preparing the bait and handing her a pole ready to use. She took a spot at the side of the boat.

"I could have put the bait on myself," she said, stifling a yawn. She hadn't slept well last night and two cups of coffee accompanied by a sugared pastry hadn't done the trick in fully waking her.

"I know you could. I was just being a gentleman about it."

She gave him a look.

He cocked his head, a mock-wounded furrow to his brows. "You don't think I'm a gentleman?"

Turning away to cast, she replied beneath her breath, "After last night, I do."

She should have been grateful he had more fortitude than her. But amid her tossing and turning, she damned herself for wanting to forget common sense and jump him.

The fishing pole was basic and functional. It had a level wind reel. Drawing back, she gently let the bait into the water, keeping her thumb on the clear line as she let it out. She knew from experience if she didn't, she'd have a ball of line at the bottom of the boat.

Sitting on the cushioned back of the passenger seat, she tried to keep warm while also marveling at the spectacular scenery. Over the waterfall, crows danced in the current, then lighted. From the east, a mature eagle soared high. Its white head darted about, quite alert. In the solitude of their spot, Dana could hear the *whoosh* of its wings cutting through the morning air.

The boat hardly bobbed, the world around them alive with the purity of nature. Mark had taken a spot behind her, his line lowered on the opposite side of the boat.

"Why do you think they call these an Ugly Stik?" Dana asked, referring to her fishing pole's brand name.

"Because if they called them Pretty Sticks, no

guys would buy them." Mark's voice was rich and deep, its timbre vibrating through her. "Plus they're guaranteed if they break."

A nibble had her reeling in her line. But when the baited jig came in, it remained empty of a fish. She cast once more.

The companionable silence between them didn't feel awkward or uncomfortable. Dana liked that they could sit here and just enjoy the day without complexities.

"There's more coffee in the Thermos," Mark said, rebaiting his hook and wetting it once more.

"Thanks. I'm okay for now."

Settling back into his perch on the seat, Mark said, "So who'd you used to go fishing with?"

"My dad."

"Tell me about him."

Tell me about him. No missing a beat, just a simple statement.

Dana paused. Mostly people talked to her about Oscar, retelling tales of him at the Blue Note when he'd been there to run the bar himself. They had stories about Oscar's saxophone playing, hearty laughs about the times Oscar told jokes. Memories of Oscar bringing in his son as a toddler to show him off. Then his precious daughter, Danalee.

Inwardly, Dana smiled.

So many with so many stories, she'd hardly ever had to pull any from her own memory well.

"My dad was kind. He'd do anything for

anyone. He had a great smile and an assured laugh. He always greeted everyone with a friendly handshake." Dana gazed at the spiring mountains, their peaks crested with spiny trees. "Daddy had Southern charm. He'd cook every once in a while, but not often. When he did, he made a batch of biscuits like you wouldn't believe. So light and flaky in your mouth you'd swear you were biting into a cloud." Wistful and with a reflective tone, she went on, finding it almost cathartic to talk about her beloved father. "On Halloween, he dressed up and took me and my brother trick-or-treating. My mom stayed home to pass out the candy."

Mark's motion behind her as he reeled in to check his bait didn't stop her train of thought.

"He liked to play Scrabble. He was good with words. Oh, and he wrote music. Nothing that ever got published, but he liked to mess around with notes and sounds, writing down scribbles on a yellow legal pad. Sometimes he'd improvise at the Note and play a tune that had been floating around inside his head. Then the next night when someone asked him to play it again, he'd say, 'Sorry, it's gone with the wind.'" Forgetting the fishing pole in her hand, she twisted around to glance at Mark for a moment. "And he drove his Mercedes into the ground. He loved that car."

Mark's back remained to her as he made an adjustment to his line. She faced forward once more. "He'd take me and Terrance to the movies with Mom. He'd treat us with popcorn and candy when she said no—it was too close to dinnertime or our bedtime." Dana vented a soft smile. She'd forgotten about that. Funny how she was adamant about no candy for Terran when she loved that her father bypassed her mother's boundary and let her have it. On a sigh, she added, "He liked to go fishing. . . ."

"I know," came Mark's hushed response.

She didn't bother to ask him how. Anyone in town who'd been a friend of Oscar Jackson knew he'd enjoyed the outdoors and fishing.

A pull on her line caused Dana to become alert and she reeled in the catch. Flopping and splashing, an orange rock cod had taken the bait and was now being scooped by the net Mark held under it.

"Nice," he complimented, removing the hook from the fish's mouth. "You got first fish."

"Liar," she stated simply. "I felt you moving around behind me. You've already let two go."

Mark's mouth broadened and he let rip a roar of laughter as he hunkered back down on the seat. "You got me there, sweetart."

"I knew it. I have mother's eyes. You know what they are?"

"You've got gorgeous eyes."

"Not the color," she quipped with exasperation, baiting her hook with a salmon head piece.

"Mother's eyes are the ones in the backs of our heads. We see everything even if you think we aren't looking."

"Is that right?"

"Moms carry a lot of responsibility."

"I wouldn't have said otherwise."

Dana cast and sat back to wait for a bite. Fighting off a damp shiver, she meant to ask about the Thermos. But looking in the cup holder, she found Mark had poured a hot coffee for her when she'd been baiting her hook.

"Thanks," she said, grateful for his foresight.

"No problem."

Sipping the warming beverage, she said, "So tell me about your dad."

Mark repositioned himself, patient and reflectively gazing at the sparkling blue-green ocean. "He was a good guy. Respected."

Another eagle flew overhead, this time dipping into the trees and coming out on a rocky cliff to overlook the water.

"He was pretty old-school Italian. A man's man."

Either lost in thought or thinking of things about his father, Mark grew quiet.

Dana prodded him. "What favorite memories do you have of him aside from skateboarding?"

After a moment, Mark said, "Listening to him talk at Sunday supper. Our family usually ate together once a week and my dad had a lot to say about life. He was pretty damn opinionated, but it was who he was. I guess I didn't take all his advice the right way. Maybe I should have more often."

"He was proud of you?"

"Yeah. No question. He was proud of all his kids. For a guy who immigrated here with just change in his pocket, he did real well for himself. There was a time just before his death that things got dicey on a project when he had to take on a silent partner. Shocked the hell out of us when we found out after he died, but the Grove got completed and we made money in the long run. I wish he could have known that things turned around and the partnership with Kyle Jagger was a good one."

"My mother believes that even in death, the ones we love know what's going on with us on earth."

"My mother believes that feeding people Italian meals is love."

Dana gave a half smile. Their mothers were different, yet they had somehow connected via e-mails. Her mother had told her that Mark's mom was a very nice lady. For Suni to say that meant a lot. Dana knew her mother could be a little judgmental. When first meeting Mark, Suni hadn't gone out of her way to extend him a welcome. Now she had changed her opinion, which Dana was glad for . . . for all the good it did. Mark may have won Suni over, but he wouldn't be around to ride things out for the long run.

The morning wore on, and she and Mark reeled in rock and ling cod, halibut and red snapper. They filled the boat's receiving tank, and as noon approached, Dana realized she was starving.

"What'd you pack for lunch?" she asked, nosing around the cooler he'd brought.

"Nothing."

He'd been so good about planning for everything, she swallowed down on the gnawing in her belly and resolved not to think about food.

Peaceful and quiet, Mark continued to fish while she'd lost the desire to reel any more in.

She gazed at the pristine rain forest, its greenery so lush and awe inspiring. Blue, like the sea, reflected in the sky. She'd have to bring Terran here. He'd love it. Cooper tended to do the camping and fishing thing with him, but there was no reason she couldn't do the outdoor stuff, too.

"You about fished out?" she questioned in what she hoped sounded casual as she sidled next to him to check his progress.

At ease in his position, reel in hand, leaning against the seat, he shook his head and her stomach growled. He seemed in no hurry to get going. She'd kill to have that other pastry in her hand.

"Well, if we don't get a move on soon, you're going to have to build a fire, clean one of those fish and cook it so I can eat. Aren't you hungry?"

"Starving."

"So then why—"

In the distance, the whir of a plane's propeller infiltrated their tranquil little spot. Shading her eyes against the glare, Dana's gaze narrowed in on the floatplane heading in. It descended toward the bay, then touched down with a skim of its pontoons. This far away, and with a direct line toward them, she couldn't make out the side colors of the plane or its tail identification.

"What's that idiot doing landing here?" she wondered aloud.

Mark rose to his feet. "Bringing us lunch."

It was then she recognized the aircraft as one of her own. Fish Tail Air and with Sam Hyatt piloting.

Sam taxied closer, then cut the de Havilland Beaver's single engine. Drifting toward their boat, the aftermath of his landing disturbed the placid water, causing it to lap on the boat's hull and plane's pontoons.

"You found us," Mark said, grabbing one of the anchor ropes from the wing.

"I know the area well." Sam had opened the cockpit door and hopped onto the plane's pontoon. "Hey, Dana."

Surprised over Sam's unexpected landing, Dana said, "Hey, yourself."

"I brought what you asked me to," Sam said to Mark. It felt a little awkward to Dana to have the two men on amicable terms. Not that she minded. It was just that since Sam's brother had died with her father and Terrance, Sam had taken on a huge burden of guilt and considered himself her watchdog. He hadn't allowed any men to get close to her, at least not without feeling out their intentions. For a time, she wondered if Sam cared for her beyond a friend, but she'd asked him and he'd told her he didn't want her to hurt anymore and he was compelled to make her life easy where he could.

Mark slipped his sunglasses onto the crown of his head. "You deliver, Sam. Thanks for doing this."

"You paid me to."

Laughing, Mark said, "Had to cover your gas and the cost of the food."

Sam reached inside the airplane and produced a couple bags from Burger Queen.

"You have got to be kidding me," Dana exclaimed, her mouth watering.

Bracing his hand on the airplane's wing, Sam replied, "That's what I thought when he asked me to bring the stuff."

"Burger Queen isn't open on Sunday," Dana stated. The aroma of cheeseburgers and fries almost had her tearing into the bags and devouring the contents.

"I know," Mark said, setting the food bags on the driver's seat of the boat.

Sam shrugged. "Never in all the years I've lived in Ketchikan has Burger Queen turned on the fryer on a Sunday, but this loco boy did something to sweet-talk them into it. I wouldn't have believed it if I hadn't picked up the order myself."

With a sly wink toward Dana, Mark didn't elaborate on how he'd managed to pull it off. She was mulling over the possibilities, when his playful mood dimmed.

Not anticipating his next words, they took the edge right off her hunger. "Your twenty-four hours are over, Dana. You can head back with Sam—take the lunch."

She didn't readily reply, eyes darting to Sam and wondering if he knew in advance he might transport her back to town if she said so.

Mark continued, "Or you can hang out here and I'll have you home by five to get your son. But I did say twenty-four hours and I want to keep my word."

Inwardly at war with her thoughts and emotions, Dana had to get a grip on the situation. Flying to Ketchikan would take twenty minutes from takeoff to touchdown. Driving back would be under an hour. She didn't want to be in this position. Damn Mark. He had taken care of everything else; why hadn't he just decided on a detail like this? As long as she was home in time to get Terran, what harm would a few more hours be?

Glancing at Mark, she drank in his handsome features. Brown eyes, compelling mouth and strong nose. The build of his shoulders, so broad and strong. She felt Sam's eyes on her as she thought over her choices. In the end, she did what she'd wanted to do from the beginning.

"I'll stay," she said, the words hardly a whisper.

Sam gave her a short nod. "Good enough. I'm out of here."

He got back into the cockpit and Mark pushed him back with a shove of his boot. Then the plane's engine fired into a roar and Sam was gliding over the water and took off. Only when he was a speck in the sky did Dana look at Mark.

She found him staring at her, a fond smile on his mouth. "I knew you'd stay."

"Me, too," she admitted, seeing no point in playing coy.

Those thoughts were far behind her.

THEY WERE PACKED and ready to return to town, their bags laid at the house's front door for loading into the pickup. Mark made a quick check of the time on his watch. He had an hour before they had to leave, and he still had something he wanted to show Dana.

"Come on," he called impatiently to her from the living room, waiting for her to descend from the second-story master bedroom. She'd gone upstairs to make a final check to see if she had forgotten anything. Why did women always have to do that? Men could care less if they neglected to throw a sock or their toothpaste in their bag. You could always buy more.

He repeated his call for her. "Dana, let's go."

"What's on fire?" she questioned, stepping down

and leaning over him on the landing. Her hair flowed over her shoulders, and the angle afforded him a dead-on view of her cleavage. Her breasts were small and round and, pushed together like that, distracted him.

"Me," he replied, then brushed off the thought. "Don't stand like that. Come here."

She finished taking the steps and met him. "Are you ready?"

"I've been ready for ten minutes." He took her hand and pulled her through the open door.

"Where are we going?" she questioned, keeping her stride as broad as his as he walked up the drive, cut through a small path in the woods and made it to the highway.

"You'll see," was all he told her. Glancing in both directions for traffic, he deemed it clear and took her to the other side. A smaller path connected at the road and wound upward through the hillside of ferns and lush, low-growing greenery.

Hiking single file, Mark held branches aside so Dana could be behind him and not get hit in the face. The climb wasn't too bad, a few hundred feet, before it leveled out and connected with another trail. Towering on either side, cedars rose tall and stately. Spongy ground buffered their footsteps.

The air came alive with scents that intoxicated. Mark pulled in a deep breath and let the coolness swirl inside his lungs. White flowers blanketed a tree copse where sunshine rained through the leafy canopy. He'd gotten lucky that it hadn't rained yesterday or today.

"Where are we going?" Dana asked once more.

"Don't you ever want to be surprised and enjoy the thrill of it?"

"No."

Mark let loose with a sharp laugh of enjoyment. He got a kick out of her sometimes. "Dana baby, you sure are a different kind of woman. I guess when a man proposes to you, you'll want to know the details in advance so you aren't taken off guard."

The comment slipped past him before he could stop it.

But he heard Dana suck in her breath as she stopped dead in her tracks and called after him, "You aren't . . . are you?"

He hadn't meant the comparison—it had just happened.

"Not today." Mark turned toward her, regret a bitter taste in his mouth. "Look, I'm sorry. It was a bad example."

"Why would you think about a proposal?"

"I have a sister. We talked about stuff like that. I guess it was in the back of my head for some reason."

Mark reached for Dana and took her slender hand in his own, giving her a slight squeeze. "We're almost there. Come on." With a gentle tug, he pulled her along and she kept by his side.

They hiked several hundred more feet up the maritime cliff face, winding through a thick tree stand. Then the terrain opened to reveal a sunlit clearing scattered with blue flowers.

Nudging Dana beside him, he took her to the edge and smiled.

"Some view, huh?"

And it was. The ocean stretched before them in an undulating shimmer of the sky's cloudless reflection, verdant forests jutting from various fingers of craggy land. The Alaskan coastlines weren't known for straight sandy beaches. They were diverse. Dense at some points, rocky at others. Always a collection of trees to frame the edges.

In the far distance, a white-and-blue-hulled cruise ship slowly motored its way down the channel toward Ketchikan. Even this far away, its colossal size was emphasized in the scale of things.

The view was beyond perfect, and the clarity of the day made it even better. A panorama to rival any postcard in the gift shops.

Mark put his arm around Dana, bringing her close.

Dana's gaze drank in the scenery. "How did you know about this place? I didn't, and I've lived here my whole life."

"Jeff Grisham showed me from the air when Sam flew us to Red Creek Lodge. We passed right over it. Must have been fate the rental house turned out to be near here."

"I don't believe in fate," she said, her voice barely audible as her arms slid around him with a fraction of space separating the curve of her breasts from crushing into his chest. A heaviness held his heart, his throat having a hard time working to swallow. "But I do love the view very much. And it would make a nice proposal spot for some woman."

Her mouth was inches from his, her moist breath caressing his lips. Though her body didn't touch his, he could feel the heat from her limbs. The air around her seemed magnetic, drawing him to her. He couldn't deny that he had wanted to hold her like this in the worst way ever since coming here.

"Why didn't you come upstairs last night?" she asked, her chin tilting so she could stare into his face.

A current of heat ran through his every nerve ending. His jaw tightened and it was all he could do not to burn his mouth over hers and kiss her. "Because everyone who loves you—your mother, Leo, Sam . . . they made it clear I shouldn't break your heart."

"It's my heart. I know how to protect it. I'm not stupid."

"Honey, I have never for a moment thought you were."

Dana whispered against his cheek. "Good."

Mark's breath jerked from his chest as she circled his neck with coaxing arms. Molding against him, she gave herself to a kiss that smoldered like the heat that joined metal. Her tongue traced the moist fullness of his mouth, then explored the recess within.

She had to stand on tiptoe to reach him and he lifted her into his arms, her legs wrapping around his thighs. She blended into his strong embrace, melting against him. His fingers burrowed into the depths of her hair as he kissed her back.

They kissed as if thirsting, their mouths greedily taking from the other and shattering the foundation of the resolve Mark had fought so hard to keep in place.

An aching need coursed through his veins and he could hardly keep from laying her on the ground and taking her.

He let her mouth trail over his cheek, brushing kisses on his eyelids and brows, finally settling on his earlobe. Torturous ecstasy rose from the depth of his throat.

It was too much.

Setting her feet back on the ground, he took a step back. As he clawed for breaths to fill his lungs, he raked his hand through his hair.

Dana struggled to stand firmly in place, a mixture of desire and an undefined emotion filling her eyes.

Clearing the hoarseness from his voice, he said,

"We gotta be heading back if you're going to pick up your son on time."

She managed to give him a half nod, then she turned and was heading down the trail. It was several long heartbeats before he was able to move without an aching tension in his muscles.

When he caught up to her, neither of them said anything the rest of the way down the hillside.

CHAPTER NINETEEN

"HEY, MARK? Can you sleep over?" Terran asked, out of breath, wearing his helmet, knee and elbow pads. He'd been practicing on the skateboard ramp, showing Mark what he could do. His little boy face was bright with excitement.

Dana quickly curtailed that idea. "Terran, quit. Enough with the sleepover talk. Stop asking me."

Mark shrugged with an amused expression. "It could be fun, Mom."

His smile told her he was messing around. Ever since they'd come home from their weekend getaway, many of Mark's comments had reverted back to a casual flippancy, as if he needed to begin the process of distancing himself from her.

She should have been grateful he was making an effort to end things this way.

"See, Mommy—Mark wants to." Terran painted a knowing smile on his mouth, a toothless one.

Feeling powerless to stop his burning desire for

other people to spend the night with him, Dana cooked up a quick idea. "Terran, I think it's time we had a big boy sleepover here. We'll ask the entire hockey team to come and bring their sleeping bags and we can have hot dogs and cupcakes."

"For real!" he exclaimed, and jumped up. "And my daddy, too, 'cause he's my hockey coach."

Discomfort held Dana in a cold grasp. Mark's eyes caught hers and she looked away, unable to meet his. "No, baby. We've already talked about this. Daddy has his own house."

Dejected, Terran's chin drooped. "Okay . . ."

Mark cut the grim mood as he said, "Come on, Terran, let me show you how to do something really cool."

Dana watched as Mark took the skateboard and went up the ramp, flipped the board, then came back down. The stunt was quite impressive. For a man his age, his athletic agility was apparent and he impressed her son beyond measure.

"Now me, Mark!" Terran squealed, wanting to try the feat himself.

Patiently, Mark spent the next thirty minutes trying to prepare Terran to make the run in the same way. Of course Terran bit the dust more than he succeeded in getting the board to the top and turning it back down. But that didn't bother her son. From the red cheeks on his face, he was thrilled just to be hanging out with a big guy and being taught a new daring stunt.

Terran had always enjoyed a physical challenge—he got that from Cooper. Funny how there was something in a child's genes that paralleled the adult.

At that thought, Dana, who stood back watching, wondered if Mark would ever want children to raise. They'd not talked much, if anything, about it. Part of her was curious, another part told her to let the subject go. It was futile and proved nothing beyond her own simple curiosity. And maybe . . . hope.

Hope that possibly Mark wanted children and to be a parent. To be a father. But really, it didn't matter.

Dana didn't want to acknowledge the limited time they had left so she didn't. Instead, she smiled and clapped, encouraging her son to do his best while holding back when he fell. She refrained from helping him dust off. Any effort would have been a waste of her energy anyway. The spry little boy was up again barely after he'd smacked down.

Terran's bedtime approached and she gave him a five-minute warning for time to call it quits. As if he would never have another chance to use the ramp, he tried to get in as many attempts as possible at making the twist at the top.

He never succeeded and fell at least a dozen more times, his slender body sliding down the plywood slope. But he gave it his best shot, and she had no doubt he would eventually master the trick and command it.

She handed him a cold box juice from the garage refrigerator and he plopped down and huffed and panted from the exercise. He knew how to unfasten his helmet, and he did so. Then he greedily drank from the straw, sucking apple juice into his mouth.

"Can I get you a beer?" she asked Mark, who just inspected the ramp and checked the joints to his satisfaction.

Facing her, he declined. "I'm good. I have to take off soon."

Regret momentarily held her in its clutches. She hated that he had to go, but knew that tomorrow was a big day at the Blue Note for him. The fire-exit steel was arriving, and he'd secured a crane to swing it into place.

Dana ruffled her son's sweaty hair, then smoothed its shaggy length away from his fore-head. He needed a haircut. "Finish your juice, baby boy, then it's time for your bath. You have to get to bed real soon."

Terran smelled like damp clothes and marsh-mallow cookies.

As he removed his elbow pads, he asked, "Mommy, what time do I have to get up for kinny-garden?"

"No different than you do now."

"Doncha want to set an alarm clock?"

"You won't need to, baby."

"I don't mean me, Momma, I mean you. You don't get up too early."

Dana traded glances with Mark, and she felt heat spread over her cheeks. "I will when you start school. I'll be there every day to drop you off."

"And Daddy will be there the other days, won't he, Mommy?"

"Yes."

"Who's going to pick me up?"

"Grandma or Daddy or the kids club bus—but just for a short time until Dad can get you when you're at his house."

Terran's face grew serious as he processed the complexities of it all. "Okay," he finally said, apparently whatever thoughts had been moving around in his head geared into place. Then to Mark, "Hey, Mark? Can you come over tomorrow to show me how to do this some more?"

Once again, Dana traded a look with Mark. She interjected, "Baby, Mommy has to work and I won't be home until really late."

"But Mark could just come over."

"That won't be—"

"Sure, if it's okay with your mom. I can come by after dinner and we'll work on it."

Terran snapped his attention on her. "Doncha think that'd be okay?"

Dana kept her eyes on Mark, a tenderness inside her heart she would never expose, for it was too fragile for her to make sense of it. "Sure. If Grandma doesn't have any problem with it, that would be fine."

That Mark Moretti would want to spend his Friday night at her house with her little boy, showing him how to do a skateboard trick, touched her more dearly than anything.

THE THREE FISH TAIL AIR floatplanes had to be relocated and the waterway in front of the Blue Note cleared to make room for the 175-foot-long barge. Before a hazy dawn broke the sky, a tugboat arrived, towing the barge carrying three sections of prefab, powder-coated steel to be assembled on-site.

By six o'clock, Mark's adrenaline had been in overdrive for an hour. With a meticulous and efficient pace, he guided the crawler crane along the pier. Its driver slowly proceeded forward, the sixty-five-ton crane moving like a snail. Its boom was in a safety position as it finally came to rest in front of the bar and the barge. A smaller crane with a man-lift basket had been employed, as well.

People who'd been out early or eating breakfast at the Pioneer Café, or who started work in nearby businesses, strolled over to have a closer look at the goings-on.

Moving the heavy lengths of steel off the barge and into place at the Blue Note was a drawn-out process that interfered with the bar's normal business hours. Mark sent word to Dana that he'd get things wrapped up as soon as possible, but wouldn't rush the job as things got under way. One wrong move could mean disaster.

By evening, the barge had been unloaded and was on its way. Then, as the sun still hovered rather high in the Alaskan sky, Sam Hyatt had the floatplanes taxi back into place to resume business operations the following morning.

Throughout the day, Dana had come out of the Note to check on the progress of things. Mark had little opportunity to engage her in conversation. Days like this were stressful and he had to stay on top of every maneuver. Only once did he allow himself a moment to enjoy the way she looked when she approached him.

He never failed to appreciate how beautiful she was, how with just one look, she could make him feel as if she only smiled for him. Her eyes always captured his attention and made him long to pull her into his arms and kiss her.

But the day didn't lend itself to thoughts beyond that, and he quickly moved on to complete another phase of the project. When he finished for the day, he popped into the Blue Note to find Dana, but found her occupied with Friday-night customers at the bar. He turned around without talking to her and headed for his truck.

Mark, dead tired from a day that had stressed his muscles and patience, wanted nothing more than to head to his condo, shower and relax the rest of the night. But he'd made a promise to a little boy, and he intended to keep it.

What Mark didn't expect was to find a message on his cell phone from Suni Jackson saying she'd prepared a dinner for him and that she and Terran would be waiting.

Arriving for a late dinner, Mark was led inside by Dana's mom and ushered directly into the kitchen. He felt sort of out of place by the fact that he was here without Dana. Never expecting this scenario, he tried to reconcile to the strangeness of it.

The house smelled like roasted meat, onions and garlic, and his stomach growled.

Terran, excited to see him, bolted from his chair. "Mark, do you want to skateboard now?"

"Terran, sit back down," Suni chastised, quilted pot holders in hand as she moved for the oven. "Dinner first. Afterward you can play with Mark."

Mark held on to a smile. He hadn't counted on being anyone's playmate, either. But the prospect of showing Terran some more moves gave him a second wind. The boy was eager to learn, and he had no fear. He was a fun dude to be around, and Mark began to relax and settle in at the table.

Suni pulled out a roast beef with carrots and potatoes that had cooked in its own gravy. He couldn't remember the last time he'd had a home-made pot roast.

"Smells awesome," Mark said, sitting politely.

"All men bow to the robust flavor of a pot roast. Oscar did, for sure."

Mark had never bowed to any meal, but he'd been thankful for quite a few. He slid his napkin onto his lap. "Thanks for having me over."

"Thanks for coming," Terran piped in with his adultlike reply. Then he gave Mark a toothy grin and a giggle. "Hey, Mark, do you like Spiderman?"

"I've seen the movie."

"My bed's a Spiderman." Half off his chair, he asked, "Do you want to come see it?"

"After dinner, Terran," Suni remarked, placing the pot roast in the table's center. To Mark, "Can I get you something to drink?"

"Whatever you've got handy. A pop would be fine."

Terran lifted his glass, milk sloshing over the rim. "Grandma, can I have a soda pop?"

"No, you need to drink your milk."

"Make mine a milk," Mark offered, changing his mind.

Terran's nose crinkled, as if he were happy the two dudes at the table would be chugging milk together.

Mark drank in the boy's face, studying it and smiling softly to himself. While he resembled Dana with dark hair, the shape of his nose and brows, his features, mostly reminded him of

Cooper. The slant of his eyes wasn't like Dana's at all. More Anglo. His color was neither Cooper's nor Dana's, and Mark thought back to the photo of Oscar Jackson and thought he could see a similarity now.

His bright and inquisitive face never seemed to let down in its innocent pursuit of things that made him smile. Even now he found pleasure in stirring his knife in his milk to make a pretend chocolate drink.

"Terran, knife out," his grandmother cautioned before turning toward the stove. Terran eased back in his chair, wrinkling his face and making himself look like a baboon with hunched shoulders and silent grunts.

Mark almost laughed hard and loud, but didn't think Suni would appreciate it.

Suni brought gravy to the table, then sat. Unlike Sunday supper at his parents' house, the meal wasn't begun with a blessing and the rancor of a dozen voices fighting to talk first about the goings-on in their lives. Rather, Suni had Terran send his empty plate her way and she served him a modest-size portion.

Terran talked about kindergarten and starting school—he held up fingers—in four days, not counting five and six days for Saturday and Sunday. He was very excited about it and wanted to know what Mark liked best about it.

"You know what—I really don't remember."

Mark knew that he had been a hellion in grade school, but going back in his memory to age five was digging rather deep. "I was young a long time ago."

"Yep, you look pretty old." Terran talked around a roast beef wad stuffed into his mouth.

"Terran, too much," Suni chided, her brow arched in disapproval.

With one enthusiastic swallow, Terran finished the meat in his mouth, then cut into another slice. "Hey, Mark, have you seen that movie *Cars*? Do you like Lightning McQueen?"

"I haven't seen the movie, no."

"My momma bought me a Lightning McQueen backpack for school. All my stuff is in it. I had the list for *J* instead of *B*."

Mark didn't follow that line of thought, but he didn't question it. The rich flavor of onions and carrots, potatoes with gravy, tasted great and he realized he'd been really hungry. "Great dinner, Suni. I appreciate it."

"It was the least I could do after all you've done for Dana."

"No problem."

Suni's warm brown eyes and her bobbed hair made her seem regal in a way. She had perfect posture and a demeanor that rarely changed in temperament. From his brief time with her he knew that what you saw was what you got. She didn't put on false airs, and when she gave a compliment, it was genuine and heartfelt. "It's a big deal to her. She told me everything you've done and all the help you've offered. Not many men in today's society would be so generous."

Her flattery made him slightly uncomfortable. He was no hero by any means, but Dana had dealt with his innuendos well and that gave him all the more fondness for her. Plenty of women wouldn't have put up with him, for he had a way of turning things around to make light of situations when he shouldn't.

Overall, he'd call himself a good guy. Someone who wanted to make a difference in a life. And it had been his luck to find Dana, a woman who needed him. Mark had enjoyed the privilege of helping her, and he'd leave here a better man for it.

After dinner, Suni refused Mark's offer to help clear plates and he went into the garage with Terran to practice on the ramp and the skateboard.

After many runs on the ramp, Mark asked, "Terran, want to see something way cool?"

The boy nodded vigorously.

Mark took the skateboard, then found a plastic storage bin on one of the many shelving units. He removed it, carelessly glancing at the label— Christmas Ornaments. Placing the box in the middle of the empty car stall, Mark set the board on the concrete.

"Whatcha going to do?" Excited, Terran came toward him.

"I'm doing an Ollie."

"What's that?"

"Something that I hope I don't break my arm on."

"Mommy says skateboards break bones."

"Yeah, well—could be. I haven't done this one in thirty years."

Mark positioned his feet on the bolts where the trucks were to keep balance. Posture not too straight, not too low and crouched. A check of his balance, arms out, then the back foot on the tail and he pushed forward, gaining a slow speed. Just before the bin, he made a tricky weight shift and hopped the box just like that, landing directly back on the skateboard without missing a beat.

"Son of a gun," Mark breathed, surprised he could still do it.

Terran stood there, short legs spread apart, and echoed, "Son of a gum."

Mark smiled. "You know what?"

Terran looked up, face focused on him. "What?"

"You're a pretty cool dude."

Puffing out his slight chest, he replied, "I know."

Then Mark grew unexpectedly reflective. This was probably the last time he'd see the boy. He extended his hand and, rather than hold it out for Terran to shake, he crouched lower and raised his palm for Terran to give him a high five.

Mark rose. "You be good in school for your mom, okay?"

"I will."

"No joking around."

"I won't."

"No talking back to the teacher."

"Nope."

"No chasing girls."

He giggled. "No way."

"No making fake dog-do from playground mud."

Brown eyes alert, he closed in and said, "Huh? How do you do that? Did you ever?"

"Yes, but I was a rascal."

"What's a rascal?"

"A kid who's always doing something so other kids will laugh." Lowering his voice, Mark pretended that the following information he revealed was a covert operation. "I'll tell you how to make the do—just as long as you don't leave any on the hallway floor."

"Okay."

Mark enlightened the little boy, then his grandmother came to tell him it was time to get ready for bed. Mark followed him inside and, before Terran climbed the stairs, he turned around with a big smile. "Mark, can you come back over tomorrow?"

The request cut Mark and he hated the answer he'd have to give. "No, Terran. I'm going to be heading home soon. I live in a place called Boise, Idaho."

"I don't know where that is."

"You have to take an airplane to get there."

"So you won't come over again?"

Mark's answer stuck in his throat, and he had a hard time forming the word with Terran's wide-eyed gaze on him. Suni came into the room and waited, her expression curious, as well.

"I don't know," Mark finally replied, unable to give an answer either way.

"Terran, I'll be up in a minute. Pick out your pajamas."

Taking two of the stairs, Terran paused, then came back down to give Mark a hug around his leg. "You rock and roll, Mark. Thanks for my skateboard and stuff."

Briefly placing his hand on Terran's head, Mark managed to say, "You're welcome."

Then Terran bounded up the steps without a backward glance.

The emotions filling Mark's chest were foreign to him. He could relate to the warmth and longing that pertained to Dana. She was a woman he had feelings for, felt a love toward. But with Terran, the pang next to his heart was more of regret that he had no son like this. No boy to do things with, to teach, to hang out with.

Collecting himself, Mark closed off his features so Suni could read nothing in his eyes. He managed to nod to her, then find his voice. "Thanks for dinner, Suni."

She approached with a slight hesitation, as if

she weren't quite sure what to say. "May your spirit be well, Mark. I thank you for all you've done for Dana. You came at the right time on her calendar."

Mark shifted his weight. "Suni, with all due respect, there is no right or wrong time. Dana's going to be all right from now on."

"I know this as well and don't disagree. Hardship and pain are a part of life and unavoidable, but I've been waiting for a long time to see a smile on my daughter's face again. Having patience is the most written-about practice in my belief. You have rewarded my patience with your kindness to Dana, by giving her the gift of heart." Then Suni reached for the coffee table where silk cloth wrapped an object. She handed it to him. "So I have a gift for you."

He pulled the silken red drawstring and lifted out the noisy object. They were wind chimes with a set of four ornaments. The chimes sounded serene when he ran his fingertips across them.

"Brass chimes," Suni said, noting the etchings on them with a point of her hand. "Each one represents goodwill and prosperity. They're called *grading* bells and are found in Buddhist temples."

"Thanks, Suni. Very thoughtful of you." He lowered the bells back into the bag and pulled the string. "I'll hang them off the patio in my backyard."

"A wise choice." Then awkwardly, she began to

say something, but paused. Then after a few seconds, she spoke again. "Dana was very lucky to have you cross, then enter, the path of her life."

"I was the lucky one. She's an amazing woman."

"You love her."

The declaration threw him slightly off-kilter. While the words were true, he'd kept them to himself. Hearing them gave them veracity that he couldn't deny. He responded truthfully, "Yes, I do."

"Will you tell her?"

Mark withdrew into himself. "I don't know."

Suni's dark eyes were like pieces of stone. "Should the winds blow you back this way, you would always be welcome at our dinner table. Your mother, as well."

"She'd enjoy that."

With a subtle shake of Mark's hand, Suni said, "Safe travels if I don't see you again."

CHAPTER TWENTY

"Look what I am seeing with mine owned eyes. You come to buy de bling, mon." Cardelle came around the counter of Jewels of the Nile to welcome Mark.

"You wore me down. You're a good pitchman, Card."

"I be dat, fo' sure." Cardelle wore a white dress shirt and a colorful blue-and-yellow tie without a coat. Tailored black slacks emphasized his lean muscle structure. "What can I show you?"

"Pearl necklace for my mom."

"Beautiful. I have jus' de one for you." Cardelle wound his way through the shop with its glass case assortment. High-intensity minilights illuminated the selections and Mark glanced at the many gems. It struck him that Dana didn't wear much jewelry of any kind. He knew what she liked, and it was a different kind of fashion statement.

Mark stopped at the pearl case while Cardelle opened it with a key anchored to a plastic, spiral-curled chain. "I'll see you at the bar at eight o'clock. We'll install the canvas after Leo sends Dana into the kitchen."

"Dat is de plan. It be my best work. I am happy, mon. Life is good."

Mark still hadn't seen the mural Cardelle had painted for the Blue Note. Described as one long piece on free-form canvas, Card had Mark build a frame and mount it on the wall with very specific measurements. Card would bring in the canvas and they'd attach the length of the picture on the frame already in place.

"Dis here." Cardelle laid out a pearl necklace on a black velvet pad and noted the uniform pearls in a simple circle. "Elegant for de mothers." He beamed. "And I give you discount—even d'ough you not be one of de cruisers."

Mark laughed. "Sold."

· · ·

HER BABY WAS a big boy now.

Dana fought back the tears that every mother experienced on the day they released their child to the care of others: kindergarten.

She and Cooper opted to drive him together rather than put him on the bus his first day. Cooper had picked them up at nine-thirty. Terran's school day would be from ten o'clock in the morning to three-twenty in the afternoon. It seemed an eternity to Dana, but Terran was ready to go.

He'd been awake since seven, dressed in his favorite shirt, hair slicked in a neat part and Velcro straps on his shoes in place. He chowed down pancakes Grandma made him, then brushed his teeth in a sloppy quickness. Then he'd positioned himself at the living room window looking for his dad's car to pull up, anxious to be off.

The school, its colorful paint, beckoned like an easel, waiting for students to lend their creativity and presence.

The stuffed backpack strapped to Terran's back made him seem smaller than ever. Terran grabbed both their hands. Cooper's left. Her right.

The trio walked into the school.

They found Terran's classroom and the teacher was warm and friendly, so very welcoming. When everyone arrived, she introduced herself, then gave them a classroom tour and made a quick trip to show them where the restroom was. Once they were in the hallway, Dana reached for Terran's hand again. Only he pulled away this time and it choked her up beyond measure.

Then the teacher said it was time to say goodbye to moms and dads. Dana held tight on to Terran, giving him a hard squeeze.

"Mommy . . ." he said in a muffled smother, trying to wiggle free. He seemed unfazed by the whole process of leaving his mom and dad and being with a teacher. He stood before them, a little man, and said, "It's okay, you guys. I'll see you later."

Dana slid her gaze to Cooper, who, for a macho hockey player, fought to keep a tick in line in his jaw. A brave front.

Terran wouldn't let them kiss him, and she and Cooper left the classroom together. They didn't speak on the ride back to her house, the radio playing rock and roll.

Dana sat stoic and quiet, sniffing and fighting the silly tears of motherly emotions.

Tomorrow she would have to do this all over again. With Mark.

It would be a week of goodbyes.

THE BLUE NOTE PACKED customers in on a Friday night, and jazz played through the jukebox in mellow notes. Lighting in the bar was veiled and soft, the back bar awash in a marine-blue color. The liquor bottles glinted on the shelves.

Leo quickly served orders and mixed drinks without a moment to pause. Presley ran the kitchen with an efficient zeal, along with a competent staff. Dana greeted those customers around her with a smile and general enthusiasm to have them here. She knew many by name, and many asked after her and Terran and her mother. Locals and vacationers alike congregated inside her father's dream.

Dana wished he could be here now, but she sensed his spirit always lived within these walls. She realized how much she'd come to love this place, how it had fit into an intricate part of her life.

While warmth and affection flowed through the room, Dana's feelings were bittersweet.

Tonight was Mark's last night in Ketchikan. He'd be leaving on the morning flight out to go home, back to his own life and the family he had to support him in his new venture.

She thought back to the moment she'd first laid eyes on him in the bar. He'd come in with the fish-brain who'd caused trouble and had been asked to leave. That seemed an eternity ago. But she still remembered her thoughts when Mark had spoken to her.

That man is more handsome than one man has the right to be.

Beyond the superficial and a casual assessment made in her head, she'd written off any thoughts about Mark Moretti. Little had she known what an integral part he'd play in her life. Like a woven tapestry, he'd knit himself into her business, her home, her heart.

Now she'd have to say goodbye to him. She wasn't very good at that, having few experiences. Not after a father and brother had been snatched without the chance to tell them how much they'd meant to her.

She would be honest with Mark tonight, but guarded. There was no point in telling him she'd fallen in love with him. What purpose would it serve other than to make her feel needy and have him awkwardly explain he couldn't stay? She wouldn't bother with sentimentalities—just the truth. That she could only thank him as deep as the bottom of her heart for all he had done for her and for her son.

While battling to keep her teetering emotions in check, Dana sensed that tonight would be special somehow. She could feel the energy in the room. Or maybe that was because she would play the saxophone tonight and she always felt her adrenaline begin to pump just before she went on.

To this day, she hadn't gotten over the fear of performing in public. Her father had been a master, as relaxed as could be—and he could quiet a room while everyone's breathing hinged on the silken notes he played.

The Blue Note's interior renovation was complete, beautiful new additions to be enjoyed for years to come. The other day, Mark had told her he had officially finished bringing the inside violations up to code. Aside from completing the second fire exit on the exterior, only one thing remained to be revealed. When she pressed him to tell her what it was, he'd said she'd have to wait until this evening. She couldn't guess what the surprise would be—but she'd been wondering about the large, blocked framework by the bandstand.

While visiting with the husband and wife owners of a local bed-and-breakfast, Dana noticed Mark come into the bar. He stood just above the crowd and made his way toward her with a smile. Inside, her heart warmed and she was glad to see him.

She wouldn't think about how much she'd miss him. . . .

Bidding the couple to have an enjoyable rest of their evening, Dana met Mark across the crowded room. "Busy night," he said, a look of amusement flickering in his eyes. "You offering dollar well drinks, sunshine?"

She laughed. "Actually all these people are here because I put up posters that we'd be bidding on a hot guy tonight—and your picture is all over them."

"I'm flattered, but there's a few too many dudes in here for my comfort zone if that's your plan. I'm a one-woman-only kind of guy." He glanced around, as if looking for someone. "Is Bear here?"

"He's around here somewhere. Why?"

"Got something for him. I left it in the kitchen when I was here this afternoon. Presley's hiding it for me—among other things."

Dana inwardly groaned. "If you got me something . . . Mark, I didn't get you anything, but I was going to—"

He didn't give her the opportunity to say anything further; he interrupted and said, "Later on, you can give me a kiss, sweetheart, and we'll call it better than good."

She grew warm with the thought.

Dana was called to a table by some old friends. She gave Mark an apologetic smile, but he sent her off with an affectionate squeeze of her hand.

Fifteen minutes later, Dana stood at the bar after helping one of her waitstaff bring out a multiple-plate food order. Talking with Leo, she kept searching the crowd for Mark, wondering where he'd gone.

Her steady heartbeat skipped every now and then, and she had to force her erratic emotions to stay on hold. Every time she thought about tonight being Mark's last in town, she tangled herself in feelings that served no purpose.

Bear nudged his way to the bar, a grin splitting his face. The glint in his eyes was pure elation as he hooked his fingers into his belt loops.

"Look-see what Moretti done give me. A hand-tooled leather belt with a silver buckle. And see that? That's a bear engraved in the sterling." The buckle itself was the size of a fist—quite intricate and showy with its design of a bear feeding in a rushing stream of water. "And y'all got to see this." He turned, his rounded bottom toward them, all but in their faces. "My name's on the back. *B-E-A-R* stamped in the cowhide." Turning around, he beamed as bright as a beacon. "This here is a right fine piece of hardware."

Leo set a cold beer in front of him. "I wouldn't say your butt is fine hardware, Bear, but the belt's a cut above. Looks good on you."

Bear laughed, slipping his large frame onto the bar stool to take a load off.

"Where's Mark?" Dana asked, looking over the top of Bear's head to see if she could find Mark in the crowd.

"Said he had to meet Card for sumpthin'. I don't rightly know the particulars."

Leo stopped mixing a drink, glanced at his watch, then said to Dana, "I'm almost out of lemon slices. I need you to run into the kitchen and get me some. Cut them clean—take out the seeds."

"Leo, you sound like you're the boss," she replied, giving him a harmless nudge with a half smile. "If I didn't like you so much, I'd have to fire you for that."

"Then you'd have to rehire me because you'd never find a better bartender."

"True that."

Dana went off into the kitchen to busy herself with lemons. Each time she finished one, Presley handed her several more and told her they could never have too many, and to put plastic wrap over the tray extras. By the time she was finished, she'd spent a good twenty minutes in the kitchen.

Taking Leo his lemon wedges, she scanned the patrons sitting at the bar in the hope of finding Mark. He wasn't among them.

Just as she made a move to search for him through the crowd, the jukebox quit and she heard Mark's deep voice speak through a microphone.

Her gaze found him on the bandstand, a spotlight focused on him. "If I could have everyone's attention. There's a special something tonight at the Blue Note if you look this way."

A curious length of white curtain had been strung behind him. That hadn't been there before. Cardelle Kanhai, head impeccably shaved clean, occupied the stage with Mark. His dark face shone with pride and excitement.

"I need Dana to come here," Mark said as he shaded his eyes against the beam of light on him.

Dana inched her way forward and the crowd parted. She took the single tall step onto the platform, wondering what this was about as Mark gently guided her to his side.

"What are you doing?" she whispered beneath her breath.

He ignored her question and addressed the audience that had gathered closer to get a look at what was going on. "In case you didn't know, this incredibly beautiful woman is Dana Jackson, and she owns the Blue Note."

People applauded and cheered—Bear being one who added a "whoo-wee!" in for good measure. Leo gave her a mock bow, hands pressed together. Walt, her bouncer, flexed a muscle, as if to say he would toss out anyone who didn't appreciate the boss. Sam gave her a mock salute, and Presley had come out of the kitchen without her apron and stood at the bar with her arms folded beneath her breasts. She gave Dana a loving smile, then lifted her engagement finger and wiggled it with a wink and a nod.

Somehow Dana got the impression that everyone who worked for her, or knew her personally, was in on whatever Mark was doing.

Mark held the microphone with ease in his large hand, his tall body muscled and confident. A green-and-brown-plaid button-down shirt fit him nicely over his broad shoulders, and was tucked into dark denim jeans. His black hair was neatly combed off his forehead, but a piece managed to stray and rest over his brow. Brown eyes were warm and friendly.

"So in case you don't know," Mark said, turning toward Card, "Dana's father, Oscar Jackson, opened the Blue Note bar back in the seventies as a tribute to the jazz music he loved.

He played his sax here until his death six years ago. I heard that his Southern sound was like no other, and that he could bring them in from miles away just to hear him play. I would have liked to meet him."

Dana blinked back the tears that had gathered in her eyes, not wanting them to spill. While her father had passed, his legacy lived on through the memories of those who'd known him. She, too, had a moment's wish that Mark Moretti had been able to meet her dad.

"As a tribute to Oscar, and a monument to stand at this bar, I asked Cardelle to do something for me." Mark moved toward Card and laid a hand on the man's shoulder. "Many of you think all this guy can do is sell bling."

With a big smile, Cardelle said, "Good people, you can find me at Jewels of de Nile—I give a discount to anybody who mentions dis night. For de ladies—tanzanite rings, fifty percent off."

Women cheered.

Cardelle's blatant sales pitch was just the thing Dana needed to pull herself back together and forget her tears.

Mark took control once more while Cardelle went to the white draping and held on to a corner. Bringing Dana to the curtain, Mark positioned her in front of it. "Dana," he said, then lowered his voice softy, "this is for you."

With a jerk, Cardelle pulled the curtain and Dana

sucked in her breath with shock, tingles rising over every inch of her body.

There on the wall, painted on a long stretch of canvas, was her father's image. His handsome black face took up the entire left side with a saxophone raised to his lips. Musical notes erupted from the sax's brass bell to dance across the canvas and intricately spell out the words *The Sax Man.* The musical notes tripped and turned on giant Ketchikan raindrops as they fell in a whimsical scatter to the bottom of the mural. In the bottom-right corner, leaning into the last note, her brother Terrance.

The entire effect made Dana speechless. Her father's face, his likeness, spread four feet tall in a lifelike recognition that filled the room with his spirit and vision.

"I . . . I don't know what to say," she whispered, barely able to contain herself and the myriad of emotions threatening to unravel her composure. "Thank you . . . I'm in awe. Truly."

Then she gave him a hug in front of everyone—something she would have never done three months ago with Mark, or anyone else in the Blue Note. She regarded herself as private and reserved, not quite approachable by men, but friendly enough. Now she had no qualms about a public display of affection for a man who held her heart in the palm of his hand . . . and didn't know it.

They parted and she took another lingering look

at the mural, smiling. She gave Cardelle a fond hug, as well, thanking him several times for his art-work. She'd treasure it forever.

Card shyly patted her shoulder, then stepped back.

"Now I guess it's my turn," she said, walking to her saxophone on its stand. Her backup musicians that she'd called earlier in the week to join her tonight—drummer, clarinetist and double bassist—had arrived and she waved the guys onstage. They took their positions, loose, limbered and ready to jam.

Mark and Cardelle stepped down onto the main floor, Mark's gaze never leaving her. She felt momentarily self-conscious as she took her instru-ment. The song's tune was heavily nostalgic, and Mark wouldn't know its title. But she'd selected Benny Goodman's "Goodbye" to play. Mark wouldn't know the tune, but the emotion to the song said everything in her heart.

She hated to say goodbye.

As she closed her eyes and let the music flow through her, she blocked out what tomorrow would bring, and only thought about this night. This last moment with the man who'd changed her. Forever from this day, she'd know that even after loving and losing her father, it was okay to grieve, and that she had so much to be happy about. Her days could be spent reflecting on the past with joy rather than sorrow.

In her own way, she'd done this, but she'd never been able to really let go. The mural, and the new look in the Blue Note felt like a new beginning.

The smooth song flowed through her nimble fingers, melodic and sweet. Each note moved through her breath as she created the sounds.

When the song ended, she lowered her saxophone to cheers and applause. Mark's eyes locked into hers, and she didn't blink. They stared, each lost in the other with unspoken thoughts until the band broke into an upbeat syncopation and they snapped things up while she exited the stage.

People enjoyed the music and the bar took on a life of its own. But Dana didn't see much around her. Her entire being focused on Mark. On walking toward him. When she'd reached him, he took her hand and simply said, "Let's get out of here."

DANA DIDN'T WANT TO TALK. She was all talked out from months of conversations with Mark. She'd simply wanted to absorb quiet in a private place and the best idea she had was Mark's condo.

It had seemed cliché to ask him to bring her here, but she hadn't wanted to sit in a restaurant or go for coffee. All she wanted was to be close to Mark and enjoy these last stolen minutes.

They'd entered the condo, set their things down and Mark had asked her if she wanted a glass of wine. Quite honestly, she already felt drunk just by his proximity. She'd declined, walked to the view at the sliding glass door, then opened it to stand on the redwood deck.

"Cold?" Mark asked, drawing up behind her.

"Not too bad. When the sun goes down, the temperature can drop like a rock. Days are getting shorter."

Sunset came late in the summer and as fall approached, the hours of daylight were growing shorter and shorter.

His strong arm came around her, the contact fanning the growing fire within her. He settled his hold on her waist and his solid chest pressed against her back, scalding her through her knit shirt like a brand. She leaned against him, fighting the urge to turn around in his embrace.

She breathed deeply of the night filled with the scent of ocean, woodsy flowers and pungent moss. All day, a thick moisture had hung in the air like a wet towel. There was a crispness to the night, several visible stars in a sky that had begun to fog over.

Mark made no effort to move away. And neither did Dana. A delightful shiver ran through her at their touch.

He slid his hands down her waist, tracing the curves of her hips over her jeans. Then he captured her hands and hugged her arms around her, his hands over hers.

The chill in the air brought a coolness to Dana's burning lungs. She breathed in deeply, inhaling the night and the man beside her. Clean soap and an aftershave, a musky scent that intoxicated.

"We shouldn't have come here," Mark breathed next to her ear.

She knew what he meant, and she knew exactly why she'd wanted to come here even though she hadn't admitted the truth until now.

"I want to be with you," she replied, the meaning clear. She couldn't face him, but his intimate hold over her left no room for reason. She'd done all of that prior to arriving.

She had made her choice.

"I want to be here, in your arms, with you, enjoying us." She turned toward him, slipping her arms around his neck. "I want you to kiss me."

Her honest admission suspended between them, and Mark's face hovered over hers. "Come inside. It's cold out here."

He took her hand and she followed him in. He closed the sliding door, then pulled the cord on the sheer curtains and turned down the lights. The fireplace had a switch for the gas to light a flame, and Mark brought the hearth to life with a soft glow.

"Let's sit by the fire," he suggested.

In front of the fireplace, Mark gathered all the pillows off the sofa and made a place for them to lean against. Once she'd settled in, he lay on his side next to her, his arm extending to brush her hair from her shoulder.

As Dana faced him, she felt as if she were

floating on a cloud of uncertainty, of longing, of desire. This would change everything. Her feelings would be turned inside out from this moment on, and it would be harder than ever to let him go if she made love with him. But if she didn't, she'd always regret not having this part of him, of them, to remember.

There had never been anyone else to evoke such a response from her by a mere touch. She stared into Mark's eyes as firelight caught in them and she saw her desirous feelings mirrored in his gaze.

Without thinking, she pressed her palm to his cheek, and stroked him with her thumb. She marveled at the roughened skin so unlike her own. The contrast made her pulse skitter. She ran her fingertip down over his mouth to his square jaw. She felt him tense under her touch and she drew away thinking she'd bothered him. He captured her hand in midair and brought it back to his face.

"You keep doing that and I am going to kiss you. And once I start, I'm not going to stop."

"I don't want you to stop," she whispered, and framed his face with her other hand.

The strong barrier she'd tried to build between them toppled with her words. Mark brought his lips down on hers with an urgency that sent her senses reeling. His mouth was firm yet pliant, yielding to her. He cupped the back of her head in his hands to draw her closer. She moaned and he deepened the kiss.

Dana felt as if she were as hot as the fire, closing her eyes and melting next to Mark. She moved her fingers over the muscles of his broad shoulders, playing with his shirt's fabric.

The erratic beating of his heart moved against her own. She kissed him with a need that almost frightened her. She controlled the kiss, gently plying open his firm lips with the tip of her tongue. She sought the entrance of his mouth where he tasted sweetly of mint chewing gum. Her actions caused him to groan, drawing her closer to him, digging his fingers into the slope of her shoulders and grinding his mouth harder on hers.

She felt lost, dizzy and swirling in a wave of sensations that were building, demanding to be quenched.

She wanted to feel every part of him.

"Please . . ." she whispered on his lips.

"Dana . . ."

Her name, spoken, said volumes. He was giving her one final chance to change her mind.

"Please," she murmured, ignoring every ounce of reason she'd ever had.

Mark removed her shirt, then pressed the weight of his torso over hers, weaving his fingers into her hair. He kissed her with light easy strokes, taking her lower lip into his mouth and running his tongue across the velvet sweetness. He grazed the hollow of her throat. The sensations Dana felt made her weak and radiated a fan of heat throughout her body from the tips of her toes to the top of her head. It swirled and centered on the place between her legs. She wanted him there.

Mark pulled away from her only for a moment as he removed his shirt and unbuckled his belt to slide out of his jeans. His chest was broad and hewn with muscles, hard from physical labors. Her hands slid unabashedly up his bare chest and she reveled in the texture of the tautly stretched skin. He was all male, so handsome. She fingered the line of coarse hair across his chest and slowly outlined his nipples. Mark's breath caught in his throat.

He made fast work of removing her bra and jeans, then her panties. Momentarily self-conscious, she bit her lip.

"You are *so* beautiful," he said, brushing her bare skin at her collarbone. Her coloring was darker in contrast to his, and he was intent on gazing at every inch of her naked flesh. "Beautiful."

As he cradled her next to him, she felt the full flush nakedness of his body beside her.

She had to bring up a subject that she found uncomfortable, but necessary. She'd never make the same mistake twice and no matter how awkward, she had to say it.

"Mark . . . I need my purse. There's something I have to get."

Without question, he reached behind his head, then handed her purse to her. She nervously dug for the protection inside.

One surprise baby was enough for a lifetime for her.

"It's not that I was thinking about it," she stammered. "But I didn't want to be in the middle of something then have to ask about it and then you have to—"

"Shh." His fingertip came over her mouth. "I understand."

The mood between them slightly chilled and she found the situation difficult, but Mark brought her close and held her for the longest time, stroking her back and the skin that curved across her hip. Finally, his palm rested on the swell of her butt.

Languid and relaxed once more, she kissed him and they fell back into the moment. Hands skimmed, mouths touched, fingers explored. Nothing was forgotten to be loved on their bodies.

Breathless, Dana thought she couldn't take another second of the sweet agony. Mark nudged her legs apart and settled over her. He raised himself up on one elbow and they became one. The flood of emotions welling inside her threatened to topple her over the edge.

The emptiness that had been inside her was gone. Her body tingled and throbbed, an eddy of hot tides racking her with pleasure. She felt the muscles on Mark's back tighten and she clung to him, raking his damp skin with her fingernails. His ragged breath hotly caressed her ear and she savored the aftermath of their entwined bodies.

A long moment passed with nothing but the sound of their beating hearts filling the room. The words on her lips that she wanted to speak remained still. Hushed and unspoken—too dangerous to reveal. Instead, she said what she must, that she had to say and truly mean.

"Mark." She blinked the tears that dampened her eyelashes. "When you leave, I don't want you to come back. I won't say goodbye twice."

CHAPTER TWENTY-ONE

THE BOISE AIRPORT TARMAC rippled with heat waves as Mark disembarked the aircraft. Carry-on bag strapped over his shoulder, he walked toward the covered awning of Alaska Airlines. He had a surreal feeling seeing the familiar surroundings, as if he'd been gone a year rather than a few months.

Not used to such arid weather, the dryness assailed him and perspiration formed at his hairline. The desertlike air was hot and scorching for late August. Must have been in the low one hundreds today—a far cry to the fifty degrees he'd left in Alaska.

He walked the ramp toward the terminal, pausing once to roll up his shirtsleeves as the air-conditioning within the building blasted him. Once inside, he took the escalator to the second floor and exited the security zone to find his sister waiting for him.

She was an attractive woman, statuesque, with long black hair and a go-getter smile.

"Hey, Franci, I didn't know anyone would be here," Mark said, giving her a quick hug.

"I haven't seen you in forever. Of course I'd be here. I want to hear all about your trip. And everything about *her*—details."

Mark nudged his bag higher on his shoulder. "You never have given me any slack about anything." Good-natured, he replied, "I'll tell you about Dana."

"Great—you can start by why you didn't bring her with you if she's as fabulous as Mom thinks she is."

THE SATURDAY MARK LEFT, Dana had taken the night off. In the morning, she'd brought her mother and Terran to see the mural in all its glory. Her mom had been in awe of Oscar's likeness. Terran had thought Grandpa Oscar looked fun with musical notes. Afterward they all went on a hike at Ward Lake, wearing jackets to fend off the cooling temperature on one of the last August days.

The afternoon was spent finding sticks, throwing rocks into the lake and playing hide-and-seek. They brought a picnic lunch and Dana and Suni told Terran stories about his uncle Terrance, whom he'd been named after, and Grandpa Oscar.

In many ways, the mural had been cathartic, bringing them to a place where Dana and Suni couldn't stop sharing and recollecting a husband and father. No longer did Dana feel as if she had to hold on to the bar to keep memories alive. She was at peace now. As if she'd been holding her breath, she'd been able to release it and find a true joy in going to the bar. And it was her father's face above the bandstand that immortalized Oscar "The Sax Man" Jackson as the Blue Note's founder. Dana would forever be grateful to Cardelle and to Mark for thinking of her.

Tuesday afternoon, Dana went into the Blue Note earlier than usual to be alone in the bar and admire the mural once again.

The Blue Note was so quiet, she could hear herself breathing. The vast room seemed to echo the big void that resided in Dana's heart. Today was the start of a new workweek and full of tasks to occupy her mind. Life began again and moved forward. Only it wouldn't bring Mark's handsome face in the doorway or his husky voice at the bar. Or his arms around her.

Things were just as before he came to Ketchikan.

Except now a loneliness settled into her the depths of which she feared to acknowledge lest it devour her.

Walking forward, she looked at the painting and smiled with fondness. Her father had been such a handsome man. Terrance, too. Their photos hung in the bar and at Fish Tail Air, and that's what Cardelle had used as his inspiration for the mural.

Dana went into her office, staring at the mountain of paperwork and receipts, then sighed. Time for work, to settle back in, to begin again and go about her day as if the past three months were a distant memory . . . when it had only been a few days since Mark departed.

The spare key to the bar that she'd loaned him had been left behind in a paper-clip receptacle.

She sat at her desk and habitually kicked off her heeled shoes and went for the spare sensible flats she kept beneath her desk. Extending her leg, her foot searched to fit into a shoe. She couldn't find the pair she had left. Dana paused and peeked under her desk.

Rolling back in her chair, surprise lifted her brows when she spied a pair of heels that she'd never seen before. She picked them up and set them on her desk.

"Oh my . . ." she breathed.

Christian Louboutin peep-toe sexy cranberry-red shoes with killer stiletto heels.

The very ones she'd repeatedly been coveting on the Internet.

She fit the right shoe on first, then the left. The toe of her foot touched something and she withdrew to find a small note inside. It was folded in half once.

Reading the boldly scripted handwriting, she couldn't contain the beginnings of a smile that caught on her mouth.

When you wear these, think about all the times you wanted to kick my ass.

• • •

THREE YEARS AFTER Giovanni Moretti told his wife, Mariangela, that he wanted to bring life back into Boise's downtown, his big vision project—the Grove Marketplace—had been completed.

The dedication that first day in September drew officials from a variety of offices. The mayor had shown, and a representative from the governor's office came, as well as city council members. A host of building department people were there, and the chamber of commerce had invited all the downtown businesses to join the large celebration. Executives from the leasing company that would see to it all the vacancies had been filled and sub-contractors came to show their support. A caterer had assembled tables in the main building's lobby, and the aroma of hors d'oeuvres mingled with the notes of a baby grand piano that had been brought in just for the occasion.

All the Morettis were present. Mark and Franci had worked together to take care of details and ensure things ran smoothly and on time. His mom stood by her oldest son, John, and his wife, Chloe, along with John's kids—Zach on a military leave for the occasion, and Kara, now graduated from high school. Robert Moretti and his wife, Marie, were by the fountain along with their young daughters.

Francesca Moretti-Jagger, and her husband, Kyle Jagger, took front and center since it had been her architectural firm, Bella Design, that had done the drawings for the renovation.

Mark remained focused on what he needed to do, and began the proceedings with an introduction of Father John Kowalsky. He offered a humble prayer in remembrance of Giovanni. Then Franci took over and said some words about the project, and how much it had meant to her father, and how sorry the family was he hadn't had the chance to see it finished. Mark spoke, talking about how it had been difficult to go forward, but that everyone who'd been hands-on at the job site had really made things easier for them.

The ceremony was brief with a recap of how they had come to this point of completion—through trials and errors, and one surprise partner, Kyle Jagger. Laughter rose from the Morettis, as there was an inside story about that one. Kyle had ended up marrying Franci because of a deal Giovanni had made with him to be a silent partner.

Applause sounded at the appropriate moments, while smiles and nods conveyed other feelings. Mark stood before the gathering and announced the surprise the family had planned for the lobby.

Franci helped him with it, and Mark glanced at his mom. Pride beamed in her eyes as Francesca called attention to the bronze wall portrait.

The local artist's work was three-dimensional, a portrait of Giovanni and Mariangela Moretti. On the inscription plaque, it read:

Love built this building and love built this marriage.

Below it was the start and completion date of Grove.

Cheers rose from those in attendance, then Mark signaled to Franci to cut the ribbon. She took a pair of giant scissors, and once the red ribbon had been severed, applause resounded anew.

Kyle came to the forefront and spoke. "I wanted to hand the key to the building over to the owners." He gave an exaggerated key to a suited gentleman who took over to add his thoughts.

"Thank you to the Moretti family for making this project a place Boise can be proud of. I know you're all wishing Giovanni could have been here. He is in spirit."

Mark saw his mother dab tears at the corners of her eyes, and Kara put her arm around her.

"It was the Morettis' honesty and integrity that made this project a pleasure to watch." With a chuckle, he added, "Normally when we're at the end of a job, it's been so stressful that none of us want to speak to each other."

Laughter rose from the subs and contractors.

Then a familiar face took front and center. His gruff approach was no stranger to several in attendance, but he'd won over skeptics and had endeared himself to many. "Bob Garretson, here, in case you don't know."

The mega grocery store chain owner was known far and wide in the business circles.

"I wanted to say a few things," Bob continued after clearing his throat. "This family's dedication and hard work ethic from the old country that Giovanni brought with him made this renovation an honor to be a part of. I'm happy that my biggest store is located right here in the heart of things. So, with that said, I'm officially making an announcement that the Morettis will be the construction managers on all my building projects in the western states."

Enthusiastic cheers rose. The honor was huge, and Mark knew it. He'd had a foreshadowing from Kyle that this partnership would transpire, but being back less than two days hadn't given Mark the time to sit the family down and tell them of his plans to go out on his own or to catch up on the local buzz.

Mark took the spotlight once more. "Thank you all for coming, and please join us for some refreshments and food. Thanks again. We appreciate it."

The crowd stretched forward, congratulations and offerings of goodwill exchanged. Mark milled around, spoke to those he knew, went through the motions of being there when he actually wasn't.

His mind, his heart, his every breath, was elsewhere.

On a woman he couldn't forget, nor did he want to.

· · ·

Three months later

DECEMBER CAME to Ketchikan in a white blanket that lay on the streets and rooftops like a dusting of powdered sugar. Most of the time, the snow melted by noon due to the steady drizzle of light rain. Daylight had become a valuable commodity, the length of days barely eight hours long.

Building space rented by the cruise ships had been vacated, the windows boarded and occupants long gone. The wintry city had grown quiet and tranquil. Only the locally owned stores remained open for business. The Cedar Chest on Main Street received their Christmas items, and Julie's Fine Jewelry was the place to shop for that special someone. For a new book, Parnassus had the selection to peruse. And the library was full every evening, as serious reading came into season.

With the heater on in her small truck, Dana headed toward town after picking up Terran from school. She'd altered her work schedule in order to get him when the bell rang. There was nothing important at the Blue Note at that hour that couldn't wait. She took joy from seeing her son run to the car where she waited for him at the parking lot's main curb.

"Tell me why you did that?" Dana asked, not liking that she'd received a telephone call about a disciplinary action that had to be taken against Terran in class today.

He'd been escorted to the principal's office for a reprimand.

Chin to his chest, Terran gazed forward. "I didn't leave it on the hallway floor."

"But, baby, you put mud on that little girl's desk. It ruined her artwork papers."

"She was supposed to laugh."

"It's not funny."

"But, Mom," Terran pleaded with innocence. "I was trying to be a rascal."

"Rascal? Where did you get that word?"

"Mark told me."

Dana's pulse skipped, as it always did when Terran referenced something that had to do with Mark Moretti. It seemed like he'd left an eternity ago, yet he'd never left her heart.

Terran insisted in a convincing tone, "I wanted to be a rascal and make Kaitlyn happy."

Dana didn't understand how a mud pie could make a little girl happy. "That makes no sense."

"She needed to be happy. Her goldfish died last night and she was crying in class today. Mark said rascals make people laugh and I knew she needed to laugh so I made her fake dog poop. Only she didn't laugh, Mom, and I got in trouble because she started crying some more." Quietly, he said in a distant voice, "I'm sorry."

Now everything made sense and Dana gazed at

her boy. He'd changed since entering school. No longer did he call her Momma or Mommy. Only Mom. Walking him into the classroom became a no-no—he wanted to do it himself. The mornings where he would let her kiss him goodbye were no more.

But at home, he reverted to her son who needed his mom, and who threw his arms around her and gave her kisses. The son who'd found a simple pleasure in learning to read and liked to read to her at bedtime.

"Oh, Terran . . . it's okay. You did a good thing. I'm not mad at you."

Sniffing, he muttered, "Thanks, Momma."

Ah, a slight regression—one she cherished.

Dana turned through town and as she did, Terran perked up and sat taller in his booster seat. "Mom! There's Mark!"

She was just past the corner Terran had pointed to and wouldn't turn around to see a ghost. "No, baby. Mark doesn't live here."

"But, Mom. I saw him."

"No, Terran."

Dana swallowed the heaviness in her throat. Mark wouldn't be back. She'd made her feelings clear to him. Sometimes she wished she hadn't. But things were better this way. She hadn't gotten over missing him and she didn't know if she ever would.

In her loneliness, she'd agreed to go to a pizza

place with Terran and Cooper, to try a "family" night. But it hadn't worked out, and Dana confessed to Cooper it had been a mistake on her part. Since then, Cooper had been dating a twenty-something woman who worked at the Tongass Trading Co. She seemed nice enough and respectable, and didn't stay the night when Terran was there.

Dana pulled into the Safeway parking lot to grab groceries for tonight's dinner. She still took Tuesday and Thursday nights off, as things had slowed down at the Blue Note.

Grabbing a cart, she asked, "You want to sit in the basket?"

"No, Mom. That's for babies."

She headed for the produce section, thinking she wasn't sure if she liked this new big-boy demeanor of Terran's. This summer, he had been fine sitting in the cart at Wal-Mart when they'd bought his school supplies.

That had also been the day they'd run into Mark in the aisle.

Dana shoved the thought aside, not wanting to revisit feelings for a man who was no longer in her life. But as she selected grapes and threw them into a plastic bag, she couldn't help wondering how he was.

Her mother gave her general snippets, but Dana never asked. She merely replied with "hmm" when Suni mentioned something about him from her exchanges with Mariangela. According to her mom's reports, Mark was keeping busy during a transitional stage with Moretti Construction since his sister had announced she was pregnant and wouldn't be returning after she gave birth.

Dana didn't encourage Suni to discuss news with her, but a part of her was always curious to know what he was doing. She'd hoped he'd gotten his new business off to a great start and that he was building projects he enjoyed.

Fire Marshal Bill had returned in October and filled out a form showing everything in the building was now in compliance—which had been a huge relief. Dana had received her one and only e-mail from Mark on that day that simply read— *The inspector called my cell and let me know everything passed inspection. Glad everything worked out.*

There had been no personal inquiries, nothing about himself. Of course she could pick up the phone and call him, check in with him . . . but she wouldn't. The degree of difficulty from hearing his voice would be too much for her to bear.

Far better to move on, to continue to forget, and to focus on the what-is rather than the what-was.

"What sounds good for dinner, Terran?" she asked, pushing away the cobwebs of her memories.

"Chicken nuggets."

Dana cringed. She didn't care for them, but

411

Terran loved the frozen kind. She'd make salads and fruit to go with them, and Suni most likely would have fried rice as a side.

Moving down the frozen-food aisle, Dana caught sight of Tori Daniel. Naturally. She had on thin leggings and a short shirt dress or maybe it really was a shirt. A box boy and two guy shoppers pretended to be interested in the pies next to the case Tori stood in front of—high beams on.

Tori's long hair was swept away from her face and she spotted Dana.

"Hi, Dana. Hey, Terran." She held onto a handcart in the crook of her elbow. "What's going on?"

"Just shopping," Dana replied.

Terran opened the glass door and rummaged for the nugget bag he preferred. They had to be cut in the shapes he liked. His little boy body was all but swallowed up inside the case as he dug around.

"So I saw that guy get off at the airport ferry," Tori remarked while she openly glanced over her shoulder at the drooling guys, a purring smile on her mouth.

"What guy?" Dana questioned, not particularly interested in any gossip Tori delivered.

"The one you were with at Burger Queen that day."

Dana's heart jumped, then ramped into a double-time beat of wonder. There had only been one guy she'd gone to Burger Queen with in recent months for Tori to remember.

Mark Moretti.

"Yeah," Tori said, smiling and flirtatious toward the guys, then addressing Dana. "Bear picked him up."

That night, sleep came in restless fits to Dana and she wasn't sure what to think. Tori was a ditz with a capital *D*. She'd probably been mistaken. Lots of men could look like Mark—tall and dark haired. He hadn't called her, so it couldn't have been him.

Then again, she'd asked him not to make contact.

By her own words, she'd isolated herself from the man she'd fallen in love with. If it was him with Bear . . .

This was one time she wished he'd ignore what she'd asked of him—like so many times in the past—and just do what he wanted.

But maybe he never wanted to see her again.

That thought haunted her long into the wee hours of morning.

ON A FRIDAY EVENING, even in the dead of December, the Blue Note still gathered a respectable-size crowd to hear jazz tunes from either the jukebox or a live band. The winter crowd all knew one another by first name.

Sitting unnoticed in a far corner dimmed by lighting, Mark Moretti held back and watched Dana at the bar. She hadn't seen him, nor did he want her to—not yet. For now, he wanted to drink in every inch of her face, her hair, her body, her mouth.

She wore jeans and an olive-colored turtleneck sweater. Although a distance away, he knew that her eye color would be emphasized by that shade of green. Her straightened hair, parted at the side and with a slight fringe of bangs, looked like she'd had it highlighted a reddish bronze. She traded words with Leo, smiling, then looked at something next to the cash register.

She was as stunning as he recalled, her image never leaving his mind. Dana Jackson had been in his thoughts every day since he'd left Ketchikan.

Finishing her task, Dana turned around, glanced about the room, then froze. She saw him, her eyes locking on his.

He felt everything inside him still to a slow crawl. His nostrils flared and he waited, reminding himself to breathe.

When she began to come toward him, he pulled air into his lungs. Once at the table, she wordlessly stared. He was the first to speak.

"Hello, Dana."

"What are you doing here?" she blurted, her hands unsteady so she stuffed them into the pockets of her jeans.

"I came to offer you a proposition."

"W-what?"

Calmly, he kept his emotions in check, riding

this out for as long as he could. "I ran this past Sam and he's in as long as you are." He had to rest his hand on the tall cocktail table, doing everything in his power not to take her into his arms and hold her, never letting go. "I want to start a business that ships freshly caught fish to the lower forty-eight. Most of the time, your planes come back empty after dropping fishermen off at lodges. Why let the cargo space go to waste?"

Mark pulled in a slow drag of breath. "I found an old Douglas DC-3 twin engine for sale in Anchorage. Sam will fly it to Ketchikan for me. You can't go wrong with a big Gooney Bird—it's like buying a sixties Chevy pickup." He knew he wasn't allowing her the chance to say anything, but he had to keep talking. "I'll cut out the middleman—the commercial flight. Sam's going to fly direct to my drop-off cities. My brother's restaurant already has a standing order. I put feelers out to places in Sun Valley, Seattle, a hotel chain in Portland. They're all interested. I'd pay you for the fuel Sam uses on Fish Tail Air, and I'd pay Sam for the loading and time. If it's okay with you."

Brows knitting into a sexy frown, her mouth trembling, she said, "You came here to ask me this? Why not just—"

"I was in town for other reasons," he broke in, his words a soft caress around them. Her facial expression looked fragile, so unlike the Dana he loved.

A loving ache held him in its clutches as he confessed with a full heart, "I couldn't stop thinking about you."

Softly shaking her head, she gazed down, then at him. "This is only going to make it harder."

"No, it's not," he said in a low tone. "This is the easiest thing I've done in three months."

She blinked, slowly and deliberately, as if trying to hold herself together. Her imploring gaze begged him for an explanation of why he was truly here.

Mark, in his earnestness to alleviate the confusion on her face, took both of her hands. They were warm and soft, and he felt a rush of blood heat through his body. She didn't move, but he took a step closer. The intimacy that surrounded them made him forget where he was and he fought against his natural inclination to kiss her.

"This isn't easy." Her voice sounded delicate, like silk thread ready to break.

Rubbing his fingers across her knuckles, he said, "Bear called me a couple of months ago. He wondered if I could recommend a good contractor in Ketchikan to build that fishing lodge for retirees he's always talking about. It so happens, I knew a guy. Me."

"You?" She studied his face, as if looking for clues to a joke. She'd find nothing. He was quite serious for a change.

Mark had let this woman see inside his soul,

places where he'd never allowed anyone to truly get to know the good and the bad that made him who he was. In this moment, he confessed to her, "I've had more conversations with my sister about you than anyone in my life. She probably knows you just as well as I do from everything I've told her about you." He took a step closer, mere inches separating them as his arms went around her to bring her near. "I love you, Dana. Love you so much it scares me. I'm coming back, and this time I'm not leaving."

As if in disbelief, she blurted, "But what about your family in Boise?"

"You're my family, Dana. If you'll marry me— as my wife you'd be my best friend. You and your son and your mom, I'd love to take care of all of you."

Still doubting, she reasoned, "You had plans to start your own company with connections you had back home."

"Doesn't mean anything to me without you. Whether or not I got a call from Bear, I was coming back. I tried to forget you and tell myself this wasn't real, but it is, Dana. I love you, and I'm not going to stop loving you . . . unless you tell me no—"

She threw her arms around him, her mouth covering his and kissing him soundly. The force threw him back a fraction, but he spread his hands and ran them up her waist, welcoming her kiss as if he'd been starved for it. When he pushed back to see her face, a look of pure emotional joy caught in her eyes. And he knew just as she spoke.

"I love you, too."

He gave her a lopsided grin, brushing her hair behind her ear. "That's what I always have liked about you, sweetheart. You do have a damn fine mind of your own."

Then, startling them both, a rousing chorus of applause hit the room as bystanders gave their approval to the embracing couple.

It was a smiling Presley who stepped forward, Leo and Walt flanking her. "Looks like we're going to have to throw us another bashment!"

EPILOGUE

One year later

"HOLD HER HEAD, Terran." Dana helped her son support the newborn's head as he cradled his sister on his lap. Wrapped in a pink blanket, the baby yawned then gazed intently at her brother.

The contemporary-style living room had been decorated for Christmas, lights on the tree winking and holiday music playing on the stereo. In two short weeks, Santa Claus would come down the chimney—but for Dana, she'd just received the best present of all.

Her daughter.

"Hey, Mom," Terran said. "Denali just tooted."

Mark laughed, standing by with the camera taking pictures like a proud father.

Suni came forward. "It might not be a toot, Terran. I'll take her to check."

"I'll get a fresh diaper." Mariangela Moretti hovered, just like Denali's other grandmother to make sure the newborn's every care was met.

Dana smiled at her husband while the older women fussed and made a big deal about either gas or something more substantial. It was nice to have the extra help since bringing the new baby home yesterday.

Denali Sunshine Moretti was beautiful, but Dana thought she was even more precious than an angel. Her tiny oval face wrinkled, mouth open, as she stretched when Suni picked her up to sniff her bottom. Mariangela moved in to give an opinion. The pair of them were like hens.

Doing surprisingly well for lack of sleep, Dana slipped her arm around Mark and they let the grandmas figure out a plan of action, a curious Terran nosing in.

Mark commented, "You'd think there was a national disaster in our daughter's diaper."

Laughter rose from her throat. "I think it is a *natural* disaster."

Tired but content, Dana closed her eyes and leaned into Mark with a love-filled smile. The happiest she'd ever been, she was more in love with her husband today than the day she married him.

She never would have guessed the changes in her life the day Mark walked into it. They'd married in late January, then taken their honeymoon in Jamaica and had a wonderful time visiting Cardelle and meeting his large extended family. Then she and Mark moved into a home of their own with Suni a regular visitor. Dana left the daily management of the Blue Note to Leo, whom she'd given a promotion to and hired another bartender. The bar would always be in the family. And she considered those who worked for her to be family. Before the baby, she stopped by a few times a week to check in with old friends, but she looked to her home life more. Her days would now be devoted to full-time motherhood, a job she embraced.

Terran had taken to being a big brother, and had adjusted to Mark as his stepdad. He still had weekly visits with his father and looked forward to that time. There had been a few bobbles along the way, a time of acclimating, and everyone getting used to things, but overall, Dana couldn't have been more blessed.

Mark's newly formed construction company was the contractor for Bear Barker's fishing lodge project. That kept him busy driving to and from the inlet just past Settlers Cove where the lodge was going up—slower in the winter due to weather.

Bear had named his place the Bear's Cave and it was scheduled to open this spring.

Beyond that, Mark had taken some smaller jobs in town. He'd sold his stock options in Moretti Construction, and over the next six years, they would be financially comfortable each month with the payments coming in until Mark got further established.

Mark kissed her temple, and she straightened. "This summer is going to be great when your sister and brother-in-law come up for a visit. Denali's going to like seeing another baby girl."

"You're going to like my sister."

"How can I not?" She cupped Mark's smoothly shaven cheek, warmth and endless affection flowing inside her heart for this man who completed her. "I love her brother very much."

AUTHOR NOTE

In June of 2008, my husband and I took a cruise through the Alaska passage. I was in awe of the beautiful landscape, the small coastal towns and the friendly locals who greeted us in every port. From this journey, an idea took shape in my mind. Ketchikan was just the setting for Mark Moretti. As the youngest of the brothers, and the one who walked on the wilder side in life, the town would be perfect for him to find love.

It's a bit daunting to write about a real location and take some creative license with it. While Ketchikan is laid out exactly as I've described, I've taken liberties with some of the facts. The marina where the Blue Note is located wouldn't have adequate dockage for floatplanes. And believe it or not, there is no ice rink so Rink Time had to be invented. The fishing locations for Mark and Jeff are fabricated, as is the Chop Suey restaurant.

None of my characters are real, and Jewels of the Nile is a fictional jewelry store. However, the fact is that cruise-ship-owned jewelry stores comprise a very large part of the downtown businesses. Burger Queen is exactly as I described and indeed on Tongass Highway. It serves one of the best cheeseburgers I've ever eaten.

Although no one would know it but me, the daily

weather that occurs in the book is exactly how it was on the days my story takes place. But Terran's hockey practice schedule has been embellished to suit my plot.

Lastly, I want to thank Charlotte Glover of the Ketchikan Library for answering my questions in such a timely manner. Thank you so much for the tour of the city and your wonderful hospitality. Any mistakes made in the descriptions or accuracies of Ketchikan life are purely my own.

I hope you've enjoyed reading about the Moretti family. The other books in this series are *All The Right Angles* and *All That Matters*.

Happy reading!
Best,

Stef Ann Holm

Center Point Publishing
600 Brooks Road ● PO Box 1
Thorndike ME 04986-0001 USA

(207) 568-3717

US & Canada:
1 800 929-9108
www.centerpointlargeprint.com

mL